HEARTBEAT OF DESIRE

A MODERN HISTORY ROMANCE

DONNA LOVITZ

Heartbeat of Desire

ISBN: 978-1-7340842-1-4

Published in the United States of America

Email contact: donna@donnalovitz.com

Website: http://www.donnalovitz.com

Edited by Sherri Hildebrandt

Cover Design by D. Lovitz

❀ Created with Vellum

*To my mother, Rose, for her patient ear during the creation of this book
and my father, Roy, for his encouragement to write it.
I know you're both reading it from heaven.*

PROLOGUE

C heryl Langtree lifted the lid on the roaster to examine her main course. Too long in the oven had left her beef roast looking tougher than a dried-out leather boot. She slapped the cover down and shoved it back into the oven. "Come on, Jon, where are you?" She tapped her fingers on the counter.

"Let's eat now," Taylor, her four-year-old son, howled. He stood in front of her and dropped to his knees.

"We'll give Daddy a few more minutes. I promise we'll eat soon."

The boy stood up and wrapped his arms around her thigh. Staring up with sad blue eyes he moaned, "But I'm *starving*."

Moments after being convinced he wasn't going to die from hunger, Taylor went back to playing with his toy tractor. Cheryl, feeling restless, wandered onto her front porch and gazed in the direction Jon had gone that morning with the tractor.

Beef roast was his favorite meal. What was keeping him? Most days she brought his lunch to the field, but today, with few dry fields left to plow, he said he'd be back in the yard before noon. *Maybe that field by Swenson's was drier than we thought and he didn't want to quit.*

She plopped onto a wooden chair and rested her head against its wide back. It didn't take long for the sun's warmth to melt away her cold thoughts of winter. *Most people believe the hardest part of living in Minnesota is the long, cold winters, but they're wrong. It's the spring — taking its sweet time to arrive.*

It was May before the snow turned into rain and dissolved the huge snowbanks around the small town of Watson. The long-awaited thaw was followed by a dreadful week of heavy down-pours. Constant rain merged with the melting snow and soon flooded the Chippewa River and the saturated fields it bordered.

Cheryl shut her eyes and listened closely for the sound of the tractor but only heard busy, chirping birds. When her eyes opened, her attention was drawn to the lawn where specks of green poked out of the matted brown grass. The new growth was easy to see against the backdrop of the peeling white picket fence around the yard. If the ground was that warm, maybe Jon found the lower fields dry enough to plow. *Would it have killed him to come in and let us know?*

It had been more than two weeks since the Chippewa had receded back inside its banks, but the lower fields next to the river always needed more time to dry out. Farmers were anxious to get into those fields where the heavy black soil was the most fertile and often yielded close to double that of the higher ground.

The late spring, along with a short growing season, had sent her husband, like most area farmers, into a planting frenzy. At times, Jon forgot farming was a waiting game that required patience — a concept he never grasped.

When the radio inside the kitchen played the one o'clock news theme song, Cheryl stood and looked at the field road again. They had waited long enough.

"Can't we just eat?" Taylor wailed from inside the house.

"Yes, we ...." She stopped when the radio announcer spoke about Governor George Wallace of Alabama. He had been shot a few days prior while he campaigned for the 1972 Democratic nomination. A chill ran through Cheryl's body as it was announced he would be paralyzed for the rest of his life. *I'm glad I married a farmer and not a politician.*

When "American Pie" began to play on the radio, Taylor forgot about his stomach. "They're playing the pie song, Mommy. Come in and turn it up."

She held his small body close while they danced and twirled to the music with his short legs wrapped around her waist. When the song progressed to the refrain, he cupped her cheeks with his soft hands and sucked in a deep breath. He started to belt out the words, but something suddenly snatched his voice away. Cheryl was still singing when she turned around to see what had captured his attention. She flinched seeing a tall figure on the other side of the screen door, wearing a cowboy hat.

Taking a moment to collect herself, she set her son on his feet and turned down the radio. The man was one of the Cameron boys from the Sugar King farm that adjoined theirs from the west. Rumor had it they were the richest farmers in the area. It had to be true. Everyone knew two of their three sons went to college to avoid the Vietnam draft. This was the oldest son, who had finished college and was going with a wealthy girl from Minneapolis.

"Can I help you?" She observed him through the screen with Taylor close at her side.

Her neighbor removed his hat. "Sorry, I was about to knock but I didn't want to interrupt." A smile softened his masculine features. "Is your husband home?"

"He's not, but he should be in shortly. Is there something I can do for you, Mr. Cameron?" She was determined to appear unaffected by his handsome face.

"Please. Call me Jake. I was hoping to talk to Jon about a farming issue."

"My husband and I are partners on this farm. Anything you need to say to him, you can say to me."

He blinked his dark eyes. "Okay. You are aware the

3

processing plant in Chaska closed last fall and now we don't have a place to sell our beets?"

She nodded. "Yes." *I'd have to be an idiot to be unaware of that.*

"The farmers in our area are trying to form a co-op where the potential goal would be to build a processing plant — that we would own — close to the area. We're having a meeting at the Montevideo High School gym on Tuesday night. Can we count on Jon to attend?"

"You can count on both of us."

His eyes darted to Taylor. "You realize this is an important issue, and we aren't inviting children. I really doubt if many women will attend."

"Why wouldn't they?" She cocked her head.

"Look, Mrs. Langtree, this isn't going to be a church social. We don't need a room full of distractions when we're trying to get down to business."

"I'll get a babysitter for my son, but I plan on being one of those few women attending. I only hope I won't be too much of a distraction to anyone." Her voice was patronizing.

He took a deep breath and let it out. "I guess I'll be seeing your husband *and* you on Tuesday night. But as far as you not being a distraction, I doubt that's possible. Good day." He nodded and quickly stepped off her porch. Cheryl watched him get into a shiny, blue Chevy pickup and drive away.

"Let's e ... eat." Taylor tugged on the side of her pedal pushers.

Worried thoughts poked at Cheryl while she put lunch on the table, but she pushed them aside and reminded herself of her husband's ego. How many times had she heard him boast to the other farmers about being the first to have finished planting or harvesting? It was too late to go out to the field now. It was time to eat.

Taylor had barely taken his first bite of food when he began to rub his eyes. He'd been up several times the previous night with nightmares. It was pitiful to watch his head bob while he slowly chewed his food. He needed a nap, and she needed to go out to the field to give Jon a piece of her mind. Seconds after her son fell asleep, Cheryl called her neighbor, Nell Thompson, to see if her husband, Earl, could go to the field and check on Jon.

"I finally got him painting the living room." Nell's words were drawn out in her Norwegian accent. "It took him awhile to get started on it. I'm not going to stop him now. I'll come over and watch your boy while you go look."

Twenty minutes later, Nell drove in the Langtree driveway and parked. It seemed a lifetime for the older woman to heft herself out of her Mercury and navigate to the house. Cheryl anxiously brushed past her on the porch, but yelled over her shoulder that Taylor was down for a nap. A large clump of dried mud fell from under her Chevy pick-up truck when she slammed the door much harder than necessary. If the tractor had broken down, he could've walked home by now. His pride had to be behind this. She hung onto the steering wheel as well as her emotions and headed for the field he planned to plow that morning. Whatever excuse he had for staying out there, it better be a good one.

Close to a mile of field road was behind her when Cheryl stopped at the top of a hill. With the door open, she stepped on the running board and popped her head above the roof to get a better look. She shielded her eyes from the bright sunlight and scanned the vast area of blackened ground.

A flashback played in her mind of the first time she came here with Jon. She had grown up close to Webster, South Dakota where the fields were basically flat. In this area the river bottom land was lush and green and bordered on rolling hills. Back home, it was dry and there were few trees. Here the large oak and elm trees grew tall next to the river and formed a dense canopy to shade it. It still seemed strange to her.

She released a disappointed breath and ducked back into her truck then scrutinized the field on her right side. It was the color of coal and still shiny from being freshly plowed. She didn't see a tractor but followed a set of tractor tracks outlined with hunks of dark, moist soil thrown from the tires. The trail turned onto another field road that led to the river. Why would he go down there? When they'd checked it a few days ago she and Jon agreed it was too wet. She continued to search both sides of the road as she drove.

Descending a slight hill, she saw an overturned tractor and sucked in a rapid breath. She slammed on the brakes and frantically grabbed the door handle at the same time. When it occurred to her the truck was still moving, she stomped on the brakes again and threw it into park. In one swift move, she bolted from the seat and hurdled over the rows of overturned ground in a dead run to the tractor. Her throat tightened into a knot when she saw part of Jon's blue plaid shirt on the ground. When she got closer, her heart released an electrifying jolt that numbed her entire body. He was lying under the tractor. His head was turned toward his right hand and shoulder. Only a boot and part of one leg stuck out from under the machine on the other side.

"Jon!" Cheryl screamed and flung herself on the ground next to him. When he didn't respond, she dug her fingers in by his neck and felt for a pulse. Above her own wild heart, a faint heartbeat brought a moment of near hysteria. She sprang up and with all her might tried to push the tractor off him. Seconds later, exhaustion took over, and she stopped. In the middle of trying to catch a breath, it came to her what she needed to do.

"Hang on. I'm going to get help," she said, panting. She spun away from the frightful scene and ran to the truck as fast as her legs would carry her. Chunks of mud flew high in the air behind her truck on the field road when she sped away.

Nell stood in the screen door when Cheryl raced into the driveway.

"Call an ambulance. Jon's had an accident. He's under the tractor." Cheryl's breaths were coming in gasps.

"Oh, my God." Nell put her hands to her mouth but didn't move.

Cheryl pushed her out of the way and dashed to the phone on her kitchen counter. Once she found the emergency numbers in the phone book, her shaking fingers dialed for an ambulance. She related the details of the accident and gave the location of their farm. When the call ended, she clicked the receiver and dialed Thompsons' number. The phone rang five times before she got Earl and told him of the accident. She hardly recognized her own desperate voice when she informed him Jon was alive and they needed a tractor with chains to pull theirs off him.

"I'm on my way. Go to Jon. Nell and I will get the ambulance there," Earl assured her.

Cheryl recited every prayer she knew on the way out to the field, asking God for Jon to be alive. When she knelt by him and found his pulse again, tears of relief filled her eyes. She blinked them back and reminded herself to breathe. The most important thing was to be there for him. Her eyes focused on his face and she noticed a line of blood had trickled down his cheek from the corner of his mouth. She quickly wiped it with her fingers, trying to erase it.

"Everything is going to be okay, Jon," she told him softly. "You know how I know? Because I love you, and God wouldn't give us this great life together to have it end now. What would be the point?" She fought the urge to cry. "The ambulance will be here real soon, baby. I promise."

Brushing dirt out of his hair, she tenderly kissed his forehead and checked her wrist-watch. It had been seventeen minutes since she left the house, but it felt like an eternity. The strong afternoon sun beat down on them and made the wait more unbearable. Cheryl stood to block the sunlight from his face and wiped sweat off her forehead with the back of her hand. She looked up the hill then back at her husband.

"I need you, Jon. If you hear me, please hang on." She closed her eyes and took a needed deep breath. Seconds after her eyes

7

opened, she saw a subtle movement in his fingers. "You heard me." She dropped to her knees next to him. Leaning in closer, she pressed her mouth to his fingers and joyfully kissed each one.

A faint wail made Cheryl turn her head to listen. It soon got higher-pitched like a cry in the distance. Hearing it again, she looked toward the hill and made out the sound of a siren mixed with the beat of puffing tractors.

Earl was in front of the ambulance with his tractor. Behind was another neighbor on a tractor followed by a line of trucks driven by neighborhood farmers. A few minutes after they arrived in the field, the farmers hooked up chains and pulled the tractor off Jon. Examining the area, it was obvious what had happened. The soft ground had caved in next to the drainage ditch when Jon plowed too close.

Cheryl stood back and stared at her husband as emergency staff worked over him. Earl watched with his arm around her.

"It's hard to believe he was under that tractor." Earl was right. Jon's limbs weren't twisted; he didn't look crushed, bloody, or bruised. "Maybe the soft ground helped him out." He told her not to worry about Taylor. They would keep him for as long as she needed.

Cheryl held Jon's hand in the ambulance. He mumbled something on the way to the hospital in Montevideo. Hearing his voice — even a mumble — calmed her. It was a sign he was going to be all right.

The emergency room staff rushed her husband into a room, while other personnel questioned Cheryl about the accident. Shortly after the doctors began their examination, Jon was sent to X-ray and she was escorted by an attendant to the waiting room. She was told that whenever the X-rays were back someone would come and get her.

Horrific flashbacks from the afternoon plagued Cheryl while she waited alone. A wave of guilt passed over her when she recalled the anger she'd felt earlier. *Stop it. It won't help anyone.*

Jon's injuries had to be less severe given his appearance and state of consciousness.

Dori Kensing, Cheryl's best friend, rushed in the room to her side. The two women held each other while they talked.

"Are they saying anything yet on his condition?" Dori inquired.

"No. They said when he gets back from X-ray they'd come and get me." The words were barely out of Cheryl's mouth when the attendant reappeared.

"Mrs. Langtree, we need you to come immediately."

Cheryl jumped from her chair and followed. This time she was led to the ICU, and the scene had changed. Two doctors with solemn faces talked quietly amongst themselves in the front of the room. She watched her husband's chest rise and fall with the help of a machine. They turned and slowly looked at Cheryl.

"Mrs. Langtree?"

A lump in her throat forced her to swallow. "Yes."

"Let's step out." One of the doctors motioned to the door and the three went down the hall into a smaller room. The doctors introduced themselves as surgeons Kraemer and Allan.

Doctor Kraemer ended an eerie silence. "Please, sit down, Mrs. Langtree. Do you have any family here with you?"

"No. I've got a friend here. Just tell me. How bad is he?" She felt her blood rush throughout her body.

Doctor Kraemer took a deep breath and let it out. "There is no easy way to tell you this, Mrs. Langtree. His condition is extremely critical. He has extensive internal injuries." He paused. "In my medical career, I've never seen anyone survive with that kind of trauma. We cannot express to you how sorry we are, but at this point there is nothing we can do. If you need to call anyone we suggest you do it now."

Cheryl's mouth fell open. "No." Her voice sounded strange again. "That can't be. He looks perfect. He was starting to wake up in the ambulance. I heard him myself."

"The moment that tractor was pulled off him, his lungs started to fill with blood," Doctor Kraemer explained.

"If what you're saying is true, why don't we try to get him to Minneapolis?" she demanded.

Doctor Allan jumped in, "Unfortunately, he won't make the trip. The nurses have told us he woke briefly in X-ray and said he wants to see you and your son. You need to get your son here as soon as possible."

Cheryl's body trembled, but she didn't cry. Nothing would come out. Left alone, she made a quick call to Earl and Nell and told them to bring Taylor to the hospital. She then phoned Jon's sister, Jane, but didn't get an answer.

In Jon's room, Cheryl watched him and listened to the pulse of the ventilator that kept him alive. He looked perfectly fine, like he had that morning when he slept peacefully in their bed. She clasped her hands together to pray. Blood under her fingernails from when she'd wiped his cheek caused tears to well up in her eyes. She shook when a tap on her arm brought her back.

"Your son is in the waiting room," a nurse told her in a soft voice.

"I'll be right there." She moved closer to the bed and whispered, "Jon, Taylor is here. I'll get him and be back as soon as we can."

Taylor stood between Nell and Earl when Cheryl came into the room. Dori was seated on the couch holding her forehead. Her curly, auburn hair flopped around her face. When she looked up, Cheryl could see her eyes were red.

Taylor saw Cheryl and ran to her. "Mommy, is Daddy going to be all right?"

Everyone looked at Cheryl.

"They don't know, sweetie," she lied.

It didn't matter what the doctors had told her. They were only human; and they, too, could make mistakes. *Anything is possible if you believe in God.* Lots of times she had heard stories about people who miraculously recovered from illness or injury. *Don't Taylor and I deserve a miracle, too?*

Taylor started to tell his mother about the Mickey Mouse-shaped meat loaf Nell made for dinner. A nurse entered and quickly stood next to the group.

"He's asked for the ventilator to be taken off, and he wants to see you and your son. The doctors want you close by before we take it off." Dori and Nell silently stared at each other while Earl put his head down and nervously rubbed his chin.

Cheryl and Taylor stood outside the room while a nurse shut off the ventilator and removed it from Jon before leaving the room. When they were allowed inside, Cheryl noticed the lights had been dimmed. Another nurse stood with Doctor Kraemer by the front of the bed. Cheryl dropped Taylor's hand and gently pushed him forward. The doctor nodded at the nurse, and they quietly left the room but remained outside the open door.

Jon didn't respond at first, then blinked and slowly whispered, "Are they here?" His voice was raspy.

Cheryl reached for her husband's hand. "Yes, Jon, we're here. You're going to be fine, honey."

Opening his eyes, he took a ragged breath and shook his head slightly. "No, Cheryl."

She swallowed hard.

Taylor laid his head onto Jon's arm. "Daddy, are you going to come home with us?" He looked into his father's face.

"Big guy, c ... can you do something for me?" Jon's eyes slowly went to his son.

"Yeah. What do you want me to do?"

"Take care of Mommy for me." Jon swallowed and tried to lick his dry lips. "I want you both to be h ... happy ..." He gasped for air. A moment went by before he tried to speak again. "Cheryl, promise me ... you'll keep farming."

"Jon, I don't know ...."

"I know you can do it." He struggled for another breath. "S ... stay on the farm, and you'll be happy." His eyes opened a little farther. "Please, promise me ... both of you." His voice was barely a whisper.

They answered. "Yes."

A fragile smile came to Jon's face before a gurgle. Taylor let out a whimper and buried his face in the blanket on the bed. Cheryl laid her hand on his shoulder to comfort him. Tears ran down his face when he looked up.

"Daddy, please don't die."

His plea wasn't heard. Nothing was heard except for the sound of Jon taking his last breath. Seconds later the heart monitor went off. Cheryl closed Jon's open eyes. Taylor didn't need to remember his father like that.

1

The fan in the front of the lectern made a pathetic attempt to move stifling air in the old Lutheran church. Despite the lack of ventilation, the pastor continued his sermon on how the music of today was responsible for the corruption of young lives.

"When I graduated from high school in 1943, music was about the big bands like Benny Goodman and Tommy Dorsey. Those good, clean songs were about love. They kept us dancing and helped everyone cope with a terrible war," Pastor Timms recounted. "Thirty years later, much of today's music would embarrass any musician of the big band era with its shameless lyrics that encourage immoral behavior. Not only are the words obscene, but many of the songs include satanic music. I over-heard a song that repeated a few chords over and over in an obvious attempt to hypnotize young, impressionable listeners. It glorified burning down buildings by the water's edge in a drug-induced state while watching the smoke rise over the water." The pastor dabbed the side of his pudgy face with the white handkerchief clutched in his hand.

Cheryl sat back in the pew and felt her polyester dress adhere to the middle of her back. To get her mind off the heat, she let her thoughts drift to that summer day when she and Jon went skinny-dipping in the Chippewa River. She remembered his shocked expression when she took her clothes off in front of him and jumped in the river. The cool water and warmth of his lips on her skin still made her quiver.

"Oh." A small, high-pitched moan escaped Cheryl's lips; and her hand went to her mouth. A few patrons turned, and she coughed. She thought no one was the wiser until across the aisle — Jake Cameron's dark eyes stayed on her long after everyone had turned away. Cheryl felt herself blush. *There's no possible way he read my mind.*

She told herself the whole thing was silly and averted her eyes to the front of the church. Moments later, Cheryl glanced in Jake's direction and discovered she was still on his radar. Whatever kind of arrogant game of intimidation this was, she wasn't going to play. Dori, a debater in high school, told her visualization was a sure way to put an opponent in their place. Cheryl needed to see Jake in a vulnerable way. She pictured him nude in the river. Her plan took a U-turn when the scene played out and he stepped onto the riverbank. He brushed the hair back from his face, and water ran from his elbows, down a set of well-built arms to a flat, sexy stomach. Jake's muscular body, in full display, glistened in the sunlight where he stood — staring at her — from across the river.

A sudden spike in body temperature made Cheryl blink a few times. *What is wrong with me?*

When Jake's eyes finally left her, she released a breath and concentrated on the preacher's face. *Pastor, do the real Christian thing and dismiss the congregation soon instead of torturing us in this oven of a church.*

Most Sundays it didn't matter how long church was, but today with the heat and a heifer in the barn in labor, it did. Cheryl checked her wristwatch. Close to an hour had gone by since the service started. If she were lucky, the birth would occur later tonight when her hired hand was due back.

A small girl started to cry, and her mother consoled her by fanning her with a church bulletin. The pastor pounded his fist onto the pulpit, obviously in a desperate attempt to capture anyone's attention. It wasn't his fault his message didn't spark a fire. Nothing was going to ignite the congregation today in this July heat wave.

Taylor became more fidgety with every moment that passed, swinging his feet back and forth under the pew. When his short legs stopped, he stared up at his mother with big, blue, sad eyes. It was a silent plea to get out of there. That same sad expression appeared too often since his father's death.

It was hard to comprehend more than a year had gone by. It seemed like yesterday she had found Jon lying under that tractor. She silently prayed to rid her mind of the sight and to remember only his smiling face. *Please, God, help me. I miss him so much — sometimes it's hard to breathe.*

Jon believed she could make it on her own; but as time passed, Cheryl found it more difficult to make ends meet. The hired hand's share alone dug deep into the profits, and the loan for seed needed to be paid each year. Taxes and insurance along with the staggering cost of keeping their older equipment in working order was an endless sea of debt. She struggled every day to keep her head above water. Tears welled in her eyes; and she blinked them back, looking away from Taylor.

Cheryl touched her cheek. Her hand was not only clammy but oddly cold. The pastor's voice faded then filtered away to some far-off place. When she struggled to find a breath, panic set in and took control. The pastor and the area around the pulpit twirled into a blur before her eyes. Cheryl reached forward to grasp the back of the pew in front of her. *Oh, God, no. I'm going to faint in front of all these people. This can't be happening.*

Taylor's shaky voice begged. "Please, Mom, open your eyes."

She blinked twice at a large Adam's apple. She was staring at the throat of Godfrey Simpson, the church usher.

"Mrs. Langtree, you all right?"

"Y... yes, I'm okay," Cheryl mumbled.

"You gave us a scare, passing out like that," Godfrey rattled. "Pastor Timms's sermon sure was running a long time, but this ain't no way to end it." Laughter broke out from the crowd gathered around.

Nell Thompson pushed through the crowd. "For heaven's sake, everybody back up and give this woman some air. Poor thing can hardly breathe. She doesn't need a crowd hovered around to gawk at her. Get her under the shade of those trees." The loose skin under her arm wobbled as she pointed out the open side door toward some large pines outside.

The usher scooped Cheryl in his arms and took a few steps toward the door.

"I'm all right. Put me down," Cheryl demanded. Godfrey carefully released her legs but hung on to her shoulders.

"We'll see to it she's okay. The rest of you go back to worshiping the Lord," Nell instructed the congregation. She nodded. "Pastor, carry on."

The good pastor nodded with a relieved smile, no doubt thankful she had taken charge. Taylor tagged behind his mother as Godfrey and Nell, each with an arm around Cheryl, walked out the door. They slowly made it down the granite steps and across the parched, wilted, grass before reaching the shade of the pines. A slight flutter of a breeze touched Cheryl's face. Godfrey gently lowered her onto a wooden bench. He and Nell sat on each side of her.

"I thought I could show my son and the rest of the world we're going to be okay. I started to believe it was true ...." Her eyes went to Taylor, and she stopped talking, but her shoulders trembled.

Nell put her chubby arm around Cheryl and looked in her eyes. "Don't you worry about what anyone thinks but you. Besides being both mother and father to this boy, you've done a darn good job running a farm by yourself. You don't have nothing to prove to anyone."

"I feel so embarrassed. I passed out in front of the whole church."

Nell shook her head. "My lands, this heat is hard on every living thing and especially on a woman who works as hard as you do." Both women looked at the usher who still had his arm around Cheryl, sitting close on the bench.

"You can go, Godfrey. Back to your duties of ushering, thank you." Nell's tone bordered on sarcastic. Startled and maybe a little embarrassed, Godfrey stood and muttered about it being a lot cooler out there on his way back to the church.

"Don't be so hard on yourself, girl. You're doing fine," Nell said in a soothing voice. She pointed to a set of swings behind the church. "Taylor, honey, I'll sit with your momma until she catches her breath. Why don't you go over there and swing for a while?"

A smile came over Taylor's face. "You mean, we don't have to go back in there?"

"No, dear," Nell told him sympathetically. "You can go and play."

Cheryl looked at her son's back as he raced off and grabbed the heavy rope of the swing. His white shirt was stuffed into his navy church slacks, and his shoes shined so that the sun reflected off them. Taylor had beamed with pride when he showed them to her that morning before church.

"See Mom, I can shine them like Dad."

Jon and Taylor had their shoe shining ritual every Sunday while she was in the bathroom fussing with her hair. Cheryl was still watching Taylor when Nell patted her hand.

"How much are you eating and sleeping?"

"It's hard to do either in this heat."

"I wouldn't want to lose that ornery old man of mine. Earl sure does leave a lot to be desired, but we've always had each other to lean on. If something happens to me first, I'd like to believe he'd try and take care of himself." Both women were startled by the sudden sound of ringing church bells.

Cheryl rose slowly and motioned for her son. "We'd better get going. I don't want the whole congregation over here fussing over a foolish fainting woman."

"Are you sure you're alright to drive? I can drive you home, and Earl can follow."

"No, that won't be necessary. I'm okay."

"Remember, you need to take care of yourself. Don't hesitate for one minute to ask us for help if you need it."

"Thank you so much." Cheryl gave her a hug but kept her eyes on the tall oak doors in front of the church.

Nell leaned in and commented with a lowered voice, "Taylor doesn't need to lose his mama, too."

Taylor sprinted toward the two women, creating a small cloud of dust with his sudden stop.

He smiled down at his shoes. "It don't matter, now. Church is over."

"Doesn't," Cheryl corrected him automatically. "Doesn't matter." She took his slightly damp hand, and the three walked to her truck.

"Oh, by the way are you coming to quilt on Thursday? I guess that's the day Lucille Cameron decided will work for her."

"Yes, I'll try to make it," Cheryl answered.

"That woman thinks she's the queen." Nell rolled her gray eyes. "Someone should tell her highness that being married to the Sugar King doesn't make her royalty."

Cheryl smiled and warned Taylor to be careful not to brush against their dirty truck when he climbed into the cab. When people began to pour out of the church doors, Cheryl waved goodbye to Nell and left the parking lot with a swirl of dust behind them.

On the ten-mile drive home, they passed fields of deep green sugar beets, golden wheat and corn over knee high in height. Most of the leaves of the crops drooped, begging for rain. When Cheryl crossed the bridge over the Chippewa River, large rocks from the bottom stuck out of the low water. Earlier that spring the river flooded, but not like the previous year. The water level this year went back down as fast as it had come up. It hadn't taken long for it to dry out nicely. Taylor hadn't said anything since they left the church parking lot.

"What are you thinking about?"

"Mom, you're not going to die, too, are you?" Taylor wrinkled his brows.

"You mean that dizzy spell? That wasn't anything," Cheryl said breezily, hoping to dismiss his fears. "I didn't eat any breakfast. That's all. Honey, I'm fine. I'm going to live a long time."

Apparently satisfied with her answer, he smiled the last few miles home. She smiled back but thought about Jon. She was still angry with him for his carelessness that fateful day, and now she was upset with herself for what happened in church. Taylor had been through so much. He didn't need to see her cry, or worse, pass out. *I need to be strong for him.*

Cheryl pulled up to their sunny yellow house trimmed in bright white. Its cheery appearance gave the feeling nothing bad could happen to anyone who lived there. When they had remodeled it four years ago, she was determined to make this into a ranch-style dream home. Jon hadn't been on board in the beginning.

"And where is there a horse on this farm?"

"Even if we don't agree about having horses, we can have a ranch house," she spouted back. He smiled and gave in, knowing how much it meant to her. That conversation seemed like a million years ago.

When she stepped into the kitchen, it was evident she had achieved her goal. The sun glinted off shiny copper kettles hanging from the rack above the counter. It was no accident the rust-colored Formica tabletop coordinated with the metal canisters. White eyelet curtains were trimmed in the same hue. *Does any of it really matter?*

Taylor slammed the screen door. "Mom, is there any iced tea left?"

"Yeah, I think so, honey. But change your clothes first, before you do anything."

"I don't want it now. I'll have water. After while when it gets dark, let's sit out on the porch and have tea, like we used to with Dad."

Cheryl smiled, amazed at her son for remembering those evenings. She could almost feel the weight of Jon's arm around her shoulder and the closeness of Taylor's small body snuggled between them on the wicker love seat. It was the safest, most perfect place in the world. Maybe that was it. It had been too perfect to last.

The sight of her son with his head stuck in the refrigerator with the door wide open was enough to snap her back to reality.

"What are you looking for now? Shut that refrigerator door. We're not cooling the house with it. We're going to have a quick bite to eat. Then we're going to change into chore clothes. We need to check on the heifer. When we're done, we're going to clean out the lamb pen and put down fresh bedding."

Taylor closed the refrigerator door and whined. "Aw, Mom do we have to? It's hot out."

"You begged me to let you have those lambs. When I walked by their pen this morning, my hair almost curled from the strong smell. If you were them, would you want to live in a dirty pen?"

He shook his head no.

CHERYL PUSHED OPENED the wooden door and stepped from bright sunlight into the darkened barn. Before her eyes adjusted she knew the status on the heifer. Her low but steady mooing indicated the time was close, but she sounded worn out. Somehow last fall, the heifer had gotten in by the bull and was bred young. Ideally, it should have been bred now to deliver with the rest of the herd in the spring. In any case, it was the small heifer's first time calving. It would need help. Cheryl stood above the animal lying in the straw. A pang of panic hit. She knew what needed to be done, but had little idea how to do it.

"Mom, is it time for the heifer to have her calf?"

"Yes, she's close. I need to stay and help her. You go into the lamb shed and start cleaning the pen. The wheelbarrow and the pitchfork with the short handle are sitting out. Go get started." Taylor sighed and left the barn.

The birth of the calf couldn't have happened at a worst time. Cheryl's hired hand, David Cowen, had gone to Freeport for a family wedding with his mother. First-time calving heifers were likely to be late. This had given Cheryl a false sense of security, thinking David would likely be back before labor began. Knowing how excited David's elderly mother was about the wedding, it wasn't the time to mention she had never pulled a calf. She didn't want to be the reason his mother missed her grandson's wedding.

When Cheryl fed the cows in the morning the heifer had acted strangely, an indication she would calve today. She had watched her father pull a calf countless times, but he believed it wasn't a job for a woman. When Jon was alive, he had always insisted on doing it.

Cheryl opened the gate and went into the pen toward the animal. She knelt in the straw close by and saw the calf's hooves were poking out of the birth canal. It was a relief to see the legs were going in the right direction. She took a deep breath before reaching inside the heifer's birth canal to check for the head. Her heart raced as her hand ran up the legs feeling for the calf's tongue or nose. She was in up to her elbow when her fingers ran into something solid. Feeling for a nostril, she knew it was too flat and wide of a surface to be the nose. The head was likely turned sideways. She groaned. *Oh no!*

Cheryl remembered her father had mentioned this sometimes occurred. The head had to be turned. If it didn't face the right direction it could break its neck, which would delay birth and risk death to both the calf and the heifer. She tried to turn the head, but the area tightened with a contraction.

Once she was able, Cheryl pulled her arm out and sat back on her legs and weighed her options. She could call Earl and get his advice, but he would want to come and deliver the calf. What kind of farmer would she appear to be then? One who wouldn't get any respect from the other farmers. *How could Jon have believed I was capable of all the things he used to do?*

Filled with disappointment, she slowly got to her feet to call Earl. She reached for the gate but stopped and tried to recall bits of a conversation between Jon and another farmer. The farmer reported when he reached into the birth canal of a heifer, he found many things amiss. The calf's legs were bent back and so was the head. In between contractions, he turned the calf's head and feet after he pushed it back further inside the birth chamber.

Cheryl returned to the heifer's side and knelt to observe the animal, waiting for signs of a contraction. Soon the heifer quieted; she reached in and put her fingers on the far side of the calf's head. She pushed it back as hard as she could and dug her fingers deeper. Feeling a soft hole, she became elated, knowing it was a nostril. Once her fingers cupped around the nose, she managed to get somewhat of a grip and pulled. Cheryl gasped when she felt it turn forward. She drew her hand out and took a big breath.

Her legs shook when she stood up and took the calf puller off the hook where it hung nearby. She carefully attached the chain around the front feet of the unborn animal above its hooves. In rhythm with the contractions she cranked the ratchet on the puller and slowly brought the calf into the world.

Sweat dripped from Cheryl's nose when she leaned over the small, motionless animal and cleaned mucous out of its nostrils and mouth. The mother stood and licked her newborn lying in the straw. The calf began to move. *It was alive!* Tears came to Cheryl's eyes, and she brought her hands together and thanked God.

She stared at the blood on her fingers and under her nails. Blood on her hands the day of Jon's accident had brought tears of sadness. How ironic that today it brought tears of joy.

"You did it, Mom! The baby calf is here." Taylor ran to the pen. Cheryl removed a handkerchief from her pocket and wiped her face.

"It sure got me all sweated up." She moved her thick blonde braid to wipe the back of her neck, smiling at Taylor's pink cheeks. "We both need a shower."

After the birth of the heifer calf and some finishing touches from Cheryl on the lamb pen, the afternoon passed quickly. As a reward for Taylor's hard work, Cheryl decided to make his favorite meal: macaroni and cheese and hotdogs. When the supper dishes were done, she filled two tall glasses with ice and sweet tea then called for him to join her. Taylor rushed to shut off the television and met her on the porch.

They sat on the screened porch until bedtime listening to the crickets and watching fireflies float in the night air. A nice breeze came up and gave them some relief from the heat. Cheryl wrapped her arms around him while they sat in the wicker love seat.

"Mom, how long do fireflies live?"

Cheryl thought for a moment. "I don't really know, but I would imagine for at least the summer."

"I'm sure glad that we're not fireflies," he said with certainty.

One moment he was talking, and the next he was asleep. She looked at her son and said a silent prayer. *God give me the strength to deal with my grief, so I can give him back his life.* How proud his father would be of him — and of her for pulling the calf. Despite what happened in church that morning, they were going to be okay.

Carefully, she picked up her sleeping boy and carried him to his bedroom. She tucked him in and examined his innocent face in the moonlight before planting a kiss on his temple. "Good night, my angel." Her eyes stayed on him as she left the room.

Cheryl returned to the porch to finish her tea, but paused at the window. The silent wonderland created by bright stars reminded her of the night she and Jon had met eight years ago. He was staying with his aunt and uncle near Webster to help with the harvest after his uncle broke his leg. That night Cheryl and her little sister, Jolene, decided to go on the neighborhood hayride that Jon's cousin, Mark, was hosting.

Jolene whispered, "Why are you holding that guy's hand?" By the end of the night she warned her older sister, "Sure he's kinda cute, but he isn't going to be nothing but an ordinary farm boy. I can't believe you let him kiss you goodnight."

Cheryl could still feel his kiss on her lips. She would do anything to have that ordinary farm boy here now.

THE AROMA of cinnamon rolls and fresh coffee invaded every room of the house at the Sugar King farm. Breakfast was about to be served in the formal dining room where Chet and Lucille Cameron waited for their sons to join them. Chet read the morning paper while Lucille tried to talk to him about the quilting project she was involved in at church.

"Well, after I said I would donate all the materials, they decided to let me be in charge of the project this year. Everyone knows I could do a better job than some people, not to mention any names."

Chet, seemingly preoccupied, turned the newspaper to the next page. Lucille waited for his comment but when he didn't give her one she sighed and pushed her chair back. A smile came to her lips. She gazed at the long, red mahogany table in front of her. Set with lovely floral placemats she'd purchased in Minneapolis. They looked elegant with the fresh white and red roses she had arranged in an antique vase that once belonged to Chet's mother. She frowned at the empty leather-backed chairs and checked her wristwatch. *I said eight o'clock. If those boys know what's good for them, they better be here on time.*

Lucille walked into the kitchen and started a conversation with Irene, the old housekeeper who had been with the Cameron family for more than twenty years.

"Where are those boys? I told them to be up to the house by eight o'clock for breakfast," Lucille said, annoyed.

Irene pulled cinnamon rolls out of the oven and set them on a cooling rack. "You didn't hear it from me, but when I got here this morning, I heard them talking about breaking that horse their dad told them to leave alone."

"*Why* can't those boys listen?" Lucille asked, more as a statement than a question. "No wonder my hair is turning gray." She hadn't finished her sentence when the door opened and her twenty-seven-year-old son, Jake, entered. He took off his cowboy hat and hung it on a hook by the door. Sun-streaked caramel highlights ran through his brown hair and created a rich contrast against his tanned skin. His brown eyes sparkled when he bent down and kissed his mother on the cheek.

"And Mother, why is your hair turning gray?" he teased playfully.

"Your two brothers are down at the stables trying to ride that wild beast your dad bought. I wish he'd never brought that thing home."

Chet's crazy explanation for buying the horse at an auction baffled her. The owner had died when the rare Arabian was a colt, and his wife had done nothing but mistreat it since. The horse was too wild to bring into the ring for viewing, but Chet decided to take a look at it anyway. He peered over the stall and it cocked its head at him. Chet saw desperation in the animal's eyes, and decided they formed a connection. When the number of the wild horse was announced, the owner muttered, "I don't care if they kill that thing for glue. I just want my money." Chet raised his hand and bid.

Jake left to wash up in the small bathroom off the kitchen.

Lucille went to the window and peered out. Her two younger sons, Michael and Brett, walked up the sidewalk brushing the dust off their clothes. She sighed, thankful neither one had broken limbs. She glared when they entered the kitchen.

Brett was twenty-two and finally done with college. He looked more like his father every day, with the same green eyes and blonde hair, the opposite of his two older brothers. Jake was more of a perfect combination of her and Chet. Michael, the middle child at twenty-six, was undeniably her son. His dark hair was the same color as hers as a young girl and his facial features resembled her side of the family.

She didn't want her husband to overhear her talk to the boys about being on the horse and decided not to bring up the subject. Instead, she reminded her sons, who were both over six feet tall, to clean up before coming to the table.

Everyone was quiet while they ate except Lucille, who once again talked about the quilting project at church.

"Hey, what happened to that Langtree woman at church?" Michael interrupted his mother. "It was hot and all, but it sure was an eye-opener when she hit the floor."

Brett chuckled at his brother's comment.

"She's probably exhausted. It's just a shame she has to work so hard since losing her husband. Now she's raising that boy on her own," Lucille remarked. "Horrible."

Jake's eyes were on his cinnamon roll as he smeared butter on it. "I heard she's still got that hired hand she had last year to help her get the crops out. Word has it she's trying to farm with him by herself. I don't know if I've ever heard of such a crazy thing. That boy can't be seven years old, and she isn't that big of a gal."

Brett was wearing a strange expression when Michael waved a hand in front of his face.

He swatted Michael's hand away. "I think she may be a little old for me, but she's certainly not hard on the eyes. With that nice piece of property she lives on ..." Brett nodded with a smile. "You know, she wouldn't be a bad catch."

Michael's brown eyes darkened, and he cuffed his younger brother on the back of the head. "When you fell off that horse this morning, did it give you brain damage?"

Chet's face flushed red. "You boys stay away from that horse or I'll be giving you both brain damage." Michael and Brett were silent and looked down at the table.

Chet regained his composure and turned to his youngest son. "You're right about that property, though. Sitting on the Chippewa River, it's some of the best cropland around. Twenty years ago, I offered Jim Langtree a fair price on it. He didn't want to sell, and said he intended to give it to his son. After Jon died, I thought it was disrespectful to rush over to his widow and inquire about selling before he was cold in the ground. So, I waited, and now she's got this crazy notion about running the place herself. All a person can do now is sit back and offer to take it off her hands when she falls on her face."

Lucille stared at her husband and pursed her lips. "I wouldn't hold my breath, Chet. The women in the quilting group say she's a very hard worker."

A second later, Brett piped up, "I, myself, do not think there is anything wrong with older women. Maybe the best-looking man on this farm," he paused and motioned his pointer fingers to himself, "should show the rest of you not-so-fortunate fellows how to win this woman's heart."

The two older brothers looked at each other. Jake burst out, "What the hell did they teach you at that college? Idiocy 101?"

Lucille broke in, "I don't want to hear that kind of talk. And leave that poor girl alone. She's been through too much already."

THE REST of the day and into the evening, thoughts of Cheryl Langtree lingered on Michael's mind. He lay in bed that night in the dark thinking about her again. He admitted to himself he had often fantasized about her during a boring sermon. He chuckled. Maybe sitting behind her was part of what kept his church attendance so high.

His amusement ceased remembering the very first time he saw her there with Jon. The sunlight had shone through the stained windows and played on her wheat-colored hair. At that moment, he'd noted her pretty face along with her nice figure and couldn't take his eyes off her. He recalled the sudden stabbing sensation in his chest the first time he watched Jon smile at his new bride and put his arm around her slender frame. Everyone had always said Jon Langtree was a lucky son-of-a bitch up until the day he died. He was lucky enough to find a beautiful girl, and smart enough to marry her before he brought her around here. Jon had also been fortunate the Cameron men were brought up to believe it wasn't right to chase married women.

A year had gone by and the respectable amount of mourning time had passed. It was time to call on her. Who knew what could happen if he played his cards right? He could easily see himself settled down with a woman like her at his side. The fact that her land connected with the home place made it easier to envision. He thought about his father's mistake with acquiring the Langtree property and concluded he had no time to waste.

"WHO'S NOT COMING?" Lucille asked after she entered the church basement. She caught the end of a conversation between Joan and Nell. Dropping the bags of fabric and batting down on the table, she scanned the group of women.

"Cheryl Langtree," Joan replied.

"Maybe she's too busy with her hired hand," remarked Joan's mother, Mary Swenson.

Some of the women giggled and Joan added, "Out in the barn by themselves."

"Wait a minute, ladies," Nell Thompson barked out. "Cheryl Langtree is a decent gal, and if you're saying anything different, then I don't want any part of this group. How can you even say such a thing, after what's she's gone through?"

Pastor Timms' wife, Patsy, immediately calmed the group down. "Ladies, let's not forget our purpose here — to serve the Lord with our gifts and talents. Please keep the conversation at a positive level."

Lucille cleared her throat and proceeded to speak, "First of all ladies, I would like to say the Star of Bethlehem quilt has always been one of my favorites." Opening one of the bags, she took out a simple cream-colored muslin. "This will be the backing for the quilt and the sections around the large star in the middle. For the rest of the quilt ..." she reached into another bag and took out some more fabrics. The remaining fabrics were coordinated well in shades of olive green and bright orange. Nell shook her head but Lucille didn't acknowledge her.

"For our second quilt, I think we should make the Double Wedding Ring quilt." Lucille looked for a reaction from the women. "I know we did that one two years ago, but I think it's always a hit. Everyone knows someone who's going to get married. Invariably, it has always been a big money-maker for the church." Everyone nodded except Nell, who sat with an icy stare and arms crossed in front of her large bosom.

While the ladies measured and cut the fabric for the first quilt, talk in the room went from the blessing of rain they'd received the night before to who was ill in the neighborhood. The group was about to adjourn, when Lucille noticed Nell sitting quietly by herself. Her silence was more than enough to pique Lucille's interest. She moved closer and heard the woman chant to herself under her breath. It was hard to understand with her accent, but when Lucille figured out Nell was reciting the

Lord's Prayer, she smiled. It was an obvious admission of her defeat.

LATER THAT DAY, Lucille poured a glass of chardonnay in a lead crystal wine glass and pulled back the long drape from the window of the den. She marveled at the coral colored clouds from the setting sun. It was a beautiful ending to a great day. Chet and Jake had gone to the fields to check on the work the migrant workers did earlier in the day. She was glad to have a few moments to herself to reminisce about her victorious afternoon. None of the women, including Nell, had any objections to her decisions. She was pleased with this year's first session of the quilting circle.

She finished her wine then decided to go down to the stables to see what Michael and Brett were doing. Earlier, she'd seen them head in that direction. Lucille's eyes checked each trimmed shrub along the cement walkway to the stables, but her mind was on how she was going to give it to those two if she caught them on that horse. Once inside the open door, she overheard her two sons talking and slipped behind one of the stalls to listen. She could see them through a slot in the wooden stall. Lucille didn't feel good about eavesdropping, but those two rarely let her in on anything that was going on with them.

"So, what makes you think she's going to talk to you?" Brett asked.

"What on earth makes you think she'll talk to *you*?"

"Let's see — my good looks, charm, and charisma. I know my way around women. Around campus I was known as the 'The Sock Remover.'"

"Why'd they call you that?" Michael wrinkled his brows.

"I can charm the socks off any woman. I'll leave the rest to your imagination." Brett beamed.

"Cheryl Langtree isn't one of your little naïve college girls who's searching for attention because she's mad at daddy. Besides being beautiful, she's a good mother and she smells like a little bit of heaven. Put it this way, she's way out of your league!"

"I guess all those times sitting behind her like a lovesick fool, you noticed quite a bit about her." Brett smirked. "Women like her don't go for men with your reputation."

Michael's face turned crimson. "Well, little brother, why don't you put your money where your mouth is?"

"What do you mean?"

"How about a hundred-dollar wager on the winning of Cheryl Langtree's heart?"

"That's a lot of money." Brett sounded reluctant.

"So, you don't want to lose that much — is that what you're saying?"

"No, I'm saying that's a lot of money for a recent college graduate to take from his older brother for teaching him a lesson about women." Brett stuck out his hand. "You're on."

Lucille watched them shake hands. She quietly crept from behind the stall and walked toward the house, confident neither one of her sons had seen her. A safe distance from the stables, she slowed her pace and recapped their conversation. It wasn't a surprise to hear Brett's feelings for Cheryl Langtree, but learning Michael felt the same was a shock. Michael deserved a girl with a little more class. Someone more like Jake's girlfriend, Susan — a woman truly worthy of the Cameron name.

2

C heryl smoothed her hands across the tiny white polka dots on her blue dress and tightened the belt. She remembered Jon's comment on how the dress brought out the color in her eyes and decided to wear it to church. In the mirror, she pinched her cheeks and knew it wouldn't work. Before Pastor Timms finished one of his lengthy sermons, she'd be bruised. She went in her makeup drawer and brushed some blush across her cheeks. Makeup was something she didn't have time for this past year. *I'm not trying to impress anyone.* Today, she'd wear blush to reassure the congregation she wasn't going to make a habit of passing out in church.

They arrived at church fifteen minutes early and Cheryl followed Taylor to their usual pew. It was the same pew where she and Jon sat since they were married. It always seemed like a safe place ... that is, before last Sunday. People shuffled in and many smiled at Cheryl and Taylor. An elderly woman, Sophie Blackstone, sat in the row ahead of them.

Leaning back, she said to Cheryl, "Dear, I hope you're feeling well today. We sure missed you at the quilting group."

"I'm feeling better. Thank you, Sophie. I do plan on coming to quilt this week."

Sophie nodded and turned to the front of the church.

Taylor was busy marking the songs they were going to sing in the hymnal with the satin ribbon markers inside the book. Michael Cameron sat down behind them, a row up from his usual spot. Shortly after, Brett Cameron came in and sat down next to Michael. Cheryl noticed because Brett generally sat by his folks across the aisle. He leaned forward and tapped Taylor on the shoulder.

"You're pretty good at numbers, aren't you?"

Taylor looked at him carefully before he slowly answered, "Yeah ..."

"Maybe someday you'll be a math teacher or something like that," Brett told him.

Taylor wrinkled his face and looked at his mother. She turned and smiled politely at Brett and saw Michael roll his eyes at his brother.

Cheryl faced the front of the church where Godfrey ushered Patsy Timms to the front pew. Being a large woman, it took all her strength to slide herself to her spot, directly under the pulpit. The service was about to start when Cheryl got the feeling of being watched. She turned her head and caught Lucille Cameron observing her from across the aisle. When their eyes met, Lucille looked away and readjusted herself in the pew. She then slid back behind her husband. Jake Cameron was on Lucille's other side reading the announcements on the back of the bulletin.

Pastor Timms started the service and progressed to the passing of the peace, where members of the congregation greeted one another with a friendly handshake. Taylor grabbed his mother's hand and shook it with a smile. Cheryl turned to shake hands and both Cameron brothers reached for hers at the same time. Feeling awkward, she let out a small giggle. Brett immediately dropped his hand and held it out to Taylor, who was hesitant to shake it. Michael shook Cheryl's hand firmly but clung a moment longer than necessary. She pulled her hand away and Brett claimed it. He brought it up close to his mouth, like he was going to kiss it. To her relief, he released it quicker than his brother.

The service ended faster than the previous Sunday. For reasons unknown, the pastor hadn't given one of his famous, long-winded sermons. The church bells were ringing when Cheryl bent to pick up her purse.

"Did you enjoy Pastor Timms' sermon?" Michael Cameron asked.

She straightened and looked around to see if he was talking to someone else before answering, "Yes, it was good, and may I add, a little shorter than last week. Maybe he was afraid someone would pass out or something."

Michael laughed.

"Maybe you," Brett said to Taylor and playfully poked him in the ribs. Taylor giggled and pulled away. Cheryl put her hand on her son's shoulder then nudged him out of the pew.

Outside, Taylor rushed ahead to the truck while Cheryl trailed behind and dug in her purse for her keys. She was about to pull her truck out of the parking spot when that strange sensation of being watched struck again. When she scanned the lot, her eyes fell on Brett, staring at her from behind the wheel in his truck. She didn't want to acknowledge him and turned away in a different direction but instantly gasped. Michael sat in his truck in the next row with his eyes fixed on her, too. *What's the deal?* Cheryl shook her head and tried to ignore their conspicuous surveillance as she drove away.

Brett sat at the table in the kitchen eating a piece of chicken when Michael came in and went to the refrigerator. He glared at his younger brother as he walked by, but didn't say anything. Opening the refrigerator, Michael reached for a piece of chicken and noticed nothing left on the platter but a small wing. He held up the wing and stared at his brother. "You ate the other three pieces of chicken that were left from dinner?"

"Yeah, what's it to you? Last I checked it's a free country," Brett answered sarcastically.

"And that brings me to the question: Why did you have to sit by me in church?" Michael's jaw was clenched.

"The last I heard, the pews are for the parishioners of the church. And being a parishioner of the church, I have the right to sit in any pew I choose."

"What was that stupid comment you said to the kid? Oh yeah, I remember. Someday you'll be a math teacher or something." Michael shook his head. "So clever for a college graduate."

"At least I didn't hold on to her hand until she had to rip it away from me," Brett snickered.

"No, you just looked like a moron acting like you were going to kiss it or something goofy."

"Well, my ignorant, uncouth brother, *that* is what they call *chivalry*." Brett's voice was condescending.

"Whatever you want to call it, it's up to you. The rest of us, including Cheryl Langtree, know what a pile of shit smells like."

Brett pushed himself away from the table and stood. The decor on the wall rattled when he made his exit out the kitchen door.

LATER THAT EVENING, Michael lay on a leather couch in the den and watched "Mod Squad" on television. When Lucille came into the room, she winced from the noisy police sirens that blasted from the show.

"Can you turn that down, please?" she asked. He did as she requested, but when she started to speak he put his finger to his mouth and motioned for her to be quiet.

When the show ended, he told her, "Sorry, Mother. It's the last episode of the season. I really wanted to watch it."

"Where did your brother go tonight?" She sounded irritated. "I didn't know he was going anywhere until I saw the tail lights of his truck going out the driveway."

"Maybe he went into town to meet some friends. Who knows where he's going, probably some stupid beer party in the woods."

"Why didn't you go with him?"

"I'm not going to hang out with Gilligan and the rest of his crew," Michael snapped, then changed the subject. "When are Dad and Jake supposed to be back from the church meeting?"

"I really don't know. But it's so exciting to know that after years of being shoved into a musty, old basement for every event, we're finally building a fellowship hall."

Michael stared ahead, not saying anything.

"What are you thinking about?"

"Nothing …. Nothing that important right now," he told her and stood.

"Wait, sit down a second," she pleaded. "We used to be so close, you and I. What happened? I don't know why I'm the enemy now."

"Mother, you're not the enemy. I just got a few things on my mind, none of which you would understand or can do anything about. So, why should I bother you with my problems?"

She pursed her lips together. "Do your problems have anything to do with the Langtree girl and what happened in church this morning with your brother?"

He jerked his head and sat down. "Did he look stupid to you, too?"

"I don't know if he looked stupid," Lucille replied. "All I know is that it was obvious you both wanted to get her attention. I don't know what your brother is thinking. Why would he want to get involved with her? She's way too mature for him."

"So, you don't think he has a chance with her?"

"No, I'm not saying that," she answered mindfully. "Cheryl Langtree is an attractive girl, but she has a child. Think about it. It would be a lot for any man to deal with, raising another man's son. Your brother isn't mature enough to handle any of it." She suddenly stopped talking. "I know you and she are the same age. But have you considered what the responsibilities of being involved with her would be?"

"I have thought about it Mother, a lot, and now I can't get her out of my head. I want to get to know her, but I don't know how to go about it." He shocked himself with his confession.

"Are you really sure? I guess this girl could be a diamond in the rough."

"Yes, definitely. I just don't know how to get into her world."

"I may be able to help you with that." Her smile looked dangerous.

"What are you talking about? I don't want you or anyone else meddling into this. It's bad enough Brett is messing things up. He made us both look like idiots in church."

"I don't plan on meddling, if that's what you think. But wouldn't it be helpful to know what's going on with her or where she's going?" Lucille watched his reaction.

"Mother, how could I possibly find out any of that?"

"She's in the quilting circle I'm in charge of. I'll be seeing her every Thursday afternoon for the next several months. We *do* talk about other things besides quilting."

"Could you find out information without her figuring it out?" Michael was now interested. He realized he didn't have a whole lot of options and this could be a huge advantage over his brother.

"Yes, I would be willing to find out anything to help you. I only want a couple of things in return."

Michael sighed. "And what would they be, Mother?"

"I don't want your brothers or your father to know what we are doing, and I want you to trust me enough to confide in me

37

once in a while. Like I said, I'm not the enemy. I want to help you."

Michael thought for a second. "If you help me with this situation, I can let you in on a few things. Not everything though, okay?" His question sounded more like a statement.

Light from headlights spilled into the den. Lucille looked relieved their discussion had ended with perfect timing.

CHERYL SAT in the wicker love seat on her porch and sipped on a glass of iced tea. She looked out over the shadowed field. Even in the dark, it was evident recent rain had increased the size of the sugar beet plants. She heard the crickets chirp a while ago, and now, nothing but silence.

After church that morning, she and Taylor went to Jon's sister, Jane's, house for lunch. Taylor was completely worn out from riding bike on a dirt track behind their house with his cousin, Jeremy. Cheryl helped her son with a quick bath and he fell asleep a minute after going to bed.

She placed her feet on the edge of the coffee table, crossing her ankles. How good it felt to relax and think about the full day they'd just spent. She thought about Michael and Brett's odd behavior in church that morning. *I wonder what's going on with them? And their mother, too?* Up until now, their family had rarely made any effort to speak to the Langtrees. Lucille patted her hand and whispered condolences when the Cameron clan came through the receiving line at Jon's funeral; Chet and the boys only nodded. Jon's late mother, Rose, confided in Cheryl her thoughts from a confrontation with Lucille Cameron. It led her mother-in-law to a private confession at church. Some of the comments Jon had made about the Cameron family weren't too positive, either. He'd been in the same grade at school as Michael and didn't have any trouble with him, but Jon disliked how he treated some of the other classmates. Michael made sure everyone knew he was better than them because his daddy had money.

When Cheryl mentioned to Jon that Michael had been staring at her in church, his comment was, "That's good, let him stare. It must kill him that I have something he can't have." Cheryl chuckled at Jon's usual statement whenever Brett's name came up in conversation. "I'd like to kick that little smart aleck's ass." Since Brett was taller than her husband, it always made her laugh.

Whatever they were up to was anyone's guess, and Cheryl decided she wasn't going to worry about it tonight. Tomorrow was going to be a busy day. Migrant workers were scheduled to weed her sugar beet fields. She and David Cowen needed to supervise the process. Thinking about all the work to be done the next day, Cheryl yawned and went to bed.

AT NOON THE NEXT DAY, Cheryl brought a large roaster filled with chicken hot dish along with bologna sandwiches to the workers in the field. Between filling plates and handing out sandwiches, Cheryl gazed up at the sky. It was hot, even though the sun hid behind the clouds and appeared as a dull, glowing flashlight behind a white cheesecloth. The workers were grateful for hot dish and sandwiches but more excited about the watermelon that soaked in cool water from the deep well on Cheryl's farm.

Her arms were full with the dirty roaster and dishes when she got back from the field. She heard the telephone ring from outside the house. Hastily, she set the items down on the porch and ran to answer the phone.

"Hello," Cheryl answered breathlessly.

"Hi, where have you been? I've been calling all morning," a concerned voice asked. It was her sister, Jolene, calling from Sioux Falls.

"I've been out in the fields most of the day with the migrant workers," Cheryl's words shot out. "What's going on? Is everything okay?"

"Stop being such a worry wart. Everybody's fine. I just called to see what you were up to."

For most of her life, her sister had lived in luxury with nothing to worry about. She was thirteen months younger than Cheryl and had never endured any physical labor in her life. As a kid, she stayed in the house to cook and — supposedly — clean.

"Well, how are things going in the sugar beet capital?" Jolene asked jokingly.

"Today has been pretty busy with weeding beets. It'll be a few days before they're done with our part of the rotation. Then on to the neighbors to the east."

Cheryl was about to go into more detail when her sister interrupted, "Where's Taylor when you're doing all that?"

"I dropped him off this morning at a friend's house for a sleepover."

"Haven't you been doing anything just for fun?"

Cheryl wanted to reach into the phone and slap her. *What did she expect?* "Look Jolene, with everything that's going on here, fun times aren't exactly my first priority." Her tone was cold.

"I don't mean to upset you. I just wanted to hear how you're doing. Sorry if I care what's going on with you."

"I'm sorry for being so touchy," Cheryl apologized.

"Do you want to know what I've been up to?"

"Sure. What's going on with you?"

"I don't know if Mom mentioned it or not, but Bob and I just got back from Acapulco." Jolene's enthusiasm flooded over on the telephone line.

So *this* was the true meaning of this call. Another brag session from her little sister about the exciting adventures of her and her extremely successful husband. Bob was a lawyer in Sioux Falls and, according to Jolene, it was only a matter of time before he would be promoted to partner at his firm.

"We had the time of our life. The food was wonderful and our room was just *fantastic.*" She didn't give Cheryl time to say anything. "I'll tell you something if you can keep a secret." Jolene was silent for a moment.

"What's that?" Cheryl asked.

"You can't tell anyone, especially Mom or Dad, okay?"

"Okay."

"On the last day of our trip we rented a car and did a little sight-seeing. We drove out to a quiet area away from the city. Bob heard there was this waterfall which was supposed to be breathtakingly beautiful. We found the waterfall and whoever said it was breathtaking wasn't kidding." Jolene giggled. "We got so caught up in the whole thing we decided to skinny-dip right then and there. It was the most exciting thing I've ever experienced. It was so freeing! You have no idea what you're missing. The water was so cool and invigorating. You have to try it sometime."

That comment stung. Cheryl did have an idea of what she was missing — a husband to do those kinds of things with. "It sounds like you had a great time, but I've got to go now. The hired hand is waiting for me outside and I have to get going," she lied.

Cheryl hung up the phone and sat back in her chair. She felt guilty about lying, but Jolene hadn't been completely honest with her, either. But why had she reacted like that? It wasn't her sister's fault Jon died and now she was alone.

Frustrated, she went out and gathered the dishes stacked on the porch and brought them into the house. A thought came to her while she waited for the sink to fill. *Have I become so cold I can't feel happiness for anyone?* She banged the dishes around in the sink and scrubbed them like her life depended on their cleanliness. Her mind was preoccupied when it was time to go back to the field and she almost forgot to fill the empty water tank in the back of her truck. She decided to forget all about her conversation with Jolene and concentrate on things at hand.

The sun had started its descent, but was still high above the horizon when David and Cheryl drove around to look at the weeded fields. The workers were gone, but scheduled to return the following day. They were pleased with the job the crew had accomplished so far, and both agreed it had been a long day when they returned to Cheryl's truck. David drove off toward his mother's house and Cheryl got into her vehicle. She was about to turn the key when the thought struck her. *Is this what my life has become? All work and void of any fun?* She turned her head slowly in the direction of the Chippewa River.

Maybe it was the heat or just the end of an exhausting day, but the river seemed to beckon her. The next thing she knew, she was looking down at the lazy flowing water from the river's bank. Large willow trees hung over both sides of the river with their lower branches dancing in the slow-moving current. Cheryl sat down on the soft grass and took off her boots and her socks. She rolled up the pant legs of her jeans and dipped her feet, one at a time, into the river. At first it felt almost too cold, but so marvelous as the water flowed around her tired feet, running through her toes as she raised them to the surface.

Thinking about Jolene and Bob, she suddenly had a crazy idea. How good would it feel to skinny-dip in the river right now? She thought about the time with Jon. No one was around, and the trees made it somewhat private. This section of the river bordered a field with the Sugar King farm, but if anyone drove up she would hear them a ways off. Besides, this was her land and she could do anything she wanted to do on it. She dropped her cotton blouse, damp with sweat, on the bank and pulled off her dusty blue jeans. The emerald water hypnotized her while she removed her bra and underwear. Afraid she might chicken out, Cheryl took a big breath and jumped in. The cool shock of the water instantly charged her weary, overheated body. She swam out to the middle of the river and dove under. As the water rolled over her, she imagined being under a waterfall. *Let*

Jolene and Bob do what they wanted. This feels great! Who needs Acapulco?

She let herself float free in the current then popped her head above the moving water. Snap! She flinched, and spun her head toward the trees on the bank behind her. What was that? In a panic, she swam to where her clothes were and bolted out of the water. Cheryl grabbed her things in a few quick moves and sprinted back to her truck where she frantically dressed behind the door. All the while, she kept an eye on the area where the noise had come from.

She closed her eyes for a second before driving away. *What was I thinking, doing a dumb stunt like that?*

Cheryl lay awake throughout the night and stared at the alarm clock. It was hard to sleep, thinking someone may have watched her parade around nude in the river. What had gotten into her? *That's what you get for being jealous of your sister.* Finally, she convinced herself there hadn't been anyone there and her sleeplessness was for nothing. A deer or any other animal could have easily made the noise.

The next day came too fast for Cheryl when the alarm rang just as she had drifted off to sleep. She was glad Taylor wasn't there to take care of today. It was going to be a long day and she could hardly get herself ready. The sun was coming up when she drove to the field and met David. Minutes later, the migrant workers arrived and David gave instructions to the foreman, who in turn informed the rest of the workers what to do in Spanish. The sugar beet plants grew in large clumps with several shoots. Each cluster needed to be thinned to one plant to every foot of ground. The group of men and women silently started the tedious process of thinning the beet plants as the sun crawled up into the sky.

It seemed a lifetime before lunchtime was over and Cheryl loaded up the roaster from the loose meat sandwiches she served. She picked up Taylor around six and returned to the field to talk to David while the workers finished up. The truck hauling the migrant workers pulled onto the field road to leave when David hopped into Cheryl's truck. They drove around looking at the day's work. Taylor sat in the middle, his small body bobbing up and down as they traveled over the bumpy field roads.

Driving up a slight hill, Cheryl caught a glimpse of something and took her foot off the accelerator. An object was coming closer from the west almost directly in the sun. Someone on a horse was riding toward them, but she couldn't tell who. Her truck idled in park while they waited curiously for the horseman to ride to them. She blinked and made out the silhouette of a cowboy hat. As he came into view, she could see the boyish smile on Brett Cameron's baby face. He was a little shorter than his brothers, but good looking like the other two. At that moment, she didn't care who he looked like, he was on her land and that didn't sit right with her. The farmers in the area respected each other's private property. Most wouldn't step foot on the other's land without permission.

Getting close enough, he called out, "Nice evening, isn't it?"

"Yes, it is. Can I help you, Mr. Cameron?" Cheryl leaned out the truck window.

"We're neighbors. Please call me Brett. It's a funny thing. My horse just seemed to wander over here to see how you were getting along with those migrant workers. We had a little trouble with one showing up drunk and picking a fight with another wetback."

Cheryl raised an eyebrow at his comment. "We didn't have any trouble. They did a fine job. Wouldn't you agree, David?" She glanced at her hired hand.

"I think things went well. I'm real satisfied with their work."

There was an uncomfortable silence, before Brett spoke again,

"Well, I thought I would check on you and see if everything went all right. I think it's a neighborly thing to do." His horse shifted its weight and he steadied it. "I don't think there's anything wrong with neighbors helping out one another, especially in your situation. You just call me and I'll be willing to help you out anytime."

"Thank you, but I believe David and I have everything under control." Her words were sharp.

"Okay, then, I'll be getting home. You folks enjoy your evening, and don't forget I'm just a holler away." He smiled and tilted his hat to Cheryl. He nudged the horse with a clicking sound and rode back in the direction he came from. All three people in the truck looked at each other.

A grin slowly appeared on David's face. "Cheryl, it looks like you have a suitor."

"Don't be ridiculous."

"Mom, what's a suitor?"

Cheryl hesitated a second. "It's when a boy wants to be a friend to a girl."

"That sounds yucky!" Taylor blurted.

David laughed, and it was hard for Cheryl not to giggle along with him. Her amusement came to a sudden stop. *Oh, my God. He could have been down at the river watching me. It was around this time yesterday. I wouldn't have heard him ride up on his horse.* She broke out into a sweat.

"Cheryl, are you okay?" David interrupted her rapid thoughts.

"Yeah, I'm fine. The day is just catching up to me. I didn't sleep so well last night. I'm turning in early tonight." They continued to look over the crops, but it was difficult to concentrate on anything when her thoughts kept returning to the evening before.

TAYLOR WAS TUCKED into bed when Cheryl took a long but not so relaxing bath. In bed, it didn't take her long to realize she wasn't going to fall asleep. Her fingers instinctively dialed a number.

"Hello," Dori answered. Her friend's voice on the end of the line was a comfort.

Cheryl was glad to have Dori around when things got crazy. She was even more grateful they didn't have the party line anymore where everyone could listen in on each other's calls.

"Hey, I didn't wake you, did I?"

"No, I was just lying here. As much as he's not here, you'd think I'd get used to sleeping alone." Dori's husband, Steve, a pharmaceutical salesman, was often out of town for work.

"I know what you mean," Cheryl answered softly.

"Oh, sweetie, I wasn't trying to make you feel bad."

"I know you weren't trying to. I can do that well enough on my own."

"What's going on?" Dori asked.

Cheryl told her the story about the skinny-dipping incident and Brett's odd behavior. Her friend started to laugh.

"Why are you laughing?" Cheryl failed to see the humor. "This is embarrassing."

"I'm laughing because I'm shocked that level-headed Cheryl Langtree would do such a thing,"

"Dori, be serious. I've made a fool of myself."

"Honey, don't be so hard on yourself. You don't know if anyone was there."

"I guess I don't. But thinking I may have made a naked spectacle of myself is enough to scare me into a life of solitude."

"I think you're getting worked up over nothing. You need to get away somewhere and relax for a while. Quit worrying."

"What do you mean?" Cheryl asked.

"How about this Friday night you and I go out for some drinks and a little dancing at the M & M. I heard they're supposed to have a good band. You could drop Taylor off and I'll get my niece to babysit. Steve's out of town and he's always telling me to get out and do something. So how about it?"

"Let me think about it and I'll get back to you."

"Oh, no, I'm not letting you off the hook. Eight o'clock sound good?"

"Okay, it's a date. I'll go. But I don't know how much fun I'll be. I haven't been out by myself in years."

"I guess it's time then. But I do have one request of you." Dori sounded serious.

"What's that?"

"No skinny-dipping, okay?" Dori giggled.

"You don't have to worry," Cheryl assured her. "My skinny-dipping days are behind me. See you Friday. Good night."

3

The humming sound that echoed up from the old church basement reminded Cheryl of a swarm of bees. She walked down the granite steps and found it hard to believe such a small group of women could make so much noise. The smell of fresh brewed coffee welcomed her when she entered the banquet room where the ladies gathered.

Each week the quilting circle followed the same routine. Sophie Blackstone, who was very serious about her responsibilities, arrived first to unlock the door and get the coffee maker started. When the rest of the women got there, a short prayer was said, usually led by the pastor's wife, Patsy. Two of the ladies, whose turn it was to host, would bring something for lunch. Nothing too fancy, just a hot dish or a kettle of soup and bread. Many of the ladies would make home-made bread which evolved into an unspoken competition. For dessert, oftentimes it was pie, cake, or a new bar recipe someone thought would impress the group. Like the bread rivalry, it was common knowledge whose cake was always dry and who could beat the meringue on their pie until it cried.

Once lunch was over, the group of women would start to quilt and the hostesses, after they were done cleaning up, would join them. Today it was Joan Uterman and her mother, Mary Swenson's, turn to host. Cheryl sat next to Nell, who was very excited about the arrival of her newest grandchild, Emily Louise. It was her fourth, and according to her proud grandma, the most precious baby God ever created. The hospital picture really didn't reflect the baby's best features, but Nell promised to have new pictures the following Thursday.

Lucille arrived late once again. Cheryl was sure Nell was so distracted showing everyone the baby's picture she hadn't realized Lucille entered the room.

The construction of a new fellowship hall and the arrival of a new baby dominated the conversation until Patsy Timms cleared her throat to speak.

"You all have heard about the exciting news of the new fellowship hall. Nothing is created without it being God's will. With that in mind, we need to focus on how we can serve him and make his will a reality. I'm asking for your help, ladies, with this project."

Everyone looked at each other. Surely, she didn't expect them to pound nails?

Lucille spoke up, "What do you need us to do, Patsy?"

"If every family would host a meal for the workers during construction, it would help to make this project a success. Construction is starting next week, and there is a sign-up sheet in the back of the church upstairs."

Murmurs of agreement greeted her request, then everyone went back to the quilt. Four women had portable sewing machines, which made the piecing process amazingly fast. Two tables of women cut pieces for the Star of Bethlehem quilt. Cheryl pressed the pieces with an iron while Nell sewed them together. It didn't take long for the quilt to be spread out on quilting boards and ready to be hand stitched.

"How have you been feeling lately, dear?" Nell asked, not looking up from the sewing machine.

"I'm feeling fine."

"Are the workers done with your fields?"

"Yes, they finished yesterday. It's good to be done with the thinning." Cheryl sighed with relief.

"Now that it's over, you should do something to celebrate. Go and do something fun with people your own age."

"My grandma taught me to quilt and I enjoy it. This is fun for me, and I don't care if there's no one here my own age." Cheryl looked around.

"I know you enjoy quilting, but don't you think you should get out and socialize with younger people too?"

"If it makes you feel any better, Nell, I do have plans with Dori to go to the M & M Club in Montevideo tomorrow night."

"Oh? What's going on there?" Nell asked.

"I guess there's supposed to be a good band there."

"That sounds like fun, dear. I hope you have a good time." Nell nodded.

Lucille sat at a nearby table, quietly cutting the fabric for the small stars that bordered the quilt. A complacent expression was on her face as she concentrated on the task at hand. When a subtle smile formed on Lucille's lips, Cheryl concluded that the older woman enjoyed quilting as much as she did.

CHERYL LOOKED in the mirror while she braided her long blonde hair. Tonight, she had intended to wear it down and curled the ends, but at the last minute changed her mind. She pulled it back into her usual braid and thought about makeup, then decided against that, too. This evening wasn't about impressing anyone. It was to unwind and nothing more. *Why am I so nervous?*

After going through her closet four times, she finally decided to wear her white bell-bottom jeans with a black, ruffled scoop-neck top. She spritzed on some Wind Song perfume, rationalizing if she wore it to church every Sunday, it was okay to wear tonight. Taylor leaned on the frame of the bathroom door and watched his mother hook a small silver hoop earring in her lobe.

"Why do you have to look so fancy to go out with Dori?" he asked.

"You think I look fancy, huh?" Cheryl lunged forward and tickled him in the stomach. Back in the mirror, she gave herself a final inspection. *What am I doing? I haven't been out by myself in eight years.* The phone rang and brought her back to the present.

"Hey, are you coming?" Dori asked.

"Yeah, we're just leaving now."

"Hurry up. I'm so excited for a night to ourselves."

Dori's eagerness helped smooth over the rough reality of going out without Jon.

The lot at the M & M was close to full when they found a place and parked. Cheryl's heart pounded along with the bass from the band inside as they neared the building.

Two guys who appeared to be intoxicated sat by the door and scrutinized them as they entered the bar. The women took a few steps inside when the inebriates started to howl.

"Are you sure you want to be here?" Cheryl asked.

"We've gotten this far. Let's find a table and sit down." Dori glanced around.

After they found a table by the dance floor, Dori ordered a rum and Coke and Cheryl ordered a vodka Collins from the waitress. A few minutes later, the band played "Go All the Way," and they got up to dance. Cheryl thought Dori looked cute in her white tunic top and tight jeans. Her shiny auburn curls bounced with every move. A guy from across the room asked Cheryl to dance when they returned to the table. She quickly declined and he walked away.

"Why didn't you dance with him?" Dori asked. "He didn't look too bad."

"Dori, it's such a big step for me to even be here tonight. I really debated canceling. Your phone call was just in time before I lost my nerve."

DONNA LOVITZ

"I know it's a big thing, and I'm very proud of you. I didn't mean to put on any pressure. We're here to relax and have a good time." She raised her glass. "Let's make a toast to girls' night out." They giggled and clinked their glasses together. The music was good, so they danced to more songs and ordered another drink. When the band went on break, Dori went to the restroom on the other side of the bar. She returned to the table and sat down with a silly expression on her face.

"Wow, Michael Cameron and Jim Stanton are standing at the bar," Dori exclaimed.

Cheryl looked up at the two tall men who stood by the bar with their backs to them.

"In high school, we called those two the dynamic duo. Every girl wanted to date one of them, but they only dated the upper crust girls," Dori sighed. "Jim married Angela Burten. Her father is the doctor in Watson. I heard they're divorced now. I guess her crust must have gotten soggy." Dori batted her eyes.

Cheryl laughed at her comment. *Oh, my God, I really miss this. It feels so good to laugh.* Her laughter dwindled when she saw Michael and his friend walk toward their table. Both men carried a drink in each hand. She observed how gracefully Michael moved for a man over six feet tall, even in those cowboy boots. Maybe it was the alcohol or the lighting or both, but as they got closer, Cheryl noticed just how undeniably handsome Michael Cameron was. She managed to pull her eyes away from his perfectly sculpted facial features to look at the rest of him. His dark, tanned skin contrasted nicely against the light blue short-sleeved shirt he wore. The sleeves were neatly cuffed and exposed more of his well-defined biceps. At church, he was always well groomed, but tonight his thick, dark hair didn't have a strand out of place. She saw the sparkle in his eyes and his smile grow bigger with each step he took across the dance floor.

"Well, hello. I thought that was you, Cheryl. Hey, Dori." He nodded at Dori. "We noticed you two from up by the bar so we

52

thought we'd come over and say hi, and buy you girls a drink." He set a vodka Collins in front of Cheryl.

"Dori Olson, is that you?" Jim exclaimed and came around the table. He set down one of the drinks he held in front of her.

"Dori Kensing now," she said, chin held high.

"I can't believe it. You look — exactly the same." He casually sat in the chair next to her. Dori stared at Jim with big eyes.

"Jim, don't be rude. Do you ladies mind if we sit here and catch up on old times?" Michael asked.

"Well, I guess that would be okay," Dori answered, and glanced in Cheryl's direction. Both men looked at her, too.

"Do you mind? Because we wouldn't want to intrude on anything," Michael said. He sounded sincere.

"No, I don't mind if you guys want to sit here. Go ahead. Sit down." Cheryl moved her purse off the chair next to her where he stood. Michael pulled out the chair and moved it closer before he sat down. He looked toward the stage where the band was set up.

"Pretty good band they got here tonight," he said.

"Yeah, they sound real good," Cheryl agreed with a nod.

The band returned from their break and started to play. The music made it difficult to hear so Michael pulled his chair up against Cheryl's and asked, "How did the thinning go with the migrant workers?"

"I guess you haven't talked to your brother Brett, have you?"

"Why do I need to talk to him?" Michael wrinkled his brows.

"He was over on his horse asking the same question."

He blinked and quickly asked, "When was this?"

"Tuesday. After the workers were done. David and I were checking the fields when he suddenly appeared."

"That kid can be a pest." Michael shook his head. "If he's bothering you, just tell him to get lost."

"No, he wasn't bothering us," she said. "It's just that you don't expect someone to ride up on a horse on your property when you're out checking your fields."

"Well, I'll have my parents talk to the youngster. Kids nowadays. You never know what they'll do."

Dori and Jim were in a conversation about who played the lead in the spring school play, "Charlie's Aunt," in their senior year.

"I'm sure it was Patty Kleis. I know it was her." Jim nodded with certainty.

"No, she played Stella in our junior year in 'West Side Story.' Mary Jo Stevens played the lead," Dori answered back.

The band started to play "Your Mama Don't Dance." Michael jumped up and extended his hand to Cheryl. "May I have this dance?"

She blinked at him, stunned.

"Come on, it's just a dance. Live a little," Michael coaxed.

Out on the dance floor, she was impressed he could dance so well. When the song ended, the lead singer in the band announced, "We're going to slow it down a bit." Cheryl turned to walk toward their table, but stopped when he grabbed her elbow.

"Where are you going? Please, I don't get many chances to dance with someone as pretty as you."

A little smile came to her lips when she turned to face him. With his pleading eyes and the people who watched at the tables near the dance floor, she felt somewhat obligated.

"Okay, just one slow dance."

Not wasting any time, he put his arm around her waist and drew her close. She could smell the sweet, musky fragrance of his aftershave. But the strangeness of being in the arms of someone else besides Jon made it hard to breathe. Cheryl backed up slightly and forced herself to take a big breath, then released it as they began to dance. The dance wasn't half over when she looked up and found him boldly staring at her. It made her feel self-conscious, so she ignored his eyes and pretended to look around at the room. Every time she caught sight of Dori and Jim they seemed to be deep in conversation. With Michael's eyes still on her, Cheryl focused on the two loud men by the door who had greeted her and Dori.

Finally, the song ended and Cheryl removed her arm from his shoulder. Instead of dropping his, Michael pulled her closer and inhaled by her neck. It felt like eternity to Cheryl but it was only a few seconds before he slowly released her. On their return to the table, she was more than aware of how close behind he was. Dori tilted her head and looked up at Cheryl. Jim was in the middle of a story about the bitch that stole all his money and took his two-year-old son to Portland. No one noticed Cheryl push the chair Michael had sat on earlier away from hers with her knee. When Michael sat down, he moved his chair back to its previous spot. While Cheryl took a long swallow of her drink, she lightly kicked her friend's leg under the table. When Dori turned, Cheryl shot her a desperate look above the rim of her glass.

Dori caught her cue. "Gee, it's been great seeing you guys, but I got two six-year-olds who are going to be up at the crack of dawn. So, we better get going, don't you think, Cheryl?"

"Yeah, it's late. Nice meeting you, Jim." Cheryl pushed her chair back and rose to go.

"Let's make it formal." Jim sprang up and extended his hand. "Jim Stanton."

"Cheryl Langtree." She smiled and put her hand in his.

Michael looked urgently at Cheryl and Dori. "Well, this sure was fun seeing you gals. I hope we can do this again. See you at church, Cheryl."

She nodded but didn't answer him. He was staring at her again with those big sparkling brown eyes and a smile that reminded her of the Mona Lisa.

The women picked up their purses and said goodbye. On their way to the door where they came in, Cheryl could feel Jim and Michael watching them. After a final howl from the two drunks at the door, they were gone.

THE VERY MOMENT Cheryl and Dori were out of sight, Michael turned to Jim. "What did you think of her?"

"The blonde? Cheryl?"

"Yeah, Cheryl. Who the hell did we come here to see?" Michael asked annoyed.

"Well, she is pretty, but kind of an ice queen." Jim looked for Michael's reaction.

"She may be a little cold now, but I plan to melt the ice and rescue that queen."

Jim busted out laughing, but soon composed himself. "Didn't you say her husband just died?"

"Yeah, a little over a year ago. Why?"

"You have your work cut out then, my friend. All I'm going to tell you is that men are different than women after breakups or a death."

"What do you mean?"

"Man, when Angie left, I found the first woman I could find and screwed her brains out. Women aren't like that. They need time to take it all in and somehow find themselves." Jim rolled his eyes.

"Before some other jerk can get through to her that her life will go on and spoil my chances, I'm going to give it my best shot," Michael said.

"Suit yourself." Jim finished his drink with a large gulp. "Thanks for telling me who the redhead was. I really didn't remember her at all. Cute little thing, though. Too bad she seems so happy with her marriage. I wouldn't mind trying to get into that little spitfire. I'm going back up to the bar and score some action. Are you in?"

"No, I'm going home." Michael stood.

"Poor guy. That's what love does to you. You go home alone and horny. Chances are you won't see me going home alone tonight. The other thing I plan to do something about, too," Jim said and wiggled his eyebrows toward the bar where a young woman sat. "See ya."

Michael smiled lightly and socked his friend in the arm. Jim tried to return the gesture, but Michael was out of his reach. He waved goodbye on his way to the door.

BEFORE THEY LEFT the parking lot, Dori turned to Cheryl. "Michael Cameron has the hots for you."

"Oh, please, don't say that," Cheryl groaned.

"You didn't notice he took every opportunity to get close to you? He didn't take his eyes off you when you two were dancing." Dori shook her head with a dream like expression. "He sure is one good-looking guy."

"I don't care how good looking he is. He knew darn well what he did out on the dance floor was inappropriate. I didn't lead him on," Cheryl blurted.

"You mean that hug? I think you may have a problem."

"What do mean?" Cheryl quickly asked.

"The problem is simply this: You're a nice-looking woman who's going to have to learn how to handle unwanted attention."

"I'm just not ready for any of this. I don't know if I'll ever be."

Dori stopped for a red light then turned toward Cheryl. "Honey, take as much time as you need. You're the only person who can decide when you're ready … or if you'll ever be."

Cheryl was exhausted when she got home, but once in bed she flopped around and punched her pillow a few times. Every time she closed her eyes, the distant hum of the music and Dori's words resounded in her head. Maybe she would never be with anyone other than Jon. *If that's what I want, why does the thought make me feel so hollow?*

4

As Jake Cameron turned onto the long driveway of the Sugar King farm, the sun's morning rays caught Susan Petrich's dark shiny hair through the window of his truck. They were laughing about Chuck, an old college roommate of Jake's. Susan's laughter revealed perfect white teeth that looked brighter against her olive skin tone. He remembered back to the first time he saw her smile and how it attracted him in his senior year at the University of Minnesota. But it wasn't the only thing that drew him to her. What really knocked him off his feet was how sexy she looked in the denim mini skirt she wore. *Whatever happened to that mini skirt?*

Susan waited until he walked around the truck and opened her door. After she gave Jake her hand, he helped her out of the truck. She stood and straightened her cream-colored skirt in front of the large, white house before her. Jake put his arm around her small waist and escorted her inside. They entered a large foyer and he led her by the hand toward the dining room. Outside the room, she stopped with a puzzled look on her face.

"Where is your housekeeper? Shouldn't she be announcing us?" she whispered. He stopped and turned toward her.

"Irene? She doesn't answer the door," he whispered back. "That isn't her thing."

"And your parents let her get away with that?"

He grabbed her shoulders and gazed into her brown eyes. "I don't want to hear about anything but how much you love me."

She was about to say something, but just smiled and looked down at the one-carat diamond ring on her ring finger. "I love you, Jake Cameron. More than anyone I've ever known."

He kissed her deeply and gave her a tight squeeze before they entered the room. Jake knew his entire family would likely be in the dining room for breakfast on a Saturday morning. Lucille was reading the paper while Michael and Brett sat next to one another talking about some kid from Montevideo who tried to out-run the cops. Jake looked around and noticed his father wasn't there.

"Where's Dad?" he asked.

His mother looked up from the paper. "Well, hello, you two. That stupid horse got out. I don't know why that thing is so important to him. He'll be here in a minute." She folded the paper and placed it on the table. "How are you, Susan, dear?" she asked in a milder tone. "Come and sit down." Lucille glanced at Michael and Brett then cleared her throat. They immediately ended their conversation.

"I'm fine, Mrs. Cameron, how are you?" Susan smiled politely.

"Just great. How is your family?"

"Oh, everyone is busy, but all doing well. Daddy is going to be honored next week at the Capital for businessman of the year. It's going to be quite the celebration at the governor's mansion." Her smile turned smug.

"Is your uncle Roland going to be at the party?" Lucille asked.

"Yes, of course, it wouldn't be a party without Uncle Roland. Not just because he's the lieutenant governor — he wouldn't miss an honor like this for his baby brother."

Laughter erupted from the kitchen. They could hear Chet converse with Irene as he walked through the kitchen toward the dining room. Everyone stopped talking when he entered the room.

"Did you tame that beast?" Brett asked.

"Put it this way. He knows who's boss." Chet flashed a broad smile. "I know his weaknesses now. Sugar cubes and apples. The second he got a whiff of the crab apples I had in my hand, he wanted to be my friend. He followed me all the way back to the pasture from out in the east field. When I closed the gate, his wild streak melted as quickly as that sugar cube I gave him. I think he has a bit of a sweet tooth." He chuckled.

Lucille sighed and reached for a tiny bell. Irene came in and set down a large silver coffee pot and a pitcher of orange juice. The old housekeeper left the room when Jake reached over and offered Susan some coffee.

"Doesn't your housekeeper serve that?" Susan asked, bemused.

"That isn't her thing," Brett answered.

"I can't believe you people put up with that kind of service from your employees." Susan's focus stayed on the archway where Irene had made her exit.

"You see, Susie, she's really more like family than an employee," Brett told her.

"Please, call me Susan," she corrected him.

Jake pushed back his chair and stood up with his eyes on Susan then looked around at his family. In a clear, strong voice he said, "Susan and I have an announcement." She immediately stuck out her hand and wiggled it back and forth showing off the diamond ring, which sparkled from every direction.

Lucille gasped, then shrieked, "Oh, my God! You're engaged!" Irene hurried into the dining room. She smiled and joined in the circle of Camerons who admired the ring.

"Irene, will you get the champagne we hid yesterday in the refrigerator?" Jake asked. "Bring a glass for you, too."

"I'll be right back with it," she yelled on her way to the kitchen.

"Jake, when did you propose?" Lucille asked.

"This morning." Jake stared lovingly at Susan.

She took his hand and squeezed it. "I thought I was still dreaming this morning when I opened my eyes and this magnificent man asked me to be his wife."

Brett and Michael smirked at each other.

"Chet, did you know anything about this?" Lucille asked suspiciously.

"Yeah, but I was sworn to secrecy." Chet's eyes gleamed.

"Who helped you pick out the ring?" Lucille inquired. "It's beautiful."

"You don't think I did it myself, Mother?"

"No," she shot back.

"Okay, that person would be the lady behind you," Jake said with a nod at Irene who had returned with a bottle of champagne and glasses on a tray.

Susan flinched, but didn't say anything.

"When did you two do that?" Lucille seemed anxious to hear the whole story.

"Do you remember last week when you wanted me to stay later in the afternoon, but I said I couldn't?" Irene asked.

"Yes, that was last Tuesday," Lucille said.

"That was the day Jake and I went ring shopping and out for lunch."

"We had a great time. Didn't we, Irene?" he asked.

Irene nodded at him with unmistakable pride in her eyes.

"I tell you, this woman was a barracuda with the jewelers down at Johnson's," Jake said. "She saved me a quite a little money." Susan frowned, and Jake wondered if she was annoyed by his frugality.

Michael popped the cork on the champagne bottle. He poured the glasses and Irene walked around with the tray while everyone took a glass.

Chet raised his glass. "I would like to make a toast to my son and his beautiful fiancée. May they be as happy as his mother and I have been all these years and beyond."

"Hear, hear!" everyone answered and tapped their glasses together.

Once they finished their champagne — Brett doing so in a single hearty gulp — the men shook hands.

Lucille took Susan by the arm. "I could talk wedding plans all afternoon," she said.

"Then let's," Susan replied.

IT WAS evening when Jake and Susan arrived at her hotel room in Montevideo. Fueled by the day's events, they found it impossible to keep their hands off one another. They stopped kissing long enough to put the key in the lock and push the door open. Susan reached for the light switch, but Jake took her hands and pinned her up against the wall. In the darkness, his hungry mouth found hers and savagely devoured her lips. She turned her head while his lips traveled down her smooth neck, then back up to nibble on an earlobe. Letting go of her wrists, his hand went to her left breast where his splayed fingers lovingly squeezed. She moaned when he stuck his tongue into her mouth and pressed her harder to the wall with his pelvis. Her silk blouse came off and was thrown somewhere in the room. Seconds later, her skirt dropped to the floor. They made their way to the bed where she switched on a small table lamp.

Standing by the bed, Susan unzipped his pants and reached in to rub his buttocks with her warm hands. Her eyes locked with his while she pulled his pants down. He quickly unbuttoned his shirt to reveal a well-developed chest heaving with excitement. They fell together onto the bed and continued to kiss with more urgency. Jake opened his eyes and looked at the woman who kissed him back. *She really does look a lot like Elizabeth Taylor. I am one lucky guy to have her.*

She moaned again as he entered her. Neither spoke. Only the intimate sounds of their lovemaking filled the room.

Suddenly she stopped. "I'm not going to invite your old roommate, Chuck Davis, to the wedding. I would be too embarrassed to have him around my family."

"Okay," Jake answered slowly. "I haven't seen him in years. What makes you think about him now?" He was annoyed. "Can't we talk about it at another time?"

"I'm sorry, darling, it's been a long day. She took his face with both hands and pulled it toward her and kissed him hard on the mouth.

He plunged his tongue between her lips and wrapped his arms around her tighter. He was determined to make her forget all about guest lists.

AT NINETY-TWO YEARS OLD, Alma Green, the oldest parishioner in the church, struggled to get down the granite steps to the church basement. One fragile hand, freckled with age, carefully held on to the rail while Cheryl held the other. When they reached the bottom step, both women were stunned to see Lucille Cameron busy setting the table for lunch.

As a rule, Lucille took pride in her appearance, but today there was an unmistakable glow to her face. Unlike most of the women her age who lived around the area, she wore the modern styles. The delicate, blue print blouse and bell-bottom slacks she sported fit her mid-sized figure well. Her salt and pepper hair was done to perfection, leaving no doubt she had just stepped out of a beauty salon.

Alma said to Cheryl and Sophie with a low voice, "What's gotten into her? I've never seen her here so early. I believe it's the first time since the quilting group started she has ever been here on time."

"I don't know what's going on," Sophie answered. "She was here shortly after I put the coffee on. I actually heard her humming when she set up the folding chairs."

Lucille glanced up at the women. "Good morning, ladies. Alma, it's so nice you can join us. I hope you are feeling better."

"Yes, much better. That was a nasty flu I had. I was so sick, I threw …." Before Alma could finish her sentence, Nell Thompson barged into the room.

Lucille interrupted Alma, "How's that beautiful new grand-daughter of yours?"

Nell was momentarily speechless, but recovered. "She's cute as a button. Wait 'til you see her latest pictures."

"Save them for when everyone gets here," Lucille said, smiling.

The entire group was nearly assembled when the pastor's wife leaned close to Cheryl.

"I see that you signed up to host one night during the construction."

"Yes. I haven't the slightest idea what I'm going to make yet, but I'll think of something."

"I think that seeing how you're by yourself, maybe you could do it together with Nell and Earl. It would be easier for all of you."

Cheryl agreed with a smile directed at Nell, who nodded back.

They had begun to eat when Joan Uterman, in charge of church clean-up day, reminded the women of the approaching event.

Mary, Joan's mother, spoke up, "I will help only if I don't get the pew where the Jenson family usually sits."

"What difference does it make if you get that pew?" Kathy Kleis inquired.

"Those two little brats, Rory and Ricky, have so much gum

stuck under that pew it takes forever to scrape it all off," Mary said with a frown.

"I wonder if their mother has any control over those twins at all? They're only nine years old and already they don't mind her one bit." Joan shook her head.

"I saw one of them spit into the hymnal then close it back up and shove it back into the book holder," Sophie said and took her last bite of cake. Swallowing, she added, "If that were my child, I would take him by the ear and make him wipe it out. And he wouldn't be able to put gum under the pew because he'd be too busy rubbing his behind."

"Ladies, we must say a special prayer for those two boys. Especially for their mother to have the strength to guide those youngsters to adulthood," Patsy remarked, doing her usual best to keep negative gossip at bay.

"Don't you have some baby pictures to share of that new granddaughter of yours, Nell?" Lucille asked.

"Yes, I most certainly do." Nell reached into her purse and took out a stack of pictures of a very bald baby. There was no way to tell if it was a girl or a boy except for the pink clothing she wore.

Still, the women looked at the pictures and commented, "Ah, so cute."

"Ladies, I have exciting news," Lucille announced. Her eyes darted at the group like she was going to explode if she didn't spit it out. "My eldest son, Jake, got engaged to Susan Petrich." She waited for a reaction, but most of the women looked back at her with blank expressions.

"Who's Susan Petrich?" Joan finally asked.

"Come now, ladies, you all must know our lieutenant governor, Roland Petrich?" Lucille held her arms open, her eyes wide. Some nodded yes, while others continued to look at her, confused. "Well, Susan is his niece."

"Ooh," they said.

Kathy Kleis spoke up, "How did your son meet this woman?"

"They were college sweethearts. She's a lovely girl. In fact, I told Jake just last week that she looks somewhat like Liz Taylor. They're still trying to figure out a date for the wedding."

"Hopefully, we will have completed the fellowship hall in time for the wedding," Patsy commented. Lucille smiled but didn't say anything.

The women finished lunch and began to sew. The quilt top of the "Star of Bethlehem" quilt was nearly assembled when Cheryl asked Nell if Earl was done with her lawn mower blades.

"I think he finished sharpening them this morning. You can stop over and get them this afternoon," Nell replied.

"I can't today, but how about tomorrow afternoon?"

"We're not going to be home tomorrow afternoon. I'm helping out with the new baby, but in the morning, we'll be around," Nell answered.

"No, that won't work, because I have to take Taylor to Dori's and then I have a dentist appointment at ten-thirty in Montevideo."

"Do you need to get some work done on your teeth?"

She sure can be a little nosey. "No, just a cleaning."

"I'll tell Earl to just drop them off, dear. It sounds like you're so busy. We can visit another time," Nell said, folding a large piece of scrap fabric.

Cheryl offered to give Earl money, but Nell declined and said they were happy to help her out. Time always flew by at the quilting circle and today was no exception. Before Cheryl knew it, the hands on the old clock in the room showed it was close to three and it was time to clean up and leave.

THE SUN WASN'T UP, but Taylor was. Cheryl was still in bed when she heard him making noise on the screened-in porch. Dori's in-laws were taking Stevie and Taylor to Minneapolis for a three-night sleep over, but the highlight of the trip was to Metropolitan Stadium for a Twins game. Both boys were extremely wound up about seeing their favorite baseball stars, Rod Carew and Harmon Killebrew.

Cheryl stood in the doorway of the porch and smiled at her son. His head was inside his large wooden toy box. "I thought we had everything you needed packed. What are you looking for?" she asked.

"I want to find that lucky ball dad gave me," he said. "You know. The one he had when he played ball in school." She knelt and helped her son look for the ball. After they found it, he handed it to her.

She looked at him, confused. "Why do you want me to have it?"

"When I'm gone with Stevie and you get lonely you can look at it and think of me and Dad," he said with somber blue eyes.

"I won't get lonely." She hugged him. "There is so much work to do around here, I won't have time to be lonely. You go and have a fun time, and I'll be here waiting for you when you get back. Then I'll play catch with you with this lucky ball."

He smiled and nodded.

When breakfast was over, they put Taylor's duffle bag in the truck and drove to Dori's to drop him off for the trip. A chaotic scene was in the midst of unfolding when Cheryl and Taylor stepped into the kitchen of the Kensing residence. In the corner of the room, Sam, Dori's three-year-old son, howled at a high pitch. Apparently, he didn't want his brother to go to Grandpa and Grandma's without him. Dori was trying to calm him down while she pulled toys out of Stevie's bag, things Sam likely added in a last-ditch effort to go with the older boys.

Cheryl planted a goodbye kiss on Taylor's cheek and Stevie snickered loudly. Taylor blushed and instantly wiped his cheek.

When Stevie looked away to say something to his brother, Cheryl whispered, "I love you. Have fun." She then pretended to be late for her dentist appointment and quickly left. It was the first time they'd be apart for longer than overnight and she didn't want him to see her tears.

Dr. Fossom's office was on Main Street in the south end of downtown Montevideo. Cheryl was happy her checkup went well and that it had taken less than an hour. The warm sun felt good when she stepped out of the air-conditioned office onto the sidewalk. She looked down at her orange flowered top and culottes and smiled to herself, remembering how Jon liked the way the shorts showed off her legs. Once Cheryl crossed the busy street in front of her, she opened her purse and pulled out a grocery list. Her eyes glanced into some of the store windows then back at the list as she walked past. Surprisingly, some of the shop displays had fall fashions in the new popular maxi length. A sharp whistle made her stop suddenly and look around.

His light-colored cowboy hat tilted down made it hard for her to see his eyes, but there was no mistaking the body of the man with his back against the grill of her truck. It was Michael Cameron. His toned, tanned arms were crossed in front of the beige and brown plaid shirt he wore. When he moved away from the grill, she noticed his tight jeans along with his silver belt buckle when it caught the sunlight. Pushing his hat up, he looked her up and down with a heart-stopping smile.

"Aren't you a sight for sore eyes?" he declared. "When I walked by, I thought this had to be your truck, so I waited and here you are."

Cheryl's heart thumped in her chest, but she managed a response, "Hi, Michael, how are you?"

"Just fine, now that you're here," he said. "So, what brings you to the fine city of Montevideo?"

"Nothing too exciting. Just a dentist appointment." She tried to sound nonchalant.

"Boy, doesn't that smell just get you?" He tipped his head back and took a deep breath. An inviting aroma of fried onions hung in the air from Tise's small diner two doors down. "How about getting a burger with me?"

With a sudden loss of words, she stammered out, "Well, thanks, but I should get going."

"Oh, of course you have to be getting back to your son. Is he home with your hired hand?" His smile left while he studied her eyes.

"Actually, I just dropped him off at Dori's."

"Good, then you don't have any excuse. Let's go get a hamburger." A dazzling smile spread across his face when he extended his arm to her.

Just because you're insanely good looking doesn't mean every woman is going to fall at your feet. She was about to say no, but got an idea. *Why not go and explain to him once and for all that I'm not interested in him or his brother?*

"Okay, I'll have a hamburger with you. But that's it, nothing else."

"What else did you have in mind?" His smile turned devilish.

"Nothing. Lead the way."

He dropped his arm when she motioned with her hand for him to proceed. They walked the short distance to the café and he opened the door for her. It wasn't too crowded, despite it being lunchtime. The waitress came over and asked if a table by the door was okay.

Michael pointed to a little table tucked in the corner. "How about that one over there?"

She led them to the table where he pulled a chair out for Cheryl. They both opened their menus and she briefly scanned the burger selection. When she looked at him above the menu, his eyes examined her from across the table.

She slapped her menu shut. "What are you looking at?"

"A beautiful woman," he said in a velvety voice.

A stressful thought surfaced. What if he was the one watching her down at the river? *It's done. Forget it. There's nothing I can do about it now.* "Please don't stare at me like that," she said nervously and readjusted her chair.

"Why? Does it make you uncomfortable? I'm sorry. I don't want you to feel uneasy around me." The waitress came back and Cheryl ordered a cheeseburger. Michael ordered the same, then asked if she wanted to share some fries.

The waitress left and there was an awkward silence. "I just want you to know, Cheryl, that I've been thinking about you a lot since I saw you the other night at the M & M. I really would like to be your friend." He stopped talking when the waitress returned with the Cokes they'd ordered.

When she was far enough away, Cheryl released a deep sigh, "You're a nice guy, Michael, but I don't need any kind of romantic ...." She stopped when he put his hand on hers.

"Just being friends with you is enough for now. I realize you've been through a lot and need time to sort it all out." He paused, like he was thinking carefully about what to say next. "But honestly, don't you think Jon would want you to be with someone again and find some kind of happiness?"

"I don't think he would want me to be unhappy, but he certainly wouldn't want me to jump into anything that I wasn't sure of." She stared him in the face.

"You can be sure of me. I'll be your friend or anything else you want me to be. You name it."

"Then friends it is," she said with a satisfied nod.

"Sounds good to me."

Michael didn't push the issue further, but sat back in his chair and watched her with a pleased smile. He leaned forward and said in a bad English accent, "I wonder, my good friend, where are our burgers?"

She shook her head and laughed at him. Not long after, the waitress came though the swinging doors of the kitchen with their food. While they ate, the conversation evolved to what they would change at church if they were in charge.

After lunch they walked to her truck and she reached for the door handle but he beat her to it. He continued to talk but his hand didn't move. She was about to say something, when he finally opened the door. He carefully closed it behind her after she got in and leaned his face in the driver's window. Her body tensed. *I hope he isn't going to try and kiss me.*

"I feel that we're more like special friends," he said, "and I'm looking forward to a long friendship." He lightly rubbed her arm and she stared down at his strong, tanned fingers.

"I gotta go," she blurted and started her truck. "See you in church."

"If not before," he said, raising his voice.

When she started to back her truck, he immediately stepped back and waved goodbye with a big smile on his face. She faked a weak one in return and drove away thinking about his claim that he only wanted to be friends. He could say whatever he wanted — his actions told an entirely different story.

BEFORE CHERYL FINISHED PUTTING away her groceries, there was a knock at the door. Pulling back the kitchen curtain, she saw a van with a flower painted on the side. *Oh, my God. He sent flowers. What is he trying to prove?* Moments later a small man wearing huge sun glasses stood at the door with a long, gold-colored box tied with a large red bow.

"Cheryl Langtree?" he inquired.

"Yes."

"These are for you." He abruptly shoved the box towards her.

Cheryl stared at the box in her arms like it was radioactive. She set it on the table but didn't open it. Instinctively, she reached for the phone and dialed.

A small voice came on the line. "Hewwo," Sam said.

"Hi, Sam. Is your mom there?"

"She's welling at Daddy," he said with no emotion.

There was a muffled sound then Cheryl heard Dori say, "No, we aren't yelling, sweetie, we are just talking."

"Hello." Dori's professional voice came on the line.

"Hi, it's me. Do you have a minute?" Cheryl asked.

She heard her friend give a big sigh. "I really need to hear from the outside world, so start talking. What's up, and it better be good."

Cheryl hesitated. "Could it be bad or ugly also?"

"I guess any of those could qualify. Shoot," Dori said laughing.

"Well, I had a dentist appointment," Cheryl told her.

"That's it? That's all you got? That doesn't sound as exciting as mopping up after a leaky pipe all afternoon and your husband coming home a day early, wondering what's for supper. I told him Sam and I were having pancakes and he said he wasn't hungry for that. That's my exciting day. All you got is a dentist appointment?"

"That and I went out for lunch with Michael Cameron. It backfired on me."

"What? Did you just say you went out with Michael?" Dori's voice got higher pitched. "I thought you didn't want to lead him on."

"I don't. I thought I'd save everyone the time and effort by sitting him down and telling him that I'm not looking for anyone."

"Just a minute, Cheryl, hang on." Cheryl could hear muffled voices again.

Dori came back on the line. "Do you have a bottle of wine?"

"Yeah. Why?"

"Save that story and put the bottle in the refrigerator. My husband has just agreed to bathe our son. Right after I get done with my own bath, I'll be right over."

"Sounds good to me. I'll put that bottle in the fridge as soon as we hang up." Cheryl chuckled.

"'Bye." Dori hung up fast.

A little while later Cheryl heard the door on Dori's red Buick slam.

"I'm on the porch," Cheryl yelled out. "Come around back."

Pulling the screen door shut behind her, Dori came into the screened-in porch. Two glasses of white wine along with the box of flowers sat on the wicker table in front of Cheryl.

"I know that you're happy to see me, but wine *and* flowers, really, Cheryl, you shouldn't have." Dori grinned.

Cheryl collapsed into the love seat with a sigh. "They came as soon as I got back from town. They were delivered."

Dori sat down on the chair close by and reached for a glass. "Well, tell me what happened at lunch and spare no details." Her eyes had a mischievous glow.

"Things didn't happen like you think." Cheryl shook her head.

"Out with it. What happened?" Dori sat up closer to the edge of her seat.

Cheryl proceeded to tell her friend that Michael had been waiting for her when she returned to her truck. "I had every intention of turning his lunch offer down, but then I thought, why play games? I'll be nice and tell him in a kind way that I'm not interested in any romantic involvement. Just when I thought he got it through his head and agreed to be only friends, he pushed it into something else. Now I got flowers."

"You didn't open them?" Dori asked.

"No. If you want to take them home with you, please feel free."

Dori untied the ribbon and opened the cover on the box. Inside, the flowers were wrapped in green tissue paper with another red ribbon around them. A small white envelope was lying on top of the tissue paper. She picked up the envelope.

"Do you want to read this or do I get the honor?" she asked amused.

"No, go ahead. I've had enough excitement from him today."

Dori opened the envelope and took out the card. She opened her mouth and was about to read it when she wrinkled her face. "Cheryl, this isn't what you think, or should I say *from whom* you think!" she exclaimed.

"What do you mean?" Cheryl grabbed the card and read it out loud, "'Thinking of you. Best regards. Brett.'" Both women stared at each other.

"Why did *he* do that?" Cheryl was bewildered.

"You don't have any idea?" Dori's eyes were huge.

"No. The last time I saw him was the day he rode up to me out in the field. I was kinda rude to him. Oh, my God, maybe he's the one who saw me nude." Cheryl shuddered.

"Calm down. You don't know if anyone was there. There is something going on, but I don't think it has anything to do with your skinny-dipping adventure, or maybe … it does."

Cheryl felt horrified as she stared at her friend.

"There's no reason to get all worked up." Dori squeezed Cheryl's hand. "Even if either one of them saw you, you've already told Michael how you feel. All you need to do, is tell Brett the same thing when he asks you about the flowers. They'll get the idea and give up. Let's see what kind of flowers the young Cameron sent you." She opened the tissue paper and gasped at the red roses that filled the air with a heavenly floral fragrance. "He must have spent a fortune on these." Dori put a rose to her nose and inhaled deeply. "I don't know what you got going on, but could you loan me some or tell me where to get it?" She laughed.

"Whatever it is, I don't want it," Cheryl told her. "I couldn't be friends with either one of them. Michael is way too slick, and they both are way too pushy."

"Maybe it's idle gossip I shouldn't repeat, but I've heard Michael has been with lots of women since high school. A friend of mine from town told me her sister met him at a bar down-town. Of course, her sister thought he was handsome and charming so she slept with him. He told her he'd call the next day, but never did. That was a while ago, but that isn't the first story I've heard about him. On the other hand, maybe he's real-ized he isn't happy and wants to do something about it. I'm not sticking up for him, but people can change. Who knows? Maybe he has. Just be careful." Dori picked up the wine bottle and filled both of their glasses. "Let's enjoy this night by ourselves and forget about those crazy Camerons. How do you think *our* boys are doing at behaving themselves?"

"I don't know, but I bet they're having a good time and we should try doing the same," Cheryl answered feeling her body relax from the wine. Things seemed to be more in perspective tonight. It didn't matter what Michael or Brett thought. She couldn't picture herself with either of them.

5

The glare from the morning sun across her yellow chenille bedspread woke Cheryl the next day. Padding barefoot in her nightgown to the kitchen, she looked out the window and saw her hired hand's truck in the driveway. David was already out in the barn doing chores. Cheryl washed her face and quickly braided her hair. Seconds later, she dressed in her chore clothes: a worn, blue shirt with the sleeves cut off and a faded pair of Levis. She scampered out the door to the barn. David was preoccupied and didn't see her when she stepped through the doorway. Making her way closer, she observed him briefly close his eyes and shake his head.

"Good morning. Why are you here so early?" she asked.

"It's Mom. I took her to the emergency room last night. They think it may be her heart, but they won't say until they do more testing." The anguish in his voice was clear. "They're keeping her in the hospital to see if they can find something. The nurse told us the doctor should be in this morning, or early afternoon, to let us know the results of the tests. I thought if I started chores a little earlier, I could be there when he comes in."

"Of course you should be there," Cheryl told him. "I can

finish the chores. You go and be with your mother. She needs you."

"Someone's going to have to go to town and get a load of feed," he stated.

"I'll be more than happy to go and get it."

"Thanks, Cheryl. I really appreciate this." He looked down at the wheelbarrow.

"Let me finish that," she said and took the handles. "You better get going. Those doctors can get there pretty darn early. Just let me know how she's doing."

After finishing the chores, Cheryl continued to walk around the farmyard and assessed things that needed her attention. Jon had always kept the place fixed up and she intended to do the same. The picket fence around the house needed to be painted, but more than that, everything needed to be prioritized. The reality of being in charge excited yet frightened her. *This is a new chapter in my life. There are still people in this world who believe in me, and I'm not going to let them or myself down.*

She brought her basket of eggs in the house to wash when the phone rang. Answering, she heard a desperate voice on the line.

"Cheryl!" Her sister sounded frantic.

"Yeah?"

"Oh, thank God!"

"What's going on?" *Maybe she needs to brag about another vacation.*

"You need to come home," Jolene blurted.

"What?"

"It's ... Mom and Dad."

"What is it? Did they get in an accident? Are they all right?" Cheryl fired out.

"No, nothing like that," she cried in a weak voice.

"Then what?" Cheryl demanded.

"They're getting a divorce!" Jolene shouted and released another bout of sobbing.

Cheryl waited for her to catch her breath. "Honey, don't be

ridiculous. You must have something mixed up," her voice was laced with laughter. "Why would Mom and Dad get a divorce?"

"Cheryl, it's true. Mom said she was going to call you, but I couldn't wait. I needed to talk to you." She continued to bawl.

"Just try and calm down," Cheryl told her. "Answer me. Why would they get a divorce?"

"Mom found out about Dad's affair with Leona Hillmer," her sister snapped. "He's been lying all along."

"You can't be serious. Gus and Leona are their best friends. They've played cards every Saturday night for as long as I can remember." Cheryl's voice trailed off.

"That's not all Leona and Dad were playing. Over a year ago, right before Jon's accident, Gus caught them after a town board meeting and told Mom."

"That doesn't make any sense. When they were here after the accident they were getting along just fine. In fact, Mom put her foot down and Dad agreed with my intentions to run this farm."

"You have no idea why he agreed with her, do you?"

"Yes, I do. He told my hired hand he had confidence in me."

"Like I said, he's been lying all along."

"What do you mean? Who told you all this?" Cheryl's chest tightened.

"I got a call from Billy. Our poor little brother couldn't take the pressure at home anymore and called me yesterday, crying. I thought he had gotten something mixed up so I checked with Mom and she confirmed it. Cheryl, do you realize our whole childhood was a lie?" Hurt and bitterness were in her words.

Cheryl didn't know how to respond.

"Someone needs to be with Mom. And I can't get away. Bob and I are entertaining a very important client this weekend. It could have a huge impact on him making partner. Can you go to the farm and stay with her for a few days?"

"I can't right now. My hired hand is with his ailing mother and one of us has to be here to do chores."

"I know it's a big deal for you to prove to everyone that you can run your farm by yourself, but what about our family?" She sobbed. "We need you too."

"What do you expect me to do? It's all *so* hard to believe."

"Are you saying you don't believe me?" Jolene's cries stopped with her question.

"No. I'm not saying that. I believe you, but I need to let this all sink in. I never thought in a million years we'd ever have to deal with anything like this," Cheryl said, trying to process the situation. "Is Mom okay?"

"I don't know; she's very quiet."

"Seeing how neither of us can be with her, I'll call her and ask if she needs anything."

"Well, then, I guess we all know how important your family is to you."

Cheryl heard a click, then the dial tone. "Jolene? Hello? Hello?" Stunned, she hung the phone back up on the receiver and wilted into a chair at the kitchen table.

Her thoughts drifted to the day her parents arrived after Jon's accident. It was a shock to see how tired and worn out her father appeared over the loss of his son-in-law. It was also surprising how his attitude changed after her mother voiced her opinion. The conversation she had with her parents rushed into her thoughts.

"Cheryl, I know you promised Jon you would stay here, but damn it, girl, he was dying and wasn't thinking straight," her father rationalized. "You've never run a farm on your own. We both know if you sell out and move back home it would be the best thing for you and Taylor. We'll stay and help out for a week, but I got fields to plant and your brother can't handle running our farm by himself."

"What do you think, Mom?"

"You're a grown woman — only you can decide." It was the first time that Cheryl could remember when her mother completely ignored her husband's opinion and spoke her mind. Her father's face flashed a bright red and his lips tightened at her comment, but he remained uncharacteristically silent.

I should've known right then something wasn't quite right.

Within the week, they heard about a farm up north by St. Cloud that had been destroyed by a fire. One of the farm hands, David Cowen, was looking for a job in the Watson area close to his elderly mother who lived two miles away. Cheryl felt bad for the farmer but hoped David would be the answer to her prayers. He was prompt when he pulled into her driveway that afternoon in his old, rusted, two-toned Ford truck. It backfired after he killed the engine and the door rattled uncontrollably when he slammed it shut. Cheryl's father watched him from the kitchen window, sizing him up as if he were buying livestock at the sales barn.

"Look at that long hair. You don't want *him,* Cheryl. He looks like one of those lazy hippie types."

"I've heard he's a hard worker. Let's just meet him, Dad."

Her mother sat at the kitchen table and nodded in agreement with her daughter.

When she opened the door, a tall man in his thirties with a slim but muscular physique stared back at her. Cheryl liked his firm handshake and how he looked her in the eye when she introduced herself. Once inside the kitchen, David Cowen removed his cowboy hat and dishpan blonde hair fell in his face. Using his fingers, he brushed it back and revealed a distinct white ring around his hairline where the sun didn't hit. He stuck out his calloused hand when he was introduced to Cheryl's father. Both men stared at each other while they shook hands.

"Can I have a word with you, Cheryl?" her father asked.

"Sure. Sit down, David, and make yourself at home. I'll be right back." Cheryl heard her mother ask David about the fire as she followed her dad into the hallway a few feet away.

"I don't think we need to waste any time on this guy. I'll get rid of him for you." He turned to go when Cheryl grabbed his arm.

"No, I think he might be what I'm looking for."

"Are you crazy? He's nothing I'm comfortable with leaving you or my grandson with."

"I'm willing to give him a chance."

"I'm not going to give my okay on someone whose hair is longer than your mother's."

"This is my farm, Dad. I don't need your approval."

He took a deep breath. "Okay. You're right."

Back in the kitchen, her father's voice was stern, "Mr. Cowen, I'll get right to it. We are looking for a man to help my daughter out with fifty-five head of beef and harvesting five hundred acres of crops."

"I understand, Mr. Garrison, that your daughter's in quite a pickle." David Cowen's voice was somewhat apologetic. "But being the only farm hand with a woman and a young boy, I could be biting off more than I can chew. Pardon, ma'am." He looked at Cheryl. "You don't look like most farm women I know."

"Mister Cowen, I have two daughters and one son. This girl grew up doing about everything that most would expect a son to do. Besides knowing how to work, she is stubborn. I believe she can do anything she puts her mind to."

Cheryl stared at her father. He was usually short on compliments and rarely showed that kind of encouragement to anyone.

I really thought he believed in me.

A couple of hours went by with a serious conversation about farming and David was offered a nice percentage.

"Would I be able to have Sundays off whenever possible to spend with my mother?" he asked.

Cheryl nodded.

"Well, jobs aren't exactly stacking up and I would like to stay closer to Mom. Okay, I'll give this my best shot." He stuck out his hand and she shook it sealing the deal.

It was amazing that day how her father defended her to David. Was his confidence in her only a lie to get into her mother's good graces? Could it be possible Jolene was wrong about him and Leona? Even if it were true, a marriage of more than twenty-seven years had to be worth fighting for.

Having no idea of what she was going to say, Cheryl picked up the phone and dialed her parents' telephone number. It rang two times before her mother's familiar voice came on the line.

"Hello."

She doesn't sound distressed. "Mom, it's me. How are you doing?"

"Let me guess. Jolene called and told you?"

"Mom, is it true about Dad and Leona?" Hearing her mother's labored breathing, Cheryl knew what the answer was, but still prayed it wasn't true.

"Yes, it's true, honey. I'm sorry. I wanted to tell you myself."

Cheryl released a sad sound, but held back her tears. "Mom, this is so awful. I don't know what to say. Do you want me to come home?"

"No, honey, there isn't anything you or anyone else can do."

"So, the answer is to get a divorce?" Cheryl blurted. "Is there any way for you and Dad to reconcile?"

"No, I've had enough." The line went quiet for a few heartbeats. "Actually, I have another appointment with my lawyer in an hour. I can't talk too long."

"Mom, I don't believe Dad is *that* bad. Remember how supportive of me he was to my hired hand?"

"I don't want you kids to hate your father." She paused, "but we weren't out of your driveway when he informed me I was a fool to believe you were capable of running your farm. He said the only thing you should be doing is making pies and babies. He ended by saying if I thought any woman can make it without a man, I was crazy. Maybe that was for my benefit, not yours. You know, honey, I hate to let you go like this, but I have to go. We'll talk soon about everything, I promise. 'Bye, now."

Once again, Cheryl heard the dial tone on the line. In slow motion, she lowered her hand and stared at the receiver before placing it back on its base. She then wandered onto the screened porch and slowly paced, trying to collect her thoughts. Minutes went by before she stopped and mindlessly stared out a window, feeling numb. She was focused on the cattle grazing in the pasture when it struck her — she needed to get feed. From there, she vaguely recalled when she changed her shirt or got into her truck.

Now she was five miles down the road heading toward town. Somehow, she must have found her purse and walked out of the house. Had she shut or locked the inside door? *Oh well, what does it matter, anyway? Nothing stays the same in this world. You can't depend on anyone or anything but yourself. According to Dad, I can't even do that.* She stared ahead at the road with her fingers tightly clenched around the steering wheel. How could he do something this terrible to her mother and his family?

Bang! Then another loud *bang*! The noises were followed by a sudden eruption of steam that rapidly boiled out from under the hood of her truck. The vehicle lost power and it took all Cheryl's strength to steer it to the side of the road. She threw it into park and cut the engine. Thoughts of a possible fire made her push her door open and quickly hop out. Seeing no flames, she opened the hood part way but dropped it and backed away when a wave of steam rolled toward her. When the steam had decreased, she opened the hood all the way and saw pieces of the fan belt scattered everywhere.

Cheryl walked to the middle of the road and looked out in both directions. Seeing no one, she returned to her truck and leaned against the outside of the driver's door. The longer she stood there the more overwhelmed she became with thoughts of her parents' divorce. A lump formed in her throat when it occurred to her she really was alone in the world. The gravel in front of her turned into a brown blur as her eyes filled with tears. She remembered back to the times in her life when her father was the one she leaned on. Now, she would never trust or depend on him again. A deep sadness filled her when she thought about the honorable man that had been taken from her. *Why did you have to die, Jon? You were the only one there for me, and now you're gone.* She sucked in a breath and began to weep uncontrollably.

In between outbursts, she got back into the truck and dug through her purse for a tissue but didn't find one. She leaned over toward the glove compartment and opened it. The small space was filled with a metal hitch, the manual for the truck and old toys of Taylor's. Rummaging through those items, Cheryl angrily threw them onto the floor mat in search of something to dry her eyes. Not finding anything but her frustration, she flopped onto the seat and cried even harder. A few minutes went by while she sobbed with her face buried into the cushion. Suddenly, she felt someone urgently poking her lower back.

"Hey, are you all right?"

Cheryl spun her head to look up.

Jake Cameron's brown eyes were open wide as he anxiously waited for an answer.

Feeling embarrassed, she turned her face away and looked down at the seat. "Yeah, I'm okay. I'm fine." Her voice was weak and shaky.

"What happened here? Are you hurt?" he quickly asked.

"I blew a fan belt." She tried to sound unemotional.

"Are you injured?"

"No," she said, shaking her head.

"Why are you lying down then?" he asked, a little more calmly. She sat up and wiped her eyes with her fingers.

"I just ..." she paused not able to finish the sentence.

He opened the driver's door. "Why don't you come out here and get some air?"

She nodded and moved toward the door. He took her hand and held it until she was steady with her feet on the ground. She took a deep breath, but tears ran down her cheeks. He squinted his eyes and looked her over carefully, obviously confused. After he shut the truck door behind her, she leaned against it and stared straight ahead at the ground. She noticed he kept an eye on her while he slowly walked over to the front of the truck and looked at the motor where the pieces of the fan belt were dispersed.

He moved his head to look at her from around the hood. "This is nothing to get so upset about. A fan belt just needs to be replaced, you know."

"Yeah, I know." She sniffled.

"Then why all the tears?" He walked closer to her.

"It just hasn't been my day," she sobbed and wiped her face with her hand.

He reached into his pocket and held out a blue bandanna handkerchief. "Here, use this."

She took it and dabbed her eyes.

"What could be so wrong that you're like this about a fan belt?" he inquired. Taking his cowboy hat off, he brushed a hand through his caramel brown hair and scratched his head. He put his hat back on and continued to observe her.

"It's hard for me to tell you, because it hurts to say the words out loud." She started to cry again. "And besides, I don't think you want to be bothered with my problems."

"Let me be the judge of that." He crossed his arms and waited for an answer.

She took a deep breath. "I just found out today … that my parents," she swallowed hard and wrinkled her face, "are getting a divorce." She blurted it out fast, hoping it would be less painful. It didn't work. She started to tremble and shake which was followed by another big sob. His mouth gaped open and he stepped closer, putting a hand on each of her shoulders.

"It's going to be okay." Jake's eyes were huge and his mouth moved and made sounds like he was searching for something to say. When her cries became more intense, his mouth opened wider but he didn't say a word. Panic was on his face when he suddenly pulled her shaking body close and held her. She clung onto him and closed her eyes. They stood on the side of the road with their arms around each other while she cried into his shoulder. Eventually, her cries lessened and she took in some deep breaths. They awkwardly stared at each other before he backed up.

"Let's go get you a fan belt. Hop in." Jake nodded toward his truck parked behind hers.

She got her purse before getting into the passenger's side of his truck. It smelled new and was immaculately clean inside the cab. *Those Camerons. Every one of them has a new vehicle. Must be a tough life. I guess if your parents are going to give you everything, it's a lot easier.* They started the drive to Joe's Gas Station in Montevideo where everyone around the area brought their vehicles in for repair.

A couple of miles down the road, Jake asked, "If I ask you a question about your parents, you won't start crying again, will you?"

"No, I think I'll be fine now. I've had a good cry." She looked down.

"Can I ask you why they're splitting up?" he asked. "I know it's none of my business, but I'm just curious about why these things happen."

"My father cheated on my mother," she answered and looked out the window.

"Oh," he answered, sadly.

At Joe's, Jake accompanied Cheryl inside the building where she purchased a fan belt. Driving back, they talked about how dry it was getting and how another good rain would really help out the crops. The topic then changed to the old folks in the area. Cheryl mentioned that David Cowen's mother was ill and she hoped it wasn't serious. When they got to her truck, Jake put the fan belt on while Cheryl watched and picked up the pieces of the old belt.

"Well, that should do it," he said and slammed the hood. "Get in and start it up." She started the truck and it sounded normal.

When he walked over to her driver's window, she asked, "What do I owe you for helping me out?"

"Nothing. Who knows? Sometime I may need help, too."

"Thanks a lot." She smiled.

"Take care, now."

Cheryl watched him in her rear-view mirror get into his truck as she drove away. Jake was nothing like she expected. He was kind and easy to talk to, unlike Michael or Brett. It was hard to believe he was their brother, but easy to see why he was taken.

JAKE DROVE BACK to Montevideo to pick up an item for his mother at the post office. He went around back where the post-master, along with two other employees, lifted a large crate into the back of his truck. It was too big for the rural mail carrier to bring out in his car. It was a mystery to Jake why his mother ordered such a large statue for her flower garden. *That's Mother — always the biggest and the best.*

On his way home, he thought about the woman he'd found on the road. For whatever reason, seeing the tears in her pretty blue eyes had disturbed him. He recalled the way they held each other and assured himself he'd done nothing inappropriate. Lucky for her, it was he who had found her instead of his brothers. Given Brett's recent declaration of his feelings for her and Michael's way with vulnerable women, who knew what could have happened?

At the Sugar King farm, he found his parents sitting on elegant, cast-iron lawn chairs in the flower garden, waiting for the statue. Jake backed his truck to the garden and his Dad stood to help him unload it. He parked his truck, but wasn't out of the seat when he saw the annoyed expressions on both of his parents' faces.

"Where have you been?" Chet asked. "Your mother is driving

me crazy. What took you so long? If I'd known it would take you all day, I would have picked it up myself."

"Sorry, Dad, I had to help out a neighbor," Jake answered.

"Who did you help out?" Chet asked.

"Cheryl Langtree." He pulled himself up onto the end gate of his truck.

"Why did she need help?" Lucille inquired.

"She blew a fan belt and was stranded over by Jacobson's. I took her to Joe's and got a belt, then went back and put it on for her."

"Where's her hired hand? Shouldn't he be doing her handy work?" she asked.

"Edna Cowen is in the hospital and David went to be with her," he answered. "Why all the questions? Is this statue so important a person can't help a neighbor?"

"Of course not. It's just that we were worried when you didn't come back right away," she answered.

The two men tipped the box down and were amazed how heavy it was. Both father and son grunted and strained to carry the wooden crate the short distance to its resting spot. They pried open the sides with crowbars, then pulled them away. Lucille gasped when she saw it. She seemed very pleased with the statue from St Louis. Father and son looked at each other and didn't say anything about the large male angel with birds perched on his wings. Neither shared the same enthusiasm about the statue as Lucille.

Brett pulled up with his truck and parked next to Jake's on the lawn.

"Looks like you didn't need a real man's help with that statue," he yelled, walking over to where the three stood by the sculpture.

"We could have used you. That thing weighed a ton," Chet snapped.

"I was here an hour ago and no statue. Where did you go for that thing? All the way back to St. Louis?" Brett retorted.

"No, he was out rescuing damsels in distress." Chet shook his head.

"What damsel would that be?" Brett asked.

"That Langtree woman," Chet answered.

Jake told Brett he'd found her broken down with a blown fan belt. He didn't tell any of them how he'd actually found her; broken down in more ways than one.

ON HER WAY to the barn, Cheryl expected to see raindrops fall any moment from the dark, rumbling sky. David had taken his mother to a heart specialist in the Twin Cities, which left Cheryl alone to do morning chores. The song "Run Through the Jungle" blasted from the radio and echoed throughout the barn while she filled a cart with shelled corn. She heard a sound outside but assumed it was thunder and finished filling the cart. Taking the handles, she made her way down the alley to the middle of the barn.

"Cheryl." A voice came from behind her. Startled, she turned and the cart turned with her. The heavy load of corn spilled onto the alley and into the gutter.

She tried to catch her breath with her hand on her chest. "What are you doing here?"

"I'm sorry. I heard that you were here doing your chores alone. I thought I would come over and help you," Brett Cameron apologized.

"Mr. Cameron, I am perfectly capable of doing my own chores." Her words were cutting. "If you felt the need to help me, why didn't you call and ask, instead of scaring me half to death?"

"Please call me Brett. I'm so sorry that I frightened you. Please ... let me clean this up." He reached for a shovel that leaned against the wall.

She took another deep breath. "Just go, and leave me alone. I don't know what your brother told you, but I am just fine. I don't need your help or anyone else's."

"Excuse me for saying this, but it sounded like you needed my brother's help yesterday." He raised his eyebrows.

"I just don't get what's going on with you Camerons. All of a sudden, you're all trying to be my friend. What's the deal?"

"I guess we're all trying to be neighborly to a neighbor who needs a helping hand."

"That's why you sent flowers?" She gave him a cold stare.

"I believe you deserve something nice because you're a special woman. I only wanted to brighten your day," he said, and smiled sweetly.

"For your information, I'm not interested in you or your brothers. Believe me, and please relay that message to them."

"My brother Jake is engaged, you know, and is planning on getting married this December. You flatter yourself to think he's interested in you." He seemed bemused.

"Okay. I really don't think *he's* up to anything, but I definitely get the feeling there is something going on with you and Michael."

"I can only speak for myself." He shook his head "I'm just trying to be your friend. Who knows with Michael? He doesn't tell me anything, but if I were you, I wouldn't trust him. He has quite the reputation with the ladies."

Cheryl cocked her head. "So, you're warning me about your own brother?"

"Like I said, I don't want anything from you but the satisfaction of helping out a friend. A person can figure out what *he* wants," he said curling his lip. "So, let me clean this up and show you I just want to help."

Cheryl leaned up against one of the stalls with her arms crossed and watched him clean up the corn. He looked more like his father than his brothers with those bright, mossy green eyes. She categorized him as cute rather than handsome, but very confident, just like his brothers. When the clean-up was done, Brett put the shovel back and wiped his hands on his jeans.

"Well, I'm sorry about scaring you. But the reality is you're here all by yourself." Hooking his thumbs in his back pockets, he pushed out his chest and stated in a lower voice, "If you ever do get scared about something and need a man to come over and check it out, don't hesitate to call me."

"I'll keep that in mind, but there isn't too much that scares me. Besides, I do have my hired hand," she paused, "to check things out." She tried to keep a straight face.

"Okay, I guess I'll be going." He sounded defeated. Making an about-face toward the door, he took a few steps but stopped and pointed to a saddle thrown over a stall. "You don't have any horses, do you?"

"No, we don't."

"Then where did that saddle come from?"

"It's mine. I had it when I was a kid. My sister and I did a little gaming at the county fairs around home."

"Why don't you have any horses now?"

"When Jon and I got married, he made it clear he didn't want horses. He always called them 'hay burners.'"

"We have several horses and now my Dad has an Arabian." He sounded excited.

"Wow! That must have cost a mint."

"Not really. The former owner didn't take care of it. Dad got it for a steal because no one could get near it. That thing is as wild as the wind, but my Dad thinks the horse likes him and is going to be tamed someday." He smiled. "Why don't you get a horse? Maybe a nice quarter horse or a Pinto?"

"I don't have the time or money for that right now." She was annoyed again.

"I bet your boy would like a horse. I don't know of any kid that wouldn't want a horse."

"I bet he would, too, but my son is six years old and can barely take care of his two pet lambs."

"If you or your boy ever want to go riding, call me." He opened the barn door, but held it half way open. "Or, if you need me for anything else." He tipped his cowboy hat and left with a smile.

WHILE BRETT DROVE TO WATSON, he thought about Cheryl and how she had treated him. When he arrived at the bank, he parked but didn't get out of his truck. He let his thoughts go and imagined he was riding on a horse, double back, with Cheryl riding in front. She wore a white, low cut gown and was barefoot with her long, sexy legs hanging down in front of him. Her silky blonde hair was out of the braid, blowing across his chest while they galloped into the wind. Bending his head, he kissed her neck …. In front of the bank, he shook his head and blinked, but continued to sit in his truck for a moment to compose himself.

Michael was right. Something about her made her different. She wasn't like the girls from school. She was a mature woman who was straight to the point about things, which was intriguing … a total turn-on. He opened his truck door slowly and got out. *Bet or no bet, Michael, you're not going to win this one.*

6

I t had rained most of the day when Cheryl decided to clean the closet where she stored Jon's personal things. She gazed at the cardboard boxes stored in that closet. *How sad to think a person's whole life could be contained in just four boxes.* One box held everything from Jon's baptismal candle to his high school yearbook from 1966, the year he graduated. Cheryl picked up one of his baby pictures and laughed because his hair stood up like Alfalfa from The Little Rascals. She opened the yearbook and found three pictures of her husband. One was his class graduation picture, another was one from the Future Farmers of America club, and the third was a photo with the baseball team. Cheryl wondered what Dori looked like in high school. Her fingers ran down the index of the Mohawks yearbook and found Olson, Doreen. In the pictures, she looked basically the same, only with longer hair and a few more freckles. Dori had been active in the debate team, drama club and the yearbook committee. One picture showed the determination on her face during a debate.

Thumbing through the book, she came across a picture of the homecoming royalty. The queen was Julie Johnson and the king was a young Jim Stanton. Michael Cameron was one of the attendants, and even back then looked very attractive and put together. There were several pictures of him with a girl named Diana Iverson. Cheryl believed Diana to be a blonde from the black and white photos, with eyes of green or blue. Turning the page, she saw a close-up picture of Michael and Diana dancing a slow dance at the high school prom. It showed a handsome couple gazing into one another's eyes, so much involved they appeared unaware of the photographer. Cheryl wondered why their relationship ended when they obviously had cared a great deal for one another. She shut the yearbook intending to put it back in the box, but stopped to look up Brett Cameron's picture in the freshman section. There were a few photos of him, all of which showed him having a good time at some event. One picture showed him on a hayride with a group of classmates during homecoming. His hair was lighter and he appeared somewhat dazed, maybe a little drunk. Cheryl took a closer look at the group of kids with their glassy eyes and funny expressions and concluded some had been drinking more than punch. Where were the chaperones? Maybe they knew and didn't do anything about it. *Rich kids, they seem to get away with everything.* She put the yearbook back in the box and pushed it back into the closet.

Cheryl pulled another box closer and picked out one of her favorite shirts of Jon's. She held it to her face and took in a deep breath. Despite it being laundered, it still smelled like him. She wrapped it around her shoulders and sank onto the closet floor. Tears flowed from the corners of her eyes like lava oozing from a volcano. Giving herself permission to cry without anyone there to watch felt healing in the dark closet.

Finally, her tears ceased and she noticed one of the smaller boxes was tipped on its side. She reached to pick up the contents spilled onto the floor and saw their marriage license and Jon's death certificate. The beginning and the end neatly stacked on top of one another. If she looked in between those two documents would she find her broken heart tucked there? More tears ran down her cheeks at the thought. It brought an ache in the hollow spot where her heart used to be. At the funeral, someone told her time healed many things. The pain was still in her chest, but time had indeed changed it from a stinging fresh cut into a tender sore spot. *But will time ever heal me enough to feel love again?*

The sun suddenly peeked out from the hall window and drew a line inside the closet onto the documents. Something shiny caught her eye and she bent down to pick it up. In her hand she held Jon's wedding ring. She remembered her struggle to get it on his finger during their wedding ceremony. On that day, she'd placed the ring on Jon's hand as a sign of her love and fidelity. She believed her love for him would never die, but who was she being faithful to now? Certainly not herself, by denying she had feelings and missed being loved by a man. The words "'til death do you part" echoed in her head. She raised her left hand and stared at the band of gold on her finger. The only time she recalled taking it off was during her pregnancy when her hands swelled. Rolling the ring around, she wiggled and pulled until it slid off. She rubbed the area where the ring had been for more than seven years. It felt so vulnerable and exposed. Clutching both rings in her fist, she held them to her chest for a moment then slipped them into her pocket.

Cheryl marked two boxes for the Salvation Army, then went outside and set them inside the truck. Going back into the house, she went directly to her bedroom and placed the rings where they belonged — together, in her jewelry box.

THE WEATHER DIDN'T CHANGE much in the afternoon and Cheryl used the time to work on the large pile of mending in her laundry room. When she talked to David later that night, he told her his mother was going to be okay for now and he planned to return to work in the morning. He was thankful for the time with her. After their conversation, Cheryl went to bed excited to see her own son in the morning.

Only a few wisps of clouds were left in the sky the next day when Cheryl went to pick up Taylor. It was a welcome change from the two dark days of rain she endured by herself. The two boys were playing catch when Cheryl drove in the yard at Dori's. Stevie saw her first and tapped Taylor on the shoulder then pointed to Cheryl. Seeing his mother get out of the truck, Taylor dropped his ball and glove and raced to greet her. She bent down and he ran into her open arms.

"Mom, you're finally here!"

"Sounds like you missed me." Cheryl held him.

"He sure did," Stevie teased.

"You missed *your* Mom." Taylor turned to his friend. "You told me the first night when I cried. You said you missed your Mom, too."

"Did you have fun?" Cheryl asked.

"It was great. Rod Carew got a hit in the seventh inning and drove in two runs. Everyone cheered. Harmon Killebrew got a pop-up, but he just got off the DL. In case you don't know what that means, Mom, it means disabled list. He got hurt and didn't play for awhile. But he's okay now." Taylor smiled, knowingly.

"Stevie, what did you enjoy at the game?" Cheryl asked.

"Rod Carew. I did like the hot dogs," he said, then slowly added, "but not anymore."

"Stevie ate three hotdogs and threw up on a guy in front of us. The lady sitting by him got mad but he didn't. The back of the guy's shirt was icky with the Orange Crush Stevie drank," Taylor reported.

"Okay, that's enough. I get the idea. Are you feeling okay now, Stevie?" Cheryl inquired.

"Yeah, right after I got sick, I felt better. Grandpa said us kids were all over-excited and that's why I got sick."

Dori and Sam came out onto the porch. "I've got lunch ready if you'd like to stay," she yelled.

"Thanks, but I think we're going to head on home and get

Taylor unpacked." Cheryl glanced at her son. He looked worn out.

While they drove home, Taylor sat close to Cheryl and talked about his visit to Stevie's grandparents' home. He told her Mrs. Kensing's food wasn't as good as hers and sleeping in his own bed was a lot softer than the bed they'd slept on. When they drove up a hill, their farm came into view.

"I love our farm, Mom. No matter what, I want to live there forever."

"I do too, sweetie." *Thank you, Jon.*

IN THE COOL MORNING AIR, Cheryl painted the picket fence in her front yard. Close to noon, the climbing temperature made it uncomfortable in the shade where she worked. She had spread almost an entire can of white paint onto the thirsty boards when David Cowen came out of the shed and stood next to her.

He cleared his throat and stated, "Sure's a hot one today." He was silent for a moment. "I thought you always went to that sewing church group on Thursdays."

"It's a quilting group, and yes, I usually go. But Dori's son, Sam, is sick with the flu so Taylor is stuck here with me. And seeing that I'm staying home, I figured I'd take a stab at this fence." She ran her brush across the bottom of the can and wiped up the last of the paint.

"I'll be here all day if you want to go. Taylor can stay with me. I've got to change the oil in the grain truck and rotate some tires but I'll be in the yard most of the day. We can get a burger at Trailways when we go to Montevideo for oil."

"You'd really watch him for me?"

"Sure, why not? He's a good kid."

"Thanks, David," Cheryl told him and didn't waste any time. She stuck her brush in a coffee can filled with water and went into the house.

All the women were gathered around the table when Cheryl got downstairs at church. They had finished the prayer and lunch was on the table.

Nell smiled when Cheryl walked into the room. "You made it. You have got to try my honey wheat bread. Earl liked it so much, I had to hide a loaf for today."

Cheryl smiled and took a piece of the bread. It was a wonderful combination with Nell's sauerkraut hot dish.

It seemed louder in the old church basement than usual on quilting day. The women chatted about the church bazaar and the fast approaching Chippewa County Fair.

"Cheryl, I heard my daughter say they're short on animal entries this year for the 4-H club so they're letting the younger kids enter. Is Taylor going to be entering an animal at the fair?" Alma asked.

"Yes. He's entering one of the lambs he's been raising all summer." Finishing her stitch, she added, "And he's really excited about it." This was Cheryl's favorite part of the quilting process, the stitching — when the women shared what was going on in their lives. It brought back the times when she and her grandmother bonded over more than just a quilt.

"May I have everyone's attention?" Patsy Timms wanted the floor. "The bazaar sign-up sheet is up in the back of the church. We're in need of people to sign up for some of the booths and the lunch table needs some volunteers for setting up and for serving. Lucille's in charge of organizing our work force, so please contact her if you have any questions." Lucille, who sat close by, smiled and nodded. Patsy concluded with, "God help us make this another successful year for our biggest fund raiser."

Cheryl signed up for the food table as did most of the ladies. Alma, Sophie and Gert, because of their ages, were always back-ups in case someone didn't show up.

It was close to three-thirty when Cheryl turned into her driveway and saw a horse trailer parked by the barn. It was a new trailer with a cartoon drawing of a cowboy lassoing the words, "Sugar King Farm" in bright red letters. Not yet out of the truck, she could feel her blood pressure rise. She mumbled under her breath closer to the corral, "I don't need this." Just then she heard Taylor's excited voice.

"I think he likes me. He's listening to me like you said."

"Yeah, he's just gotta get used to you. You wait and give it some time. He'll be your friend," Brett answered.

Taylor was on a quarter horse, riding around the corral when Cheryl approached. Once Brett's eyes met hers, he went quiet, but Taylor, with his back to her, continued to talk about the horse. Sensing that something was different, he turned and looked over his shoulder at his mother.

"Mom, look at me. I'm riding this horse! Brett said I'm good at it and if it's all right with you, we can keep him." Taylor could hardly get the words out fast enough.

Seeing him so proud of himself, Cheryl couldn't remember the last time she'd seen the boy so happy. Taylor's blue eyes beamed, and that smile. *Where had that been hiding?*

"Can we keep him, Mom? Pl … ease?"

Cheryl didn't answer. She turned to David who was leaning against the fence. "Can I ask? When did this all happen?"

"He showed up here with that trailer over an hour ago and told me he had something to show Taylor. He claimed he'd talked to you about it."

Cheryl watched her son ride around the corral another time. "Brett, can I talk to you in the barn for a moment?" she finally asked.

"Sure. Taylor, just go slow. Remember, pull to the right he goes right. Pull to the left, he goes left. If you want him to stop, pull both the reins back and say, Whoa!"

Cheryl walked quickly to the barn with Brett close behind. She closed the barn door and turned to him with her eyes narrowed.

"What were you thinking, bringing that horse here?" she asked through gritted teeth.

"Before you get all fired up, let me explain," he quickly said.

"Explain what? That you got my son all fired up about a horse that he can't have?" she ground out.

"I know you said you don't have the time or money for a horse, but I do."

"Good for you. What am I supposed to tell Taylor? That our rich neighbor wanted to tease him with something that he can't have?" Her tone was cold.

"Before you go on judging me, let me speak." He looked directly into her eyes. "I thought I could do something good for the kid. Now you're being mean to me because my folks have a little money they worked hard for."

"Tell me what you're trying to do here," she demanded.

"How would it work for you if I took care of the horse here? I can bring over the hay, shoes and anything else he would need. I'll do the grooming and even shovel the shit. You name it — I'll do it. While I'm here, I could show Taylor some tips on riding. Maybe someday he'll ride at the county fair like you and your sister." He paused. "You may wanna ride him, too. I saw that look in your eyes when you saw the horse." He raised his brows making his green eyes bigger. "His name is Eddy."

"Why would you want to do all that for Taylor? What's in it for you?" she asked with her hands on her hips.

"I think it's a shame, a kid growing up without a dad. I thought maybe a little male companionship would help him out." The barn door flew open and Taylor stood in the sunlit doorway blinking his eyes.

"Mom, could we please keep the horse? It would be so much fun. Please, Mom. Just say yes. I'll help, too. I promise." He stepped closer and hugged her waist. Cheryl looked up at Brett.

"It's up to you, Mom," Brett told her.

"If I say okay, you're only here for Eddy and nothing else?" She shot him a glare.

"No. I'm here for Taylor and you, too."

Cheryl frowned.

"I can teach you more about competitive riding," Brett added.

"So that means we can keep him here?" The excitement grew in Taylor's voice.

She stared at Brett, trying to size him up. "Yes, if Brett gives me his word that his intentions are honorable."

"What does that mean, Mom?" Taylor looked up wrinkling his forehead.

Brett smiled at Taylor, then said to Cheryl, "I give you my word I have no hidden agenda. I've said what I'm here for."

"Then it's yes, Mom?" Taylor's eyes pleaded.

"Okay. Yes, but you have to help out too, young man, and do what Brett tells you to do when you're on that horse," Cheryl answered sternly.

"I will. I promise," Taylor answered. He jumped up and down then bolted out of the barn screaming, "David, we can keep him. She said yes!"

Cheryl's eyes followed Taylor out the door then returned to Brett. "If you let him down, I will never forgive you." Her voice was hard.

"I won't." He sounded sure. "You know, if you let your guard down and have a little faith in people, they may surprise you," Brett chided. Turning on his heel, he went back out to the corral.

LATER THAT DAY, Cheryl watched from the kitchen window and saw Brett put Eddy in the pasture with the beef cattle. Brett playfully rubbed Taylor's head and shook his hand before he got in his truck. He drove out of the yard waving to the boy. Taylor stood by the pasture fence long after David had gone home and watched the horse munch on grass. When Cheryl called him in for dinner, he washed his hands and came to the table, looking exhausted.

Smiling at the macaroni and cheese, he declared in a satisfied voice, "It's been the best day ever. Thanks Mom." He sat down and started to eat but then stopped. "Brett said if it would be okay with you, he'd come over on Saturday and we'll go riding. He's bringing over another horse and he'll ride that one. Did you know his dad has a wild horse?" His eyes were big. "He said if it's okay, we can go to his house one day and he'll show him to me." Cheryl didn't say anything.

She helped Taylor wash up after supper, and he went to bed. Ten minutes later when Cheryl checked on him, he was fast asleep. She tucked his blankets in and kissed his forehead. Her hand was on the doorknob when she looked back at her sleeping child and smiled. *I would even put up with that little smart aleck Brett Cameron for you.* She quietly closed his door and went to bed herself.

BRETT BACKED the trailer into the large shed next to the stables. He grabbed a shovel and opened the trailer door, then went in to clean up what Eddy had deposited in there. He was almost finished when he heard Michael.

"What are you doing? Where did you take Eddy? He stood behind the door of the trailer.

Brett was slow to answer, "I'm boarding him somewhere else."

"What? Why would you do that when you're not paying anything here? Where is he?" Michael asked again.

"I'm boarding him over at another farm." Brett pushed the trailer door open farther, making Michael move out of the way.

"And my question is: Where would that be?"

"The Langtree farm," he said without emotion and hung up the shovel. Michael's jaw dropped slightly and his eyes darkened.

"Why, you little shit. How the hell did you get her to agree to that?"

"I guess she just likes me, that's all." Brett smiled.

"Did you ask Dad if it was all right to board Eddy someplace else?"

"That's the difference between you and me. I'm not some little boy living with Mommy and Daddy doing whatever they tell me to do. I don't plan on living here any longer than I have to. I don't know why someone your age is living here when you know Jake is going to get this place. Are you afraid to go out into the big, bad world and get a real job?"

Michael's face reddened and he grabbed Brett by the shirt collar, pushing him up against the wall of the shed.

"Listen, baby brother. I'm not taking your shit like Mom and Dad do. If I wanted a job other than this one, I'd get one. Where's *your* fancy job, college boy? Huh? And about Cheryl, she's *mine*. Do yourself a favor. Go and get your horse back and quit making a fool of yourself."

Brett pulled away and heard something rip. When Michael released his grip, the collar hung down on the side of Brett's western style shirt.

He glared at Michael. "Go tell Daddy. It won't matter. Eddy is my horse. I'll do what I please with him."

Brett could hear his mother talking as he approached the dining room late for dinner. The rest of the family members were quiet as they filled their plates and listened to an update about the wedding.

"Today, Susan called and told me what the flowers in her bridal bouquet are going to be. She said her mother had white roses and white calla lilies and she wants the same. At first, I have to say, I was a bit shocked. I don't know how good that will look in colored pictures. Maybe a little boring for a Christmas-themed wedding." Lucille paused and eyed Brett up and down. "You certainly didn't have to change your shirt for spaghetti and meatballs."

"I hooked my shirt and tore it." Brett sat down.

Michael seemed unconcerned as he poured more tomato sauce over his pasta.

"Hey, Brett, where did you go this afternoon with the new horse trailer?" Jake asked anxiously. It was likely an attempt to change the subject from his fiancée and her wedding plans to anything else.

"I used it to help a friend." He didn't look up from his plate.

"Oh? Who would that be?" Chet asked.

"Taylor Langtree." Brett took another bite of food.

"Are you talking about Cheryl's boy?" Lucille frowned.

"Yeah, her boy," Brett said. "I took Eddy over there and I'm going to leave him there for a while."

"Why would you want to do that?" Chet asked.

"It gives the kid something to do now that his dad is gone." Brett sounded sincere.

"You wouldn't have to leave Eddy over there. Why couldn't you just bring the boy over here and let him ride?" Lucille asked, annoyed.

"Well, for one thing, it has always been my understanding that Eddy is my horse. And what I do with him is my business," Brett answered.

"Wait a minute young man, I don't like that kind of tone when you're talking to your mother," Chet snapped at his youngest son. Everyone stopped eating.

Realizing this was not heading in the direction he wanted, Brett thought he could save himself by saying, "Mother, I didn't mean to sound disrespectful to you. I'm sorry. I was just hoping that at my age, you and Dad would begin to trust me. I was under the assumption you both believe I have a good head on my shoulders and I can make my own decisions."

"We do trust you, and we do believe you have a good head on your shoulders. But I'm not sure that's the head making your decisions," Chet rattled out.

"Chet!" Lucille gasped.

Jake and Michael busted out laughing, but after a glare from their father, they stifled themselves.

"I'm sorry, Lu. He's gonna hear what I think," Chet answered. He turned to Brett. "I think it's fine to help out a kid, but if I'm wrong about the kid not being the main reason for this sudden burst of kindness, I'll kiss your behind."

Brett swallowed hard hearing his father's words. Another bout of snickering broke out but ended just as quickly with another look from Chet. All eyes went to their own plates and each person continued to eat.

Chet broke the silence. "I guess it won't hurt that horse to be in a different pasture for a while, but come fall, I want him back here where he belongs."

Brett tucked his head down and nodded slightly. Shoving the last forkful of pasta in his mouth, he stood up and pushed his chair back. His family watched him leave the table and exit into the kitchen. A few minutes later he slammed the back door and left.

A SLIGHT BREEZE was enough to keep the mosquitoes away while Michael and Jim sat in the pickup with the windows down, each drinking a beer. Michael had parked his truck on a hill overlooking the Langtree farm. His eyes fell on the rows of nice looking sugar beets that stretched out in the field below. He remembered back to spring when he saw her, not the hired hand, on the tractor planting the field. The rows were amazingly straight and weed free, and that somehow excited him. His eyes followed the parallel lines of the field into the farmyard. Orange rays from the setting sun touched only the tops of the trees and illuminated the windmill blades along with the galvanized steel roof on the barn. It was evident, even in the shadows, how she kept the place up. Besides everything being in its right place, things were well maintained. He noticed the picket fence around the house looked freshly painted. That house was cute, but he wouldn't tell her until after they were married he planned to tear it down and build something classy.

"What are we doing here?" Jim asked, interrupting Michael's thoughts.

"Let's just say we're keeping an eye on my investments." Michael told Jim about Brett and the crafty, under-handed scheme he'd used to get closer to Cheryl. Jim took a swallow of his beer and almost spit it out when Michael reported what Chet said during dinner.

After he contained himself, Jim commented, "Well, you got to hand it to him, Mike. It's a brilliant plan. She's always going to be there and soon enough he's going to win her over, if he's good to the kid. Women eat that stuff up."

"Yeah, I didn't expect it out of him, that's for sure. Now, I got to figure out a way to get her to see what he's doing is all bullshit."

"How are you gonna do that, Romeo?"

"I think I'm going to work the same angle with the kid," Michael said and swigged back a mouthful of his beer.

"With the horse?"

"No. I found out the kid is showing a lamb at the Chippewa County Fair. Doesn't your dad basically run the fair?"

"Yeah, he's been on the fair board for years. How'd you find out about the kid and the lamb?" Jim looked at him curiously.

"I have my sources, my friend." Michael smiled. "Tell your Dad I'll be coming to visit him and learn what it takes to be a judge at the 4-H building."

"Wow, what's that chick got that you two are running so crazy?"

"All I know is, I haven't felt like this about anyone since Diana. I'm not going to let my brother or anyone else get in the way." Michael tipped his beer to get the last swallow before he crushed the can in his hand.

Not long after morning chores, Dori pulled into Cheryl's driveway. As soon as it was warm enough, the three boys played on the Slip 'N Slide while the women butchered thirty chickens. Knowing it was going to be another hot, sticky summer day, Cheryl braided her blonde hair and wore a shrunken, old gray T-shirt with a pair of jean cut-offs.

They were half done with the birds when Cheryl noticed somehow, she'd managed to get a large, round blood spot on the toe of her blue canvas tennis shoe. After making a mental note to throw them into the washing machine, she forgot about her shoe and concentrated on plucking feathers.

When they were giving the chickens a final inspection, three wet and hungry boys reminded them it was time to eat. With the heat and feeling famished themselves, the women were happy to be done with the task. They ushered the boys to the house and left the chickens outside to soak in washtubs filled with cold water.

Dori and Cheryl passed out towels and were busy drying off children when they heard a vehicle pull in and the engine shut off in the driveway.

Stevie ran to the window and yelled, "I don't know who it is, but they got a nice truck." The boys gathered at the window to look out.

Dori went to the window above the kitchen sink. "Cheryl, it's Michael Cameron."

"Oh, God, no. What does he want?" she gasped in a whispered voice. Cheryl joined Dori and watched Michael walk past the soaking chickens toward the door. He knocked on the screen door and the boys ran to it with Cheryl behind them.

"Hey guys, is your ..." Before Michael could finish, he saw Cheryl. "Hi, I'm sorry to bother you. I can see you're busy." He turned his head toward the washtubs. "But Dad wanted me to come over and see exactly where that horse is at and make sure it's okay with you to have him here," he said, then smiled.

Cheryl managed to maneuver her way through the group of little boys and stepped out onto the porch, shutting the screen door behind her. Michael's eyes quickly went to her tight T-shirt, then over the rest of her before they fixated on the blood spot on her shoe.

"There isn't any problem having the horse here as far as I'm concerned." A bead of sweat ran down Cheryl's forehead and she wiped it away with the back of her hand. "Why would there be?"

"Well, there really isn't any problem. It's just that the kid should've asked permission. Dad and I were a little concerned if Eddy would be taken care of properly. That's all."

"Are your parents okay with it, then?" She glanced back and saw Taylor's worried face through the screen door, listening closely to every word.

"Of course, they are. I just told Dad I would come over here and make sure."

"If you want to go look, he's in that south pasture next to the woods," Cheryl answered, and pointed in that direction.

"Okay. Again, I'm sorry to bother you about this, but you know how kids are always doing something without thinking it through." He turned and started to walk toward the pasture but suddenly stopped. "Oh yeah, one more thing. If the kid starts to come over too often bothering you, Mom said to just send him home." He flashed his usual gorgeous smile. "As always, it's been a real pleasure to see you, Cheryl." Then he continued to walk toward the pasture.

7

W ide beams of golden sunshine flooded the kitchen with light. Cheryl sat at the kitchen table with a cup of coffee in front of her thinking about what a beautiful sunrise it was — too beautiful to witness alone. She missed the time with Jon in the mornings while Taylor slept. Over morning coffee they'd start their day with a plan or just stayed in bed a little longer to make love. Tears welled in her eyes and she got up for a tissue. She didn't need to do this to herself, especially today. Brett was coming out to ride with Taylor and she didn't want to appear distressed in any way.

Her plan was to leave the two alone for the majority of the visit. It sounded like he really didn't have permission to leave the horse. *So maybe he's on the up and up and really wants to do something for Taylor. Why else would he go against his family?*

Around nine-thirty, Brett drove in and parked the horse trailer. Cheryl watched at the open kitchen window after Taylor bolted out of the house to greet him.

"Hey, buddy, ready to go riding?" Brett stepped out of his truck.

"Yeah, I'm ready." Taylor bubbled with excitement. He

followed Brett to the trailer door where they unloaded another quarter horse.

"This here horse's name is Milo," Brett said. "He and Eddy are good friends." They saddled up Milo and Brett helped the boy get on the horse. He handed the reins to Taylor and got on the animal with him.

"We gotta find Eddy and get him saddled up." Brett hung onto the extra bridal while they rode out to the pasture. After a while Cheryl saw them leading Eddy back toward the barn. It only took Brett a few minutes and Eddy was saddled and ready to go. They rode down a field road and were gone for over an hour.

When they returned, Cheryl let some time go by before she went out to see how things had gone. Brett was busy washing down Eddy and had finished brushing Milo. She could hear their playful conversation and laughter when she approached the lean-to on the barn where they groomed the horses.

Reaching them, she commented, "Sounds like you two had fun."

"It was great, Mom. Brett told me to show him who's boss and I did." Taylor held his head high.

"Yeah, this kid shows the makings of a champion horseman." Brett smiled at him.

"I bet you guys are good and thirsty. Brett, would you like to come in and have a glass of iced tea and a cookie?" Cheryl asked.

His eyes widened, then he released a sigh. "I really would love to, but I gotta get back home. My brother's fiancée's family is coming to our house for a luncheon and I have been given strict orders to be back as soon as I can. Listening to my mother, you would swear the governor himself was coming over, not the lieutenant governor's brother's family. She wants everything to be perfect. I don't really need to explain." He shook his head. "You know my mother."

"Yes, she *does* like everything organized," Cheryl agreed.

"I guess you could call it that, but I'll call it what it is — controlling everything. I think the rest of our family will be happy when this wedding is over."

Cheryl thought about his comment and concluded she wouldn't want to go through the process with Lucille either. *Poor guy.*

JAKE AND MICHAEL sat on the patio and sipped lemonade under a large, dark green awning. A beautiful green tablecloth with matching yellow and green cloth napkins covered the table in front of them. Around each plate of white bone china delicately trimmed in gold lay the silverware, polished to perfection. Bouquets of white and yellow roses were carefully arranged in crystal vases adorning each end of the table. A light breeze helped dispense the fragrance of the peony bushes nearby. Their aroma dominated the several species of roses, hydrangeas, geraniums, and lilies around Lucille's well-manicured flower garden.

"There you two are," Lucille exclaimed, coming out of the French doors. "Don't mess up the table setting," she ordered. "We don't want to look like we're hillbillies."

"Calm down, Mother, they're not going to think we're hillbillies." Jake shook his head.

"It's the first time our two families have gotten together. We need to make a good impression." Lucille straightened the collar on the back of his shirt and went back into the house.

"Where's Dad and Brett?" Jake asked Michael.

"Dad's putting the finishing touches on the stables. He's going to offer tours. Brett is still upstairs, powdering his butt. He was over pestering the Langtree family again this morning with his hospitality. I don't know what he's trying to prove."

"Why does it bother you if he's over there?" Jake asked. "I think Cheryl Langtree would tell him to leave if he was bothering her."

"It doesn't bother me. I just don't want it to get around that our goofball baby brother is making a fool out of himself chasing a woman who is way too old for him."

"Just admit it. You've got the hots for her, too." Jake looked for his brother's reaction. Michael's eyes shifted to the table in front of him, but before he could respond, they were interrupted by Lucille, yelling at Chet. Their father quickly retreated onto the patio.

"What are you boys drinking? I think it better be whiskey, because at this point, I may need one." Chet scratched his head.

Lucille was suddenly there and stuck her head out the patio door. "Nothing more than lemonade. Get that straight."

Brett stood behind his mother and cleared his throat. "Excuse me. The Royal Family has arrived," he said with a bad English accent.

Lucille elbowed him lightly in the stomach and warned, "Cut it out. You better be on your best behavior, young man." Brett didn't answer but backed up to let her pass by.

SUSAN PETRICH and her family were in the foyer when Jake and his parents went to greet them. Michael and Brett soon joined the group and introductions were made. Her father, John, was a balding, pudgy man with a dark complexion, like Susan. His firm grip seemed to impress Chet when he shook his hand. Her mother, Sheila, a tall, thin, blonde, wore an expensive looking gold suit jacket and dress. Her makeup was heavy but skillfully applied. She nodded and smiled as she was introduced to everyone. When she wasn't looking, Brett raised an eyebrow at Michael.

Susan's sister, Monique, glanced at Michael and lingered for a moment before she gave Brett the quick once over. Averting her eyes, she continued to survey her surroundings. Unlike her sister, Monique's hair and complexion were lighter, like their mother's. She towered over Susan and was a bit too thin, and noticeably less attractive.

Brett nodded to his soon-to-be sister-in-law and said, "Hey, Susie. How's it going?" Susan's entire family turned to her with astonishment.

"Oh, Brett, must we go through this every time I see you? Can you do me a tiny, tiny favor and just call me Susan, please?" she asked in a sweet voice.

Lucille narrowed her brows at her youngest son and promptly changed the subject. "We're having lunch out on the patio, so why don't we all go out there."

The group went to the patio and after they were seated, Irene came and asked if they wanted some lemonade.

Chet looked at John. "Or would you rather have something a little stronger, John?"

"You read my mind, Chet. That would be great."

Lucille glared at Chet when the two men retreated to the den for drinks.

"You ladies can start planning the wedding without me. I think I could use one of those, too," Jake said and stood.

"Sounds like a plan," Michael agreed. Brett rose from his chair and followed his brothers. Lucille watched Brett from the corner of her eye. Irene again asked if anyone wanted lemonade.

The women all said they wanted some and Irene was about to leave the patio when Monique waved her finger at the housekeeper. "Make mine without pulp in it. Pulp in my lemonade really makes me ill."

Irene stared at Monique momentarily before she went inside.

"Well, I guess this gives us girls some time to talk and get to know one another," Lucille said, eyeing the women around the table. Susan smiled back and so did her mother, but Monique didn't appear to be listening. She was staring at the statue of the angel with obvious skepticism.

"We are so fortunate to get the Lake Calhoun Beach Club for the reception," Sheila said. "It usually takes a year, but I got the inside scoop on another wedding that was canceled. When I heard about it, I immediately called and booked the date. The Mass, of course, is going to be at the Basilica of St. Mary in Minneapolis. That's where John and I got married along with everyone else in our family. When Jake attends religion classes there, he'll see how it's the perfect place to get married."

Lucille suddenly stopped smiling. "Why would Jake be attending religion classes there?"

"When he changes religions," Sheila answered.

"This is the first I've heard my son is changing religions," Lucille said sternly, and stared at Susan.

"Actually, Jake and I have only briefly discussed the issue," Susan said, but stopped talking when Irene returned with the lemonade. Irene set down her tray and examined each glass as she served them, making sure Monique got the one without pulp. The drink she set in front of the girl appeared to be pulp-free as requested.

"I said I wanted no pulp." Monique lifted her glass. "I see a piece of pulp floating in this glass." Her eyes narrowed and she scowled like a small child.

"I'm so sorry. I'll get you a different one." Irene took the glass from Monique's hand and went into the house.

Lucille recognized Irene's irritated tone of voice. Monique would be lucky to get her drink this afternoon.

The men returned from the den, drinks in hand, and sat down at the table. Irene was back with her hands full with bowls of fruit. She set a bowl down on each end of the table. Each time Irene brought out another item of food, Monique looked up, likely expecting her lemonade.

Irene was in the house when Monique whined, "What is going on with that maid of yours? You really need to get rid of her and find someone who at least will accommodate your guests. Where's she going for the lemonade? Florida?"

"Did she run out of lemonade?" Chet asked his wife.

"No, Chet. Monique wanted a glass without the pulp," Lucille answered.

Chet subtly shook his head in Monique's direction.

"By the way, Jake, when were you going to tell us you're changing religions?"

"What are you talking about, Mother?" Jake jerked his head.

"Sheila has informed me you're going to be taking religion classes at the Basilica of Saint Mary." Lucille waited for her son's explanation.

"I think there's been a little misunderstanding. Susan and I are required to attend a class in order to get married there, because I'm a different religion. That's all there is to it," Jake said calmly.

Sheila glanced at her eldest daughter with obvious concern. Irene returned with the lemonade and a plate of crepes. Monique gave her a dirty look when she set the glass on the table in front of her.

Putting the crepes down, Irene announced, "Lunch is served. Does anyone need anything else I could get them?" Everyone except Monique shook their head no.

"Could I have a different knife, please?" She held it up. "This one has a finger print on it. That is *so* unsanitary." Monique put her hand to her chest.

There was an awkward silence before Irene said, "I will get you another one." With a pleasant smile, she took the knife from the girl.

"So, have you two decided on who's going to stand up for you?" Lucille asked after they recited a traditional Lutheran mealtime prayer and started to pass the food.

Susan looked at Jake and answered, "Of course, Monique is going to be my maid of honor. Jake has talked to Michael about being the best man," she smiled at Michael. "My best friend, Lona, and her husband, Jack, are going to be our bridesmaid and groomsman. I think a small, quaint wedding party is so nice. So, that's our little group."

Jake stopped eating. "Didn't you ask your friend Melody to be a bridesmaid too?"

"I thought about it and decided a smaller group is what I want. Besides, Mel didn't seem to be too excited about the wedding. I think she is — I hate to say it — *jealous*."

"Isn't there anyone else you could ask besides Melody?" Jake asked.

"No, I can't think of anyone." Susan shook her head.

"I think it would be great to have both my brothers in my wedding," Jake said looking at Brett.

Susan glanced at Brett, who smiled and kept on eating.

"Jake, darling, I really have my heart set on a small group of attendants," Susan told him.

Jake quieted for a second. "I don't really even know Jack. Why couldn't Brett take his place with Lona?"

"I don't know how I could do that. I've already asked Jack." Susan's voice went lower as she continued, "I wouldn't want to hurt his feelings. Can we talk about this later? There are so many other things we need to discuss with your family before we have to leave. Daddy's got to get back to Minneapolis for a very important dinner this evening."

"By all means, continue." Jake returned to his food. The rest of the luncheon went nicely and the conversation was pleasant. Most of the group was sipping coffee when Irene came onto the patio and cleared away the dishes. Each time she made a trip back and forth Monique gave her a disgusted look. Irene smiled at her occasionally but continued to remove items from the table.

Monique couldn't keep silent any longer. She cleared her throat and said to the older woman, "Didn't you forget something?"

"What was that, dear?" Irene tilted her head.

"My knife."

"Oh, that's right. No need to bother getting it now, since you've finished eating." Irene smiled sweetly and went into the house.

"It has been wonderful meeting all of you," Sheila said, when she and her family were back in the foyer.

"Yes, it certainly has been a delight," Lucille quietly answered. Chet stood beside her and stuck out his hand to John.

"The kids have been dating for a while and this little get together has been long overdue," John told Chet while he pumped his hand.

"It certainly has," Chet answered. "I'm sure we'll be meeting more often in the next few months."

"Jake, honey, you're coming back to the hotel with us. Aren't you?" Susan asked.

"How about I catch up with you later? I have some things I need to attend to," he answered and kissed her on the cheek.

The Petriches hadn't gotten out of the driveway when Jake turned to his mother. "I can tell by how quiet you are, something's bothering you. So, out with it, Mother. What is it?"

"Well, I don't want to meddle. But I feel it's your wedding too, and you should be able to have both of your brothers in it."

"I completely agree, Mother, and it's not out of the question. I'm thinking I can convince Susan. She isn't as difficult as you think. I just need a little more time. In the meantime, Brett could try to be a little nicer to her. Maybe that would help." Jake turned to his younger brother who stood close by.

"Come on. What do you want me to do?" Brett asked. "Kiss her ass?"

"Watch your mouth, young man," Chet snapped at him.

"I'm sorry, but what have I been doing to her that's so bad?" Brett shrugged his shoulders.

"For one thing, why do you insist on calling her Susie?" Jake sounded annoyed.

"Well, I thought seeing how she's going to be family, I could give her my own pet name."

"You know she doesn't like it, so cut it out." Jake frowned.

"Okay, whatever you want. I didn't think it was that big of a deal," Brett answered.

Chet chuckled.

"Why are you laughing?" Lucille asked. "He's right. We are going to be family and we all need to get along."

"No, I'm laughing about that spoiled Siamese cat going up against the tiger we have in the kitchen," Chet answered. "That's a perfect pet name for that girl."

"You mean Monique and Irene?" Michael asked. "Now, that was entertaining." He smiled at his dad.

"You two are not helping with this situation." Lucille glared at her husband and son.

"Lu, take a step back and let the kids decide what they want," Chet told her.

Lucille pursed her lips. "I'm not trying to decide for them, Chet. I just want to make sure my son gets a vote on things. I believe if he wants both of his brothers in his wedding, he should be able to."

JAKE DIDN'T PUT on the radio while he drove to Susan's hotel in Montevideo. He drove in silence and analyzed how the meeting between the Petriches and Camerons had gone. He knew his mother liked to run things and no matter who he would be involved with, she would have her say. He thought to pick up some flowers in case something was said he needed to smooth over. Besides, maybe it could help to get Brett in the wedding. He pulled into Hemstad's green house and bought some dark pink roses.

Arriving at Susan's hotel, he knocked on the door with the bouquet of roses in his hand. It wasn't long before she answered the door dressed in a long, black, lacy nightgown. It was very sheer and low cut in the front and left little to the imagination.

He backed up with a big smile. "Wow. Are you part of the welcoming committee?"

His eyes ran up and down her voluptuous body.

"Just your welcoming committee," she replied in an alluring voice. Taking his hand, she pulled him into the room. He set the flowers on a small table and wrapped his arms around her. His hand trailed up her back to the nape of her neck, pressing his lips to hers while his tongue probed her mouth.

Suddenly, she stopped and put her hand on his shoulder. "So, how did you think things went with our families?" He continued to kiss her neck while she tried to speak. Finally, she said, "Jake I'm serious. Did you think everything went well?"

"Do we have to talk about it right now?" he managed to say in between kisses.

"Yes, it's important. How do you think things went?"

He stopped and backed his head. "I think things went about as good as I expected they would."

"What do you mean by that? How good did you expect?"

"You know my mother doesn't like to stand on the side lines, she's more of a team player. The only thing she wanted to know is why Brett isn't in the wedding."

"I thought I explained it very thoroughly. It just doesn't work. Is that why you stayed and didn't come with us?" she anxiously asked.

"I believe we should try to solve any problems we're having about the wedding right away."

"What is there to solve? I don't want a large wedding party. I think it looks tacky. Besides, I don't know of anyone else I'd want, other than the people we already have."

"Maybe you should give Melody another chance. From what you've told me about her, I kinda like her perky attitude. Maybe she and Brett will hit it off and she'll become your new sister-in-law," he said with a goofy grin.

"You're talking silly, Jake. Do we really need to discuss this any further? I think who we have are enough attendants. Don't you agree?"

"I told you in the beginning, I really want both of my brothers in the wedding." His playful tone was gone.

"And I said I would try and make that possible. I tried and it isn't possible." She released an exasperated sigh.

"I don't think it's impossible. Even if you're right and Melody *is* jealous, why don't you ask her anyway?"

"I'm not sure ... if I even want her in our wedding," she said, looking at the floor.

"But I *am* sure I want Brett to be in the wedding, so could you ask her for me?"

"Okay," she said slowly. "If it means that much to you, I will." She kissed him and took his hand. This time she led him to the bed, where there was no more wedding talk for the rest of the night.

IN A BOOTH at the Trailways Cafe in Montevideo, Cheryl sat and waited for Jon's sister, Jane. Taylor had spent the night at his cousin Jeremy's house, and now everyone was to meet for breakfast at nine. It was nine and there was no sight of Jane or the boys, but Cheryl didn't mind. The coffee was always good at Trailways, and a moment to herself to relax was a rare thing. She was lost in thought, mechanically sipping her coffee and gazing out the window when a familiar voice brought her attention back inside the restaurant. Looking up, she saw Jake Cameron and a woman with dark hair being seated by the hostess in a booth a short distance away. Jake smiled when he recognized Cheryl and nodded to her before he sat down. The woman was seated with her back to Cheryl but turned in time to see her smile and nod back at Jake.

"Who's that?" Cheryl heard the woman ask Jake.

"That's my neighbor, Cheryl Langtree."

He mumbled something else to her. The woman turned and her eyes darted rapidly in Cheryl's direction.

That must be her — the woman he's engaged to.

The waitress took their order and was headed back to the

kitchen when Cheryl caught the woman looking at her again, but this time more slowly. She was a striking woman who projected a rich, polished image of sophistication. Her hair and makeup were perfect along with her dress, a stylish, modern print, in shades of pale green. Cheryl remembered the blue shorts and white cotton blouse she had on and smoothed her braid with her hand. She then looked out the window at the parking lot and pretended to focus on the cars. *What did Jake tell her that's causing her to stare so rudely?*

Coming out of the kitchen with her arm loaded with plates, the waitress made a bee-line for Jake and the woman's table. Cheryl was grateful the woman would be busy with something else, rather than gawking at her.

A loud commotion came from the entrance of the restaurant when Cheryl saw Jane and the boys had arrived. Heads turned as they created somewhat of a scene. Taylor held a jar and both boys looked to be very excited about the contents.

"There's your mom, Taylor!" Jeremy yelled after he spotted Cheryl.

The boys rushed over to the booth followed by Jane, who didn't appear the slightest bit embarrassed. Taylor put the jar on the table in front of his mother. Inside was the largest brown toad Cheryl had ever seen.

"Isn't this the biggest toad ever, Mom?" Taylor asked loudly.

"Yes, but why did you boys bring him in here?"

"I told them to leave it in the car, but they were afraid he'd die from the heat out there." Jane plunked down in the booth.

People at the tables close by pointed at the toad and stared at them. Jane instructed the boys to sit and put the jar on the floor while they had breakfast. The waitress cautiously eyed the jar as she took their order.

"Shove that jar farther under the table so no one will see it," Cheryl advised. The women were talking about the county fair when suddenly, the jar rolled out from under the booth. Both boys scrambled to retrieve it. Jeremy leaped for the jar but barely made contact. The jar spun away toward Jake and his fiancée's booth. She saw it and screamed, while Jake leaned over and scooped it up. He casually stood and waited for Taylor to scamper over to him. Before Jake handed the jar over to the boy, he examined it carefully.

"Nice looking toad you got here. Can't say I've ever seen one that big before."

"Thanks," Taylor said shyly. He took the jar and walked back to his mother's booth.

"You boys take that thing out to the car and then come right back in," Cheryl ordered. "He'll be fine out there until we're done." The boys did as they were told.

Jake was still standing when the waitress came and handed him his change. The woman with him stood and hastily grabbed her purse. Jake waited for her to go first, but halted when he got by Cheryl's booth. His female companion hurried past, but stopped when Jake called her name.

"Susan, wait up." She turned and walked back to him. "I want you to meet my fiancée, Susan Petrich," he said to the two women.

Susan smiled dutifully.

"This is Cheryl Langtree and her sister-in-law, Jane Peterson," Jake told her. "Cheryl lives on the farm east of us and Jane grew up on that same farm. I've known Jane all my life."

"Is that right?" Susan asked.

"We are so sorry the boys disturbed you while you were eating your breakfast," Jane apologized.

Susan was going to say something when Jake beat her to it.

"Little boys never change." He shook his head laughing. "My mother can vouch for that. The things my two brothers and I did. I bet she could write a book about all the critters we brought into the house."

Susan looked at him. "We better get going. I have to drive back to Minneapolis this afternoon. Nice meeting you two." She hurried to the door.

"See you, ladies." Jake smiled and followed his fiancée out of the cafe.

Jake and Susan got into his truck and pulled out of the café's parking lot. He noticed she was quiet and seemed to be contemplating something.

"What are you thinking about?" he asked.

She replied with a question, "So, let me get this straight. Both your brothers are competing for that blonde?"

"Yep, and they're both making fools out of themselves, because I don't think she's interested in either one of them." Jake shook his head.

"I don't think she's anything special. Do you?"

"She's pretty enough." A frown formed on Susan's face and he quickly added, "If you like that country girl type. Maybe the allure is the fact she's sitting on some nice, fertile, river bottom land which connects with our farm. My family and most of the neighborhood feel sorry for her with her husband dying last spring. She's trying to run a farm and raise her boy by herself."

"Do you think your brothers are just trying to get her property?"

"Well, I think they both want the whole package. The land and the girl."

"When we were in college, wasn't your brother Michael involved with some girl from high school?"

"Yeah, he went with a girl named Diana Iverson."

"I remember you said your parents were worried because they thought it was way too serious. Whatever happened to her?"

"I guess that was the problem. Michael and Diana planned on backpacking through Europe after high school, before college started. Mom and Dad thought the idea was crazy and they convinced Michael not to do it. It was Diana's dream to go to

Europe, so she decided to go with another classmate. While she was in Europe, she met a guy studying to be a doctor and those two hit it off. Last we heard, from her sister, she got married to him and they live in Connecticut where he has his practice. I think she broke his heart. That's when Michael decided not to go to college. Since then, I've seen him pick up any girl he wants faster than anyone else I know, but he never gets serious about any of them. Just uses them like he doesn't care about their feelings. Like he has no feelings himself."

"He is *very* attractive. He'd better find what he's looking for before he's an old man and his looks are gone," Susan remarked.

"Better looking than me?" Jake raised his brows.

"No, you're both good looking, but your personality does give you the edge over him." She sweetly blinked her eyes.

"Don't you think he has anything else going for him besides his looks?" Jake asked.

"Yes, of course. He can be charming. Maybe he'll meet someone at the wedding."

They arrived at the hotel and stood by the driver's door of her Mercedes, saying goodbye. Locked in a kiss, she suddenly stopped and put her arms between them. "I better get going. I have a full day tomorrow. After work, I have an appointment with Mother and Monique at the bridal shop. I've narrowed my wedding dress selection down to five."

Jake stood back when she opened the car door and got in.

"See you next weekend." She tilted her head out the window with closed eyes and puckered lips. Knowing she expected a kiss, he leaned in and kissed her forehead. Her eyes popped open. "What was that?" she asked.

"That was a kiss for a busy girl who needs to get going before I ask her to stay and call in sick tomorrow."

"I have such an important day tomorrow with my dress and all. Besides, I don't know how Mother and Monique would feel about me canceling. They both have things going on. I couldn't just ...."

"No, you couldn't," he interrupted. "But what if I came with you back to Minneapolis?" His excitement grew as he asked the question.

Susan suddenly stammered, "I — I'm not trying to discourage you. But it could get a little boring for you tomorrow at the bridal shop and I thought you wanted to go to that ... that county fair thing?"

"I'll wait for you at your apartment. We'll have a late supper when you get back. A romantic candlelight dinner with a nice bottle of merlot." He smiled and winked at her. "I can miss the fair. It will be there next year. The only drawback is Michael. For some strange reason, he decided to attend every day this year. Someone's got to be home to do chores. I could maybe get out of it. I'll talk to Dad."

"Jake. Are you sure you want to come with me and put your Dad out like that?"

"I think I'll drive my truck to the Cities. That way I'll have a vehicle if I have to come home." His enthusiasm suddenly hit a wall. "Don't you want me to come?"

"Yes, of course I want you to come. What girl could resist a romantic candlelight dinner with the man she's planning to marry?"

"Can you stay here for a half hour longer? I'll run home and grab some clothes."

"Thirty minutes and that's it. I really need to get going. And you're following me. I know the route a little better than you." She checked her wristwatch. "Get going and don't take too long."

Jake wasted no time. He got in his truck and speeded most of the way to the Sugar King. His plan was to sneak into the house, but he really didn't care if anyone saw him. Yet, it was exciting to know only he and Susan knew what they were doing. He felt confident he was successful at his mission when no one saw him slip out of his parents' patio door carrying an overnight bag.

Passing the Langtree farm he thought, *It sure would be nice to have that place — so close to the home farm. Don't even think about it. Susan would never go for an old remodeled house. She wants the new house I promised her and that's what I intend to build her next spring.* He remembered the happy tears in her eyes when he showed her the deed to the property closer to town.

Jake joined his fiancée back at the hotel, and with the sun behind them he followed her to Minneapolis.

8

A scent from a mixture of cotton candy, hot dogs and manure hung in the air at the 4-H sheep barn. Excitement brewed all around as children tended their animals and adults tried to keep things in order. It was warm and noisy when Cheryl watched her son's and Stevie's lambs get used to their new environment in the small pens. When Dori and Sam arrived, she collapsed on a folding chair with an exhausted sigh. Both mothers wanted to sit for a moment, but the boys, excited about being at the fair, had other plans. It didn't take too long before the children begged to see the animals in the other barns and the women to grow tired of their whining. They were in the horse barn admiring the huge workhorses when someone tapped Cheryl on the shoulder.

"Hi, Cheryl." She turned and stared into a pair of gorgeous brown eyes. "How are you?" Michael asked. He nodded his head. "Hey, Dori."

"Hey," Dori answered in a monotone.

"I'm good. How are you?" Cheryl asked. She was proud of her calm response.

"Just fine. And as always, I see that you're *looking* mighty fine." He gazed at the pale blue print cotton blouse and the denim shorts she wore. His eyes dropped, then slowly traced down her long, slender legs.

"Thanks. Do you have any horses here?" Cheryl's eyes searched the stalls of horses in front of her.

"No. I just like to see the entries. Dad used to take us boys in here to look at the workhorses. Kind of a family tradition."

Taylor interrupted Michael and Cheryl's conversation, "Mom, can Stevie and I go to the Midway and go on the rides?"

"Not by yourselves," she told him. "Some of the rides you have to be tall enough or they won't let you ride. We'll all go." Turning to leave, she glanced back. "We'll talk to you later, Michael."

"Wait, I'll go with you," he said. "I haven't been to the Midway in years." Cheryl saw Dori's raised brows and subtle smile.

The music from the merry-go-round and the sounds of the motors from the rides gradually grew louder as they approached the heart of the fair. Once they bought tickets, the boys decided to go on the Scrambler. The three adults watched Taylor and Stevie, with Sam in between them, smile and wave as they passed by in the air. The boys went on a couple more rides before the group reached the end of the Midway.

Stevie stopped suddenly and pointed to a large roller coaster. "We should go on that!" Above the entrance to the ride was a large painted snake. The name of the ride was displayed on the end of its long lashed out tongue: "The Serpent."

"Yeah! Let's get in line." Taylor immediately agreed.

"Wait a minute." Cheryl pointed to the front of the line. "See that height line? You've got to be that tall to go on the ride."

"Mom, I'm big enough to go on it," Taylor said. It was evident Stevie was tall enough, but Taylor's height was questionable.

"Do you want to know how we used to get Brett on the rides when he was too short?" Michael asked.

"How?" Both boys asked at the same time.

"Well, we would have him stand on one of our shoes while we waited in line. Then when it was his turn to be measured we would distract the carney. Brett would walk on his tippy toes past the guy and find a seat. I'll show you two boys how it works."

"Do you really think that's going to work?" Cheryl was doubtful.

"If you and I go behind them in line and go on the ride too. It will work. Just watch and see." Michael grinned.

Cheryl glanced at Dori.

"Don't look at me." Dori shrugged her shoulders. "Those rides make me sick. I'm not going on it."

"I don't know if Taylor should be on the ride if he's too short for it." Cheryl pursed her lips together.

"Mom, please. I'm big enough. I'm the same age as Stevie," Taylor begged.

"I'm not a big roller coaster fan, but okay, we'll try," Cheryl said.

Michael bent and whispered something in Taylor's ear. The group made it to the front of the double line when the carney checking heights glanced at Stevie who stood next to another boy. Cheryl was closest to the operator behind Stevie.

Taylor carefully balanced himself on Michael's boots next to his mother.

Before the boys in front of them moved on, Michael made a scene. "Wow! Do you ever have nice legs!" He said it loud enough for everyone to hear.

The carney's attention was drawn to Cheryl while Taylor tippy-toed by with Stevie and another boy and took a seat. Cheryl's mouth gaped as she stared at Michael, who handed the man the tickets for the group. Michael took Cheryl's hand and helped her and himself into a seat, then pulled the metal bar down across their laps. When she put her tanned hands up on the bar he smiled at the white line around her left ring finger where her wedding ring used to be.

"I've got to hand it to you. I never thought it would work," Cheryl told him.

"Stick with me and you'll see a lot of things," he said with a wink. He whistled at the boys who sat three seats in front of them and they waved back with triumphant smiles.

The ride was about to start when Cheryl realized how close Michael was to her. She could smell the sweet, musky aroma of his aftershave and feel the heat penetrate from his body. As the roller coaster clicked on the way up the first steep incline, Cheryl's anxiety climbed along with their rising cart. *What am I doing here?* When they dropped to the bottom, everyone screamed including her. Michael moved in sometime during the plunge and kissed her on the way up the next rise. Cheryl didn't realize what he was doing until she felt the warmth from his mouth on hers. He kissed her quick and turned away. She stared at him while he pretended to gaze at the seats in front of him. When the ride stopped, he was slow to remove his arm from around her, but did after she pushed up the metal bar. He stepped onto the platform and extended his hand to help her out of the seat. The boys, already on the platform, rushed toward them.

"Wasn't that fun, Mom?" Taylor shouted.

"Yeah, that ride was something else," she answered.

"It sure was the best roller coaster ride I ever had," Michael said with a big smile. "Would anyone care to do it again?" he asked the boys, but his eyes came back to hers.

"I think that was enough for today, guys," Cheryl said quickly. "We need to get back to the lambs and see how they are doing. Besides, we're out of tickets."

The children ran ahead of them down the exit ramp out to Dori and Sam who waited at the bottom for their return.

Cheryl and Michael walked down the ramp. "Did I hear you right? Taylor has a lamb in the 4-H sheep barn?" he asked.

"Yeah, why?"

"I'm one of the judges on the board this year for 4-H."

"Really?" Cheryl felt her mouth gape. "I didn't know you were involved with the 4-H Club."

"Well, you remember my friend Jim, who you met at the M & M?"

She nodded.

"His dad, Fred, is in charge of almost everything around here at the fair. I saw him a few weeks ago and he mentioned they were short on judges. He asked me if I was interested, and of course, I told him I would do anything to help out the kids." He looked for her reaction.

"That was certainly nice of you," she said, surprised. Once they reached Dori and the boys, they continued to walk to the barns.

"Michael is on the judging board for the 4H Club," Cheryl told Dori.

Dori blinked her eyes. "Is that right?"

"Yes, and I do believe I am going to be one of the judges for the sheep and lambs," he stated.

When they got back to the sheep barn some of the other judges were gathered by a table.

Michael glanced at the group of officials. "It's been fun, but it looks like I have to attend a meeting right now," he said. "See you later." He walked away and both women stared at each other with wide eyes.

JAKE SCANNED the darkened room when he awoke, not knowing where he was. Then he remembered he was at Susan's apartment. At home the sun usually woke him, shining through the sheer curtains in his bedroom. The heavy drapes in her bedroom allowed only a small trace of light in the room. He leaned over and looked at the woman who slept next to him. Susan's hair was messy and tossed around as she lay there with her back to him. He rarely ever saw her like that since college and it really turned him on. Rolling close, he gently pushed up against her and let her know he was ready to make love.

Susan's eyes fluttered open and she sat up. "I forgot to set the alarm. What time is it? Oh, my God!" she screamed. "It's seven-thirty."

She flung back the covers and ran into the bathroom. He lay on his back with his arms over his head on the pillow. He sighed when he heard the water turn on in the shower. A short time later, she came into the room in a white robe and her hair wrapped in a towel. She quickly opened her closet and thumbed through her clothes for something to wear.

Without looking at him she said, "Meet me for lunch at my office at eleven-thirty. We can spend some time together, then. What are you going to do the rest of the day?"

"I thought I would look up Chuck Davis. I heard he lives somewhere in Edina."

She stopped sliding hangers and turned toward him. "You're kidding, right? Don't you remember I told you I don't want him at the wedding?" She glared.

He propped himself onto his elbow. "Yes, I do remember. Just because I'm looking him up doesn't mean I'm going to invite him."

"I know you, Jake. You'll feel sorry for him and you'll invite him." She stepped into a dark navy blue dress. "Can you zip me?" She turned around by the bed.

He sat up to zip her dress. "I'm going to look him up, and if it makes you feel better, I won't invite him to the wedding."

"Okay. Please don't," she said on her way back into the bathroom. "We don't want him to embarrass us in front of everyone we know." She finished getting ready then brushed a quick kiss on his lips.

Before leaving the apartment, she yelled, "Instead of visiting Chuck why don't you go and buy some new clothes. You're in the Cities now, darling. You need to look the part. Remember, eleven-thirty. See you then."

Jake heard the door shut and lay back down on the bed. Soon, he felt his stomach growl and went into the kitchen. He peered into Susan's refrigerator and found two bottles of Tab diet soda along with a doggy bag containing something dried beyond recognition. He slapped the door shut on the refrigerator and went into the bathroom to shower. He dressed in a brown plaid shirt he'd brought from home and left her apartment. After asking someone, he found a shop that sold men's clothing and chose two shirts with slacks to match. He didn't know if Susan would like his choices or not, but he did, so he purchased them. At eleven twenty-five he was in the elevator going up to the sixteenth floor of the tallest building in Minneapolis, the IDS Center. The elevator opened and he saw Susan's receptionist, Beth, in front of him. There was another young secretary putting files in a nearby cabinet.

"How are you, Beth?" He smiled.

"I'm fine, Mr. Cameron. It's so nice to see you." Beth smiled back. "She said whenever you arrive, I'm to send you in."

Jake nodded and started walking down the hall when he heard the younger girl ask Beth, "*Who's* that?"

"That's Miss Petrich's fiancé," Beth answered.

"*Lucky girl,*" the young woman commented.

Smiling to himself, Jake continued on his way to Susan's office where he knocked on the closed door.

"Come in," he heard her answer. She was at her desk when he entered the room. Without hesitation, he walked directly to his fiancée, intending to kiss her. Susan put up her arms to stop him and her eyes shot to the corner of the room. Jake was surprised to see her mother, Sheila, sitting there.

"Well, this is a pleasant surprise," he said, collecting himself. Sheila stood and gave him a hug.

"After I talked to Susan earlier, I just couldn't resist the urge to have lunch with my future son-in-law."

Leaving Susan's office, they went down to the third floor of the IDS center to Marquette's Italian restaurant. Mother and daughter were strangely quiet as they waited for their salads and Jake's lasagna.

Sheila cleared her throat. "Jake, what are your plans for your family? I mean as far as religion is concerned?"

"What are you getting at? I don't follow you."

"I don't know if you two have given it any thought, but are you going to attend separate churches? I mean, after you have children." Sheila tilted her head.

"We've never talked about it, Sheila. I guess we'll cross that bridge when we get to the river."

She ignored his comment. "I talked to Father Bolin and he said that since you're already taking the marriage classes it would be easier now rather than later to change religions." Her eyes bored into Jake's.

"Where would you get the idea I was planning on changing religions?" He was annoyed.

"I guess the thought came to me when I learned you two were getting married at the Basilica of St. Mary," she said in a matter-of-fact tone. The conversation was interrupted when the waiter appeared with their food.

When the three were alone again, Jake offered an alternative, "If you want, we can get married in Watson."

Susan's eyes widened and her mother gasped, "Oh, God no." Sheila recovered. "I … mean … it's not big enough to accommodate the number of guests we have."

"I think you've answered your own question on why we decided to have the wedding at the Basilica of St. Mary." Looking at his fiancée Jake added, "And there's one more reason." He smiled and put his hand on Susan's. "Your daughter told me walking down the aisle of that church would make her feel like a princess."

Sheila smiled, but became quiet again as she cut up her salad. The subject of religion didn't come up again. The two women talked of florists, decorators and dresses for a while before Susan looked down at her wristwatch.

"I have an appointment after lunch, so I best be getting back. Mother, do you want me to walk you to your car?"

"Yes, that would be great."

They all stood and Susan turned to Jake, "I'll be back at the apartment around six. See you then." She then kissed him lightly on his cheek.

As Jake watched his fiancée and her mother leave the restaurant, he thought about their conversation. If he was going to smooth things over, he'd have to see Chuck another time. That romantic dinner needed to be something special. On his way out, he asked a waiter where to find a reputable supermarket.

It was six o'clock when Jake dimmed the lights and struck a match to light the candles on the dining room table. The salads he'd proudly made of romaine lettuce, tomato and cucumber chilled in the fridge. He poked the baked potatoes in the oven with a fork, then opened a bottle of merlot to breathe and set it on the counter. The table had been carefully set around a bouquet of red roses with plates, silverware, cloth napkins and wine glasses. Everything was perfect, especially the steaks he was going to broil. When six-thirty came and went, he shut the oven off and put the steaks he cooked on a platter on top of the stove. At seven o'clock he fell asleep on the couch and around eight o'clock he awoke to the sound of Susan's key in the door.

She set her packages down and glanced at the candles, now melted to stubs. "Oh, I'm so sorry, Jake. Things got a little later than I intended." She forced a smile. "I did make a decision on my dress, if that helps any?"

He yawned and sat up on the couch, rubbing his eyes. "That sounds great, but I think we better order a pizza, because the steaks I made are more than done."

"Okay, order a small one, though. I did have a bite to eat with Mother and Monique."

"So, you've already eaten?" he asked, feeling a stab.

"I had planned the appointment at the bridal shop and

dinner with my mother and sister a while ago. I didn't want to let them down."

"So why didn't you tell me this when I decided to cook dinner?"

"You were so excited about our intimate dinner. I didn't want to hurt your feelings. I thought it would go faster at the bridal shop. My plan was to eat a lighter meal earlier with them and then come home and eat with you." He was about to ask her why she didn't call from the bridal shop when she reached her hand into his shirt and slowly rubbed his chest. She pressed her lips against his ear and whispered seductively, "Why don't you order a pizza and pour us some wine while I slip into something a little more comfortable?"

Susan kissed him fully, sucking his bottom lip in her teeth before she slowly released it. The gesture was bold and raw with a promise of so much more, and Jake forgot all about his ruined dinner.

It was close to eleven in the morning at the fair and already extremely warm in the 4-H sheep barn. Michael poked his head around the crowd gathered in front of the judges' table and waved at Cheryl. She reluctantly waved back, then returned her attention to Taylor who brushed his lamb. Moments later, she noticed Michael leave and return shortly after carrying a large wicker picnic basket. He stood between her and Taylor.

"How would you like to have a picnic at Smith Park?" he asked the boy. "I've got fried chicken, potato salad and some cold root beers." Michael then looked at Cheryl. "That's if it's okay with you, Mom."

She was surprised by his offer but promptly answered, "That is very kind of you, but I think we can find something here at the fair to eat."

"Not as good as this." He opened the cover on the basket to

let Taylor look in. Cheryl could smell the fried chicken from where she stood.

"Mom, I'm tired of fair food. Can't we have some of that chicken?"

"Wouldn't it be nice to get away and sit under some cool shade trees for a while?" Michael quickly cut in. "And besides, it would be a shame to waste all this fried chicken."

Taylor looked up at his mother and said, "Mom, you always say don't waste food when there are people starving in the world."

Cheryl couldn't help smiling at her son. "Okay. I guess it would be nice to get away from the heat for a while."

"I'll drive," Michael told them with a huge smile. "Follow me through this crowd to my truck. It's parked around the corner where all the important judges park." He laughed.

They drove the short distance to the park and walked to a shady area with a picnic table under a tree. Michael opened the basket and took out a red-and-white-checkered tablecloth. He shook it out and spread it over the wooden table.

Cheryl looked at the table. "Looks like you've thought of everything."

"You could say that." He handed them both a cold root beer and took one out for himself along with a bottle opener. He reached in the basket again and took out three white Melmac plates and placed them on the table with silverware and red cloth napkins.

Michael extended his hand. "Please have a seat. Lunch is about to be served."

Taylor and Cheryl sat down and watched in amazement while their host opened a plate of chicken wrapped with aluminum foil. Locating a spoon in the basket, he took the cover off a Tupperware bowl of potato salad and set it in front of them. He then carefully unwrapped a napkin and offered them each a biscuit. Taking one, Cheryl found they were still warm.

"Help yourselves, but be sure to save room for dessert."

"You have dessert, too?" She was astonished.

"Of course. Peach pie." He reached back into the basket and took out another plate wrapped in foil. Cheryl dished Taylor's plate and then her own.

She stopped before she took her first bite. "Who helped you with all this food?"

"Let's just say I have connections," he told her, and took a drink of his root beer. "By the way, how's my little brother doing with Eddy? Is he getting on your nerves yet?"

"He hasn't been over too often lately. Eddy's no problem in the pasture grazing with the cattle. Brett doesn't bother anyone, and I think Taylor does look forward to his visits," she said, looking at her son, who nodded with his mouth full. Michael didn't say anything for a few seconds, then changed the subject to the lamb exhibition.

"I don't think the Peterson kid has the grand champion ribbon sewed up like he thinks ...." He stopped when someone hollered from over by the playground equipment.

"Taylor! Taylor!" A boy yelled and ran toward them.

"That's Jimmy from school."

Jimmy came over and stood at the end of the picnic table. "Hey, Taylor, do you want to go over to the swings and play for a while? I can go really high."

Taylor stood and turned to his mother. "Can I go?"

"Not until you finish eating. And not too long because we have to get back to the fair," Cheryl told him. "Jimmy, grab a seat. When Taylor is done you two can go and swing."

Both boys sat down and Taylor ate while Michael asked them questions about baseball. When Taylor shoved in his last bite, he and Jimmy ran toward the playground.

Cheryl watched her son play with his friend.

"He really is an amazing boy," Michael finally said. "I think my brother coming over is great and all, but he's really just a kid himself. Taylor needs a real man in his life ... and so do you." He put his hand over hers and squeezed it softly.

She pulled it away and looked down at the ground. "I don't know why I agreed to come here today. I should have known that sooner or later you would pressure me again."

"I don't mean to pressure you. It's just been a long time since … I've felt what I feel when I'm around you. I know you've been through something awful, losing the person you love. I can understand, because I lost someone I loved, too."

"Who did you lose?"

"My first love, Diana. I thought she was the one, and we were going to get married. I made the wrong decision and now she's with someone else." He looked away at the boys on the swings. "I know it doesn't compare to losing someone you were married to and brought a child into the world with. But I loved her and I lost her and it … still hurts all the same."

He was quiet for a moment before his eyes went back to her. "Wow. I can't believe I told you that. I've never told anyone." He paused and looked down at his wristwatch. "I suppose we should be getting back. It wouldn't look good if a judge is late …." He stopped talking when she put her hand on his arm.

"I'm sorry about you and Diana."

"Thanks." His eyes glistened. "Cheryl, will you meet me sometime? Just to talk."

She drew a breath. "Michael, how long has it been since you lost Diana?"

"About six years. Why?"

"It's only been a little over a year for me. I need time to sort everything out. I don't think …."

"That's my point," he interrupted. "I still lost her, no matter how you look at it. I need to sort some things out, too. It's not like I'm asking for a date or anything. You're the only person I found I can talk to about this stuff. I really thought we were friends." His eyes found hers then trailed down to the ground.

"Okay, I'll meet you sometime. To talk. Maybe at Trailways for coffee in the morning, would that work for you?"

"Yes, it would." He released a heavy sigh. "I feel better

knowing I have someone I can trust to talk to. And, of course, you know *you* can always confide in me, too." He smiled and looked at his wristwatch again. "We better get going or we're going to be late."

SUSAN LEFT for work and Jake sat on her leather couch watching television. The news was on and the story was about beer commercials and how the networks only allowed them to run in the evening before sporting events. A clip from a Miller Lite commercial showed a bunch of friends indulging in a few beers and having a good time. Jake suddenly thought about Chuck Davis and the old gang who hung around together back in college. He picked up the phone book and found Chuck's name listed in Edina, then dialed his number. After two rings, he heard a familiar voice on the end of the line.

"Hello."

"Chuck?"

"Yeah, this is he. Who's this?"

"It's Jake Cameron. How are you?"

Chuck started laughing. "How ya doing, Cowpie?"

"Pretty good, but I was hoping you forgot that nickname," Jake said with a laugh.

"I would never forget that name. You earned it," Chuck fired back and they both laughed harder.

"Well, I know it's last minute, but I'm in Minneapolis and I was hoping to see you if you're not busy."

"For you buddy, I'll call in sick."

"No, don't do that. I wouldn't want to get you into any trouble with your employer."

"No, don't worry about it, my employer won't say shit."

"Why do you say that?" *I hope he's employed.*

"Because I own my own law firm. Charles Davis and Associates. You know, if you got out of Montevideo and visited your friends once in a while, you'd know I'm not doing too bad for the crazy, beer-guzzling guy you knew at the U."

Jake was briefly lost for words. "W... well, that's great. I'm happy to hear it."

"Get your ass over here, Cowpie," Chuck shouted in the receiver.

Jake followed the directions his friend gave him to Edina. Carefully reading the addresses on the houses, he came to a driveway with brick pillars on each side with Chuck's house number on it. The grass looked recently mowed and the hedges were plush and groomed on the sides of a cobblestone driveway curving uphill. Arriving at the top, Jake did a double take, seeing water run out the bill of a large swan fountain in the middle of the circular driveway. The house was a huge, three-story, brick mansion. *Susan is never going to believe this.*

A large man came out of a set of enormous doors and bolted for Jake's truck before he was parked. Jake stepped out of his vehicle and Chuck, who measured six-foot-five, instantly grabbed his old college roommate and wrapped his large arms around him. A moment went by while both men looked at each other and laughed. Finally, after they composed themselves, Chuck invited Jake into his luxurious home and gave him a tour that ended in the back yard. The two men sat poolside with a beer and laughed more than talked about their crazy college days. It wasn't too long into the conversation when Jake noticed nothing had changed between him and this man. Despite his success, he was still Chuck.

"Are you still dating Susan?" he asked.

"Yes. As a matter of fact, we're getting married in December."

"Is that right? Well, congratulations, buddy. She still look like Liz Taylor?"

"Maybe a little prettier than Liz."

"Cowpie's in love," Chuck teased.

"I saw the good-looking woman in the pictures in the house. Who's that, Chuckie?"

"No one, but the love of my life, Nancy. We're engaged, too. It's a funny thing you'd call and come over when I was going to get a hold of you."

"Why's that?"

"You know Jake, all that good advice you gave me in college really straightened me out. I'm grateful to you, and it would mean the world to me if you'd be in my wedding." Chuck waited for Jake's answer.

"I would be honored. When's the wedding?"

"April fourteenth. I'll know more details at your bachelor party. I don't do the kind of partying these days like I used to, but I still tip a couple of beers on occasion." He grinned and took a swallow of his beer. They talked for a while longer when Jake heard a large grandfather clock chime from inside the house and checked his wristwatch. He blinked, expecting to see an hour had passed, but discovered it had been three.

"I'd better get going. Susan and I have dinner plans with her friend and her husband tonight," Jake said with a sigh. "We'll have to get together soon with you and Nancy."

"Sounds good, buddy," Chuck answered. They walked out to the driveway and before Jake got into his truck, Chuck said, "Say hi to Susan. Tell her I can't wait to see her and have her meet Nancy." Jake nodded and after a hug from his friend he left.

It was five-thirty when Jake got to Susan's apartment. He wasn't there long when the phone rang. He said hello and heard a woman's voice.

"Is this Jake?"

"Yes. Whom am I speaking to?"

"Melody Green. My, you *are* that straight-laced guy Susan said you were."

"She said that?" he asked with a chuckle.

"Is Susan there with you?"

"No, she's at work, yet. Can I give her a message?"

"Yes, you certainly can. I wanted to thank her again for the lovely time we had at her dinner party last week. Oh, and if it's not too much trouble, I'd like to know the name of the wine she served. It was wonderful. I would love to serve it at a dinner party I'm hosting."

"You'll have to ask her," Jake answered. "Are you planning on being around later? I'll tell her to give you a call back."

"I should be," she replied. "Well, nice talking to you Jake, and by the way, congratulations on your engagement. I'm *so* happy for you two. Goodbye." She hung up and Jake was looking for a piece of paper to write the message down but was interrupted again by the ringing telephone.

"Where have you been?" Susan asked. "I've been calling all afternoon."

"I've had an interesting day. You — " He was going to tell her about the call from Melody when she interrupted him.

"No, I don't have time right now. Tell me later at dinner. Something came up here at work and I need to take care of it. I've got an important client waiting in my office right now. I won't have time to come home, so can you just meet us at the restaurant tonight?"

"That's no problem. Tell me where and what time I should be there. Anything for my girl."

Susan gave him the address and time. "Don't be late," she warned before hanging up.

At precisely six-thirty Jake arrived at Camelot, an expensive-looking French restaurant. The maître d' led him to a round corner booth in the back where Susan, Lona and Jack were enjoying a cocktail. They were laughing, but cut their conversation when Jake approached the table.

Jack stood up and held out his hand. "If it isn't the Sugar King Prince."

Jake smiled and the men shook hands, then he pulled out a chair next to Susan's and sat down.

"It's been a while since we've seen you last. Where have you been hiding?" Jack asked. "In the sticks?"

He and the women erupted into laughter and Jake looked at the group confused.

"I'm just kidding, Princey." He gestured toward Susan with his martini. "It's been a joke with us about you taking our girl here away and hiding her in the sticks."

Jake managed a small smile but didn't say anything. Susan changed the subject and talked about the wedding for a while. The waiter came back to the table and Jake ordered a beer.

Susan frowned. "Are you sure you don't want a martini or something instead of a beer?"

"No, I had a couple with Chuck earlier, so I'll stick with beer." Susan stared at him but stopped when the waiter handed her a menu. Jake opened his menu and discovered the cheapest entrée was fifteen dollars. He looked at Susan with raised eyebrows. Jack saw him give Susan the look.

"What's wrong, Princey? The prices scare you?" Jack smirked. "Things are a little more spendy here in the Cities."

"No, the prices don't scare me. But I will say with the price of these steaks we should be able to invest in a whole beef cow," Jake commented with a smile at the group around him. An awkward moment passed when no one laughed. Jake noticed a nervous smile on his fiancée's lips.

Susan broke the silence. "Speaking of investments, what a day I've had. One of our major investors came in wanting to pull out of some stocks that would have created a significant loss of income for our firm. Naturally, my boss wanted me to handle the situation knowing this guy is infatuated with me. Who knows, I may get a big promotion from this."

Jake snapped his head toward her.

Jack again noticed Jake's reaction. "Princey, maybe you two will be moving to Minneapolis instead of Montevideo."

"My name is Jake, not Princey," he said in a serious tone.

Lona, who throughout the evening had listened and said little, quickly broke in, "Just ignore Jack. He has a different way of saying things. He really doesn't mean to hurt anyone's feelings."

"He's not hurting my feelings, Lona," Jake told her. "But thanks for your concern." He took a big swallow of his beer.

The women took over the conversation while the men sat and listened, interrupting only when the waiter came to order another drink. Jake was starved when the waiter set down a small salad in front of him with an assortment of strange colored vegetables in it. He ate the salad hoping his main entree would be something he'd be able to identify. A while later, the waiter returned and removed his salad plate then replaced it with another plate.

"I'm glad we get this appetizer with our dinner. I'm pretty hungry," he said gazing down at the small piece of beef on his plate. The whole group roared in laughter. Jake looked up at them. "What's so funny?"

Susan composed herself slightly, and said between giggles, "That *is* the main course, darling."

"This is it?" Jake blinked. The sprig of parsley lying next to the meat was close to the same size.

"It's not quite the half-a-beef you farm boys are used to eating, is it?" Jack managed to say while he laughed.

Eyeing his plate, Jake shook his head. "I guess not."

Everyone started eating and the conversation turned back to investments. Jack talked about the recent killing he'd made on the stock market.

Jake recalled to himself what Susan told him about Jack. He had inherited all his money, and the way it sounded to Jake, had never done an honest day's work in his life. He made Lona sign a document Susan called a prenuptial agreement, which protected his money from her in case they divorced. She had to stay in the marriage ten years to get a percentage of his assets. Jake looked at Lona. *I pity you.* Jake's eyes focused back on Jack. *No way in hell any amount of money would be worth being with him.*

Jack came to the finale of his story long after everyone

finished their after-dinner drinks. The waiter came to the table with the dinner checks and set them next to the men. Jake briefly examined his bill to make sure it was correct then took out his wallet to get some bills.

"Don't be so shocked, Jake. Just open your wallet, blow off some of that plow dust and pay the man," Jack instructed.

Jake cocked his head and momentarily stared at him.

The waiter looked at both men. "I can come back if you wish."

"No, here you are," Jake told him, and put the correct amount in the book along with a nice tip. Jack paid his and Lona's bill and the couples left the restaurant.

They were in the parking lot about to say their goodbyes when Jack asked Jake, "It's always interesting to see how the other side of the world lives, isn't it?"

Jake took a breath and pondered. "I don't think this is much different than back home. Near as I can tell, the big differences are the higher prices and the increased number of jackasses you have to deal with."

Jack's jaw fell open. Lona gasped and put her hand to her mouth. She scuttled around their convertible parked in the next row and got into the vehicle. Jake walked over to the passenger's side of his truck and held the door open for Susan.

Susan's face was slightly red and her eyes were narrowed, but she silently got inside his truck. Lona turned and waved only her fingers at Susan while she waited for her husband. Jack coolly got into the car and slammed the door. He turned his face toward his wife and muttered something to her before they drove out of the parking lot.

WHEN CHERYL and Taylor had returned from the park with Michael, the judging started right away. Cheryl could feel Dori's eyes on her, but there was no time to talk to her friend. Taylor and Stevie were astonished when they each won a blue ribbon, but no one was surprised when the purple grand champion ribbon went to the Peterson kid. During the judging, Michael took every opportunity to smile at Cheryl and didn't let her out of his sight for more than a few seconds.

Dori came up behind Cheryl and whispered in her ear, "Come with me to the ladies' room and tell me what's going on."

In the restroom, Dori put a finger to her lips then tipped her head and checked under the stalls to see if anyone else was in there. Seeing no one, she demanded, "Tell me where you were and what happened."

Cheryl told her about the picnic at the park and what Michael said about his lost love.

"Wow. Sounds like he went through a lot of trouble for that picnic."

Cheryl nodded and asked, "Do you think his feelings are true about Diana?"

"Everyone in high school knew he was head over heels for her because he never dated anyone else. Rumor has it she met someone in Europe or somewhere overseas before college." She stopped to look at her friend. "Wait a minute. You didn't agree to go out with him. Did you?"

"He told me I'm the only one he can talk to about his loss, and asked if we could get together and talk some more about it," Cheryl answered. "I told him maybe we could meet at Trailways for coffee in the morning sometime."

"Let's hope he's on the up and up. We're all familiar with his reputation with women." Dori sighed. "Who could blame any woman for getting lost in a face like his with that body."

"Oh, my God, what did I get myself into? Is he looking for another conquest?" Cheryl closed her eyes and dropped her forehead in her hand.

"I wouldn't worry about it. All you agreed to was a cup of coffee and some conversation," Dori said soothingly. "It's a good way to see if Michael is what he claims to be ... your friend."

Both women agreed and went back to the 4-H barn to their children. Soon after, they told the boys to get the lambs settled in for another night at the fair.

BRETT WALKED past a small building on his way to the sheep barn. Seeing his reflection in one of the windows, he stopped suddenly and stepped back. Smiling at himself, he ran a hand through his blonde hair and straightened his collar. Once inside the exhibit, he scanned the barn until his eyes found Cheryl. When their eyes met, she surprised him with a pretty smile and a friendly wave. Her encouragement was enough to make his heartbeat shift into a higher gear. He took a deep breath before he made his way through the crowd toward her and Taylor. In all honesty, he really did want to see Taylor, but knowing Cheryl would be there was more than a bonus. He could tell she was starting to trust him and it would be just a matter of time before he would make his move. A thought occurred. *Who knows? Maybe she'll make the moves on me.*

Taylor noticed him and his face lit up. "Brett!"

"Hey, buddy. I came down to see how you did." Brett smiled at him.

Taylor moved out of the way and pointed to the board above his lamb and exclaimed, "Look. A blue ribbon." His smile went from ear to ear.

Apparently, Stevie didn't want to be left out, so he pointed to his board. "I got a blue ribbon, too."

"You boys did real good." Brett looked toward Cheryl and Dori. "Good afternoon, ladies. Are you enjoying the fair?"

"Yes, we are," Dori quickly answered, "but I don't think quite as much as these two boys are. A blue ribbon is more than they were expecting."

"They earned it, and that's all that matters. They did a fine job." Brett patted Taylor's shoulder.

Dori stepped closer to Brett. "It didn't hurt anything to have your brother as one of the judges either," she said in a hushed voice.

"What?" Brett narrowed his eyes at her.

She nodded toward the judges' table where Michael sat working on some paperwork.

Brett felt his mouth open in disbelief. "He is unbelievable." he exclaimed. "Excuse me. I'll be right back."

He walked over to the judges' table and waved his hand in front of his brother's face to get his attention. Michael looked up, annoyed.

"What the hell are *you* doing here?" Brett's tone was contemptuous.

"Helping out the kids. Why are you here?" Michael stood and said to another judge, "So, that should do it, right?"

"Yep, that's all of it. Thanks for helping out this year."

"It was my pleasure." Michael shook his hand.

"I bet it was your pleasure and nothing else," Brett announced loudly.

Michael's face turned noticeably red and he motioned for his brother to follow him. They went around the outside of the barn to the area where the judges parked and turned toward each other.

"So, you manipulated yourself into another part of her life." Brett stepped closer.

"Get out of my face, little man."

"What's to stop me from going back in there and telling her everything?"

"Why the hell would you do that? She'll find out about *you*, too." Michael forced a fake smile.

"You just want a piece of ass. I care about her. Before I'd let you use her, I'll take the chance on losing her." Brett started for the barn entrance.

Michael pounced on his brother, shoving him up against the barn. His nostrils flared and his chest was pressed up against Brett. "You tell her, and I will make your life a living hell."

While they pushed each other, dust rose from the commotion and caught the attention of two judges who came from around the corner of the building.

"What the hell's going on here?" one of the men yelled. The bigger of the two stepped in and pulled Michael away while the other guy took a hold of Brett's arms. Both brothers struggled to break free, but couldn't.

"Come on boys, break it up," the first man told them.

"Aren't you two both Chet Cameron's boys?" the larger man asked.

"Yeah, unfortunately, we're related." Brett's chest heaved as he spat on the ground.

"We don't need any fighting here at the fair," the big man told them. "Where's your vehicles? Go home and cool off."

"Okay, okay." Michael panted. "My truck's over there." He nodded toward his truck two rows from where they stood.

"Where's yours?" the big guy asked Brett.

"It's parked over by the entrance," Brett growled.

"All right then. Joe here, will escort you to your vehicle and I will make sure your brother finds his. I want you both to go on home and don't come back until you learn how to behave yourselves at the fair."

JAKE DROVE to the apartment under the glare of his fiancée's stare. He looked at her a couple times, then back at the road. Finally, he told her, "I know what you're going to say — that I shouldn't have said that to him. But how much can a man take from that idiot?"

"How could you say that to my best friends?" Her chin was trembling.

"Come on, Susan. You heard all his condescending remarks,"

Jake snapped. "All those things about living in the sticks and blowing off the plow dust from my wallet. And let's not forget about 'Princey.'"

"He was just trying to be funny and get you to like him. If you'd let your country bumpkin, hard-core attitude go for a second, you'd see that."

"So, you think I'm a country bumpkin? Well, even a country bumpkin can tell when someone's making fun of him."

"All I'm saying is you could have acted a little more refined than you did. Lona and Jack are used to the finer things in life. Like martinis and wine, not beer."

He flinched. "So, you're mad at me because I had a beer?"

"No. I'm upset because you don't see Jack is a great guy with a charming personality," she said more calmly.

"Maybe he *does* have more of an abundance of charm than the average guy," Jake smiled.

Her face relaxed and she released a deep breath.

"You know that could very well be, because he doesn't do any work to speak of. He definitely has a lot of time to come up with all sorts of charming and witty things to say to us country bumpkins."

"He's got to be better than that drunken Chuck Davis you seem to want to hang around with!" she yelled. "What's he up to these days? Has he made it to head grocery boy at the local market?" Jake was about to answer but she continued, "You better not have invited him to the wedding."

"As a matter of fact, I did invite him. I'm also going to be in his wedding in April."

"I *knew* something like this would happen if you went to see him." She crossed her arms. "Don't plan on *me* going to his wedding. I wouldn't be caught dead there."

Neither spoke another word the rest of the drive, and the silence continued after they got back to Susan's apartment. She sat on the leather couch in the living room and made a point not to look at him. He went into the bedroom and after a few minutes came out with his bag. He stood behind the couch where she had her back to him.

After a moment, he cleared his throat. "I'm going home."

Susan turned toward him, eyeing the bag in his hand. "Tonight?"

"Yeah, you have to work tomorrow, and I should get back. Dad's probably tired of doing all the chores. Sounds like Michael and Brett haven't been around much when I called earlier today."

"You don't have to drive in the dark. Why don't you sleep here on the couch tonight?" she suggested.

He stared at her. "Thanks," he said coolly. "But it's time for this country bumpkin to head on home." She frowned and he left, slamming the door behind him.

THE WOMEN at the old church basement tried to keep straight faces while Nell Thompson told the quilting circle about her time at the fair.

"I don't know why I told my grandson I would go on that ride with him. That Ferris wheel didn't look that high in the air until I was at the top. I know people are talking about me now, but I couldn't do a thing about it, once I was up there. It didn't occur to me my old weak bladder would let go the moment I looked down to see where Earl was on the ground. The only thing I can do now — is laugh at myself." She chuckled and the women laughed with her. "So, Joan, that's why I snubbed you at the fair. I was making a bee-line for the car."

"I knew there had to be something wrong. I've never seen you walk so fast," Joan answered, struggling to keep the laughter out of her voice.

Perhaps desperate to change the subject, Nell asked Cheryl, "So how did Taylor do with his lamb at the fair? I would have gone and looked myself, but you can understand why I didn't."

"He got a blue ribbon, and he's still very excited about it," Cheryl replied. The women around her smiled at her pleased tone.

Lucille stopped stitching and looked up. "I'm so happy for your son. How nice that he got a blue ribbon."

"I don't know if it made any difference or not with Michael being one of the judges. But if it did, it sure made Taylor happy."

Lucille stared at her. "*My* Michael?" Her voice raised.

"Yes. You didn't know he was judging the sheep and lambs for 4-H?" Cheryl asked.

"He did mention he wanted to do something for the children this year. I just didn't know what he had decided. He sure does love children," Lucille said matter-of-factly.

Cheryl didn't mention Michael again. The topic moved on to the up-coming bazaar.

"Too bad the fellowship hall isn't completed," Patsy Timms said. "It's my understanding there will be electricity for the bazaar, but the new stove with the oven hasn't come yet. There are so many things left at the fellowship hall to be completed. Everyone has been so generous with their time. I pray it continues. Ladies, please check the schedule to remind yourself of what evening you're in charge."

Kathy Klies told the group she had a new recipe for a salad, and was looking forward to trying it. Alma, who was paired with Sophie, said they were going to make a hot dish on their night, one that Alma's mother had often made when she was a young girl. Nell and Cheryl were serving roast beef with mashed potatoes on their night, mainly because it was Earl's favorite. No one knew how much work the volunteers were getting done, but everyone knew they were eating well.

The afternoon slipped away, and as Cheryl drove home she reflected on the session. It was like a family gathering. Most of the women cared about each other and shared what was happening in their lives. It was more than just quilting. For the first time in a long time, she didn't feel alone.

9

It was close to noon when Jake and Chet drove in the yard with a wagonload of hay. The thermos of water they brought to the field had been empty for quite a while. They drove up close to the barn where Brett and his father helped unload the hay onto the conveyer while Michael and Jake went up into the hay loft and stacked the bales into neat rows. When they were finished, the men were ready for a cold drink and something to eat, along with a cool spot to do both. They came in the back door off the kitchen and cleaned up in the small washroom.

All four Cameron men were headed toward the kitchen table when Irene yelled, "She wants to eat in the formal dining room."

Chet looked surprised. "She does realize that we've been baling hay and we're not exactly what I'd call clean?"

"That's what she told me to tell you," Irene answered.

Lucille sat at the long dining room table when the men entered the room. They all stopped at once, seeing Susan sitting next to her.

"What are *you* doing here?" Jake asked a bit coldly.

Susan smiled sweetly. "I thought I would come out early and surprise you."

"Well, you certainly accomplished that," he said and sat at the table.

Susan looked lovely with her makeup and hair flawlessly done. The lilac colored, cotton sundress she wore completed her chic look.

"Don't you look prettier than a picture sitting there," Chet said with a big grin.

"Thank you, Chet," Susan answered with a flirtatious smile.

"Call me Dad," he told her, "After all, we are going to be family."

Lucille smiled at her husband, obviously pleased with his comment. Brett sat and looked at Susan from the corner of his eye.

Susan noticed his stare. "How are you, Brett?"

"Fine. How are you?" He seemed on edge.

"Good. It's always great to be here with this family." Her gaze fell on Jake.

Michael and Chet took a seat when Irene began to bring the food in from the kitchen. She set a huge pork roast on the table along with three large bowls containing mashed potatoes, green beans and steaming gravy. A lined wicker basket was piled to the top with homemade dinner rolls next to two rhubarb pies at the end of the table. Susan silently stared at the food with big eyes.

"When a man works hard, a man's gotta eat," Jake said to her. "There are four hard-working, hungry men here."

She didn't acknowledge his comment and struck up a conversation with Lucille about the number of guests her mother had estimated for the Petrich side.

"Do you need our list soon, dear?" Lucille asked. "We do have the church bazaar tomorrow. I'm sorry I won't be able to get it to you until after this weekend."

"Don't put yourself out. Next week is just fine." Susan smiled.

"Speaking of the bazaar, you two *are* planning on going?"

Lucille asked but her question sounded more like a statement. "There are so many people I would love to introduce you to."

"I don't know," Susan told her and looked at her fiancé. "Jake hasn't invited me. Are we going, honey?"

Jake let a moment go, before he answered, "Only if you want to go. I didn't say anything about it because I didn't think you'd be interested in going. It isn't exactly the kind of excitement you're used to in Minneapolis." He casually took another bite of food.

No one said anything about Jake's comment, but a few glances were exchanged around the table.

Chet studied both Jake and Susan before he broke the silence. "Jake, your brothers and I can finish up the baling. I think you two love birds need some time alone this afternoon." Brett let out a groan but Michael sat quietly with an amused expression on his face. "When you're finished eating, go and get showered up. We'll keep this pretty little thing entertained until you get back." Chet flashed a big smile at Susan and she reciprocated.

Jake finished with his shower and came down the long staircase combing his hair. He stopped at the gold, framed mirror at the landing on the bottom for a final inspection. Only Susan and his mother's voices could be heard, so he assumed the men returned to the field. He put his comb in his back pocket and walked toward the dining room, but came to a standstill when he heard his mother ask Susan a question.

"Susan, I don't mean to be sticking my nose into things, but have you and Jake figured out a way Brett could possibly be in the wedding? Jake told me you were going to ask another friend to be a bridesmaid. Have you asked her?"

"I haven't seen or heard from her in over a month," Susan replied. "I think my friend may have left the country. Sometimes it's so hard to reach her."

She has the gall, to lie right to my mother's face. Jake took a deep breath to calm down. To avoid a family feud, he decided it was best to confront Susan later.

Jake came into the room and Lucille didn't say anymore. They talked for a few minutes before leaving, but the subject of Brett being in the wedding didn't come up again.

Jake followed Susan in his truck to the Hotel Hunt where she stayed in Montevideo. In the hotel parking lot, she parked her car and he backed into the spot next to her. Before she could get out of her vehicle, Jake rolled down the window in his truck.

"Do you want to go for a drive?" he asked.

"Don't you want to go up to the room?" She sounded surprised.

"Why don't we go for a drive and then come back to the room?"

"Okay, we can come back here later and make up." She gave him a mischievous smile.

They drove back to the other side of Watson, to the eighty acres of land he'd purchased and walked around the stakes that marked the site of their new house.

Looking around the area he said, "I guess ever since I started watching Bonanza, it has always been a dream of mine to live in a ranch-style house. Maybe a rambler, but not too big."

"I don't think it would give anyone privacy. Especially from the children or unwanted guests."

"So, what kind of style home were you thinking?" he asked.

"How about a house like your parents have?"

"Counting the basement and the attic that's a four-level house. My grandfather built that house in 1904 and he had eight kids to clean it. I don't think a house of that size is anything you want to take care of."

"I wasn't planning on taking care of it. Aren't we going to have a housekeeper? Your mother has one, if that's what you want to call her."

"We didn't have a housekeeper until after Brett was born. We had to get one because Mom was always outside in the field or in the barn, helping Dad. Then, after us boys got big enough — we helped Dad. Are you planning on helping me farm?"

"I don't think that would work out for either of us," she said, sounding annoyed. "I plan on getting a job in Montevideo at the bank or maybe even starting my own investment company there."

Jake cocked his head at her. "So, when did this all come about?" he asked. "I've never heard you mention anything about starting your own company."

"Well, you remember the great save I did earlier in the week? My boss has known my father for years and they discussed how well I'm doing at work. Daddy called me and we talked about what's going to happen with my career after we get married."

Jake didn't say anything but let out a big sigh.

"It's not like I expect you to finance it or anything. Daddy says rounding up some other investors wouldn't be that difficult."

A couple of mallard ducks flew over and Jake watched them land on a pond close by.

"Sounds like you and Daddy have it all figured out," he said sharply.

"Jake Cameron, I know that tone," she fired back. "You knew when you asked me to marry you I wasn't going to be the typical farm wife. I love you and I want to marry you. And I believe you and I can make anything work if we want it to."

"I thought you wanted children right away after we got married," he said. "How is that going to happen if you're starting a business?"

She slipped her hands around his waist and pulled herself close to him, "So there might be a slight delay. But I definitely want to have a baby or two with you." She pressed her head to his chest and hugged him tightly. "Let's go back to the hotel and practice."

With her arm still around his waist, she led him toward the truck, but he stopped after a few steps. "One more thing." he said.

"What's that darling?" she asked him playfully.

"When was the last time you talked to Melody?"

"Probably a month ago," she answered. "Why?"

"Well, she called that afternoon before we went out with Lona and Jack." Watching her reaction, he looked her in the eyes. "I was going to tell you when you called, but you were busy, and afterwards I forgot. She told me to tell you she enjoyed the wine at your place the previous week. And wanted to know the name of it."

"Oh, yeah, that's right. I forgot all about the dinner party. What difference does it make when I talked to her last, Jake?"

"It makes a big difference, because weeks ago I asked you to talk to her about being in the wedding and earlier I heard you lie to my mother about it."

"I didn't intentionally mean to lie to either of you. I was simply embarrassed that I forgot to ask Melody." She pursed her lips. "I'm sorry. I was busy entertaining my guests at my dinner party. If it makes you feel better, I will ask Mel first thing Monday morning and I'll call you after."

"Why don't you call her when we get back to the hotel?" he asked.

"I'm not going to bother her on the weekend. Besides, it's rude to call collect. Monday, okay?" Taking his hands, she looked up into his eyes, "Look, Jake, I came here early to make up. Not to fight. I love you."

"I love you too, but if we're going to make a marriage work you need to be honest with me no matter what." His voice was serious.

"Okay. I screwed up. Let's go back to the hotel and see if I can find a way to make it up to you." She winked.

CHERYL STIRRED IN BED, not fully awake from a sweet dream. She and Jon were in their bed making love. Wrapped in each other's arms in what seemed pure ecstasy, his lips devoured hers while a wave of sweet desire rolled through her entire body. So power-fully real, it left her with the elated belief he was still alive. It had all been a mistake. He had just been away for some reason and now had returned.

Before her eyes opened she ran her hand over the other side of the bed and felt nothing but her heart ache. The reality was — he was gone. It was only a dream. She opened her eyes and tears streamed down her face, dampening the pillow. Upset, she turned on her back and stared at the ceiling. *What a way to start the day, sad and lonely. Especially on the day of the bazaar when everyone will be there looking at my red, puffy eyes. I wish I hadn't volunteered to watch the food table. I just want to stay in bed forever.* She heard the floor board creak from the hall outside her bedroom and watched the door slowly open. A small figure stood in the doorway.

"Mom, what's wrong?" Taylor's voice was soft and inquisitive.

"Nothing's wrong, honey." She tried to sound normal.

"Then why are you crying?"

"Sometimes it just feels good to cry."

He looked at her like she was crazy. "When I cry, it doesn't feel good at all. I hate crying."

"Come here and lie by me for a while." Cheryl reached out. He smiled and hopped over her legs. He pulled the covers up over himself and cuddled in close to her.

"Mom, do you remember the promise we made to Dad?"

She thought for a second. "You mean the one about being happy and carrying on without him, no matter what?"

"Yeah, that's the one." He nodded. "I think we need to keep our promise and be happy."

She smiled and hugged him tight.

When she released him, he said, "You look pretty when you're happy. You don't have to be happy just for Dad. You can be happy and pretty for me. I love you, too, Mom."

"I love you, Taylor," she said and embraced him again.

Cheryl tickled Taylor, making him giggle and squeal until it was time to get ready. He went to his room to get out of his pajamas and get dressed while she got in the shower. Her hair was sudsy with shampoo when she thought, *I'm going to put a smile on my face and take some time getting ready because I'm going to look pretty for my son.*

THE COFFEE POT wasn't the only thing heating up in Susan's hotel room. Steam rolled out the door of the small bathroom. Susan stepped out of the shower and Jake came out right behind her. She handed him a towel then bent over in front of him and wrapped her hair in another.

"Now that's a view to get a man's blood pumping in the morning."

With a devilish smile, she turned and gave him a quick kiss. After drying off, she went to search through her bag while Jake stayed in the bathroom to shave.

"So, what's a gal supposed to wear to this thing?" she asked.

"What about that denim mini skirt you used to wear in college?" he said and put his head around the doorway of the bathroom. His face was full of shaving cream. "You always drove me wild when you wore that."

"That old thing?" She laughed. "I got rid of it years ago."

He faked a frown and went back to shaving.

"I better wear something nice because the way it sounds, your mother is going to introduce me to the whole county."

"Not quite the whole county, just the southwest side," Jake said and chuckled. When he was ready to go, she wasn't, so he left the hotel room to get some rolls to go with the coffee.

Susan removed a sundress from a hanger and stepped into it. The dress was bright yellow and looked sharp next to her dark skin and hair. She opened a small black box and put on a yellow diamond and green emerald butterfly necklace set in yellow gold. When she finished her make-up, Susan rubbed her lips together then puckered them and admired herself in the mirror. While spraying her perfectly styled hair, she heard a key slide into the lock. Jake entered with a white paper bag in his hand.

Immediately he stopped and whistled. "Don't you look like the belle of the ball!"

"You like?" Susan smiled and turned in a circle for him to see her from all angles. She put her hand to her necklace. "This is the necklace I told you about. The one my grandmother bought at Tiffany's in New York for my birthday last year. Isn't it gorgeous?"

"Not half as gorgeous as the one wearing it," he stated.

Jake came over to kiss her and she put her hand up. "Please, honey. Let's not mess up my hair or makeup or we'll never get there. I would rather get there and leave early than be stuck there all day with your mother throwing names at me."

"Maybe you shouldn't get too annoyed with her," Jake told her as he filled their coffee cups. "She's just excited to show the whole world her wonderful future daughter-in-law." Susan let out a big sigh and rolled her eyes in the mirror in front of her.

EARL THOMPSON and Chet Cameron stood above the open granite stairwell to the church basement and gazed over at the tents they'd set up earlier that morning.

"I don't know about you, Chet, but my body's telling me I'm not as young as I used to be."

"My body is not telling me anything right now, but who knows what it'll be saying tomorrow morning," Chet said, laughing. Their voices echoed down the steps where Brett and Michael were hauling up a large table. The table legs didn't fold, making it awkward to maneuver. Michael was on the bottom end while Brett walked up the steps backward.

"Lift your end! This thing is heavy!" Michael shouted.

Brett felt the blood rush to his face and shouted back, "I *am* lifting, Grandma."

Michael pushed the table into Brett and he shoved it back down at him. One table leg smashed up against the wall of the granite stairwell. It grated but didn't look like it sustained any damage.

"Look, you two, I don't know what's going on between you lately, but you'd better knock it off," Chet hollered down. "Get that table up here right now." They did as they were told and got the table to the top of the stairs. Chet then yelled over at Lucille and Nell, "Where do you gals want this table?"

Lucille pointed to a tent close to the new fellowship hall. "That would work real nice for the food table."

Nell looked around. "I don't know. Maybe it should ...."

"I don't care where you ladies want it, just decide. It's getting pretty heavy." Michael's voice was strained.

"Just put it over there. We'll use it for the food table." Nell sounded pressured.

Lucille looked pleased when Michael and Brett set the table down where she suggested. More volunteers showed up, and soon all the booths were set up for the dunk tank, cake walk, bingo, and a few others.

Brett pounded posts in the ground for the pony rides while Michael sat in the ticket booth with John Kleis and learned about ticket sales. Chet walked over to Brett to see how he was doing on the corral and stood next to him.

"Your mother and I are proud of you boys for wanting to help out this year. I can't say we aren't a little surprised, but whatever the reason, we're proud just the same."

Brett smiled at his dad and continued to pound, but his thoughts went back to last week when he'd found the sign-up sheet for the bazaar on the dining room table. Earlier he'd left the new Stetson he'd purchased for the bazaar on a chair pushed in close to the table. For what the hat cost him, he wasn't about to leave it there for someone to sit on and flatten.

He pounded a little harder as he recalled reading the list with Michael's name on the top. It was written in his mother's handwriting in the tickets sales category. Someone's name had been erased and replaced with his brother's name for setup and ticket sales during the early shift.

This more than piqued his interest, and after careful examination of the sheet he figured it out. *For as long as he could remember, the ticket booth had been located across from the food table. And during the early shift the food table is being tended by — none other than the lovely Mrs. Cheryl Langtree. That was more than coincidental and way too convenient. That weasel is using our own mother!* He wrote his own name on the sheet for the pony rides during the same shift. His buddy Taylor would like that, and Taylor's mother would certainly see his genuine interest in children.

CHERYL WAS en route to the church bazaar when she noticed Taylor had his baseball glove and his dad's baseball in his lap.

"Why did you bring those?"

"So Stevie and I can play catch."

"I think it's a good idea, but I know how much you care about that ball, so be careful with it, okay?"

He looked down at the ball and nodded.

Once they arrived, Cheryl got out of the truck with a large bowl filled with macaroni salad for the food table. "What are you going to do while I'm busy getting the food ready?" she asked her son.

Taylor looked around and pointed to Brett tending the ponies. "I'm going to be by Brett."

Taylor yelled Brett's name as he skipped toward the ponies. Brett turned to greet him and did a double take when he caught sight of Cheryl. He slowly waved to her with a goofy, dazed expression. Holding the heavy bowl, she nodded back before going down the basement steps. No one appeared to notice when Cheryl entered the room and put her salad in the refrigerator. The quilters along with a few other women from the parish were engaged in conversation while they dished the salads into smaller bowls. Nell's face was red from her attempts to inflate a child's wading pool that would be filled with ice for the items they needed to keep cool.

She stopped blowing air and pinched the end of the nozzle of the pool. "My, don't you look pretty, dear. I do love your hair like that."

Cheryl curled the ends of her blonde hair, which grew to her waist over the summer. She pulled a section of hair from each side of her face by her temples and fastened them with a gold clip to the back of her head. A trail of golden curls flowed down to the middle of her back. She had carefully applied eye makeup and finished her look with some blush. The cosmetics brought out her flawless complexion against the peachy-colored top she wore. The bright color set off her blue eyes and the ruffles framing the V-neck gave it a soft feminine look. Her top, tucked into the band of her denim mini-skirt, made her small waist look even smaller. It was impossible to ignore her shapely long legs in the short skirt and taller wedged sandals. All the women stopped what they were doing and gathered around Cheryl.

Joan stood in amazement with her hands on her hips. "You look like you belong in a fashion magazine."

"You look like an angel," Alma Green exclaimed with her hands on her cheeks.

They were suddenly interrupted by Lucille, who barked out a command as she came down the steps, "Ladies. We need to get that food out there as soon as ...." She stopped when Cheryl turned around to face her. Lucille blinked. "Cheryl, you look absolutely lovely."

"Thank you, Lucille." Cheryl turned back to the other women. "Thanks, all of you. You're so sweet."

"We do need to get the food out there as soon as possible," Lucille repeated.

Nell finished inflating the pool and the women carried the food up the steps. By the food table, Cheryl felt a little self-conscious noticing a few eyes focused on her. She quickly shook those thoughts and began to organize the food. The line at the ticket booth was small when she saw Michael get another parishioner to take over while he took a break. Immediately, he headed to the food table where Cheryl stood shooing flies away and Nell was taking tickets for the luncheon.

"I can't concentrate over there when someone as beautiful as you is over here." Michael's voice was low and seductive. He smiled and added, "Man, do you look great."

"Thank you, Michael," she answered primly, then looked away to wipe off the side of a bowl of tuna salad.

Brett was busy with the pony rides when Taylor tapped his mother's arm and interrupted her and Michael's conversation. "When is Stevie getting here?" he asked.

"I talked to Dori and they have company from out of town. When their company leaves, they'll be here as soon as they can," Cheryl assured him.

"I'll wait for him by the truck." Taylor quickly turned and started for the parking lot.

"Wait!" she called after him and he halted in his tracks. "I don't think that's a good idea with all the traffic." Cheryl looked around then instructed her son, "Why don't you stand there in the shade by the corner of the new fellowship hall. That way you can see all the vehicles pull in and I can see you from here."

Taylor nodded and tossed his ball up, then caught it in his glove as he walked toward the building.

A long line had started to form at the ticket booth when Michael commented, "Looks like I better get going. But how about we eat lunch together after we're both done?"

"We'll see what time my relief comes," Cheryl slowly answered. "I'm sure Taylor will be ready to eat by then."

"If I get done before you, I'll find him and we'll save a spot for you over there," Michael said, pointing at the tables where people were already eating.

He went back to the ticket booth, but Cheryl saw him glance over his shoulder as he walked.

A pickup truck pulled up to the fellowship hall with the new stove in the back. Chet and Earl walked over with Pastor Timms and watched while three young men from church hauled the new stove into the building.

Lucille rushed over to her husband and demanded, "What's going on here?"

"Pastor said the new stove was sitting in his garage, so I thought, let's get it over here."

"Now? During the bazaar?" Lucille frowned.

"With all these strong, young guys around, I can't think of a better time," Chet answered with a smile.

Within fifteen minutes, Cheryl saw a calmer looking Lucille come out of the fellowship hall.

She walked over to Cheryl. "Well, it certainly would have made things easier if they could have gotten the stove in before today. But it's done," she sighed. "I checked the large coffeemakers and the coffee is close to being done. At least they have the electricity hooked up and we don't have to carry the coffeemakers up the steps from the church basement. I guess we should be thankful they got this far and the bazaar is going so well."

THE SUN WAS high in the sky when Jake and Susan drove into the parking lot of the Watson Lutheran Church. When Susan got out of Jake's truck she looked around at the old church then down at her sandals.

"Why don't they have the parking lot tarred? You know, people usually wear nice shoes to church."

"Honey, I said not to expect anything too fancy here, remember?" he told her. "This is Watson, not Minneapolis."

Susan smiled politely and put her arm in his while they walked across the parking lot to the festivities. They hadn't gone very far into the crowd when Jake's mother approached.

"There you two are. I was wondering when you would get here."

"How are you today, Mother?" Jake asked.

Susan only smiled at her.

"Fine. Now that everything is all set up for this bazaar," she said looking around. To his left Jake saw Albert Andersen and his wife talking with another couple.

"Susan," Lucille said. "I do want you to meet Albert and his wife. He is so involved in the development of Montevideo. Some people call him 'The Montevideo Man.' I need to borrow your fiancée for a while," she told Jake. He caught an annoyed glare from Susan after his mother took her arm and escorted her along toward the Andersens.

Jake walked around to see what his parents were busy with for the past two weeks. When he spotted his youngest brother talking to a boy on a pony, he thought his eyes were playing tricks. Jake blinked a few times then moved in closer, but stayed far enough away so Brett wouldn't see him.

"Just sit, don't scream, and the pony will be your friend," Brett told the little brown-haired boy.

The boy's expression wasn't hard to read. He was terrified, yet determined. His mother stood next to him and said, "Bobby, it's okay if you don't want to ride the pony. Please get off and let someone else try. We can try again later."

Brett looked at the long line forming and seemed a little irritated with the boy's indecision. After a few minutes, he said impatiently, "Listen to your mother and try again later. The ponies will be here all afternoon. Okay, Buckaroo?"

The boy put his head down and tightened his grip on the pony. Finally, Brett picked the child up and pulled him off the pony. As soon as the boy's cowboy boots touched the ground he stepped toward Brett and kicked him hard in the shin. Brett instantly folded his knee and grabbed his leg, wincing in pain. The mother turned to Brett and gave him a dirty look, then put her hand on her son's shoulder and escorted him away. Jake laughed while Brett hopped around holding his leg.

"Having fun?" Jake yelled, walking closer to his brother.

"I wouldn't exactly call it fun," Brett said in a pained voice. He released his leg and pointed to the ticket booth. "But it's got to be more fun than he's having."

Jake glanced over his shoulder and saw Michael give a man a strip of tickets in a small booth nearby. It looked like he just crawled out of the dunk tank. His face was wet and shiny with sweat. "Someone told me last week he was a judge at the 4-H building and I thought they were joking. Now he's selling tickets and you're giving pony rides. What the hell's going on with you two?"

"I'll tell you in a second," Brett answered.

He turned and put another boy on the pony. A young man came and took the reins from Brett who told him, "Hope you wore an athletic cup." Brett winked at Jake while the younger man looked at him strangely.

The two brothers walked a short distance away from the pony corral when Jake said, "I thought you were going to tell me what's going on with you and Michael."

"I thought I would just show you instead," Brett replied. Jake wrinkled his brows and Brett nodded toward the food table. "That's what's going on with us."

Seeing Cheryl, Jake felt his jaw drop. The only thing that came out of his mouth was a drawn out, "Woo-ow!" *What happened to her? She wasn't hard on the eyes before, but now she looks ... beautiful, with that long blonde hair ... and those legs coming out of that denim mini-skirt.*

"Jake. Jake honey. *Jake!*" Susan's voice startled him. He hadn't noticed her next to him. "What are you two so busy looking at?"

She looked toward the food table and a knowing look came over her face.

"Isn't that your neighbor girl?" she asked.

"Yeah, that's her," Jake answered, his eyes still on Cheryl. "You remember her little boy with the toad in the jar at Trailways?" He pointed to Taylor who stood by the fellowship hall.

"I still don't understand why any parent would allow their child to bring a disgusting creature like that into a restaurant." Susan curled her lip.

Both brothers nodded, but their attention seemed to be focused on the food table. Susan continued with her comments about that frightful breakfast at Trailways until their father came toward them.

"Hey, you made it," Chet remarked. "Your mother was driving me crazy asking me to keep a lookout for you two."

"Yeah, she's already introduced Susan to over half of Montevideo," Jake answered.

"You really need to see our new facility," Chet said to Susan. "It needs a little work yet, but it should be up and running by the time you two tie the knot." She smiled but turned to Jake with a panicked expression on her face. "Jake, why don't you give Susan a tour?" Chet asked. "And while you're in there, give them boys some advice on hooking up the new stove. I told them we can do it another time, but they were still monkeying around with it when I came out here."

Jake looked at Susan. "I think we should take a tour. Come on, you can see all our hard work."

"Okaaay ...." She sighed.

Jake led the way to the fellowship hall and held the door for Susan. The thick, rich smell of fresh brewing coffee rolled out at them. He took another quick look at Cheryl before he stepped inside the hall.

"So, what's the latest report on your brothers and that blonde?" Susan asked.

"Who? You mean Cheryl?" Jake asked innocently.

"Yeah, I guess you said that was her name. Well, who's in the lead now?"

"I couldn't tell you. Far as I know, they're both still making horses' asses out of themselves for her attention."

Susan laughed. "I think they could do a lot better than her. I mean, she cleans up well, but as far as someone you'd want to date or marry, she certainly isn't sophisticated enough for your family."

"I don't think it shows any sophistication on my brothers' part making her affection into some kind of competition. As far as I'm concerned, she's too good for either one of them. They better back off or she'll figure them out. If she hasn't already. She won't have trouble finding someone else." A vision flashed of Cheryl in his arms and Jake swallowed hard trying to squelch it.

Susan shrugged, then took a few steps into the main banquet area and looked around.

"What do you think of the moldings around the doorways?" he asked.

"Nice, if you like that kind of thing."

"I know the guy who hand-carved them," he said. "If you want, I could get him to do that in our new house."

She tilted her head to inspect the doorway. "Those are all right in a church hall or something like that, but I think in a house, they're too old-fashioned. I like a modern design for a home."

He looked at the moldings and shook his head. They continued to walk around the fellowship hall, Susan saying little. The tour concluded with the kitchen where the three men worked on the stove. Jake and Susan walked back to the front door and gazed out at the bazaar from one of the large windows.

"So, what do you think of our new facility?"

"Do you want my real opinion?" She smiled.

"Yes, of course."

"It's a nice little building and it's been keeping you busy when I'm not around, so I think it's great. But I hope your dad, or anyone else, doesn't get the crazy idea we're going to have our reception here. For one thing, it's way too small."

"No, I don't think anyone thinks we're going to have our reception here," he quickly said. "I'm sure Dad was just kidding."

"I love a man who has my best interests at heart." She smiled and reached her arms around his waist. They lovingly stared into each other's eyes and kissed but footsteps behind them interrupted their passionate embrace. Turning around, they saw one of the men from the kitchen.

"Sorry to bother you two," he said sheepishly. "Jake, could you give us a hand for just a moment?"

Jake looked down at Susan and she released him, but said in an unexcited tone, "If you don't take all day, I'll be fine right here." She added sarcastically, "I can watch all the *fun* of the bazaar from these big windows."

Jake followed the man into the kitchen and Susan stepped closer to the window in front of her. From where Jake was in the kitchen next to the stove, he could see her gazing out. After a few minutes, he heard the door slam and looked up at the window but didn't see his fiancée.

He called out, "Susan, are you still in here?"

"Yes. But I'm going out to get some air. Take your time."

A few minutes slipped by when Jake thought about how Susan hated to be kept waiting. He glanced toward the window and saw her outside, obviously in a conversation with someone but he couldn't see who. When he looked again a moment later, she quickly bent over and did something. *Maybe she's taking the dirt out of her sandals.* His thoughts were interrupted by one of the men who worked on the stove.

"I think we got it," he said, and turned on the exhaust fan above the stove. It quickly pulled the smell of the coffee into the room. "That's sure working. All we need to do is hook up to the new gas tank they're bringing on Monday."

The men discussed the construction project as they slowly

walked to the door, but quickened their pace when they heard screams. Jake got outside in time to witness Michael punch Brett in the midsection and Brett go down on his knees. Jake raced over and leaped in between the two, pushing Michael away from Brett. Two of the men who worked on the stove along with some from the crowd restrained the brothers.

"I have had enough of you two making idiots out of yourselves!" Jake shouted. "Now look what your stupid competition has done." He waved his hand at the table tipped over with splattered food and broken dishes scattered on the ground around it. "You have both single handedly ruined this bazaar." He turned to Cheryl, who was covered from head to toe in potato salad and red Jell-O and asked, "Are you all right?"

She tried to wipe the food off the front of herself but only smeared it. "No, I'm not," she answered. "But they didn't cause the table to collapse. It was those kids." Cheryl turned with a glare at Taylor who stood next to Ricky and Rory Jenson. All eyes in the crowd accusingly focused on her son and the sneering twins who stood near him.

"I didn't do it, Mom!" Taylor shouted. "She threw my ball." He pointed over to the hall. His eyes got big, as if he expected to see someone — but no one was there. He slowly lowered his hand. "I didn't do it," he said stubbornly. He stared at the Jenson twins. "It was them guys." Mrs. Jenson made her way through the crowd and took each twin by the ear and led them away.

Jake turned to his brothers and snarled, "Go home. You're just as responsible as those kids."

Lucille stood in the crowd with a bowed head. She used her hand to shield her eyes. Chet was next to her wearing an amused expression, but didn't appear to be embarrassed. Some of the women began to pick up the broken bowls and those that survived the tumble. Nell came over with a towel and gave it to Cheryl. Dori and Stevie pushed their way through to the front of the crowd.

"What the heck happened here?" Dori asked in surprise.

Cheryl's lips started to tremble like she was about to cry. Dori put an arm around Cheryl and took her away from the prying eyes of the large group of people gathered.

Nell stood in front of the crowd and announced, "Show's over folks. If you haven't eaten I guess you're just plain out of luck. We have the cakewalk left to do and all the other games are still in working order. So, everyone, please, let's just forget about what's happened and continue with this bazaar." She turned away and continued with the cleanup. "And God help us," she muttered.

Jake saw his brothers leave and searched for Susan but didn't have any luck in finding her. Finally, he walked out to his truck and found his fiancée in the passenger's seat with the window down. She was fanning herself with a program from the bazaar.

He walked up to the window. "There you are. I've been looking all over for you. How long have you been out here?" he asked.

"I came out here right after I left the fellowship hall. What was all the screaming about?" she asked, blinking her brown eyes at him.

"You wouldn't believe what you missed," he said. "I've had enough of this bazaar for today."

"What happened?"

"I'll tell you over dinner at Rosy's Supper Club."

He got in and pulled a pint of whiskey out from under the seat and showed it to her. "I think I'll have a stiff one when we get there."

WHEN CHET and Lucille got back to the farm, she went into the house and he went to the stables to check if any of their sons' trucks were parked there. Lucille sat on the leather sofa in the den and stared out the window across the room. Without a word, Chet walked past her on his way to the mahogany bar in the corner. Lucille heard the ice cubes clink in a crystal glass as he poured himself a bourbon and water. He set his drink and himself down next to his wife and took off his shoes. Lucille grabbed his drink and took a sip. He looked at her with raised brows.

"Well, that's about the first time I've ever seen you do that, Lu."

"I guess it's a day of firsts," she said sadly and closed her eyes.

"Oh, Lu, it wasn't the worst thing the boys have ever done."

Her eyes popped open. "It wasn't?" she shouted angrily. "When the punches were being thrown, I saw Susan run out into the parking lot to Jake's truck. I think the poor thing was frightened out of her wits. She was holding her hand to her mouth in shock. What do you think she's going to tell her family about us? The hillbillies started a brawl at the bazaar. Thank God, the Andersens had already left. But I'm sure they'll hear about it by tomorrow."

Chet took a swallow from his drink and said, "Lu, the only thing the boys did was get into a fist fight over a pretty girl. It happens all the time in this world. They didn't flip the food table over. Those naughty little brats did."

"I've taught my sons for years about manners and how to act around people in public, and this is how they repay me, by getting into a family ruckus in front of everyone we know."

Chet sighed and put his arm around her shoulder and held her.

If only I hadn't left that sign-up sheet on the dining room table, none of this would have happened.

When Chet finished his drink, they went up to bed, physically and mentally exhausted.

It was crowded at Rosy's when Susan and Jake got there. Jake slipped the hostess a five- dollar bill and she seated them after a few minutes.

"I suppose it's busy in here tonight because of all the people in town for the bazaar," Jake told his fiancée while they waited for the waitress to come and get their order.

Susan looked around at the full tables then commented, "Yeah, but don't you think some of these people could have dressed up a little better to come in here?"

"Maybe they didn't plan on eating here tonight, just like us." He looked down at his blue jeans and added, "I'm not as presentable as I should be, either."

"You always look great. But some of these people — I think a fair or a bazaar can bring out all sorts of weirdos."

He shrugged his shoulders and the waitress appeared with the menus. She was a young girl in her teens, who smiled when she took their order. A short time later, she returned with Jake's drink and Susan's glass of wine. Jake drank half of his Coke and filled the rest of the glass with the whiskey. Susan's eyes got big when she saw the amount of whiskey he put in his drink but didn't say anything.

"Here's to brotherly love," he said and raised his glass.

She raised her wine glass to meet his. "So, tell me everything that happened. And don't leave out anything."

As he told the story, she laughed loudly and her eyes danced with exuberance. After a moment he remarked, "I think you are enjoying this way too much, but you're *so* beautiful when you laugh." He leaned in and kissed her.

Their entrees came and the waitress said she'd be back in a minute to check on them. Susan cut into her steak and let out a groan.

"What's wrong?" he asked with a frown. *She always manages to find something.*

"My steak is way too well-done," she said. "I can't eat this." She dropped her fork on her plate and it made a loud bang.

"Why did you order it medium when you usually order it medium rare, like I do?" Jake asked and cut into his deep pink steak.

"Because last time we were here it was too rare," she said, annoyed.

"In all the years I've been coming here, my meal has always been perfect. The cook knows how I like it."

"Well, good for you. I'm sending mine back." She had a frown on her face when she motioned for the waitress. "Take this old boot of a steak back to the cook, and tell him to make me another one that's edible. Make sure it's medium rare and not raw."

The girl apologized and immediately took the plate back with her into the kitchen. She reappeared in a remarkably brief time with a different steak. She stood by the table and waited for Susan to cut into her entree. When she did, a small amount of blood oozed out of the meat.

"Ugh!" Susan gasped and pushed the plate in the direction of the girl. "Take this back and give me an order of broiled shrimp. I can't believe you people can't get a steak right."

The waitress glanced at Jake who shook his head and continued to eat his dinner. For a moment, Jake thought she might start to cry, but the girl took the plate and went back into the kitchen. When Susan's shrimp finally came, Jake had finished eating.

"Seeing how you'll be dining here for a while, I'm going up to the bar to get another drink."

Susan wrinkled her face and said loudly, "Get that poor excuse of a waitress to get you another drink. That's her job."

"No, I need to stretch my legs anyway," he replied.

JAKE WALKED UP to the bartender and ordered, then struck up a conversation with a man who sat alone at the bar. Susan watched him from the table while she dipped her shrimp into melted butter. *You better not keep me waiting. I may have to entertain myself like I did at the bazaar.* She managed to hold back her laughter but her shoulders bounced as she recalled the day's main event.

While she had waited for Jake in the fellowship hall, Susan looked out the window. *This is even more boring than I thought it was going to be. At least I got it straight with him about having the reception in this place. Mother would kill me if I agreed to have the reception in this little hole in the wall.* Outside, Lucille walked by scanning the area, obviously on a quest to find someone. Susan stepped back from the window. *I'm glad we came in here though, if it gets that woman off my back for a while.*

A few seconds later the doorknob turned and Susan slipped behind some scaffolding draped with a large canvas. The door slowly opened and two sets of sky-blue eyes peered inside to see what, or who, was in there. Cautiously, they crept into the room and walked over by the two large coffee makers. Susan saw before her two identical blonde-haired boys.

The brothers stretched their necks and tiptoed around, while their eyes searched the room. Not seeing anyone, one of the twins said to the other, "You know what would be really funny, Ricky?"

"What?" the other one asked.

The first twin's eyes glowed with excitement as he took a quick breath. "You know that big old hound dog under the table with all the food on it?"

"Yeah, what about him?"

"You know how he's lying there with his balls showing?"

Susan's eyes went to the window then out to the table where Cheryl was filling one of the bowls with food, but she couldn't see the dog.

"Yeah. But what would be so funny, Rory?" the other twin asked.

"I wonder how high that dog would jump, if we poured some of this hot coffee on his balls?"

Both boys snickered hysterically. Their plan made Susan smile. *Well, this little shindig could get interesting.* She silently watched the two boys take one of the empty cups from the table next to the coffee makers and fill it close to full with steaming hot coffee. They walked slowly across the floor being careful not to splash the coffee on themselves but slammed the door when they left.

"Susan, are you still in here?" Jake yelled.

"Yes. But I'm going out to get some air. Take your time."

She quickly stepped outside to watch the show. The two boys walked over to the table and hid the cup behind a bowl when Cheryl walked past. Susan spotted the dog spread eagled on the ground under the end of the food table. She leaned up against the building and waited for the action to happen. Suddenly, an idea struck her as she watched Taylor throw his ball up in the air and catch it. *That's her son. I wonder how blondie is going to handle this? Especially if her son's involved.*

She walked up to Taylor. "That's your mom, right?" she asked, pointing to Cheryl, who was busy helping an elderly man dish up a plate.

Taylor looked up at her and answered, "Yeah."

Susan didn't say anything for a few moments because she was watching the Jenson twins. Cheryl turned her back to them and Susan knew the boys would make their move soon. Taylor threw his ball in the air and put his glove up to catch it. Bending slightly, Susan reached forward and caught his ball with both of her hands. Taylor looked at Susan and opened his mouth to say something, but before he could, she threw the ball in the direction of the dog. Taylor immediately ran after it, and by the time he got to the table, the Jensons had accomplished their mission.

A loud howl came from the hound dog, halting the conversation of most of the crowd. Much like a missile, the huge animal bolted into a table leg and it gave away, causing the table of food to flip over. Cheryl rushed toward the table and got in the path of the flying, splattering food. Potato salad, red Jell-O and coleslaw splashed all over her blouse and clumped in her hair. The crowd gasped and shouted as Brett ran over to help her. Michael rushed out of the ticket booth to see what was happening. Brett found some napkins and started to wipe Cheryl off when Michael grabbed his arm.

Ripping the napkins from his brother's hand, Michael shouted, "Don't touch her. Let me do that."

Brett's face turned stone cold and he brought his other arm up punching Michael in the face. Screams broke out again when Michael fell backward and rubbed his eye socket in shock. Shaking his head, he seemed dazed. He got back up and swung at Brett, just missing his face. Susan stepped into the crowd but looked back and saw Brett swing again at Michael. This time Michael blocked it and punched Brett in the stomach. She didn't want anyone to see her amusement or know of her involvement, so she held her hand to her mouth and laughed all the way to Jake's truck.

10

Tuesday evening the telephone rang in Cheryl's kitchen. She got up from her chair in front of the television and answered it. She heard a man's serious voice on the other end.

"This is Michael. How have you been?"

"Okay, I guess. How are you?"

"I've been better. I thought I would call because I want you to know how sorry I am about what happened at the bazaar."

"Don't blame yourself. It was a group effort, which included my own son."

"Yeah, I didn't think anything like that would ever happen in a million years. Mom and Dad are still angry with both Brett and me, and he isn't speaking to me. I just feel down and I really need someone to talk to." He sighed. "I tried to get a hold of Jim but I couldn't. Could I come over and talk to you tonight?" There was a silence until he asked, "Cheryl are you still there?"

"Yes, I'm still here. It won't work tonight, Michael. Taylor might get the wrong idea. Besides, didn't we agree to meet for coffee during the day?"

"Let's be honest here, Cheryl, is it Taylor you're really worried about, or you? Can't you trust yourself to be alone with me?" In a quieter voice he added, "I thought you were my friend."

"Of course, I can trust myself just fine, it's you I have to worry about!" she fired back.

"I promise I won't do anything you don't want me to do. I'll be a perfect gentleman."

A moment went by before she responded, "Okay Michael, but please don't make me regret this."

"I won't. Is it okay to come over now? I'm downtown on a pay phone and I can be there in less than twenty minutes." Seconds after she told him it would be all right, he said goodbye and hung up.

She hurried to the bedroom pulling off her nightgown on the way. When she reached into her lingerie drawer, she hesitated. *Should I wear an old bra to make sure nothing happens with him the first time we're alone? Oh, my God. Why would I even think of that?* Angry with herself, Cheryl chose a newer bra and told herself her will power didn't need an insurance policy. After she slipped into a pair of denim pedal pushers and a pink blouse, she went into the bathroom to brush her hair. In the mirror, she pointed at herself. *Why did you say yes? Do you want this to go somewhere? You're just lonely.* She combed her hair into a long ponytail then used a small amount of Dippity-do to smooth away the fly-away hairs. Before leaving the room, she noticed her pale reflection and brushed some blush on her cheeks but didn't bother with lipstick. She certainly didn't want Michael to think she had gone through any fuss for him.

The coffee pot was on a low burner in the kitchen when Cheryl sat in the living room and finished a rerun of "Maude" on television. With the windows open she heard the gravel crunch as Michael drove his truck in the driveway. Within a few seconds, he rapped on the screen door. When she opened it, he stood there wearing a black eye and a grin on his face. In his hand, he held a bottle of wine.

"Why did you bring wine?" she asked, staring at the bottle.

"It's my mom's favorite. I thought maybe you would like it, too. It's a chardonnay." He stood there for an awkward moment. "Can I come in?"

"Yes, of course," she said and backed up. He stepped into the kitchen and looked around. While he examined the decor, she went over to shut the coffee off and examined him from the corner of her eye. His blue jeans showed his well-defined leg muscles and a dark-green, short-sleeved shirt did the same for his tanned arms. *He's a very handsome man. Why is he here? He obviously could have any woman he wants. Maybe he's telling the truth and needs a friend to talk to about his problems.*

"You've got this place remodeled and decorated so nice," he said. "It's so different from when Jim and Rose had the place. My dad would absolutely love to live in this type of ranch house but my mom sure wouldn't." He stared at the floor and seemed to recall something. "Let me see, the last time I was here I was about ten. I spent the night for Jon's birthday."

"You were here for Jon's tenth birthday?" Cheryl's voice softly escalated.

"Rose got so mad at us for getting into a mud fight, she took a garden hose and hosed us down." He smiled. "It was pretty cold, and we tried to run away from her but she wouldn't let us in the house until all the mud was washed off."

"That sounds like Rose," Cheryl said with a laugh. "She always did love a clean house."

"Do you have a corkscrew and some glasses?" He held up the bottle of wine.

Going into a drawer, she found a corkscrew and handed it to him. It didn't take him long to pop the cork out of the bottle. She got some glasses from the china hutch in the corner of the room and he filled them.

He picked up both glasses and looked at her. "So, where do you want me to go?"

"What?" she asked nervously. "Oh, oh — on the porch. There's usually a nice breeze out there from the south."

"Lead the way."

As they walked to the porch, Cheryl caught his head turn subtly in the direction of the hallway leading to the bedrooms. *Maybe he's just noting the layout is the same as the last time he was here.*

There wasn't any electricity on the porch. The only light came from a lamp burning in the living room. Cheryl quickly sat down in the wicker chair and lit the large candle in the middle of the coffee table in front of her. Michael hesitated before he set the wine glasses on the table and sat in the love seat.

"Wow, this is nice out here. I can feel that breeze you were talking about," he told her.

"We used to spend a lot of time here. Taylor and I still do." She had a detectable note of sadness.

"With all the screens, how do you keep the snow out of here in the winter?"

"It was an idea that Jon had and it works nicely." She pointed to the windows. "There's a roll of water-proof canvas above each window under the eaves outside that we roll down. The small shutters that most people think are only decorative, flip in and keep the sides of the canvas in place. Jon made each shutter with a slot where a board can be placed to keep the shutters snug against the canvas."

Michael raised his eyebrows and nodded at the windows. He didn't say anything for a moment then broke the silence.

"Cheryl, one of the reasons I wanted to come here tonight is to apologize for what happened at the bazaar. I feel awful about the fight with Brett. But what could I do? He threw the first punch. I was just defending myself. And that thing Jake said about a competition, I have no idea what he's talking about." His eyes searched hers. "My feelings for you are genuine. That's all I know." He let a moment pass before taking a swallow of his wine.

"I accept your apology, Michael. But you can bet that tongues are wagging at church. Everyone is still talking about me passing out there. Now they think my kid ruined the bazaar and because of me, you two are fighting. Everyone's blaming me."

"Who cares? All those are things you had no control over. When Diana left me, I was embarrassed because I was the one left behind. Now I realize it was something I had little control over."

"May I ask what happened with you and her?"

"I was hoping you would," he said slowly. "I haven't actually ever told anyone the whole story. It would make me feel a lot better to tell someone about the hurt." He took a deep breath. "Men don't talk about that sort of stuff with other men, and I never met any woman I felt I could trust. That is, before I got to know you." He looked at his near empty glass. "If you don't mind, I think I need a refill before I get into the story."

"I better go check on Taylor, too," she said, and stood. "Go into the kitchen and help yourself. I'll be right back."

When Cheryl returned, she watched him fill his glass with the bottle in his hand.

"I thought I would just bring the bottle out here instead of risk spilling wine across the house."

She sat down and stared at her full glass. She was positive it was half full when she left the room. Michael sat down on the love seat after setting the bottle on the coffee table.

"Maybe if you sit over here," he said, and patted the cushion with his hand. "I won't have to talk so loud and wake up Taylor." His suggestion was followed by a gorgeous smile.

Does he really think I'd fall for that? "I can hear you just fine from here. Just talk a little quieter."

"You can't blame me then, if he wakes up." His eyes sparkled.

"You were saying," she said softly, "about Diana?"

His smile faded. "Oh, yeah, getting back to the worst time of my life. I guess I'll start in the very beginning in grade school. I always thought she was a skinny kid with braces on her teeth. You know, the brainy type who always does the right thing. I thought she was too goody-goody, so I never thought twice about her. Then in our freshman year of school, she walked in our history class and I heard the teacher call her by her name. I thought that *can't* be her. I was hooked, and everyone knew it, including our parents, who immediately were alarmed, especially my mom. We spent every waking minute with each other and basically grew up together. As soon as I got my driver's license, all we would talk about was how we planned to be together for the rest of our lives.

"In our senior year, she read in some magazine about backpacking through Europe and decided we should do it in between high school and college. We both saved our money and we were about to buy the tickets when Mom and Dad talked me out of it. They said I would never know if she really was the one because we'd never been with anyone else. They told me to let her go on this trip with another classmate and see how we felt about each other when she got back. I got one letter from her before she met the doctor of her dreams. I felt like my whole life crashed."

Cheryl saw what could've been a tear in his eye.

"I was angry with my parents for quite a while. Now, I know if she decided to be with someone else so quickly, they were right. She wasn't the one. The only problem I have now is, since it happened, I've been afraid to be seriously involved with anyone." In a big gulp, he finished the wine in his glass and set it down on the table. "So, don't think for one second I don't understand the risk." Silence replaced the conversation.

"I'm so sorry you had to deal with that," Cheryl finally said. "But the fact is, Michael, you're young and good-looking. You could get anyone you want," she blurted, then regretted her choice of words.

"Does that include you?"

"It isn't about you and me. You're still healing, and at this point, I don't think I'm ready to move on."

He stood up and asked, "Why don't we find out?" He snatched her hand and hauled her to her feet. His warm lips were on hers before she knew what was happening. Thrusting himself against her, he slipped his tongue in her mouth and she felt his excitement through both of their jeans. His hot breath, reeking of alcohol, filled her nostrils while his belt buckle cruelly pressed into her stomach. She regained her balance and forced her hands up between them pushing back until he finally released her. They both stared at each other, breathing heavily.

"You better leave." Her voice was shaky.

"Come on, Cheryl. I know I shouldn't have kissed you like that. I'm sorry. Give me another chance to prove I care about you."

"You need to go."

Michael looked down at her with a dangerous, dark look in his eyes and pointed toward the hallway. "When you're lying in there alone tonight, I want you to think about how it felt to have my lips on yours and our bodies touching each other. We both know you liked it. Admit it. You want it as much as I do."

She pointed toward the kitchen and spoke in a low, harsh voice. "Get out!"

Cheryl followed him but left a distance between them. She panicked when he opened the door but didn't go out.

"And for the record, I am a gentleman. If I weren't, I would have done what I wanted to do since the first time I laid eyes on you. But like I said, I'm not like that." He smiled. "I'll be waiting. Let me know when you're ready."

The second the door closed behind him, Cheryl ran over and locked it. She leaned her forehead against the door frame and stared at the deadbolt for a few seconds trying to catch her breath. *Oh, my God! I was a complete idiot to trust a womanizer like him.*

11

L ate for the quilting circle, Cheryl hurried across the lawn to the steps of the church basement. She looked over in front of the fellowship hall where the grass was matted down — the only evidence left from the bazaar. She swallowed hard. *Well, I better just go down and face the music.*

When she came down the steps an abrupt hush ended the conversation in the room.

"Hello ladies. How is everyone today?" Cheryl asked cheerfully and met their stares.

"Fine," a few of the women answered.

Lucille sat in the middle of the group hand stitching but didn't look up.

Everyone was silent until Joan finally said to Cheryl, "I hope you didn't get hurt when that table flipped over."

"No, I didn't," Cheryl said with a small smile. "I just felt a little foolish, that's all."

"Did you punish your son for his part in the awful attack on that animal?" Mary asked.

All eyes were on Cheryl as she pulled a chair up to the quilt.

"Yes, he doesn't get to watch television or ride horse for two weeks," she told them. "I heard the dog is fine now. His owner brought him to the vet, and Taylor and the Jensen twins have agreed to split the expense."

Mary made a face at Joan then commented, "That doesn't seem to be much of a punishment for someone who was part of ruining the biggest money-making event for the church all year. Did you see how many people left after they knew they weren't going to get any lunch?"

"Taylor claims he didn't know anything about what the twins were up to. He said he was just getting his baseball," Cheryl defended her son.

"And you believe him?" Kathy asked.

"In a way, I guess I do," Cheryl answered. "He doesn't usually lie." She recalled the big tears in Taylor's eyes after the bazaar. He stuck to his story that a lady had taken his ball and thrown it in the direction of the twins. The cry in his voice was convincing, but there was no way to prove he was telling the truth. If she, his own mother, had doubts, it was best to keep it to herself. The boy didn't need to be labeled a troublemaker *and* a liar.

"Cheryl, maybe he lied because he's never been in this much trouble before." Kathy wagged her head slightly. "I saw him running toward those twins right before I heard the dog howl. It looked like he was right with them."

"Despite if Taylor was in on it or not, he's only six years old and them twins are nine," Nell snapped. "Maybe they led him astray. But what I'm curious about is your sons, Lucille." Nell turned toward Lucille and the group of women followed her lead. "What got into those two?"

"I'm not sure what really happened," Lucille answered slowly, but didn't look up at the eyes on her. "Chet and I tried to figure it out, but the boys are being tight lipped about it."

"It appeared to me they were both trying to help you and then got mad at each other for some reason," Kathy said to Cheryl. "Did one of them say something wrong to the other?"

Lucille's head was down looking at the quilt, but she looked up at Cheryl over the top of her glasses and waited for her response.

"I don't know what happened with them." Cheryl's voice softly trailed off. *Likely, a ploy in their idiotic competition.*

Alma chuckled and all heads rotated toward the old woman. "I wasn't born yesterday," she said. "It's obvious our girl, here, was the reason for the fight. Who could blame them? She's an angel."

The rest of the women all nodded in agreement. Cheryl looked down, feeling her face get hot and finished her stitch.

"I know it's hard to believe, but when I was young I had a couple of dashing young men who got into a fist fight over me," Alma continued. "One of them I was married to for sixty-one years and he wasn't the one who won the fight." She smiled. "He won a much better prize — me."

Almost together, the group of women sighed.

Changing the subject, Patsy said, "Even though the bazaar had a few unpleasant surprises, I want you all to know the quilt raffle saved the day by bringing in four hundred and ninety-three dollars."

Cheryl released a big breath, relieved at the news of their success despite what happened.

"You know, Cheryl, next Tuesday is our evening to serve the workers at the fellowship hall," Nell said and interrupted her thoughts.

"Are we still going with roast beef, mashed potatoes and gravy?" Cheryl asked.

"Sounds good to me, dear, especially now they have the stove hooked up in there."

The rest of the menu was decided later when the two women walked to the parking lot and stood by their vehicles. Nell got into her car and looked around to see if anyone was near, then motioned for Cheryl to come closer.

"I'll see you on Tuesday," she said quietly. "And then maybe you can tell me what's *really* going on with you and those Cameron boys."

Cheryl shook her head but didn't answer. She just waved and got into her truck. Nell was like a hound on a scent when it came to gossip, but this time it was hard to blame her. Alma's story had put the spotlight on Brett and Michael's competition. Everything was out in the open except for one very important detail — the real reason behind the whole contest.

Driving down the road, Cheryl wondered if either brother could possibly be sincere. Or was it just a way to prove who the better man was by seeing who could get her into bed first? Whatever their motives, it changed nothing. Unlike Alma, she didn't have any romantic feelings for either of the men who fought over her.

THE BLARING SOUNDS of the baseball game on television could easily be heard from outside Jim Stanton's apartment. Michael knocked at length before Jim came to the door in his boxers.

"Is this how you always answer the door?" Michael looked him over.

"Yeah, I always think it could be some good-looking chick just waiting to catch a glimpse of what a real man looks like," Jim answered with a grin.

Michael rolled his eyes at Jim, who backed into the apartment and motioned for him to follow. The living room was a mess with unwashed dishes and pizza boxes scattered everywhere. On the coffee table, cigarette butts had spilled from an overfull ashtray onto a stack of magazines. Michael stood in the living room and looked around. There were clothes reeking of cigarettes and sweat thrown on the couch and floor.

"You're not going to attract any women with this mess you got going here," Michael commented.

Jim laughed and went to the refrigerator. He got two beers out and handed one to his friend. "Hey, by the way, what the hell happened to you the other night? One second you said you had to make a phone call and then you didn't come back. I was getting a pretty good buzz on by then and I thought maybe you passed out somewhere, so I went to look for you. Someone said they saw you peel out of the parking lot. Where the hell did you go?"

"I went over to Cheryl's place." Michael pushed some clothes off the couch and sat down.

"Oh, yeah?" Jim's eyes lit up. "Did you score with the Ice Queen?"

"No, but I did give her something to think about."

"What was that?" Jim asked. Michael filled him in on what had happened.

Jim shook his head. "So why didn't you just do her anyway? It sounds to me like she's been shaking her tail feathers in your face for quite a while now. If she didn't like it, too bad, it would be your word against hers, and with your old man's money, nothing would happen to you."

Michael shook his head before he replied, "I believe if I'm just patient and wait, she'll come begging. I felt her lips open for a second and I know she wanted me, but she has this odd loyalty to a dead man."

Jim looked down at his beer and took a long swig then wiped his mouth with the back of his hand. "I hope you're not wasting your time, buddy."

CHERYL SAT in her kitchen and sipped on a much needed cup of coffee. She noticed Dori watched her from the chair across the table.

"What are you looking at?" Cheryl asked.

"What's with the dark circles? Are you sleeping?"

"No, I haven't been."

"So, what's on your mind?"

"Michael Cameron."

Dori's brows wrinkled. "Why are you thinking about him?"

Cheryl told her about his visit and his inappropriate behavior. Dori's eyes got big as she listened.

"Cheryl, I can't believe you let him come over at night. He has it bad for you, and he's arrogant enough to think he can have anything he wants. Weren't you frightened out of your wits?"

"I wasn't until he said he hadn't done what he wanted to. Then I realized I had put myself into a bad situation. Maybe he said that because he didn't get the response he wanted from the kiss. I don't know. Now I lie in bed and listen for every noise or creak. I find myself getting up to double check the doors making sure they're locked. And the worst part about it is I keep thinking about what he said about being alone in bed. Now, I feel lonelier than I did — which I didn't think was possible."

The screen door slammed and both the women turned their attention to Sam who rushed over to his mother.

"Momma, the boys won't wet me pway with them," he said in a teary voice.

"Is, that right?" She smiled down at him. "Don't go back out there, then. Stay in here with us girls."

His eyes moved like he was processing what she said. Seconds later, the toddler ran back outside. Dori looked at Cheryl.

"What is it with men and rejection?" Dori asked. They both laughed.

NELL HAD PHONED at least seven times to make sure every detail was perfect and nothing had been overlooked. Each time, Cheryl assured her everything would be fine. Lucille Cameron hosted the meal the week before, and Cheryl figured it was the fuel behind Nell's desire for perfection.

It was warmer than usual for early September and extremely warm in the fellowship hall with the heat from the oven. Cheryl's mouth watered when she entered the building and smelled the delicious aroma from the beef roast. Nell was busy slicing bread and smiled when she came in the kitchen. A wall of heat was coming from the oven and Cheryl was thankful her hair was in a ponytail. She thought the red, sleeveless blouse and a white skirt were going to be cool, but her blouse was stuck to her back by the time she unloaded her truck.

Earl helped Cheryl lift a large kettle of peeled potatoes onto the stove and set up the long table where the men would eat. He found a fan to put in the kitchen for the women, then walked around and inspected the work the carpenters had already done.

A few minutes later, Earl popped his head into the kitchen. "Mother, you should see the beautiful work someone is doing on the moldings," he told Nell. "Just like my grandfather did back in the old country."

Cheryl and Nell both came out to see what Earl was talking about. Some of the men arrived and started to work, but they stopped and marveled at the skilled work of the moldings.

"Who is doing this?" one man asked Earl. "Did they hire a professional carver?"

"As far as I know they don't have that kind of money in the budget." Earl shook his head.

After they were back in the kitchen, Nell told Cheryl, "Look out there and make a head count. How many do we have to feed?"

Cheryl looked out at the roomful of men scattered throughout the banquet area. She started to count but lost the number when she saw Brett, Michael, and their father in a circle around one of the moldings. She swallowed hard and recounted. Finally, she gave Nell the number: twenty-two. Mealtime came and Cheryl brought the food to the table while Nell stayed in the kitchen and filled bowls. The first trip to the table, Cheryl felt all eyes on her. *I don't care what they think. What happened at the bazaar wasn't my fault. I have a right to be here as well as anyone else.* She got to the end of the table where Chet was seated between his two sons.

"Good evening, Mrs. Langtree. How are you?" Chet asked.

Cheryl felt relieved he broke the tension and started to talk. "Just fine, Mr. Cameron. How are you?" she politely answered.

"I think we're all fine this evening." He looked at one son and then the other. "Hopefully, it will be a peaceful meal."

"How's it going out there? Has anyone made any comments about the food?" Nell asked after the meal was served and Cheryl had returned to the kitchen.

"Not yet, but they barely took their first bite."

Nell and Cheryl pushed the kitchen door open a crack and watched the men while they quietly ate.

"Well, they all must be enjoying it, because everyone is busy eating and no one's talking," Cheryl commented.

"Tell me, which Cameron boy would you like to feed on a regular basis?" Nell whispered.

"I've got a boy at home and I don't need another one to take care of."

"Yeah, I didn't think them fighting over you would impress anyone, especially you." Nell chuckled. "But I still think it was quite amusing to see Lucille during the fight. It brought the Sugar Queen down off her high horse. That sure was something to see." It was clear to Cheryl that Nell found the whole thing amusing by the way she talked.

For dessert, they served Cheryl's chocolate cake with fudge frosting. She was collecting empty plates when Michael gently grabbed her wrist. Brett frowned at Michael and Chet raised his eyebrow.

"Did you make the cake?" Michael inquired.

Cheryl nodded, silently looking him straight in the eye.

"It was the best chocolate cake I ever ate. Honestly."

She moved her arm to pick up more plates and he immediately let go. When the men got up and went back to work, Cheryl carried her last load of dirty plates into the kitchen.

"So, what did you do with Taylor tonight?" Nell asked while they washed dishes.

"I dropped him off at Dori's. He's spending the night, but he's still getting punished." Cheryl reached for another plate to dry. "I didn't want him to hear all the teasing and see the dirty looks down here tonight."

"Who knows what happened that day," Nell said while she scrubbed a pot. "It certainly was a bazaar to remember. Earl told me he thought it was one of the best ones in years because of all the entertainment. I don't think we'll get any excitement tonight with Chet refereeing."

Moments later, Cheryl peeked out the swinging door at Brett and Michael who worked on opposite sides of the room.

After the dishes were done, Earl went to his car with a load of kettles while the women checked the banquet room to see what was left to clean up. Immediately Brett walked toward Cheryl and Nell.

"Ladies, is there anything you'd like me to do?" he asked, smiling.

Before Cheryl had a chance to answer, Nell took him up on his offer and pointed to some folding chairs. "We need those chairs put away."

Brett nodded and proceeded to stack the chairs into a large closet. Michael didn't try to approach Cheryl but watched her closely the last hour of the evening. The crowd of workers dwindled to a handful when the Cameron men decided to call it a night. Chet stood by the door and talked to Earl on his way out, but kept a watchful eye on his sons.

The evening was about to wrap up when Brett hooked his thumbs in his back pockets and casually strolled over to Nell and Cheryl. "Thank you, ladies, for a wonderful meal. It's been a pleasure." He went to the door and stood next to his father but stared over his shoulder at his brother. Michael finished his conversation with another worker and made his way over to the two women.

"Well, that sure was a great meal. I was serious about the chocolate cake, Cheryl. It was fabulous."

"Thank you," Cheryl answered stiffly.

He looked down for a second then back up at Nell. "Could you excuse us for a moment?" he asked.

Nell jerked her head and pursed her lips. "Yes, of course. When you're ready to go Cheryl, we'll help you lock up and walk you to your truck." She then waddled over to her husband.

"I want to apologize for my behavior the other night. I don't know what got into me. The only thing I can come up with is maybe I had way too many drinks downtown before I called you. I'm really sorry." When she didn't respond, he said, "Cheryl, I need to be honest, I haven't felt this way about anyone since Diana. I can't stop thinking about you. It hurts to know I completely blew it with you. Please don't be afraid of me. I really care about you, and I want you to be happy. Can you find it in your heart to forgive me?"

She silently glared at him not knowing how to react. "Why should I? So you and Brett can continue on with your little competition?"

"Did he tell you that?" His eyes narrowed at his brother.

"If you remember, Jake said it at the bazaar."

"Okay. If you let me, I'll explain to you exactly what happened." He looked around. "Can we go somewhere and talk?"

"No. I'm running out of patience with you both. Tell me now why two grown men would stoop to something so juvenile?"

"Alright. I don't blame you for being upset. No more games — I swear. I'll tell you the absolute truth. I made the mistake of telling Brett how I felt about you and he told me you were out of my league. When he bragged what a ladies' man he was in college and he planned to pursue you, I let my temper take over and I challenged him."

"You expect me to believe that?"

"Yes. Because I care about you, and I couldn't bear to see him hurt you. Can we *please* start over and be friends again?"

Cheryl noticed Nell and some of the men watched them by the door and decided to end their conversation with a discreet nod.

A smile came over Michael's face like she'd given him a gift. "I'll call you."

I'd rather you didn't.

He quickly stepped past his father and threw a triumphant glance at his brother before going out the door.

The Thompsons and Cheryl walked around the rooms in the fellowship hall making sure everything was shut off and cleaned-up before they left.

When Cheryl stuck the key in the lock of the kitchen door, Nell told her, "Don't worry about returning the key until Thursday's quilting circle. Tomorrow night they aren't going to work because of the church board meeting. And as far as tonight goes, Pastor and Patsy go to bed with the birds. I don't think they'd appreciate it if you woke them to return a key." After saying their good byes, the neighbors left to go home.

On the drive home, Cheryl rolled the windows down in her truck and sang along with the song "Summer Breeze" on the radio. The cool night air blew in the window, smelling sweet and damp as it stroked her face. Still warm, she wanted the breeze to blow through her hair and freed it from the ponytail. She parked in front of her house cooled off and relieved knowing her commitment as hostess at the fellowship hall had been fulfilled.

Her mind was on a shower when she reached for her purse on the passenger's side. Feeling an empty seat, her eyes went to the floor to see if it had fallen there — no luck. Slowly, she recalled putting it under the counter in the kitchen at the fellowship hall. She released a disgusted sigh, then started her truck and headed back to Watson.

Cheryl found the key in her pocket and unlocked the door,

then stepped into the dark kitchen. As she fumbled for the light switch a shock ran through her. But the jolt wasn't from any electric wires. It was her heart skipping a beat after she heard a noise from the banquet area.

She stilled herself enough to listen closely and made out the distinct sound of music. Confused but still scared, she made a quick decision not to turn the lights on and warn whoever was there of her presence. She tried to envision the layout of the kitchen in the darkness around her. There was a long counter in between two swinging doors that led out into the banquet area. Earlier, they used the door on the left because the door on the right was blocked by a large box filled with paint supplies. Cautiously, she stepped forward feeling for the counter in front of her. When her fingers found the edge, she used it to guide herself to the left door. The counter ended and her eyes focused on the kitchen floor. A dull strip of light from under the door beamed onto the new linoleum. Her hand shook when she slowly pushed the door open a crack and peered out into the room.

"Ah," Cheryl sucked in her breath. There was a dark-haired man with his shirt off and his back to her. The top half of his tall body was evenly tanned to a deep golden brown. In awed silence, she watched the hammer in his hand hit its target and the muscles in his strong arms flex with each blow. A hanging light from an extension cord, shined on a small stream of sweat that trickled down the middle of his well-muscled back. Her eyes fixated on his tight jeans that covered a perfectly toned backside before they slowly traveled down to his cowboy boots. She took a deep breath, but it took a few seconds to pull herself together. He was so involved with the molding he didn't hear her step closer to observe him work.

A very surprised Jake Cameron turned and did a rapid double take when he saw her. He lowered his hand that held the hammer. "What are *you* doing here?" he quickly asked.

"So, you're the one who's doing these moldings!"

"Yes, I guess I am," he admitted. "Don't tell me you think they're outdated, too."

"No. Are you kidding? They're timeless and beautiful. Where did you learn to carve like that?" she asked and moved closer to inspect his exquisite work.

A proud smile came to his lips. "My grandfather, on my mother's side, taught me when I was quite young. Michael wasn't interested, but I loved the carving — and my grandfather's attention."

"Was carving your grandfather's profession?" she asked.

"No, just a hobby of his. He had a small shop in a shed behind his house. We would spend hours out there carving and talking about the old days, when he was young." He tilted his head. "You never told me why you're here."

She kept her eyes on his to keep herself from staring at his half naked, sexy body. "Oh, I hosted the meal for the workers tonight and I forgot my purse. I've got to say, it really scared me when I first came in here and heard your radio. I knew we had shut everything off when we left." She paused. "Why don't you come and work when everyone else is here?"

He appeared to consider the question. "Well, when everyone's here there are too many chiefs and not enough braves." He smiled.

She laughed softly with a nod. "Does anyone else know you're doing these?"

"Mom, Dad and Pastor Timms know, and my brothers have figured it out, and now, I guess, you know. I told them all to keep it to themselves."

She wrinkled her brows. "Why do you care if anyone else knows?"

"Sometimes, it's rewarding to do something nice and not get the recognition for it. You know in your heart you did it, and that's a gift to yourself."

She pressed her lips together. "Hmm …. That's a lovely thought. But do you think that'll work when people see those magnificent moldings in your new house over by Swenson's? They'll figure out who did the ones here. Your secret will be out."

He suddenly looked down with a wounded look on his face.

Cheryl sensed something she said offended him. "Well, I better get my purse and let you get back to work." She stepped toward the kitchen.

He reached down for his open can of beer on an overturned pail and took a swallow. "I'd hardly call it work."

She gave him a small smile then pushed open the swinging door. In the kitchen, she turned on the light and spotted her purse under the counter. She slipped the strap over her shoulder and was almost to the door when she heard Jake call from the banquet room.

"Hey, do you want to stay and have a beer? I'll put my shirt on!"

She squeezed her eyes shut. *Oh, God. Was I that obvious?* Seconds later, she decided it best to appear nonchalant and turn down his offer face to face. She took a breath and pushed open the swinging door.

He jumped back and the door barely missed him. "I thought you left and I went to check if I was talking to myself." A smile appeared on his face. "So, you're going to stay?"

"Well, I …."

"Need to get home to your son?" He finished her sentence.

"No, he's actually at Dori's."

"It's up to you, then." He paused. "I don't want to hold you up. I just thought a beer and a conversation between neighbors would be okay. Actually, I forgot to bring the finishing nails I usually use, so I don't think I'll be doing too much here tonight."

"A cold beer does sound good," she answered, surprising them both.

He found his shirt and put it on but left it unbuttoned. The shirt didn't help. It only framed his well-defined abdominal muscles and made her more aware of his hot body. She pulled her eyes away and hoped he hadn't caught her gazing. Whether he did or not, Jake didn't acknowledge. He opened the cover of a large cooler next to him and took out two beers, then handed her one.

"Looks like you brought enough beer." Her mouth gaped at his full cooler.

He chuckled. "Before you go telling people I'm an alcoholic, let me explain. Some horses' rear end took my small cooler out of my truck and this was the only cooler I could find. So, I figured why not save myself time and fill it up and I'll be good for a while."

Jake set his beer down and went over to the closet where the folding chairs were stored and brought out two chairs. He pulled them open and they sat down next to each other.

"Are you and Susan planning on having your reception here?"

He shook his head no and took a big swallow of beer. "Are you kidding?" he asked more like a statement then a question. "Susan wouldn't have our reception here in a million years."

"Why do you say that?" She narrowed her eyes.

"She told me it's too small, but I know that isn't the only reason. This wouldn't be fancy enough for her or her mother. My mom isn't saying much, because she thinks the lieutenant governor will be more impressed with the Lake Calhoun Beach Club than the Watson Lutheran Church fellowship hall. I guess I never knew what all goes into planning a wedding until now."

"Most men don't really know until their own wedding." Cheryl smiled and drank some of her beer.

"Maybe everyone should elope. Wouldn't that be easier? No worrying about who's going to be invited or who's not, or who's going to be in the wedding."

"That's the easy part. Asking people to be in the wedding." She looked at him strangely.

"That hasn't been easy at all." He shook his head. "I want both my brothers to be in my wedding, and Susan is okay with

Michael, but for some odd reason, Brett rubs her the wrong way. She insists on the number of attendants being small and is using that to exclude Brett."

Cheryl tucked her hair behind her ear and put her hand to her chin. "Maybe if you tell her how important it is to you to have both of your brothers in the wedding, she'll reconsider."

"I can tell you don't know my fiancée very well." Jake smiled. "She's used to getting her way. She has always been somewhat of a challenge."

"Maybe that's what keeps you interested in her." Cheryl took another swallow of her beer. He stood up to get another a beer and gave her one, too.

"Hey, speaking of interesting people," he said with a grin, "I see you're looking a lot better than the last time I saw you."

She looked down at her beer can. "I was hoping you wouldn't bring that up."

He started to laugh as he spoke, "When I came out of the fellowship hall and saw my two brothers fighting and you standing there with potato salad in your hair and red Jell-O stuck to the front of you, I didn't know if I should laugh, or beat the crap out of those two." She was quiet. He must have noticed her reaction then added, "Come on. You gotta admit it was funny."

"Yeah, I guess from an outsider's view it must have been pretty entertaining. Earl Thompson and a few others thought so, too."

"I hope you weren't too hard on your son for that prank."

"I was pretty angry at first, but he kept saying he wasn't involved in hurting that dog."

"You believe him?"

"Well, it's just not like him to lie. But now, with his dad gone, maybe that's something he's starting to do for attention. You'd swear it's killing him with no television."

"What did he say happened?" he asked.

"He says he was standing on the side of the building waiting for Stevie to arrive when some lady appeared. She asked him if I was his mother and he told her yes. When he threw his ball up in the air she caught it and threw it under the table at the precise moment the Jenson twins did their dirty deed. He believes she did it on purpose. I asked him to point her out at church but he couldn't."

"There were quite a few people there who weren't from church. He could be telling the truth."

Cheryl shook her head. "That's what doesn't make any sense. What kind of a grown woman would do that? What would be her reason?"

"It's kind of a far-fetched story, but who knows why some people do anything? I'd give him the benefit of doubt, but keep an eye on him to see if he's lying about anything else. Speaking of morals, are my brothers still giving you grief?" He sounded genuinely concerned.

Cheryl took a deep breath. Letting it out, she said, "Yeah. Not so much Brett, but Michael. He's always coming on strong." She took a large swallow of her beer.

Taking another drink of his beer, he tipped it up and finished it. "Hold that thought." He walked over to the cooler and got out two more beers. He handed her one and she drank the rest of the beer in her hand. He sat back down. "So, tell me what has Michael been doing to drive you crazy."

"I would tell you, but how do I know it won't go right back to him?" She looked at him apprehensively.

He laughed. "Believe me, it won't get back. I will tell you though, he hasn't tried *this hard* to be with any woman that I know about. Most girls throw themselves at him, and he takes advantage of it."

"He's very handsome, and I can see how that could happen, but he just doesn't get that I'm not looking for anyone," she said seriously. "But, I guess I do have to admit he's made me realize I don't want to be alone for the rest of my life."

Jake raised his brows. "Sounds like he's getting to you." He winked at her, then smiled and took another swallow of his beer.

She was quiet again.

"You know that's a process, Cheryl. I talked about my grandfather, now I should say something about my grandmother. She was widowed young and she had two children. My grandfather fell in love the first day he saw her when she moved into Watson with her mother. But Grandpa had his work cut out for him. Not only did he have to win over Grandma, he had to win over her mother too. Now, that's quite a feat." He laughed and took a big gulp of his beer.

"So, what was your point about it being a process, with your grandmother?" she asked.

"She told me it was the scariest thing she'd ever done. Letting go of someone you loved at the same time you're learning to open up to love again. The pain of loving and losing was so fresh she didn't want to give her heart away. Well, Grandpa knew she was the one, and later Grandma admitted feeling the same about him but was just afraid in the beginning."

Cheryl smiled, but it quickly left her lips. "That's the thing. I like Michael, but I don't feel comfortable around him. I know I shouldn't compare him to Jon, but Jon always made me feel relaxed. Kinda like you ...." Her voice faded momentarily before she continued. "It seems like he should just back off." She quickly put her mouth to her can and took another big gulp.

"If you don't want Michael, what *are* you looking for? I mean, what kind of a guy do you think you would want to spend the rest of your life with?"

She looked up at the ceiling and took a deep breath then released it. On the radio, "Help Me Make It Through the Night" played.

"Someone who's honest. Who won't play mind games or lie to me," she said slowly. "A guy who shares my dream of running a farm together. I want to sit on my back porch at night and feel his arms around me while we talk about our day and how … much we love one another." She tipped her head down and her long hair fell around her shoulders. Staring at the floor in front of her, she whispered, "I want someone who will stand by me on this earth as we face life together. I want to feel all that again." When she blinked, a single tear ran down her cheek. The song played on when she looked toward Jake. She felt he was trying to absorb her with his mesmerizing dark eyes.

It seemed a powerful force in the room was drawing them together and neither of them was strong enough to stop it. Jake silently stood and looked away from her toward his beer can. As if in a trance, he slowly took a swallow from it and set it down. The radio continued to play and the lyrics in the song seemed to speak volumes as the music echoed throughout the room.

He reached out for her and she stood and stepped into his arms. She could feel the electricity when their bodies came together. Their lips instinctively found each other and she felt herself melt into him. He brought his hand up behind her neck and drew her closer, hungrily devouring her mouth. Her heart pounded so hard she felt weak in his arms, but she couldn't make herself stop. Her lips opened and she felt his tongue explore hers.

Taking her hands, he dropped to his knees and gently pulled her down to the tarp where they both knelt, staring at one another. When he reached up and shut the light off, a small voice in her head alerted her not to take this any further, but she ignored its warning. Instead she let herself be hypnotized by the feel of him and the moonlight shining through the large windows. She watched him hastily unbutton her blouse then shrug off his own shirt. His lips sought hers while his hand reached around and unhooked her bra. A sound came from her throat when he softly squeezed and rubbed her left breast. He pulled her tighter in his arms and kissed her so profoundly she felt a sweet ache in the deepest region of her body. Locked in a kiss, they slowly fell together onto the tarp. He rolled himself on top of her and bunched his shirt under her head. Cheryl felt the hardness of him as he rubbed his pelvis into hers and she heard him moan. Overtaken with raw desire, she readily returned his burning kisses with her own. She couldn't remember ever wanting a man this much.

Suddenly he stopped kissing her and sat up. "Oh, my God, what am I doing? I'm engaged." He looked at her. "And what about Michael? I … I'm sorry."

She quickly got to her feet and buttoned her blouse. Without looking at him she grabbed her purse and hurried into the kitchen.

"Cheryl, I'm sorry," he yelled after her.

She slammed the outside door and ran like the devil was chasing her to her truck.

12

T he sun had been up for a while when Michael banged on Jake's bedroom door.

"Are you getting up? We're almost done with chores!" Michael hollered. "I need to take your truck. Mine's in the shop. Dad wants me to pick up a part for the combine."

"Just take it!" Jake yelled. "The keys are on the hook in the kitchen."

Hearing Michael's footsteps lighten as he walked away, Jake rolled over in his bed. He had tossed and turned most of the night, then awoke with a physical reminder of the previous evening. He stared at the ceiling and tried to sort out what happened. Each time he closed his eyes, the vision of Cheryl in the moonlight seized his thoughts. He recalled the erotic sensation when he kissed her soft, willing lips, and the feel of her silky, long hair on his arms when he wrapped them around her waist.

His heart raced with his thoughts. *Would she have finished making love to me? Was that my plan, to seduce her? Subconsciously? I can't believe I got myself into this situation. What the hell was I thinking?* He still could hear the door slam when she left. Seconds later, he heard her truck start and the tires squeal after she got onto the tar road. His heart pulsed in his throat when he reached for the extension cord and turned the light back on above him. Moments passed while he sat with his head in his hands and viewed himself as a complete heel. Finally, he put his shirt back on and gathered up his tools. He felt like a thief leaving a crime scene when he threw the empty beer cans back into the cooler and left as fast as he could.

Jake got up, dressed and went downstairs to the kitchen. Irene sat at the table with a cup of coffee, cutting out coupons from The Lady's Home Journal magazine. She slowly looked up at him after he poured a cup and took a chair across from her.

"What's up with you?" Her eyes studied him.

"What do you mean?"

"Something is very different from yesterday. Did something happen?" she asked.

He looked at her like she was crazy. "I have no idea what you're talking about." Jake finished his coffee the moment it was cool enough to swallow. "Do you know where Dad is?"

"He's down in the stables with his wild horse." She kept her eyes on him.

He put his cup in the sink then casually went out the kitchen door. Once he passed the kitchen window he sped up his pace to the stables.

DRIVING BACK from the implement dealer, Michael decided he wasn't in any hurry to get home. Seeing Jake's shotgun hang from the rack in his truck gave him an idea. He turned the truck around and drove the short distance to Jim's apartment building. Technically, it was Jim's dad, Fred, who owned the building. Jim was the superintendent *or maybe that's what he liked to think he was.* It was a job that required very little work and left Jim with lots of free time on his hands. Michael banged on his door and was about to leave when Jim finally answered, again in his boxers.

"What the *hell* are you doing here this early?" He rubbed the sleep out of his eyes.

"Early? It's nine o'clock," Michael answered, then acted confused by glancing at his wristwatch. "Time for you to get your ass moving."

"My ass moving, where?" Jim asked, annoyed.

"Let's go for a ride and do a little target practice on some crows."

"Well, I guess it's something to do." Jim shrugged. "Let me get my pants on."

They had left Jim's apartment and driven out into the country a few miles when Jim looked though the rear window into the back of the truck.

"Do you think there's some beer in that cooler?" he asked.

"Who knows? Let's check it out." Michael grinned. He pulled the truck over to the side of the road and they got out.

After opening the lid of the cooler, Jim exclaimed, "Holy shit, it's pretty full."

He pushed aside the empty cans on top and dug out two cold beers then handed one to Michael.

"Good ol' Jake. I guess this is what brothers are for," Michael laughed. His gaze dropped to the cooler and his laughter stopped. He picked up one of the empty cans with a red thread stuck to it and examined the lipstick around the opening. Michael turned the can around in his hand. "Well, looky here — a can with lipstick on. How do you think this got in here?" He pointed to another empty can. "And there's another one." He gave Jim a sneaky look and tossed the empty back in the cooler.

"What about it?" Jim shrugged. "Isn't your brother engaged or something? He was probably drinking with his fiancée."

Michael smiled and shook his head no. "I know he filled this cooler yesterday because I took his small cooler out of this truck the day before. The thing is, his fiancée doesn't drink beer, and she doesn't come here until the weekends. So, my big brother is seeing someone else on the side. Who would have figured that?"

"That sly dog." Jim smiled slowly. "I guess I'm a little bit amazed with this breaking news. He always puts on that straight-and-honest-guy act." Michael agreed with a nod and cracked open the beer in his hand.

CHERYL FELT her heart and her head ache before she was fully awake. She opened her eyes and slammed them shut when the room started to spin. It seemed like it was all a dream, but she knew better as she hid her face in her pillow and started to cry. *What was I thinking? Why did I want him to make love to me? He's engaged to a beautiful woman. What made me think he'd be interested in me? He probably thinks I'm a whore! How am I going to face him or his family?*

She stood, then sat down just as quickly on the end of the bed. The second time, she slowly got to her feet and made her way to the bathroom for some aspirin. She tried to avoid her reflection in the mirror while she splashed water on her face and braided her hair. Eventually, she got herself dressed and went into the kitchen to make a pot of coffee. While she ate a piece of toast and sipped her coffee, the phone rang.

"Hello," she answered.

"Cheryl, this is David. Mom got sick again last night but she's fine now. I'm going to be late. So, don't go out and do chores, I'll be right there."

"It's no problem David, I can do them. You don't have to come to work today if your mom's sick."

"No, I need to get away from here for a while. My sister's here from Freeport and she's going to stay with Mom. I'll see you in a bit."

She hung up and moments later the phone rang again.

"Good morning. I have a delivery of a small, blonde-haired

child." Dori laughed. "We are on our way out the door. I just thought I would give you a call to make sure you're up. Last night I called around ten and you weren't home. Did you go somewhere after hosting the meal at church?"

Cheryl was lost for words but managed to say, "I went for a drive." There was a strange silence.

"We'll see you in a few minutes," Dori finally said.

It wasn't long before Dori's Buick pulled up into Cheryl's driveway. Taylor threw open the door and bolted inside with Stevie not far behind.

"Brett's here, and he brought the trailer with another horse," Taylor excitedly announced.

Cheryl stepped toward the window and saw Brett back the trailer to the corral.

"Can we go ride with him for a while?" Stevie asked Cheryl. The sound of a spring stretched when Dori held the screen door open for Sam.

"You are going to have to ask your mom if you're going to stay and ride," Cheryl told him.

Stevie looked at his mother who made it inside. "Mom, can we stay? I want to ride with them guys."

"If Cheryl doesn't mind," Dori answered slowly.

"No, I don't mind."

The older boys ran out the door and Sam scampered after them. Dori caught her youngest by the back of his T-shirt, "Oh, no you don't. You're staying here. Those two aren't going to look out for you."

Sam scowled at his mother and burst into tears. Cheryl motioned for them to follow her out to the porch where she showed him a big dump truck. Except for a few motor sounds, the toddler played quietly on the floor while the women drank their coffee on the porch. Soon their conversation went to the previous night.

"So, where did you go for your drive last night?" Dori asked.

Cheryl looked down at Sam. "Up by Milan, across the bridge.

Do you want a cookie with your coffee? I made some oatmeal raisin cookies the day before yesterday."

Dori shook her head and let out a labored breath. "Cheryl, we've been friends for a long time. I have never lied to you about anything. So, I don't expect to be lied to. You look like warmed over death. What happened last night?"

Cheryl took a breath and said, "I ...." Suddenly she broke down and sobbed. Dori leaned in and held her.

"Oh, my God. Did Michael do something to you? I'll kill him myself."

Cheryl shook her head no.

"Honey, tell me what happened?"

Cheryl stopped her sobbing long enough to reply. "I made a fool out of myself."

"And who did you make a fool out of yourself to?" Dori inquired.

Cheryl took a breath and blurted, "Jake Cameron."

"At the meal, last night?"

"No, he wasn't at the meal. After the meal." Cheryl wiped her eyes with a napkin before continuing. "I forgot my purse and he was there when I went back to get it."

"So, you left your purse there?" Dori sounded confused. "Big deal. Did he make fun of your absent-mindedness?"

"No, I got drunk and threw myself at him," Cheryl wailed.

"What?" Dori exclaimed. Her eyes grew big. "You're not serious, right?" Cheryl let out another sob and buried her head in her hands. Dori, stunned, flopped back in her chair. "Well, I gotta tell you, I really didn't see *this* coming. If you want me to help you sort it all out, you need to tell me what happened."

Cheryl nodded.

"Just a second." Dori went out into the kitchen to make sure the older boys weren't around. She came back with the coffee pot and filled their cups then left the pot on the table. "Okay. Let's start from the beginning."

Cheryl told the story and her friend listened. Dori's eyebrows raised a few times as Cheryl got into some of the details but she didn't say anything.

"Do I need to sell out and move?" Cheryl asked when she finished.

"No, I don't think you need to do that," Dori assured her.

"How am I going to face Jake?"

"The same as you always have. Believe me, he isn't going to tell anyone, and you have only told me. And it's not going anywhere."

"Don't you think he'll tell his brothers?"

"No, he isn't going to risk his fiancée finding out," Dori said, adding, "but Cheryl, I think you need to ask yourself why it happened. Figure it out, learn from it, and forgive yourself."

Cheryl silently looked down, not able to come up with anything. She tried to think about why she wanted him so badly and why being in his arms felt like she belonged there. The only thing that came to mind was the way he looked at her as the song played, right before she lost herself in his eyes.

Jake entered the stable and heard his father in a stall talking softly to the wild horse.

"It's okay, fella. It's just you and me. She doesn't own you anymore. I do. She didn't care about what you needed. She kept you cooped up in a pen when you needed to get out and stretch those legs, didn't she? I don't know if you're ready yet, but one of these days we're going for a ride and then you'll know I care about you more than she ever did."

The horse made a noise like it answered. Jake smiled to himself and thought, *Dad, only you would talk to a horse like it could understand you.*

Jake stepped in front of the stall. "Dad, what are you doing?"

Chet smiled as he looked at his son. "Just giving this horse a few words of encouragement. I see you finally got out of bed. I heard you get in last night. You must have finished putting all those moldings up."

Jake walked closer and quickly rubbed his hand carefully on the soft velvet of the horse's nose.

"No, I didn't. I forgot the finishing nails I bought yesterday."

"So, then what took you so long last night?"

Jake silently looked around. "Where are Brett and Mom?"

"Brett went over to Langtree's with Milo in the horse trailer and your mother went into town to run some errands. Why?"

"If I tell you, it needs to stay between you and me." Jake stared down at his boots. "Please don't tell Mom."

Chet looked at his oldest son and motioned to the large built-in wooden box next to the stall. "Come over and let's sit down, son." After he was seated, Chet slowly asked, "Do we need to call Ron Malend?"

"No." Jake shook his head. "I don't need a lawyer. It's not that kind of situation."

"Then, what is it, son?"

"You know the wedding is three months away."

"Yes, so what about it?"

Jake closed his eyes briefly and took a deep breath. "I almost made love to another woman."

Chet was speechless for a moment. "You went downtown last night and met some woman?"

"No. I didn't meet some woman downtown. It gets worse. It's more complicated than you could imagine."

"Who the hell were you with?" his father demanded.

Jake's eyes focused on the stall in front of him. "Cheryl Langtree."

"What!" Chet's mouth fell open. "You've got to be kidding me. What is it with you boys and that woman? I can see she's a pretty little thing, but the woman you got isn't too bad either." He suddenly stopped talking and cocked his head at Jake. "Wait a minute." His brows wrinkled. "She was leaving when we left. So, when did you two get together?"

"When I got there, no one was there so I started working. Then suddenly she appeared and we started talking. She said she forgot her purse and came back to get it. I asked her to stay and have a beer with me. We talked and maybe flirted a little too much and had way too many beers and one thing led to another. The next thing I know we were in each other's arms and about to ...."

Chet let a moment go by then asked, "Did she throw herself at you?"

"No." Jake shook his head. "She's vulnerable. I'm sure I took advantage of her."

"If that's the case, your brother should be engaged to her by now. Oh, boy, what about your brother? I suggest you don't let him know anything about this."

"Believe me, I'm not going to say anything to anyone but you," Jake replied. "I just don't want Cheryl to think I'm going to break up with a woman I'm engaged to, who I've been with for four years, for a night of drunken passion."

"So, what *are* you going to do, then?"

"I guess I'm just going to act like nothing happened," Jake said softly.

With his chin in his hand, Chet blinked at him and silently nodded.

LUNCH WAS over at the quilting circle, and most of the group sat around and chatted while they hand-stitched the quilt. The two hosts finished cleaning up and took their seats when Lucille made an announcement.

"Ladies, as you all know, my son Jake is getting married this December fifteenth. The wedding is going to be at the Basilica of St. Mary, off Hennepin Avenue in Minneapolis."

"That's a *Catholic* church. Why would your son get married there?" Alma asked.

"His fiancée is Catholic, and that's where her parents attend church." Lucille sounded slightly annoyed.

"Then the reception will be in the Cities?" Joan asked.

"Why yes, at the Lake Calhoun Beach Club." Lucille smiled and made another stitch.

"After the wedding, will they be going to church here?" Mary asked.

"I know Jake will be. I can't really say with Susan," Lucille replied.

The rest of the quilting time the women continued to fire off one question after another about the wedding plans. Cheryl felt a dull, stabbing pain in her chest, which went deeper with every detail while she silently stitched. She became frustrated and had to pull out some of her stitches to redo them because they weren't straight. As an experienced quilter, it was something she rarely had to do. *This isn't a surprise, so why does it bother me? Did I really think he was going to call it off because of what happened between us?* Cheryl tried to divert her mind with thoughts on what to make for dinner and tasks that needed to be done when she got home. She was successful for a while, but then her curiosity was piqued.

"Will both of your other sons be in the wedding?" Joan asked.

Lucille paused for a brief second, then replied, "Of course they will."

The afternoon and the conversation finally came to an end when everyone packed up their materials to leave. Cheryl had said her goodbyes when Lucille stood next to her and quietly whispered, "Can I have a word with you privately? Stay and walk with me to the parking lot."

Cheryl felt her body go cold, but she nodded yes.

"Are you feeling well, Cheryl?" Nell asked a few seconds later, "You look a little pale."

Cheryl assured Nell she was fine, but inside her screaming

thoughts were doing somersaults. *Oh, my God. He told her what happened. Does their whole family know?*

Sophie locked the door but curiously watched Lucille and Cheryl walk toward the dirt parking lot. Cheryl's heart pounded with each step and it almost exploded when Lucille stopped and opened the rear car door.

"I really didn't want the rest of them to know, but the invitations are going to be sent out in a couple of weeks," she said, putting her quilting bag in the car. "I don't think our group of ladies would want to drive all the way to Minneapolis for a wedding. But we do want you to be there." She reached for a cream-colored envelope lying on the seat next to the bag and handed it to Cheryl. "That is your invitation. I thought I'd give it to you early so you'd have plenty of time to arrange for a sitter. I didn't invite your son because I really don't think it would be any fun for a child. Don't worry about driving. I'm sure there will be plenty of room in our Cadillac for you to ride with Chet and me and the boys. I promise there won't be any sort of trouble like there was at the bazaar with those two. We'll be going to the Cities the night before the wedding and I will get you a private room we'll pay for." Cheryl looked at her, speechless. "Please, dear, it would mean so much to me if you could attend … and I know a certain young man it would mean the world to."

The only thing Cheryl could muster up to say was, "I'll think about it."

"Please do, and let me know as soon as possible." Lucille smiled. "And by the way, what size are you? About a four?"

"Yes," Cheryl answered slowly. "Why?"

"For the new dress that I'm getting you." Lucille smiled.

"Pl … Please," Cheryl stuttered. "You don't need to buy me a dress."

"I'm not going to. Michael is. I'll be over to get your measurements and shoe size sometime next week. 'Bye now."

Lucille waved and smiled on her way out of the parking lot.

Cheryl found it hard to lift her hand to wave back. Her body felt frozen to the spot where she stood. It was obvious Jake hadn't told his family what happened between them. A feeling of gratitude swept over Cheryl, followed by a wave of regret. She couldn't shake the ridiculous thought that given different circumstances, something worthwhile could have developed between her and Jake. *Stop it with your silly schoolgirl fantasies.* She needed to accept the hard realization that neither of them would ever acknowledge their feelings for each other.

Lucille sat in the dining room on Saturday morning with a cup of coffee while she read the newspaper. When Michael came in the room, she looked at him and smiled.

"Where is everybody?" he looked around.

"Your father and Brett went to look at the field over by Thompson's to see if they're going to chop that corn. And Jake is in town with Susan." Michael took a chair next to her and poured himself a cup of coffee.

"So how did it go Thursday when you talked to her?"

Lucille folded the paper and tossed it on the table. "She was surprised, that's for sure. But she didn't say no."

"Did you tell her she could ride with us?"

Lucille nodded.

"When the day comes, we'll have to make sure the car is so full we'll have to ride together, alone in my truck." Michael's eyes sparkled. Lucille felt a sudden pang of worry in her stomach and stared at her lap. Michael got up and put his arm around her.

"Mother, I believe it is only a matter of time. I know I'm getting to her. If you think about it, her husband has only been gone a little over a year. In a weird way, I respect her loyalty but I don't like it very much. Eventually she'll realize her old life is gone and come running to me."

"Well, I hope you're right. You would think she'd realize you're the best-looking, wealthiest, available bachelor in a three-county area." She stopped and looked him in the eyes. "I just hope you aren't wasting your time with this girl. She *is* nice, and I certainly wouldn't mind calling her my daughter-in-law some-day, but if love isn't there, it isn't there. I wish there was a way a person could tell."

She pondered for a moment before her face lit up. "I've got a great idea. Why don't you ask her out for a date? Maybe a double date with your brother and Susan? It would certainly make the date less awkward and it would be a nice way for everyone to get to know one another." *Who knows, maybe something about fashion will rub off from Susan onto Cheryl.*

A big smile formed on his lips. "That is a *very* good idea, Mother. A double date does make things less intimidating, and besides, didn't you say Jake helped Cheryl out a couple of months ago? I think she likes him okay. All right, I'll give my future sister-in-law a call and see if a date can be arranged. But first, I better call Cheryl and convince her to go."

He walked over to the phone on the small mahogany stand in the corner of the room and started to dial. Lucille watched her son and that strange sensation in her stomach returned. *He knows her number right off the top of his head. For your sake, my darling, I hope she's falling for you. The rest of us will learn to accept her.*

TEARS OF LAUGHTER rolled down Cheryl's cheeks while she and Dori watched Sam with a toy telephone. He pretended to be his mother in a conversation with his grandmother. In his finger, he rolled a curl like Dori often did when she was bored. He then mimicked his father's mannerisms and responded with one-word answers in a lowered voice.

"Yep, nope, okay, 'bye."

The women couldn't contain their laughter when the real telephone rang and Sam's eyes got huge.

"I'd be careful what you say, Cheryl," Dori said when Cheryl went to answer the phone.

With laughter still in her voice, Cheryl answered, "Hello."

"Hey, you sound like you're in a good mood."

Her tone changed after she heard Michael's voice. "Yeah, I guess I am," she answered, then silently mouthed to Dori, "It's Michael." Dori stood next to her and Cheryl tipped the receiver away from her ear so they both could listen.

"Then it's a perfect time to ask if a lovely lady such as yourself has any pressing plans for tonight?"

"What?" she asked.

He laughed. "Would you like to go out tonight? I thought maybe I could convince Jake and Susan to go on a double date with us."

Cheryl's heart sank, just hearing Jake's name. She was about to say no when Dori grabbed the phone away. Cheryl pulled it back from her and gave her a dirty look, then put the receiver back to her ear. "Can I call you back, Michael? Something's come up here."

"Okay, I'll sit right here and wait for you to call."

Cheryl stared at Dori while she hung up the phone. With her hands on her hips she confronted her, "Why'd you do that?"

"I had to do something. You were about to tell him no and I had to stop you."

"Why did you want to stop me?"

She looked at Cheryl with sincere eyes. "You know I think the world of you. And you trust me, right?"

Cheryl nodded.

"And if you thought I was doing the wrong thing, you would tell me, wouldn't you?"

"Yeah, so you think I should go out with him?" Cheryl was bemused.

"You should go out with him so you can face Jake," Dori

blurted. "Then you'll know if what happened the other night was something or nothing."

Cheryl shook her head no. "There is no way he's going to acknowledge anything ever happened between us, and I wouldn't want to hurt Michael that way."

"No, Jake most likely won't. But wouldn't it be interesting to see how he treats you after what happened? You may as well face the fact that you fell for him like a ton of bricks. You really owe it to yourself to find out why," Dori stated and crossed her arms.

"You don't think it was just the alcohol?" Cheryl's voice raised and faded.

Dori shook her head no. Cheryl went to the drawer for the phone book and looked up Cameron's phone number then dialed.

Michael answered after one ring.

"Hi, it's me. Sure, I'll go out with you on a double date. I just had to find a sitter for Taylor," she told him, then glanced at Dori, who pointed to herself.

"Okay," Michael replied. "I'll be there to pick you up around six-thirty and we'll go for dinner and maybe some dancing. Sound good to you?" He sounded much too happy.

"Yes, I'll see you then. 'Bye." After Cheryl hung up the phone, she told her friend, "I hope you're sure about this, because I'm not."

13

J ake was swimming nude under the water in the Chippewa River. As he surfaced he heard Susan yell at him from the bank.

"Get out of the water right now!"

She had a rope around his neck pulled so tight it was hard for him to breathe. Suddenly, Cheryl emerged from under the water and stood naked in front of him. Very carefully, she took the noose off him and tenderly kissed his neck where it burned from the rope. She whispered in his ear and told him everything was going to be all right. The rush of the cool water and the feel of her naked body pressed against him awakened a powerful longing deep inside him he couldn't suppress. His yearning for her only heightened when they found each other's lips and sank slowly back under the water.

Jake woke suddenly with a jolt. Susan immediately reached over and turned on the lamp.

"Jake, what's wrong? Are you okay? You're sweating. Do you have a fever?" She touched his forehead then quickly wiped her hand on the sheet, curling her lip. "You're cold, not hot. Do you feel sick?"

"No," he answered.

"Well, then try to relax and go back to sleep." She patted his shoulder and rolled over.

Jake lay awake for a while and thought about the dream. He became so aroused, it felt like being on fire. He recalled how Cheryl trembled in his arms at the hall and the way her kisses deepened with each touch. A picture of her half nude body lying under him in the moonlight, kept flashing in his mind. He couldn't extinguish the consuming flames of desire that blazed with every thought of her.

Jake couldn't take it any longer. He reached for Susan, who came to him eagerly, and they made hot, passionate love. But in his mind, the lips he kissed weren't Susan's; they belonged to Cheryl.

The room was lighter when Jake woke up gripped with nagging guilt. Wanting to make things right, he reached for Susan's warm body and felt nothing but the cold sheets next to him. When he heard her voice on the phone behind him, his eyes popped open.

"Yeah, I do appreciate it, Mel. I'll see you on Tuesday for lunch. 'Bye now," she said in a low, hushed voice. He rolled over to his other side and saw her carefully set the receiver down on its base, then anxiously look at him.

"Who were you talking to on the phone?" Jake asked her with a sleepy voice.

"Monique." She smiled. "That poor girl. Everything is a tragedy with her. She just needed a little reassurance from her big sister." Her eyes stayed on him while she went to the other side of the bed and slipped under the covers. She reached her arm around his waist. "Boy, after the little spell you had last night, you sure turned into an animal. Let's see how wild you're feeling this morning," she said in a seductive voice, and rubbed him intimately across his hip. He didn't say anything.

"Is there something wrong?"

He rolled on his back and stared at the ceiling as he spoke, "I know you were talking to Melody. Why did you say you were talking to Monique?" He glanced toward her and saw her mouth open slightly.

"I'll be honest. I didn't want you to know I was talking to her. I know you would have insisted I ask her about being in the wedding. I just don't want a big wedding party. Must we go through this again?"

"Yes, we must," he answered. "Because you need to realize how much it matters to me that both of my brothers are in our wedding."

"Then you will have to do something for me," Susan said after a moment.

"And what would that be?"

"I don't know where he got an invitation from, but mother said she got an RSVP from Chuck Davis. If you take him off the guest list, I'll get Melody to stand up with Brett."

He propped himself on his elbow. "How dare you tell me to make a choice between my brother and my friend." His teeth clenched. "Chuck owns a successful law firm now. And even if he didn't, I would still want to invite him because he's a decent man and a good friend. I don't know if you realize it or not, but I've been taking your crap with this wedding from the start, and I'm sick and tired of it!"

She stared at him with big eyes. "I'll have your brother in the wedding. What else do you want?"

"Chuck Davis and a guest. And I want you to go to church with me tomorrow morning."

"In Watson?" she asked. "I'm not Lutheran. Why would I want to go to that church?"

"I'm not Catholic either, but I'm getting married in your church. You can attend a regular Sunday service with me in mine."

"Okay, if it makes you happy, I'll go." Her bottom lip protruded.

Cheryl would never pout like a child. Why do I keep thinking about her? The phone rang a couple of times when Jake asked, "Are you going to answer that?"

Finally, Susan got out of bed and picked up the phone.

"Hello."

She listened to whoever it was on the other side of the line then asked, "Who is this? Michael?"

She listened again then turned to Jake cupping the phone. "He wants to know what we're up to this evening."

Taking her hand off the receiver, she asked Michael, "Why do you want to know?"

She listened. "Hang on a second."

She cupped the phone again. "Jake, he wants to know if we'll go on a double date with him and that country girl for dinner and dancing."

"Is he too afraid to date her by himself?" Jake asked, annoyed. "He doesn't need us to hold his hand. He's a big boy. Tell him we already have plans."

"And what would they be?"

"I don't know. Maybe we'll take a drive or something, or cruise downtown. We'll find something to do."

She lifted the receiver back to her mouth. "Yes, as a matter of fact, we would love to join you two."

Jake groaned and flopped back on the bed but quickly sat up into a sitting position. In a panic, he shook his head and waved his arms in a desperate attempt to get her attention. She ignored him and continued to nail out the details. It was decided that Michael and Cheryl would meet Jake and Susan at her hotel so the four could ride together in Susan's car.

Susan hung up the phone and smiled at Jake who sat with his back against the headboard. He glared at her with his arms crossed in front of his chest.

"Why did you agree to go out with them?" His words were calm but sharp.

She gave him a playful look. "Because I knew you didn't want to go. I figured if I can go with you to church tomorrow, you can go dancing with me tonight. Besides, maybe we can help Michael realize that girl isn't the right one for him."

"Stay out of it," Jake warned her. "That's between him and her."

He thought to himself, *I've got to stop thinking about her and that dream. It's going to be a hell of a night.*

CHERYL LOOKED at herself in the mirror and gave herself the final inspection. Never in a million years did she think she would wear the silk, rust-colored cocktail dress her sister sent her. Jolene paid a fortune for it then gained too much weight before she got an opportunity to wear it. Reluctantly she gave the dress to Cheryl with the comment, "Better to collect dust in your closet than in mine." Cheryl couldn't believe she was going to be the one to wear it.

The kids played on the porch while Dori helped Cheryl get ready. While she applied Cheryl's makeup, Dori explained an evening event required a little more eye makeup. She pulled the sides of Cheryl's hair back much how it was at the bazaar, but Dori ratted some of the hair in the back to give it more of an up-do look. Carefully, she fastened the silky side tresses around the ratted hair to the back of her head with a white rhinestone clip. When she finished curling the ends of her friend's long hair, she preserved it with a good dose of hairspray.

Dressed and ready, Cheryl stepped onto the porch to show the kids who wanted to see what she looked like. Taylor was sitting on the floor, but jumped up when he saw his mother.

"Mom, you look like a movie star!" he gasped.

She smiled and gave him a hug.

"Hugs are okay, but don't kiss me with that stuff on your lips." He looked up.

Dori and Cheryl laughed.

At six-thirty on the dot they heard Michael's truck pull into the driveway. After they shooed the children away from the window, Dori and Cheryl stood and watched Michael get out of his truck.

"It can't be legal to look that good," Dori said as she gazed dreamily at Michael.

He wore a silky, black and white print shirt unbuttoned far enough to reveal a gold chain settled into the dark hairs of his tanned chest. The shirt was paired with black, flared dress pants that showed off his fit lower body. Michael knocked on the screen door but the kids got to the door before Dori. With a playful smile, he looked down and scanned the boys.

"Are you boys the doormen?" he asked.

They looked at each other and wrinkled their faces. Dori pushed a child out of the way and stepped closer to the door.

"Come on in, Michael," she told him and held the screen door open.

Once he was in the kitchen, Cheryl smelled the sexy musk scent of his aftershave from where she stood by the children.

Seeing her, he slowly shook his head. "Wow. There's no other word to describe it. You're absolutely the most beautiful woman I know."

"Thank you. You look very nice too," she replied.

Cheryl continued to assess him. It was hard to ignore his perfectly styled hair and the thick lashes that surrounded eyes so dark they sparkled from any direction.

How easy it would be for any woman to be drawn to this man and be under his spell.

"I'll lock up and take the troops over to my house," Dori finally said. "Have a great night."

"Thanks for everything, Dori," Cheryl told her. "I do appreciate everything you do for me." She then bent down and gave Taylor a hug. "Be good and listen to Dori."

Taylor nodded.

Michael opened the door of his truck and Cheryl stepped up to get inside the passenger's seat. Doing so, her dress fell back and revealed a very shapely leg. An instant smile came to his lips. He obviously enjoyed what he saw, but he carefully shut the door behind her. A mile down the road she caught him looking at her legs again. Nervously she thought, *I hope I didn't make a bad decision here.*

"I have to admit this was Mom's idea for the double date. She thought it would be a nice way for everyone to get to know one another." He chuckled. "I'm really glad you decided to go tonight. I was surprised it worked out with Jake and Susan. They tend to keep to themselves. I know they're always at her hotel. Let's just say, getting to know each other better." He smiled and gave her a wink.

Cheryl looked away. *I wonder if they have anything else in common.*

When they arrived at Susan's hotel, Michael parked next to a new silver Mercedes Benz. He informed Cheryl the luxurious car belonged to Susan. The lobby was clean and organized when they passed through on their way to room twenty-two. Michael knocked, and a few seconds went by before Jake opened the door.

Cheryl could see the family resemblance: the scintillating brown eyes and gorgeous smiles that appeared somewhat forced, in Jake's case. The brothers were about the same height, but Jake's hair was lighter and shorter than Michael's, which gave him a grown-up, sophisticated look. He wore an expensive-looking burgundy short-sleeved shirt with only one button left undone but it still showed a hint of chest hair. The short sleeves complimented his muscular, tanned biceps as did Michael's, but Jake's black slacks weren't as flared. Obviously, the younger sibling tried to portray a flashier, modern look, while the older appeared more classic and conservative.

"Come on in," he told them. "She's still working on her hair." He sat on the end of the bed and motioned for them to sit on two chairs by a small table. Cheryl looked around at the nice room then back in the direction of Jake and their eyes met briefly.

Feeling her heart pound, Cheryl took a needed breath and reminded herself, *He's an engaged man. Don't forget it!*

He seemed nervous as his eyes stayed on Michael then toward the bathroom. A few moments past when Jake's anxiety seemed to have gotten the best of him.

"What's taking you so long in there?" he yelled rather loudly.

Susan came out and looked at him, annoyed. "For a guy who doesn't dance much you're sure in a hurry." She stopped when she saw Cheryl.

"Cheryl, right?"

"Yes, I met you at Trailways."

Susan wrinkled her brow like she was trying to recall.

"You remember, my son had a toad in a jar?"

"There is no forgetting something like that." Susan shook her head in disgust. "I couldn't believe any mother would allow her son to bring that thing in a restaurant."

"It wasn't the sort of thing he usually does. And it was in a jar. No harm done," Cheryl said, defending both herself and Taylor.

"No harm?" Susan responded. "I was sick to my stomach after I saw that thing. It was huge and bumpy."

"Let's forget about that stupid toad and get on our way to Rosy's Supper Club. I'm starved," Jake interrupted.

Susan raised her brows at him. "I can't believe you're hungry when we didn't eat until one-thirty today."

"Some of us are used to eating," he informed her.

She shrugged her shoulders and Cheryl noticed the glitter from the large diamond in her ring when she picked up a black clutch purse lying on the bureau. The purse was made of chiffon which matched the flared black dress she wore. Cheryl gazed at her. *She looks so nice. But according to Dori, I do, too.*

Cheryl noticed Jake give her a quick once over while he held the front passenger door open for Susan. Michael, opening the rear passenger door, was oblivious with his back to his older brother. They hadn't traveled far when Cheryl's date moved in closer. He took her hand and laced his fingers through hers. Holding it tight, Michael brought her hand to his lips and gave her knuckles a rapid kiss. Jake apparently caught the movement and glanced up in the rear-view mirror then back at the road. Susan started a conversation about the bad service they recently got from the waitress at Rosy's.

"I hope we don't get that *thing* who waited on us last time. For the life of her, she couldn't get my order right. I ordered my steak medium and it came well done, so I sent it back. The second one she brought was so rare, I swear, it practically ran off my plate. So, I sent it back. It's not that complicated to make a steak, right? I finally just ordered some shrimp because I knew she couldn't screw that up."

"I tried to tell her the cook is preparing the food, not the poor waitress," Jake said as he stared at the road ahead.

Susan shook her head. "Don't you think after the waitresses receive countless complaints they would fire the cook? I couldn't believe you gave her that big of a tip."

"Why not? My steak was perfect," Jake answered. Susan gave him a dirty look.

"Jake, doesn't Milt still cook at Rosy's?" Michael asked.

"Yes, I believe he has since the doors opened and probably will until they close the place down."

They decided to pull into a local liquor store to get some wine, knowing Rosy's only served set-ups but also allowed patrons to bring their own wine.

"Did you like the chardonnay we had the other night?" Michael asked Cheryl. Jake's eyes again darted to his rear-view mirror where they stayed on Cheryl.

"Yes, it was good," she replied.

Michael got out of the car and tapped Jake's arm resting on the open window frame.

"Aren't you going to get some wine for you two?" he asked, "not to say you can't have some of ours, but I know Susan doesn't like chardonnay."

Jake started to move when Susan put her hand on his arm. "Make sure you get that French merlot I adore."

"I don't know which one you're talking about," Jake told her. "Why don't you go in with Michael and make sure you get the right kind?"

Susan let out a disgusted sigh but went with Michael after he opened her car door. The door of the liquor store had barely closed behind Michael, when Jake turned to Cheryl.

"What do you think you're doing?"

"What do you mean?" she asked.

"I suppose it was your idea to go on this double date," he said accusingly.

"Michael told me it was your mother's. He said she thought it would be a nice way for everyone to get to know one another better."

"I guess it doesn't matter. It's obvious my brother is very fond of you, and I hope you're not just using him. But if you *are* using him to get to me, I hope you realize I'm not going to throw away a four-year relationship for what happened the other night. I've thought about it and I realize it was a terrible mistake."

Feeling like she had been slapped in the face, Cheryl looked down at her gold-colored sandals and didn't say anything. *Dori was right. This way, I know exactly how he feels. It was foolish to think he'd react any other way than he did. He was, after all, Michael's brother.*

Michael held the car door for Susan after they returned with the wine. Instantly, Susan turned to Jake. "Of course, they didn't have the wine I wanted." Holding up the brown paper bag in her hand, she stated, "I got this Italian kind. I really doubt it will be as good. You would think this liquor store would stock a few of the more popular imported brands." No one else commented about the wine and the four continued the drive to the supper club. Jake smiled at the hostess who came over shortly after they stepped in the door.

"Good evening, Jake. Would you like a table in the back?"

"You read my mind, Shirley."

She seated them at a quiet table in the corner that overlooked the river behind the club. After a moment, a waitress came over with some glasses and poured their wine. She left but came back shortly and asked if they were ready to order.

"Ladies first," Michael said to Cheryl.

"I'll have the shrimp," Cheryl told the waitress.

"I'll have the porterhouse. Medium," Michael ordered.

The waitress looked at Susan.

"I'll have the sirloin steak, medium rare," Susan told her. Everyone turned to look at her.

"Are you sure you want to risk ordering a steak?" Jake asked.

She smiled and nodded. "I'll be a good sport and give it another try."

Jake stared briefly at Susan before he turned to the waitress. "I'll have the porterhouse, too."

"And how would you like your steak done?" she asked.

"Milt knows how I like it," he replied with a smile. "Just tell him it's for Jake Cameron. He'll know."

"I'm sorry, but Milt no longer works here," the waitress said sadly.

Jake looked at her dumbfounded. "What?"

"He was let go earlier this week."

"Why?" Jake demanded.

"No one seems to know why," the waitress replied with a shrug.

"I guess we can't blame *him* tonight if our steaks aren't done right," Michael said.

Jake told her how he wanted his steak and the waitress left the table. He was quiet while Susan talked about the meal for the wedding.

"So far we have narrowed the choices for our wedding entree down to two — chicken cordon bleu with asparagus and roasted red potatoes or fillet mignon with glazed carrots and baked red potatoes."

Suddenly Jake stood up. "Excuse me. I'll be right back."

He headed toward the rest room and was gone for quite a while before he returned to the table.

"Hey, I was about to come looking for you," Michael told him.

"I ran into an old friend," Jake answered.

"Who?" Michael asked.

"No one you would know," he replied. He didn't say much else but kept his eyes on Susan throughout most of the meal. His fiancée smiled at him periodically and to everyone's surprise, she made no complaints about the food.

Shortly after the waitress cleared their plates, Michael commented, "The music here is a drag. All that Frank Sinatra crap. Why don't we go down to the M & M Club for some good ol' rock and roll?"

Susan immediately responded, "Your brother really isn't much of a dancer. I'm afraid we'll be going back to the hotel."

"No, we don't have to," Jake spoke up. "Why don't we join these two for a while?"

Susan's eyes blinked in surprise. "Well, then, let's go to the M & M."

When the four arrived at the M & M Club, Cheryl saw the same two drunks sitting by the door who were there the night she and Dori went out dancing. They hooted and hollered loudly when Susan walked past, but got even louder seeing Cheryl.

"I guess *you're* the belle of the ball," Jake stated, smiling at Cheryl.

The compliment caught Cheryl off guard and she didn't respond, unlike Susan who narrowed her eyes at him. Michael, beaming with pride at his brother's comment, stepped closer to Cheryl and put his arm around her. Jake pointed to a small, round table a distance away from the band. They made their way through the crowd to the table and sat down after they found some chairs. Seeing the waitress was busy and tables away, Michael volunteered to go to the bar and get some drinks. Cheryl went to the ladies' room and returned to find Jake sitting alone at the table. She sat with a chair between them and was surprised when he scooted over to sit on the chair next to her.

"What do you think you're doing?" she asked, echoing the words he'd spoken to her earlier. "Your fiancée is gone for a second and suddenly I become your friend. Didn't you tell me a few hours ago I was a *terrible mistake*?"

Jake shook his head and briefly closed his eyes. "I know I don't deserve it, but please try to forgive me for what I said. I realize I was way out of line."

"And what has changed in a couple of hours?"

Jake was about to answer when Michael approached the table with a tray of drinks. At the same time, Susan returned from the bar and pulled up a chair on the other side of Jake. When Michael set a glass of wine in front of her she looked disappointed.

"I can't believe they employ a bartender who doesn't know how to make a martini. Now I'm stuck with worse wine than what I had for dinner," Susan complained.

"Do you want to know what I think is truly amazing?" Jake asked, smiling. Susan turned her head toward him. "How is it that no one here in Montevideo can measure up to your standards?"

The band started to play the song, "Nice to Be With You," and Michael quickly asked Cheryl to dance. They danced to two songs, then returned to the table where Susan sat with her arms crossed and her eyes focused on her glass of wine. Jake was reclined in his chair with his legs stretched out in front of him. His dark eyes followed Cheryl and Michael from the dance floor to the table. Neither Jake nor Susan said anything to them when they returned to their chairs. The waitress appeared with another tray of drinks and set them down in front of everyone at the table.

"Who ordered these?" Michael asked her.

The waitress pointed at Jake. Michael looked at Jake and tilted his head. "Are we celebrating something special tonight?"

"Nothing but getting to know one another better," Jake answered flatly.

Michael smiled and took a drink of his whiskey Coke. "I guess Cheryl told you what Mom had in mind for this double date tonight."

Cheryl set down her vodka Collins when the band started to play the song, "Knock Three Times."

"I love this song. Let's go dance," she said to Michael. He pushed his chair back, but Jake shot up first.

"If we're going to get to know each other better, *we* should dance." Jake smiled at Cheryl. "I like this song too."

Dropping her folded arms, Susan's mouth fell open with a glare directed at Jake and Cheryl.

Michael looked amused. "I don't mind. Go ahead."

Jake motioned his hand toward the dance floor. Cheryl was slow to move but she led the way and began to dance. Jake wasn't a bad dancer and Cheryl observed him, trying to figure out what game he was playing. After a few minutes, they were joined by Michael and Susan, who danced next to them.

The song ended and the lead singer announced to the crowd, "We got so many couples on the floor right now, it's a perfect time to play a few slow songs." The piano player began the intro to the song, "Maybe I'm Amazed."

Cheryl felt Jake's strong arm go around her waist as he brought them together. She stared up into his eyes feeling the whole world brake to a sudden stop. He had the very same hypnotized expression he wore that night at the fellowship hall — right before they started to kiss.

Michael instantly stepped over to them. "This is where I need to cut in."

Jake stepped back and Michael took Cheryl's hand.

"May I have this dance?" Jake turned to Susan, who seemed a bit confused.

Cheryl heard her ask, "*What* do you think you're doing?"

Jake didn't respond but twirled Susan and himself around further into the crowd of dancers, away from Michael and Cheryl.

"I wonder what's going on with those two. He sure is having fun with Susan, flirting with you to make her jealous," Michael said. "Last week they weren't seeing eye to eye on things, and it sounds like this week isn't any better." Cheryl shrugged and Michael added, "I guess it's premarital jitters."

They danced a while longer to the song when Michael pulled Cheryl in closer and whispered in her ear, "You know what would make this evening a night to remember?"

"What?" Cheryl asked tilting her head at him. She took in the sweet aroma of his aftershave.

"If I could spend the night at your house." His eyes twinkled from the stage lights.

She shook her head at him. "Do you ask every girl you go out with that question on the first date?"

"No. They usually ask me," he replied with a radiant smile. Cheryl didn't say anything, but smiled slightly and rolled her eyes. Neither of them noticed that Jake and Susan were back dancing by them again until Jake tapped Michael on the shoulder.

"May I cut in?" he asked. Judging by the angry expression on Susan's face, this didn't make her happy.

Michael wrinkled his brow. "Okay. I guess I'll dance with my favorite sister-in-law-to-be again." He sounded a little annoyed.

He turned to Susan and was about to take her hand when she hastily turned and walked off the dance floor. Cheryl saw Michael look back in their direction, but his brother swiftly spun her and himself into the crowd. Once they were in the middle of the throng of dancers, he smiled down at her.

"Looks like you're starting to warm up to my brother."

"I don't think that's any of your business, what I do with your brother," she retorted.

"To a certain point, I guess you're right. But I wouldn't want him to be with someone if that person didn't truly care about him. Especially if that person was interested in someone else."

"What are you trying to say?" Cheryl stopped dancing.

"I don't know. I'm so mixed up right now." He shook his head. "I'm sorry about everything."

She pulled away from him. "You better go find your fiancée and see what happened to her." Cheryl left the dance floor with Jake close behind. When they got back to the table, Michael was there alone.

"Where's Susan?" she asked.

"She left. The way she stomped out of here, we better get going or we'll be walking back to the hotel."

Susan was in the passenger's seat with the radio on when they got in the car. No one said anything when Jake turned the key in the ignition.

"Do you and what's-her-name here like this song, too?" Susan asked Jake coldly. She kept her eyes on him but glanced briefly at Cheryl. She then turned to Michael. "Really, Michael, I thought you could do *so* much better than this little tramp."

Cheryl gasped. "How dare you say such a thing?" *You are a horrible person!*

Michael's mouth dropped open and Jake said loudly, "Don't talk to her like that. What's wrong with you?"

Susan turned her head toward the window and crossed her arms. No one spoke a word while they drove back to the hotel. Silently, Michael and Cheryl got out of the car and into his truck. Jake got out of Susan's car and slammed his door, then leaned against it. Susan stomped away, retreating into the hotel.

When they drove out of the parking lot, Michael released a heavy sigh. "I'm really sorry about what Susan said. She's just a spoiled brat. Her sister's the same way. Jake's going to have his hands full after he marries that little tiger."

"I don't care what she said about me. She doesn't know me at all. For a woman who's about to be married, she's very immature." It was hard to fathom Susan was the type of girl Jake wanted.

"Let's not talk about them anymore," Michael stated, after they had driven a few miles. "I would rather talk about us. Have you given any thought to what I suggested earlier?"

"I thought about it and I came up with some conclusions," she told him with finality.

He glanced at her with interest.

"Michael, this is our first date and you expect to spend the night?"

"It's 1973 and we are not our parents. No one waits anymore."

"I believe if you are going to make love to someone you better be in love with that someone." *Listen to yourself. You were going to make love to his brother!*

Michael parked in Cheryl's driveway and immediately got out of his truck. He went around to the passenger side and opened the door.

"What are you doing?" she asked.

"If you insist on doing things the old-fashioned way, I'm going to walk you to your door," he said with a smile. "I would then like you to invite me in for a goodnight kiss."

"If I invite you in for a goodnight kiss, do I have your word you won't try anything else?"

He shrugged his shoulders. "Maybe just one more kiss. And perhaps a promise."

She looked at him apprehensively.

"I'm not drunk like I was the other night," he told her.

He followed her inside the house and she switched on the light in the entry way then stopped to face him.

"I guess this is my cue." Without further ado, he reached for her and slowly brought her close. He placed a slow, passionate kiss on her lips. Cheryl could smell the mix of aftershave and sweat while her hands explored the strong muscles in his back. She didn't try to resist his kiss and even returned it. *What's wrong with me? This is the best-looking man I have ever seen in the flesh. Why don't I feel anything?*

"If you won't let me sleep here tonight, I'd like something in exchange." His warm lips brushed her ear.

She pulled her head back. "And what would that be?"

"Either make love to me tonight or promise you won't go out with anyone else."

Cheryl blinked with emphasis. "You seriously want me to commit to being exclusive when we've only gone on one date?"

"I know that we've only had one *official* date, but when I'm around you, I know what I want — and that's you."

"Michael, I was married for six and a half years and Jon and I dated for almost a year before that."

"I don't believe there's a time table on these things. All I know is, I've only been in love with two women. One is gone and the other is in my arms. I'm not going to make the same mistake I did before and let someone steal her away."

Did he just say he loves me? She took a deep breath and let it out slowly. "I know what happened to you wasn't good, but I can't make any promises to you or anyone else."

He gently tilted her chin and kissed her deeply. His hand slid across her breast and she put her hand up against his chest.

He stopped, then asked, "I know after being married as long as you were, you miss that. Admit it, Cheryl."

"Of course, I do, but I'm not going to jump into bed with you."

He released her. "Okay then, what about the promise?"

"I promise to think about it, okay?"

"I guess I'll have to settle for that right now," he sighed. "I'd better leave now, because you are way too irresistible and I don't want to screw up and have you throw me out again. See you in church tomorrow." He lifted her hand to his lips and tenderly kissed it. "Till we meet again."

"Good night, Michael." She laughed at his pretension, then shut and locked the door behind him, and watched from the kitchen window as his truck drove out of her driveway. She was in the bedroom putting on her nightgown when she heard something in the kitchen. Hearing it again, she put on her robe and went to check-out the noise. Someone was knocking at the door.

"Who is it?" she shouted.

She heard a voice that sounded like Michael, "It's me."

"Look, I told you. I'm not going to sleep with you," she said through the door.

"Cheryl, it's me … Jake. Could I please talk to you?"

Hearing his voice — she froze. It took a few seconds to find a breath before undoing the lock. Reasons for his presence flooded her head. *Does he think I'm easy? Someone he can have on the side?* She ripped open the door.

"What are *you* doing here?" Her tone was icy.

"Wow, you're fast. He just left. I didn't think you'd have your clothes changed already."

"How did you know he just left?" She cocked her head.

"I was watching from up on the hill." He glanced down nervously.

Cheryl felt her blood pressure rise at his bold violation of her privacy.

"Did you and Susan have another fight?" she lashed out. "Let me guess, you were hoping if your brother didn't get lucky with me, you might be able to."

His eyes got big. "No, that's not what I was thinking at all!" he shot back.

"Then what were you thinking, coming here?" Her fists sprung to her hips.

"I needed to talk to someone and for some odd reason, you're the only person who came to mind." He stared at her through the screen door.

"Why would you want to talk to a *little tramp* like me?" she snapped.

"Don't think for one second I had anything to do with what Susan said." His eyes flashed. "She was jealous I paid attention to you and she couldn't handle it."

"Then tell me what you want to talk about?"

He looked beyond her into the kitchen. "Can I come in and sit at your table and tell you what really happened tonight?"

Her thoughts raced but she stared at him motionless. "Okay. I'll put some coffee on."

Cheryl backed away from the doorway and went directly to the stove while Jake slowly opened the screen door and stepped into the kitchen. She saw his eyes widen then travel around the room before he seated himself at the table. He watched her make the coffee, but didn't say anything until she took a chair next to him.

"You have a very nice place here. Who designed it for you?"

She let out a slight chuckle. "I designed it. My grandmother gave me most of it. Jon thought it was too much the ranch style, but I wanted it to look more like a ranch house than a farm house, like Grandma's. Some people joke about it and say it looks like the Ponderosa."

He seemed to be lost in thought as he silently studied the décor. She curiously watched him until the coffee pot reached a steady perk on the stove. Without a word, she went to the burner and shut it off then returned shortly to the table with two steaming cups of coffee. She then sat and crossed her arms.

"So, tell me what really happened tonight."

He sighed and looked down at the red-and-white-checkered tablecloth in front of him. "After the other night with you I was really mixed up. I still feel that way, and I guess when I found out Susan and I were going out on a double date with you and Michael, I got defensive. I opened my big mouth and said some things to you I shouldn't have. It was hard enough just being around you and my fear escalated to anger. I'm sorry. Please forgive me."

"So, that's the reason you were acting so strangely at the M & M?" She sounded doubtful.

"No, that wasn't the only reason."

Jake proceeded to tell her what happened at Rosy's after he excused himself to go to the restroom.

Once he was out of sight, he cut back through the room to Shirley, the hostess, and tapped her on the shoulder.

"Can I have a word with you?"

"Is everything okay with your table?" she asked.

"It's perfect." Jake motioned for her to step away from a coworker and she followed him to an area outside the coat room. "What happened with Milt?" he asked.

"If I tell you what I know, you have to promise not to say you heard it from me." Shirley looked from side to side.

Jake nodded.

"I overheard Rosy and Ed talk about it when they thought no one was around. I guess some woman was in here a little while back and thought Milt didn't do a good enough job on her steak. She sent it back a few times and was angry when she left. A few days later, Ed gets a call from her saying she knows some very influential people from Minneapolis, especially the restaurant critic from the Tribune. She told Ed if Milt wasn't gone the next time she came in, the food critic might have a not-so-tasteful review of Rosy's Supper Club in the Tribune." Shirley shook her head. "It's just a shame. Milt was a great cook and a fun guy to work with."

Jake took a sip of his coffee, then finished the story. "Shirley said the woman never gave Ed her name and told him not to mention her call." His eyes went down on the table again. "But I know — it was Susan."

Cheryl's hand went to her mouth. "Does she know someone at the Tribune?"

"That's how I know it was her. Her girlfriend Melody, the one I want Brett to walk up with in the wedding, is the restaurant critic at the Tribune," Jake replied. "Oh, and by the way, Susan has agreed to let both my brothers be in the wedding."

"She reconsidered?" Cheryl asked softly.

"Yeah, she did, after I caught her in another lie. I told her I was sick of her crap with the wedding."

"Sounds like everything is working out for you," Cheryl said sharply. "You'll be a happily married man for Christmas." She looked down blowing on her coffee and took a sip.

A moment of silence passed when neither said a word. The only sound was the star-shaped clock ticking above the sink.

Finally, he said, "Tell me. You've been married. How do you know if someone is the right one or not?"

"With Jon, I just knew."

"But what did you know? Was it the way he treated you? The way he looked? What was it?"

She thought for a second. "You know by the person you become when you're with them. You become the best person you can be, because you bring that out in each other."

He slowly nodded. She felt his warm hand slide over the top of hers and squeeze it. Her heart jolted with his touch.

"Thanks for the advice. I need to show Susan how to be that better person you're talking about." He let go of her hand and for the second time that night she felt like he'd slapped her face.

"I guess I'll see you in church tomorrow," he said, and stood. Cheryl stayed by the table and focused on her coffee, unable to watch him go. He quietly shut the screen door and left.

At the sound of his truck pulling out of her driveway, she hung her head and cried. *How stupid could I be to fall in love with someone who loves someone else?*

14

I n the morning sun, a few dewy leaves in vibrant shades of red and yellow glittered in the trees along the road. What should have been a beautiful drive to church with the appearance of autumn's first colors only saddened Cheryl. Thoughts of facing another long winter alone left her feeling cold and empty. *Did you expect something in your life to change last night?* She was still angry at herself for being foolish enough to believe Jake would want her when he had Susan.

Once settled in a pew at church, Cheryl saw a family sit down on the other end. It was a young couple with two small children, a boy and a girl. She watched the father put his arm around the little boy and whisper in his ear. Whatever he said brought a smile to the boy's face. Cheryl thought about Taylor, who was likely still asleep at Dori's. *Doesn't he deserve to grow up with a father?* She was lost in thought when Michael slid in next to her in the pew.

"Good morning, beautiful." He leaned in close with a low voice, "Did you sleep well without me?"

"Shh …. If you haven't noticed, we're in church," she whispered back and gave him a weak smile. "I don't think that kind of talk is allowed in here."

He smiled and took her hand. Thoughts of pulling it back disappeared after her eyes traveled down the pew to the young family where the parents also held hands. It gave Cheryl a feeling of belonging, so she decided to leave her hand where it was.

When Chet and Lucille arrived, they sat in their usual spot across the aisle. Lucille smiled at Cheryl approvingly, but Chet raised an eyebrow at her and Michael.

The noise level increased as the parishioners filled the pews and greeted one another. It wasn't until Brett released a disgusted sigh that Cheryl realized he'd sat in the pew behind them.

A few minutes before the service started, Jake and Susan appeared in the back of the church. Susan smiled at Jake's parents then seated herself next to his mother. The dress Susan wore was accessorized with a large looped chain belt around her waist.

Cheryl recalled seeing the garment last month in a magazine. Susan looked innocent in that shade of light blue, smiling sweetly at the people around her. Her sunny demeanor this morning was an amazing contrast to her dark behavior last night. She gave Jake an adoring look, which proved all was forgiven between them. It was clear he loved her deeply to put up with a woman so rude and spoiled.

The church bells rang soon after the pastor's wife claimed her seat in the front row. The congregation sang the first hymn while Pastor Timms walked up the aisle to start the service. The pastor glanced down at his hymnal every few steps while he sang until his head snapped in the direction of Michael and Cheryl. He suddenly stumbled, then tried to catch himself. There was a hush in the crowd, but he quickly steadied himself and continued to the front of the church.

Michael squeezed Cheryl's hand with a pleased smile when the congregation greeted one another. When she turned to Brett, he took her hand and leaned slightly toward her.

"My condolences to you," he whispered loud enough for Michael to hear.

The smile on Michael's face fell and was replaced with a cold stare at his brother. He then nonchalantly turned and faced the front of the church without shaking Brett's hand.

It wasn't until Pastor Timms plunged into his sermon about lies and deception that Michael shifted his body closer to Cheryl's and casually slipped his arm around the pew behind her. She eyed his hand by her shoulder and noticed his thumb was turned upward. Her head slowly turned to see who the recipient of the silent message was across the aisle and found Jake's dark eyes staring back. Realizing Cheryl had caught him, he quickly redirected his gaze to the front of the church.

When the service concluded, the aisle filled up with chatter from the crowd of parishioners as they slowly migrated toward the door.

Cheryl overheard Lucille say to Jake and Susan, "I'm confused. Why didn't Pastor Timms announce your engagement to the congregation today? I just talked to him on Thursday before quilting and I specifically asked him to announce your wedding today."

Chet looked at his wife. "I wouldn't worry about it, Lu. What difference does it make when he announces it? They're not getting married here anyway."

Lucille gave Chet an impatient look, then asked Susan, "You two are coming for lunch, aren't you?"

"Yes, of course we'll be there," Susan answered.

At the bottom of the church steps, Lucille pushed through the crowd on her way to Cheryl and Michael. Immediately, Michael's eyes darted toward his mother then back to Cheryl. He wasted no time asking his question. "What are your plans for the rest of the day?"

"I have to pick up Taylor at Dori's."

"Before my mother asks, would you and Taylor like to come over for lunch?" He got the words out as Lucille reached them.

Lucille must have heard him ask because she stood with her head tilted at Cheryl and waited for a response. Once again, an invitation from the Camerons had left Cheryl with a loss of words. Michael added quickly, "How about I follow you to your house and we can leave your truck there. We can pick up Taylor on the way to our house."

Cheryl finally got out, "I do appreciate the invitation, but we're going to have to decline. Taylor won't be dressed for lunch. And besides, he'll likely be tired and want to go home and rest."

"He can go home and do that right after lunch," Lucille answered. "Bring some clothes with you for him when you come. He can change at our house. Problem solved. See you then. 'Bye now."

She turned and walked away with a satisfied smile on her face. Chet shook his head at Cheryl and followed Lucille to the car. Jake and Susan were close enough to hear what Lucille had said.

"Maybe someday we can join forces and stop that woman," Jake said to Michael. "Until then, we're stuck with her running our lives."

Michael chuckled and nodded in agreement.

Susan touched Jake's arm. "Jake honey, let's get going, I want to go back to the hotel and get my things loaded in my car before lunch. I've got a very important meeting at work tomorrow. I need to leave right after we're done eating."

"Seems like I'm getting it in all directions. See you later." Jake followed his fiancée to her car.

THE DUST from Cheryl's truck made it difficult to see Michael's truck following her. *I can't believe I let myself get into this. I can't go to their farm and listen to her go on about their wedding plans. Just*

thinking about the situation made her nauseous. *Maybe I'll tell him I'm feeling ill, which wouldn't entirely be a lie. No — it's time to stop this — he needs to know how I feel about him.*

Cheryl pulled into her driveway and soon after, Michael drove in and parked next to her truck. She was by her front door unlocking it when he came up behind her and wrapped his arms around her. When she spun around to face him, he pushed her against the door and planted a firm kiss on her mouth.

"Michael, please, we just left church," she said and pulled her face away from his.

He laughed. "Doesn't that make it all the more naughty?"

She gave him a serious look then turned to open the door. Her heart pulsed in her throat as he closely followed her to the table where she set her purse. He reached for her again, but she stepped aside and he almost fell over one of the chairs.

"Why do we need to play these games, Cheryl? Neither one of us are virgins. We've had our first date now." He smiled. "Do you realize I have never had to wait for a woman as long as I've waited for you?"

She stared at him. "You and I ...." she took a breath, "we really need to talk. I just don't feel ... I'm sorry, Michael, but I do believe you're wasting your time waiting for me. Please believe me, I never meant to hurt you."

He looked down, but quickly raised his head and met her eyes. "No. I don't believe I am wasting my time."

Cheryl saw how dark his eyes got when he leaned toward her. He reminded her of a cat ready to pounce on a mouse. Her eyes went to the door, and then at the phone on the counter. She knew both were too far away.

"You better get going. Your mom will be wondering where you are," she said, trying to keep the quiver out of her voice.

"We've got time," he answered. "Give me a chance to change your mind." He motioned with his index finger for her to come to him. "Come here and kiss me."

She turned to run around the table away from him, but he got a hold of her arm. In one swift move, he pulled her close to him and kissed her while she tried to turn her face away.

She struggled against him but managed to yell, "Let me go!"

Bringing his hand up, he cupped her breast and she slapped his face. He flinched and glared down at her.

"Jim's right. You have been teasing me *way* too long," he said. "Pretty little girl, I'm going to give you what you got coming. A lot of people have seen us together as a couple. No one is going to believe I forced you into anything."

Cheryl swallowed hard and tried to move out of his hold. He suddenly swooped her up in his arms and started toward her bedroom. She kicked and screamed but it only intensified his grip on her. Once in the bedroom, he threw her on the bed and she landed with a bounce. Michael's eyes never left hers as he undid his belt and unzipped his pants.

"So, you understand when I'm done — you officially belong to me. Don't ever think about being with anyone else again."

She sprang up but he pushed himself on top of her and forced her back down on the bed. His mouth covered hers while she squirmed, trying to get him off her. She managed to get her hand up close to his head and dug her nails into his cheek. Wincing, he pulled back his face and touched his cheek. Seeing blood on his fingertips, he clenched his teeth and put his face close to hers. "You little hellcat. I'm going to teach you a lesson you will *never* forget."

He grabbed her left wrist and held it above her head. Cheryl tried to move her right arm but it was trapped underneath him and rapidly losing circulation. He reached under her dress and felt the soft skin of her stomach, which made him moan. His hand went farther up and under her bra. With his mouth still on hers, he caressed each of her breasts for a moment and then his hand went down to her pantyhose. He hastily pulled down each side of her pantyhose sticking his fingers through them. Cheryl tried to kick him but he brought his leg up across hers and held it firmly to the bed. He stopped to look at her and smiled. Obviously, it brought joy to him that he could overpower her. Michael continued to watch her expression while he deliberately rubbed the front of her panties in what seemed to Cheryl a slow, demeaning torture. When she didn't react, he appeared frustrated and gathered the fabric of her panties in his hand and pulled hard. She felt the elastic cut into her skin and heard her panties tear. He stopped suddenly and raised his head to listen.

A siren was close outside, but it was hard to tell if it was a police car or an ambulance. Letting her go, he got up and looked out the bedroom window. When he was unable to see anything from there, he went out to the porch.

Cheryl pulled up her ruined pantyhose then rubbed her arm as she got up off the bed and straightened out her dress. Her eyes frantically searched her bedroom then landed on the heavy lamp on the nightstand. She looked over her shoulder toward the bedroom door then stepped toward the lamp, but froze when she heard his voice from the doorway.

"It's an ambulance, and it's headed to either Dori's house or ours."

Oh, my God, Taylor. She felt her body instantly go cold.

"It already passed Cowen's and I think it sounded like it turned west. Get in my truck. Let's go see where it's going."

"I'll drive my own truck," she told him outside.

He held his truck door open. "Get in," he ordered. Worried about Taylor, she didn't want to waste precious time arguing and got in his truck.

As they left her yard, she looked at the scratch marks on his face where small beads of blood had formed and felt her stomach lurch. They drove down a hill and up the next where they could see a half a mile away. The ambulance turned in by the sign that read *Welcome to Sugar King Farm*. Michael stepped on the accelerator and Cheryl felt the back of the truck swerve on the gravel road. He slowed down to turn onto the blacktop driveway and barely managed to keep the truck on the tar. The tires squealed sharply when they took the corner. When they drove in the yard the ambulance was parked on a field road between the barn and the pasture. Michael and Cheryl burst out of the truck and Irene rushed toward them.

"What's going on?" Michael shouted.

"It's your dad," she cried out. "He's had an accident with that horse."

"Where is he?"

Irene caught her breath and pointed toward the pasture. "Brett found him on the horse trail that leads over to Thompson's. That's where he and your mother are now, with the ambulance drivers. They're going to have to put him on a stretcher and carry him out on the trail."

Cheryl slipped off her sandals and ran behind Michael into the pasture toward the trail. Coming upon a wooded area, they heard Lucille weeping and saw Chet's motionless body on the ground. Not far away, the horse casually munched on grass with his reins hanging down, unconcerned with what was going on around him. Lucille reached for Michael, but he lunged to his father's side where Brett and the medical team assessed the situation. Cheryl reached for Lucille and they held each other.

"He has a pulse," one of the medics said.

Lucille dropped her head onto Cheryl's shoulder and thanked God he was still alive. Chet had a huge bump on the side of his head and his leg looked unnaturally twisted. The four men carefully hoisted him onto the stretcher, then with two on each side they started back down the trail. The women followed arm in arm behind the men into the yard. They wasted no time getting Chet and Lucille loaded into the ambulance, but before they shut the doors, Lucille's frightened eyes found Cheryl.

"You're coming to the hospital, Cheryl. Please. I need you there," Lucille said with desperation.

"Yes, I'll be there, Lucille," Cheryl nodded.

The ambulance circled around and they heard the siren again as it headed back to Montevideo. Michael, Brett and Cheryl followed it to the hospital in Michael's truck. As they hurried into the emergency room, Cheryl's thoughts went back to a year earlier when her whole world changed after she entered this room. She came back to reality when hospital staff rushed Chet past them into a room to be examined and the group followed alongside the stretcher.

Jake was already there, and when his mother saw him, she ran to him with open arms. "Jake. Thank God you're here." Lucille clung to him for a moment before she asked, "How did you find out what happened?"

"Irene called the hotel."

"Who here is family?" a nurse asked. "Whoever isn't needs to go and sit in the waiting room.

"We're all family here," Michael answered. "We are his sons and she," he pointed to Cheryl, "is my fiancée." His family and Cheryl stared blankly at him.

"It doesn't matter. There can only be two people in here while the doctors are examining the patient," the nurse told him. "The rest of you will have to go to the waiting area."

Lucille looked frantically at Jake. "Please stay in here with me. I can't do this alone."

"Of course, Mother, I will," he answered and put his arm around her.

The rest of the group went into the waiting area where they found Susan powdering her nose. She dropped her jeweled compact into her purse, then stood and fired questions at Michael and Brett, who filled her in on what they knew.

"What's *she* doing here?" She wrinkled her nose at Cheryl. "This is a family crisis, not a neighborhood get-together."

"I want her here and Mom asked her to come." Michael's eyes narrowed.

Susan released a disgusted sigh and plopped into her chair. No one said anything for a while until Brett broke the silence.

"What happened to your face?" he stared at Michael.

Michael gingerly touched his cheek with his fingers. "I must have accidentally brushed my face on a branch or something running out to help with Dad." His eyes moved slowly to Cheryl and he stared at her for a moment from the corner of his eye. A few minutes went by but it seemed like an hour before Jake and Lucille appeared.

"They're taking him to X-ray," Jake said. "They need to know the extent of his injuries. They do know for sure he has a concussion and a broken right leg. The most serious being the concussion." Lucille took a seat next to Cheryl and started to cry again.

Cheryl put her arm around her and said in a reassuring voice, "It's going to be okay. He's breathing on his own. That's something to be thankful for. Take my hand and let's pray together."

Both women began to say the Lord's Prayer and the rest of the group, except for Susan, joined in. During the prayer, Cheryl glanced at Susan and caught her rolling her eyes at Jake.

After what seemed like an eternity, the doctor finally entered the waiting room. Concern was evident on his face as he reported, "Chet has no broken bones other than his leg. The tests so far don't show any internal injuries, but we are not out of the woods with that or the concussion. The brain is a very delicate organ. When he wakes up, and hopefully that will be the case ...." Lucille suddenly let out a cry, and he stopped and looked at the group. "With time, we'll understand the full extent of his injuries."

"So, there's a chance he won't wake up?" Jake quickly asked.

The doctor took a breath. "I'm afraid that is a reality with head injuries. The best scenario is that he will wake up within the next twenty-four to forty-eight hours. After that, his chances of a full recovery go down quite a bit."

Hearing the doctor's prognosis, Lucille's sobs intensified. Cheryl leaned over and held the older woman in her arms. Susan glared at Cheryl, then looked back at Jake and shook her head. Jake went back into the emergency room with his mother. This time they were gone for quite some time.

"I think I'll give Jake a break and sit with Mom in there," Brett said and stood from his chair. A few minutes after he went in the emergency room, Jake appeared and sat next to Susan. His fiancée gave him a small compassionate smile when he took her hand. Jake continued to hold her hand but not her attention as her eyes went up to the clock on the wall every few minutes.

"You know it doesn't pay for all of us to just sit here," Susan finally said. "I'm going back to Minneapolis. You know I'm no good when it comes to things like this. Besides, your mother has her." She nodded toward Cheryl. "She obviously doesn't need me."

Jake stretched his arms out behind his head and then stood. "I guess you'll need a ride back to the hotel to get your car." He and Susan were not far down the hall when Michael got up and sat next to Cheryl.

"You know when I told the nurse you were my fiancée, I liked the way that sounded." He smiled. She didn't say anything and looked away while his eyes stayed on her. "Cheryl, I want you so bad. That's why I just get carried away sometimes."

Stunned by his explanation, she turned and glared at him. He leaned in closer to her and spoke in a lower voice, "If you're going to be this way, we need to get something straight here. If you tell anyone, including your friend Dori, about what happened between us earlier, I'll make sure you go bankrupt with that farm you're trying to run. Wouldn't it be something if next spring when you go to the Watson bank for a loan for seed, they suddenly consider a single woman trying to make it on her own too big of a risk?"

Her eyes narrowed and she snapped, "You don't have anything to do with the bank in Watson."

"I don't." He smiled. "But our good family friend Charlie Vanders is the bank president, and my father does a lot of business there. If you were to accuse me of something, my family isn't going to believe you. And word would get around that you're bad-mouthing us. If my Dad doesn't pull through, Jake and I will be dealing with those guys down at the bank. Think about it, Cheryl. Our farm is a big operation, and yours is just you, your hired hand and a six-year-old kid. If you try to get a loan somewhere else in Montevideo where you never have before, do you really believe they wouldn't consider you a big risk, too?"

A small smile formed on his lips, like he knew he struck a nerve with her. She turned her head and concentrated on the wall in front of her, trying not to break down and cry. *I will not give him the satisfaction.*

"I call the shots with you and me from now on. I don't want to even see you look at another man." He crossed his arms and reclined comfortably in his chair.

"DID anything change with Dad since I left?" Jake asked urgently. He was breathing hard when he returned to the waiting room.

"No," Michael said. "What makes you think it did?"

Jake sat down across from him and his eyes went to Cheryl. "I thought maybe it did by the look on her face." He pointed to her.

Michael looked at her face and shrugged.

"Speaking of faces, what the hell happened to yours?"

"I scratched it while helping Dad off the trail."

Jake wrinkled his brow. "How'd you do that?"

"Who knows with everything that happened?" Michael answered, annoyed.

There was a silence before Cheryl rose from her chair. "I need to call Dori and tell her what's going on or she'll have a posse out to my house. Maybe she can pick me up so you can stay here for as long as you need to, Michael."

"I'll go with you to call. She doesn't need to bring you home, I will," Michael said.

"I can't expect her to watch Taylor all day and night," Cheryl answered sharply.

"She'll watch him," he told her. "Just let me talk to her."

After Cheryl picked up her purse, Michael took her arm and escorted her to the pay phone at the end of the hall.

Jake watched them go, and wondered *why they were acting so differently toward each other. And those four scratches perfectly spaced like that. I'll bet a million dollars she scratched his face.*

When Michael and Cheryl returned, Jake eyed them while they both sat. He noticed a couple of small, dark spots of what could be blood on the front of Cheryl's dress. In one move, Michael draped his arm around her like it belonged there. She looked nervously at her left side where his hand was and then looked down in her lap. *She doesn't look very comfortable. Something is definitely going on here.*

Hours passed at a slow crawl before Jake saw Lucille and Brett come out of the ER toward the waiting room.

"Mom needs something to eat and I could use some food, too. Anyone want to join us?" Brett asked.

"Why don't we eat in shifts in case something happens with Dad?" Jake suggested. "You go on ahead. Michael and Cheryl, if you two want to go and eat now, I'll stay here until you get back."

"No, I'm not hungry. But if you want to get something, Michael, please don't let me stop you," Cheryl said.

"I really don't want to leave Dad," Michael told Brett. "So why don't you bring me back a sandwich."

Brett nodded.

Lucille looked around the room. "What happened to Susan? Where is she?"

"She said she isn't any good in these situations and decided to go back to Minneapolis," Jake answered.

Lucille closed her eyes. "She probably thinks we're a bunch of hillbillies down on the farm."

"Mom, not that hillbilly thing again," Jake said with a sigh. "Not now."

She opened her eyes and turned toward Jake. "I saw her the day of the bazaar when your brothers started to brawl. She stood there staring at them fighting, then ran to the parking lot, holding her mouth. Poor thing. Probably couldn't handle the whole embarrassing episode. And now she's going back to her family to tell them your father tries to ride a wild horse and practically kills himself." She started to bawl again when Cheryl got up and put her hand on her shoulder.

"Lucille, people get hurt all the time when they run farms," she told her. "It's just a fact of life when you're a farmer. I'm sure Susan's family is going to look at it as an accident, not craziness. The man you love is in there fighting for his life. That's the only thing you need to worry about right now."

All the Cameron brothers focused on Cheryl and witnessed their mother nod in agreement and stop crying. Brett put his arm around his mother and turned her in the direction of the cafeteria but Lucille turned back to Cheryl.

"My dear, you are a Godsend. Michael, hang on to this one."

"Believe me, Mother, I don't plan on letting her go." He gave Cheryl an adoring smile. Cheryl looked down at the floor and when she looked up, Jake's eyes were on her, full of questions. *How could their relationship evolve so quickly? I know he didn't spend the night last night. Now he's referring to her as his fiancée and leading her around like a prized mare.*

Lucille and Brett left for the cafeteria and Jake started a conversation with Michael about their father and that crazy horse. After a while, Michael stood up and excused himself to go to the restroom. The second he was out of sight, Jake jumped out of his chair and sat next to Cheryl.

"What's going on with you and him?"

"Nothing," Cheryl said, and looked straight ahead.

He reached and turned her chin toward him to look her in the eyes. "Tell me the truth, Cheryl. Did you put those scratches on his face?" She stared at him, breathing hard but didn't answer. "I thought so. That son-of-a-bitch." When Jake saw Michael return from the restroom, he quietly whispered to Cheryl before his brother was close enough to hear, "You're not going home with him."

Approaching Cheryl and Jake, a small smile appeared on Michael's lips. "I can't leave you alone, can I?" he asked and sat down.

Jake gave him a serious look but didn't say anything. A short time later, Brett and Lucille returned with sandwiches and a small tray filled with cups of steaming coffee.

No one said anything while they devoured the sandwiches until Michael commented, "I guess we were all hungrier than we thought."

Finding it hard to speak to Michael, Jake only nodded.

Brett and Lucille were about to go back in the ER when the doctor appeared again.

"We're going to put him into the intensive care unit where he will be monitored very closely," he told them.

Like the ER, the ICU only allowed two family members in at a time. Brett went with his mother while the other three stayed in the waiting room. At nine o'clock, Brett and Lucille came back to join the rest of the family.

"Mom is going to spend the night here, and I don't want her to be alone, so I'm going to sleep on the couch," Brett said, and pointed to the couch against the wall.

Jake rose from his chair. "No, little brother, you have been above and beyond today. Your big brother is going to stay here with Mom."

Michael nodded in agreement. "Okay, then it's decided, Jake's going to stay and I'll take Brett and Cheryl home, then do chores tomorrow morning." He sprang to his feet and Jake motioned for him to sit. He looked at Jake curiously but took a seat.

"Michael, you're going to stay here tonight and Brett is going to take your truck home. I'll take Cheryl home."

Michael looked dumbfounded. "Why can't you stay here? Hospitals give me the creeps."

"You're the only one who hasn't been in there to sit with Dad." Jake glared at him. "It's your turn."

"I guess if you put it that way," Michael said with a frown. "Okay, I'll stay." He reached over and put his arm around Cheryl. "I'll be seeing you as soon as I can. And don't forget about what we talked about." He leaned over to kiss her, but she didn't turn her face, so he brushed his lips against her cheek into her hair.

BRETT WALKED with Cheryl and Jake out the door of the hospital into the lit parking lot.

"I really am proud of how you handled yourself today, Brett," Jake told him, and the two brothers hugged each other. Tears shined on Brett's cheeks when he backed his head.

"Jake, be honest with me. Do you think he's going to pull through this?"

"That old bird. Hell, yeah. He's tougher than you think," Jake answered, and ruffled his brother's hair.

Brett's face relaxed. They talked a while longer before Brett got in Michael's truck and left.

Neither Jake nor Cheryl said anything as they drove away from the hospital. Stopping for the first stoplight, he turned to her.

"Did he rape you?" he asked in a rigid voice.

She felt her body start to shake, but held back an answer.

He drove down a couple more streets then pulled his truck into Smith Park. After he cut the engine, he took her by the shoulders and shook her. "Tell me. Did he rape you?"

"He tried," she blurted out and started to cry.

"That dumb shit! If my dad makes it, he is going to kick his ass in every direction. And if he isn't in shape to do it, I will," he told her. He took a handkerchief out of his pocket and handed it to her. She caught her breath and wiped her eyes.

"He started to rape me, and when we heard the siren from the ambulance, it made him stop. I feel terrible for your dad, but the truth is, if he wouldn't have had his accident, Michael would have succeeded."

"Trust me, Cheryl. Please tell me everything that happened," he pleaded.

She told him how Michael had reacted to her rejection that morning at her house and what he told her at the hospital. He shook his head and pressed his lips together as he listened. The security light outside illuminated the same mesmerized expression he wore that night at the fellowship hall. Without a word, he reached out and pulled her close. It felt familiar and safe in his strong arms.

Jake kissed her temple and whispered, "I'm *so* sorry. Everything's gonna be okay …. It's gotta be." A few moments went by before he gently laid his hand on her cheek and lifted her lips to his. The kiss was fervent, but unhurried, and she felt he was somehow attempting to heal them both.

He pulled his head back. "I thought I was going crazy in that hospital. I felt like I was going to throw up. I don't know if it was worry for my dad or the thought of Michael's hands all over you."

She moved away and straightened in the passenger's seat. "I have to be honest. You were right about last night and the reason why I went out with Michael. I wanted to see *you* and get your reaction to me after what happened at the fellowship hall. I can't stop myself from thinking about you. I just wish things were different and we could be together." She stopped and caught her breath. "There. I said it. You must think I'm terrible. My husband died a year ago and now I'm here, throwing myself at you, an engaged man." He silently stared at her.

"Can I spend the night with you?"

Seconds ticked by as she stared back at him. "Are you sure you want to do that?" she slowly asked. *Please don't do this to me again if you don't mean it.*

"It's the only thing I'm sure of at this moment," he answered.

15

The morning sun filtered through the blinds when Jake walked through the waiting room of the ICU. Michael was sleeping on the couch with his face down on the pillow. Jake stepped into his father's room and saw his mother asleep on a cot next to the bed. Quietly, Jake tiptoed back out and carefully closed the door. At the nurse's station, he asked how things went overnight.

A nurse smiled sympathetically. "Your father's condition didn't really change any, but your brother sure did complain about how hard the couch was."

"Good. It should have been harder," Jake said.

"I beg your pardon?" she asked.

"Never mind. Where can a guy get a good cup of coffee?"

She smiled and told him the cafeteria should be open. Jake went to get his coffee then came back up to the waiting room and sat down. Watching Michael sleep, he thought, *How can he sleep after what he did to her?* He brought his cup up to his mouth to take a sip of coffee and became lost in thought. *When was the last time the coffee smelled this great? Oh yeah, the day of the bazaar in the fellowship hall when the building was empty except for those coffee makers filling the air with that wonderful aroma.* How quickly the smell was drawn into the kitchen when they turned on the fan. Suddenly he asked himself, *Why did I hear a door slam before I yelled for Susan? She answered and went out, then I heard it slam again.*

A few minutes later Pastor Timms came walking up the hall. "Good morning, Jake." They shook hands and the pastor said, "I'm so sorry about your dad. Your mother called late last night and told me not to come until this morning. We can only pray God will help him to a speedy recovery."

"Thank you, Pastor," Jake answered. Michael stirred while they talked, then opened his eyes as the pastor left for Chet's room.

"Did something happen with Dad?" Michael sprang up into a sitting position.

"No."

Michael blinked then rubbed his eyes and looked at Jake. "What time is it?" he asked.

"Seven o'clock."

"I gotta go to the can and wash up." Michael stood and went down the hall. A short time later, Pastor Timms came out of Chet's room and stood next to Jake.

"They're giving your dad a sponge bath so I thought I would give them some privacy. Since you're here alone, can I have a word with you?" Pastor Timms asked.

"Okay, what's on your mind, Pastor?" Jake inquired.

He glanced over both his shoulders and took a ragged breath. "I'll just come out with it. Last Tuesday evening I was called out to the Cowen farm. David said it wasn't an emergency, but felt I should come all the same. He told me to take my time and not to rush."

Jake nodded.

"Well, I saw your truck parked in the back of the fellowship hall. I figured you were likely working on the moldings, so I thought I would see how you were doing. And that's when I saw you and her in each other's arms."

Jake flinched and looked away.

"After what I saw that night, how could I announce your up-coming wedding? I felt I had to talk to you first and see if you were going through with it." Jake sucked in a deep breath while the pastor continued. "Jake, you and I both know she is an attractive woman but you have promised marriage to someone else. You need to do the decent and honorable thing and end it with one of them before you continue with the other. So, what it all boils down to is, are you getting married or not?"

"I'm really confused right now, and I'm trying to sort some things out," Jake answered. "With everything that's happening with Dad, could you give me a little more time?"

The pastor looked at him and crossed his arms. "Yes, I can give you more time. But, the real question here is, how much time will your mother give me to announce your wedding before she goes above my head and complains to the church board?"

Lucille came out of Chet's room. "Good morning, Jake. Pastor, they're done now. You can come in." Pastor Timms nodded and walked back with her into Chet's room.

CHERYL REACHED OVER and pulled the pillow Jake had used to her side of the bed. She held it tightly in her arms and inhaled the sweet smell of his aftershave … and him. It was the only thing that confirmed he had been there and it hadn't all been a dream. Jake told her he'd be gone early to go home and do chores before Brett woke up in the morning.

Her thoughts ran in every direction while she lay there, looking around the room, trying to sort them out. What happened yesterday with Michael seemed like a blur. Maybe her mind was trying to block out his attack. But what happened in the same room last night with Jake would be etched in her memory forever. The second their lips touched everything became clear. He awakened feelings in her she had muted and desperately tried to forget existed. In his arms, she felt herself surrender with no will to resist. She replayed in her mind what happened after he started his truck and reached for her.

"Come on over here. I need you close to me," he said softly.

Cheryl slid across the seat and he put his arm around her pulling her closer. She laid her head on his chest and felt her shoulders drop as her body relaxed. "Peaceful Easy Feeling" played on the eight-track, but neither spoke as they drove out to her farm.

Inside her house, she turned on the light in the kitchen and watched him look around the room. When his eyes settled on her, he wrapped his arms around her. He held her tightly and inhaled with his face nuzzled in her hair. His mouth claimed hers in a slow but deliberate kiss. It fueled the growing fire inside her. She stared into his deep brown eyes, then without a word, took his hand and led him toward her bedroom. Jake followed close, but halfway down the hall he slowed. Cheryl turned her head and caught him checking out the decor.

A smile was on her lips when she stopped and cleared her throat. "You saw the kitchen last night. Would you like a tour of the rest of the house before we go in there?" She nodded toward the bedroom.

"All right," he said slowly. "I guess it wouldn't hurt to know a little more about the woman I'm about to sleep with." He smiled. "Besides, I wouldn't want you to think I'm easy."

"Okay, I'll give you the grand tour." She laughed.

They ended the tour on the porch. She sat down in the wicker love seat while he walked around and examined the screened-in room. He stood next to her with his hands on his hips and looked down at her.

"I love this house. It's perfect," he paused, "just like you."

"If you're just saying that to seduce me," she said, "you better try harder."

He smiled and took her into his arms, then kissed her deeply. The kiss was so intense it left her dizzy and craving more. Jake picked her up and carried her to her bedroom. His lips didn't leave hers until he set her gently on the bed.

Enough light illuminated the room from the yard light outside for Cheryl to watch him take his clothes off while she undid her braid.

When Jake stood in front of her, she saw how much he resembled Michael and felt uneasy. Somehow, sensing her fear, he took her hand and pressed it to his heart. He held it there with his hand over hers so they both could feel his rapid, strong heartbeat — letting her know she was not alone with anxiety. He brought her fingers to his lips and turned her hand over to kiss her knuckles with his warm mouth. His hand released hers, moving behind her to unzip her dress. Goose bumps broke out on her skin when he pulled her dress forward and touched his fiery lips to her shoulder. He kissed it while his fingers slowly slid her bra strap down. His hot mouth made its way across her collarbone and hungrily trailed up her neck.

Cheryl's knees shook as he undid her bra and pulled it down off her arms along with her dress. Both garments fell to the floor around her ankles. She sank down on the bed to remove them along with her pantyhose and panties. Her eyes slowly traveled up his lean muscular body when she stood. His hand went under her chin and gently lifted her face to look in his eyes. The other hand softly brushed her cheek and went higher into her hair while his splayed fingers combed through it. He gathered some hair from each side of her head draping it on both sides of her breasts. He seemed to be in awe when he took a step back.

His dark eyes appeared to drink in her body while he studied all of her. A few heavy breaths later, he whispered, "You are a goddess." He kissed her again before his head dropped to her breasts and lovingly caressed one with his mouth. Her hands went through his hair when he took a nipple in his lips and gently suckled it. It stirred something deep within, and she ached to feel him inside her. It had been so long.

They lay on the bed and rolled with their arms wrapped

around each other until he was on top of her. His hands ran over her body like he was trying to memorize every detail. Each touch took her to a new level of pleasure and further exposed the needs she had hidden away.

His lips sought hers but this time with more urgency, taking over her mouth and body as he entered her.

She gasped.

He quickly asked, "I'm not hurting you, am I?"

"No," she breathed. "It feels incredible. Please, I don't want you to stop." Cheryl felt herself spin like a leaf dropped into a raging river.

He cupped her face in his hands and kissed her profoundly. The kiss confirmed her conviction that they were here together because it was meant to be. Nothing on this earth could be more perfect. Suddenly, an intense rush of pleasure exploded from deep inside and she cried out uncontrollably as it took over her shaking body. A deep sound came from Jake's throat before his strained voice shouted her name drawing it out, "C h e r y l ..." as he released.

Moments later they lay together with her head on his chest. She could hear his slower heart beat along with the sadness in his voice as he stroked her hair. "I need to leave early tomorrow and get home to do chores before I go back to the hospital."

Hearing his words, she looked down and silently nodded. Her pensive gesture seemed to bother him because he pulled her closer and kissed her with his hand lovingly pressing the nape of her neck. She kissed him back and felt his longing return with her own. *The devil can have tomorrow,* she thought. *Tonight may be all we'll ever have.*

Now alone in the morning light, she sadly reminded herself that no promises were made. As far as she knew, he still planned to marry Susan. The longer she lay there, the harder she tried to convince herself that she and Jake would end up together. But the reality of the situation slowly crushed her optimism and she realized it was likely they wouldn't. She wiped the tears in her eyes with the corner of the pillowcase. Whatever the outcome, she would have to learn to accept it.

MICHAEL CAME from the restroom feeling for his comb in the back pocket of his dress slacks. Figuring it had likely fallen out while he slept on the couch, he went back to the waiting room. He was almost there when he heard the Pastor say to Jake, "And that's when I saw you and her in each other's arms." He quickly hid behind a large pillar and listened to the rest of the conversation. The pastor left to see their father, and Michael let a moment go by before he entered the waiting room. While he looked around for his comb, he kept an eye on Jake who stared out the window through the slits in the blinds.

"There it is," he said, locating his comb lodged between the cushions on the couch. "Where'd you get that coffee?" he asked Jake. "I need to get some."

In the elevator on his way to the cafeteria, Michael started to think. *It was Wednesday morning when I found those beer cans in his cooler. I don't think he would bring other women there from town. Wow. He must be doing some woman from church.* He got his coffee and headed back up to intensive care.

Jake still looked to be deep in thought and didn't seem to notice Michael return with his coffee.

Wearing a small smile, Michael cleared his throat. "Penny for your thoughts."

"What?" Jake asked startled.

"So, what's on your mind, big brother? It wouldn't be woman trouble, would it?" Michael tried to sound concerned.

"No, I'm just worried about Dad. That's all." Jake frowned.

Michael took a sip of his coffee and said into his cup, "I'm sure that's it."

Jake and Michael both looked up at the same time then back

at each other and grinned. Brett walked down the hall toward them carrying a pink, flowered bag.

Michael whistled, then yelled, "Don't you look all manly, Barbie."

Brett narrowed his eyes at him. "It's for Mom. She called and wanted a change of clothes and her tooth brush, so Irene got this ready for her." He looked at Jake. "She wanted to talk to you but I told her you didn't come home last night and only did this morning to do chores and shower." Jake was silent, but Michael smiled and lightly punched him in the shoulder.

"You, horny dog, you. Even as Dad is lying up here you still have the notion to get a little. I got to say, you sure surprise me, Jake."

Brett looked at them both confused. "I thought Susan went back to Minneapolis," he said, then paused. "Who were you with?" He stared Jake in the face.

Michael crossed his arms and tilted his head at his older brother, but Jake was silent. "I've been trying to crack this mystery for a few days now," he told Brett. "Let's go over the facts, shall we?" He carefully scanned his older brother's face while he spoke. "First I find beer cans in his cooler on Wednesday morning with lipstick on a few of them and a suspicious red thread from someone's clothes. We know none of it was from Susan because she wasn't here, and besides, she doesn't drink beer. Then this morning, I came out of the restroom and I overheard quite the conversation with our good brother here and Pastor Timms."

Jake's eyes got big and he looked away.

Brett turned his attention back to Michael, who continued, "It seems the Pastor had the excitement of his life witnessing the wolf, here, in sheep's clothing in the arms of some woman at the fellowship hall on Tuesday night."

Brett snapped his head around to look back at Jake.

Michael added, "Even I wouldn't have thought to entertain women at the fellowship hall. So, from the facts, I believe it has to be a woman from church." He hesitated a second and then said, "Let's see, last night he left here at around nine-thirty with you and Cheryl … and didn't come home until morning."

The blood rushed to his face and a sudden pain in his chest made his whole body instantly hot. He stared ahead trying to process the information. Turning back to Jake, his words spouted out, "She had on a red blouse Tuesday night. Oh, my God. It all adds up now."

He cupped his head in his hands. "Your strange behavior with her Saturday night. The weird expression on your face when you see me with her. And the way you're always watching her."

Michael lunged forward, his face close to Jake's, and demanded an answer. "Is it her, Jake? Is it *her*?"

"Yes," Jake answered calmly.

Michael closed his eyes. "You son-of-a-bitch." His eyes opened with a cold glare of disgust. "Why her? You're a bigger pig than me."

"You can say that after you tried to rape her yesterday?" Jake retorted, his nose close to Michael's.

Brett's green eyes popped open along with his jaw and he dropped the flowered bag. Michael seized the opportunity and punched Jake as hard as he could in the stomach. Jake's body violently folded and he knocked over a chair. Lucille ran into the room to see her eldest son on one knee trying to recover.

"What the devil is going on here?" she shouted, and rushed to Jake's side.

"I'll tell you what's going on," Michael heatedly said. "Your precious little Jake here is screwing Cheryl."

Lucille's mouth fell open. "*Your* Cheryl?"

"Yes *My* Cheryl."

"Oh, my God, Jake, is this true?" He didn't react for a moment, then pressed his lips together and silently nodded to his mother. She slowly backed away from him and wilted into a chair. Her face was white when Brett rushed to her side and put his arm around her. Lucille then looked up at Jake, who now stood hunched over. "Does Susan know?"

"No," Jake answered.

"All the wedding plans! Jake, you still want to marry her, right?" Lucille asked.

Jake didn't say anything. Motionless, he stared ahead at the couch in front of him. Lucille composed herself. "Jake, you've been with Susan for over four years. Are you willing to throw that all away? No one has to know besides your brothers and me about what happened."

"And what about Cheryl?" He turned to her. "She'll know."

"If she says anything we will all deny it ever happened," Lucille answered swiftly. "It will be her word against ours. I doubt she would want it out about you and her. It would ruin her reputation." One of the nurses walked through the room and Lucille went silent. When the nurse was far enough away, Lucille finally ended the conversation, stating, "You'd be a fool to leave Susan. She's the best thing that ever happened to you."

Jake didn't answer. Michael listened with his back to the group. *He's in love with her. I can tell by the way he's acting. Oh, Jakey boy, marry the one your mommy wants you to. And after you do, it will kill you every time you see me with the one you love. That will make you pay, and I'm going to make her pay. Oh, yeah, she's going to pay.* Michael walked away from the group and started down the hall.

"Where are you going?" Lucille called after him.

"Home to take a shower," he yelled back. "I'll be back later."

CHERYL DROVE BACK from the field where David was planting winter wheat. She brought lunch to him and returned soon after he'd finished eating. Driving her truck around the barn, she gasped and slammed on her brakes seeing Michael's red truck parked in front of the house. He was sitting on a chair on the front porch in the sun, with his boots propped up on the rail. His cowboy hat covered his face and he looked to be asleep. Cheryl drove a little closer and parked her truck by the shed then carefully tiptoed past him into the house. She went directly to a drawer in the kitchen and took out a knife and stuck it in her cowboy boot. Walking back out to the porch, she pushed his feet down with her knee and he almost fell out of the chair.

"What the hell did you do that for?" he asked, blinking up at her.

"You're trespassing. Get off my farm!" she snapped.

"You mean the future Cameron farm," he said, looking around.

"What are you talking about?" Cheryl asked, annoyed.

"When someone puts the bug in Mr. Vander's ear about what a high risk you are for a loan, maybe I'll take it off your hands." He leaned back in his chair stretching out his arms, then folded them behind his head.

"Jake won't let you cause trouble for me."

A dangerous smile came over his face. "Oh yeah, speaking of my brother, how was he? Has he been screwing you good?"

Cheryl looked away, feeling her face flush.

"I guess he needed to have a little fun before he marries Susan. He told Brett and me you were a good piece of ass, and he hopes you won't think it was anything serious. He certainly doesn't."

His words stung, but she pretended they didn't and stared him in the face.

"Oh, and a couple more things. I'm going to make sure Susan knows *all* about you and Jake. He won't be able to have anything to do with you. Knowing Susan, *she* may convince all the banks in the area not to give you a loan." He paused, shaking his head at her. "Did you really think Jake would give up a woman like Susan Petrich *for you*?"

He laughed nastily. "Well, you have a good day now, Mrs.

Langtree." He stood and casually walked off her porch. Looking back at her, he winked and tipped his hat.

THE ROOM WAS STILL when Jake looked in to see his mother sleeping on the cot next to his dad's bed. As quietly as possible, he went over to the other side of Chet's bed and got down on his knees.

"Wake up Dad, please," he whispered. "I need you. I don't know what to do. I keep thinking about you and that crazy horse. I overheard when you were talking to him. The weird part about it is, I think I'm like that horse. All cooped up and belonging to someone who doesn't understand or appreciate me."

He sighed heavily.

"I've been with her for a long time and I hate to let her down. But I feel like I've been sleeping and now I woke up. The trouble is, I woke up in a dream with an angel that could tear our family apart. Dad, wake up, and tell me what I should do." Jake bowed his head. "If you can't wake up, find a way to show me what to do."

He felt a tear roll down his cheek. Wiping his eyes, he went back out to the waiting room where he was spending the night and sat on the couch.

Two attendants wheeled another patient past him into a room. A nurse went in behind them and soon another followed. A few minutes later, one nurse stepped out, but didn't get far when her colleague came out of the room and asked for a roll of surgical tape.

"Here you go." She tossed the roll to her co-worker who reached forward to catch it with both hands.

Suddenly Jake thought about the way the nurse caught the tape. His mind went back to the bazaar. He remembered seeing Susan through the large glass window shortly after she'd left the fellowship hall. She had bent over the same way. He thought about it for a few minutes, then his heart started to pump hard as his mind went over the time frame.

There had to be someone else in the fellowship hall who left before Susan did, because I heard the door slam. It must have been those Jenson twins, because where else would they have gotten the hot coffee to put on the dog? So ... she had to have seen and likely heard them and didn't do anything to stop it. When she went outside, I saw her bend over like the nurse. And she caught something.

Oh, my God. It was Taylor's ball. She was the woman the boy said caught his ball. He got punished for something she did.

Jake tossed and turned on the couch most of the night while disturbing thoughts about Susan played over and over in his head. *Why did she have Milt fired? Did it make her feel superior to mess up people's lives with no remorse?*

He fell asleep close to dawn and was awakened by an attendant with a squeaky cart around six a.m. He sat up on the couch and found his mother sitting across from him. Her dark eyes stared at him from a tear-stained face, but she didn't make a noise.

"Jake, I'm scared." Her voice quivered as she whispered, "What am I going to do if he doesn't wake up? How will I be able to go on without him? He's my whole world."

He got up and sat down next to her with his arm around her. "We're going to get through this together, Mom," he said trying to convince himself, too.

"I don't know about that. Who knows if our family is going to stay together now that you and Michael are fighting? Your dad and I always had a dream that someday you boys would run our farm together. The sad part about it is, someday may be here right now, and you have hurt Michael so badly I'm scared he won't have anything to do with you." She was quiet for a moment while her eyes searched his face. "You had to have known how much that girl meant to your brother. And it's not just Michael you're hurting here. What about Susan?"

"Our family is going through a rough patch right now. But give it time, everything will be okay. We'll always be together, no matter what." Strangely, he believed that.

She released a deep breath. "You don't know how happy that makes me to hear you say that," Lucille said, with a huge smile. "What a relief to know the wedding is back on!"

Jake silently stared down the hall in the direction where the nurses had exchanged the tape. It was neither the time nor the place to tell his mother what he suspected the bride-to-be had done.

16

"Don't You Love Her Madly" played on the radio as Jim drove his car up the hill and parked. Looking down at Cheryl's farm, he shook his head then reached in the cooler on the back seat and got out two beers.

Handing one to Michael, he said, "I just can't believe the Ice Queen and your brother. Wow. I didn't see that coming. I've seen that spicy dish he's engaged to. Forget Superman. This guy's my new hero."

"Knock it off. As far as I'm concerned, he's a snake in the grass," Michael said, annoyed.

Jim let out a laugh. "'Jake the Snake.' It fits." Jim's laughter escalated. Michael didn't even smile, so he brought it back to a serious tone. "Okay, so it's over. Now you'll have to go on and find someone else. I got a great idea. Let's head downtown and pick up those Mason sisters."

"It's not over," Michael answered. "Sure, it pisses me off more than anything that my brother did her first, but it's far from over."

"What are you going to do?" Jim wrinkled his forehead.

Michael took a sip of his beer. "I think Jake's in love with her, but if I know my mother, she'll talk him into marrying Susan.

Just like she did with Diana and me, when we wanted to go to Europe. When my brother realizes he should've married Cheryl, it will be too late. He'll be married to Susan and Cheryl will be mine."

Jim flinched. "You still want her after what happened? How are you going to convince her to be with you?"

Michael let out a sinister laugh. "When I'm done with her, I'm going to bring her to her knees and she'll be such a mess, she'll crawl to me and beg me to take her. Her and that farm." He pointed down the hill. "They'll both be mine to do whatever I please with."

"Sounds like you have it all figured out." Jim started his car. "Good luck with that, buddy."

BRETT SAT at the kitchen table and waited for another pancake. Irene came over with the frying pan and flipped one on his plate then one on hers. She sat down across from him at the table and cut up her sausage.

"So how are you doing with everything that's going on with your dad?" she asked.

Brett had his mouth full and shrugged his shoulders, then swallowed. "There's nothing anyone can do until Dad wakes up." He took a breath. "If he … wakes up."

"I've seen your Dad in many tough situations and he has always managed to get through them." Irene patted his hand. "He's one tough cookie."

Brett nodded slowly and took a drink of his orange juice.

"How are your brothers handling this?"

"Them two, they've got a mess on their hands," Brett stated.

"Why do you say that?"

Brett told her about the situation with Jake and Michael, and Irene put her hand to her mouth.

"Your poor mother. Everything with your Dad, and now this."

"Jake seems to be indecisive and Mom wants him to marry Susan," Brett told her, then added, "Just between you and me, I wouldn't marry her for all the money in the world."

A small smile came over Irene's lips and she quickly covered her mouth again.

Brett pointed at her and grinned. "You agree with me, don't you?" He stood, still smiling, and walked around the table. He put his arms around her and gave Irene a hug followed by a kiss on the cheek. "That's why I love you so much, old woman. You and I always see things the same. I better get to the hospital. Mom will be wondering where I am. The doctor wants to talk to all of us this afternoon and she wants to come home and get cleaned up before." He headed to the door then yelled back as he went out, "Thanks for breakfast!"

IT WAS AROUND four o'clock when Lucille and Brett returned to the hospital. Jake was in Chet's room and Michael was in the waiting room reading a magazine. Brett went in to see his father and Lucille sat down next to Michael.

"Did you go in there and sit with your Dad?" she asked.

Michael nodded.

"Put the magazine down. I think we need to talk before one of them comes back in here," Lucille whispered, glancing toward Chet's room. "I know you must be crushed with everything that's going on with Jake and Cheryl."

He nodded again with raised brows.

She continued, "But I know your brother. He's very level-headed, and when all is said and done, he'll marry Susan. But I think *you* need to forget all about Cheryl and find someone new. She obviously is a loose woman, or she would've never have gotten your brother into this mess."

"She isn't like that," Michael answered. "You don't think he may have manipulated her some? Maybe he got her drunk and took advantage of her being lonely? Don't for one second blame just her. As far as I'm concerned, they're both guilty."

Lucille sighed. "Jake is your brother and she's just a pretty girl amongst all the pretty girls you've been involved with. He should matter more, and you should forgive him."

Michael's eyes flashed. "Yeah, it should have mattered to him when he was doing the woman he knows I'm in love with. And, I'm letting you know Mother, I'm still going to be with her."

Jake and Brett came out of the room as Michael finished the end of his last sentence. Jake's eyes met Michael's and they stared each other down with undeniable disgust. Just then, the doctor arrived and asked everyone to take a seat. A few minutes into the conversation, he told the family that if Chet didn't wake up soon, they had to consider the possibility he might not. He also reminded them that a head injury such as Chet's could also include some degree of brain damage.

Not long after the doctor left, they all agreed hospital rules could be broken and moved two extra chairs into Chet's room so they could all be in there at once.

The sun dipped behind the trees when Lucille walked to the window and opened the blinds enough to see out. The sunset only reinforced her sinking feeling. A reminder to her that another day was over and her husband still hadn't awakened. Helplessness took over, and she started to cry. Michael went to his mother and draped his arm around her. After a few moments, her tears stopped and she dabbed her eyes with a white handkerchief, elegantly embroidered with the letters L.C., then turned to her sons.

"I want that beast of a horse destroyed." Her voice was stern. "I want you boys to promise me that animal will not be on our farm when I come home tomorrow. I don't care which one of you does it, I want that animal shot." The room went silent and a few glances were exchanged after she made her demand.

"Don't … shoot … my horse," a soft voice said.

Everyone looked at each other and Brett shouted, "Dad!" He leaped to Chet's side while his father tried to open his eyes.

"Chet! Oh, my God, Chet," Lucille cried as she rushed over and carefully wrapped her arms around him.

Tears sprang to Jake's eyes as he looked up at the ceiling. *Thank you, God!*

Michael hung back, then came closer to his Dad and hugged him. A nurse poked her head into the room and saw Chet had awakened.

"Call Dr. Steiner. Mr. Cameron is awake!" she shouted at another nurse.

Soon the doctor came in the room and asked the family to step back so he could examine Chet.

"How are you feeling, Mr. Cameron?" Doctor Steiner shined a light from a small flashlight into his eyes. Chet winced at the light.

"Other than my leg feeling like it's been twisted into a pretzel and my head pounding like I was in the liquor cabinet way too long, just fine." A low roar of laughter erupted from his sons.

"Do you remember falling off your horse?" the doctor asked. Chet was quiet for a second.

"Yes, I do. It was my own fault, too. I was looking down at the horse and I led him a little too close to a tree. I didn't see that low branch and then all I saw was stars." He frowned. "I must have broken my leg when I fell?"

"Unfortunately, yes, you did break your leg," the doctor answered. "We set it and in about eight to ten weeks, it should be healed. But that isn't our main concern. It's the bump on your head. Can you tell us what day is your birthday?"

"June 29th, 1920," Chet quickly answered. "I was born in the morning around seven- thirty. According to my mother, I was the best-looking baby of all her four sons." Again, the boys laughed while Lucille smiled and shook her head with her arms crossed.

"I think you're going to be just fine," the doctor stated. "But you're going to need to stay here with us for a couple of days so we can keep an eye on you." Dr. Steiner left the room, chuckling with a smile.

"What happened to the horse? Did he run off?" Chet asked Brett.

"No, Dad. He stayed right by you. When I found you, he was nudging at you trying to get you to wake up."

"Well, I'll be damned. I rescued him. Who knew he would try and return the favor?" Chet smiled.

WEDNESDAY EVENING, the sun was setting but it wasn't visible from Chet's new room on the east side of the hospital. He had been moved out of intensive care into a regular room. Jake sat next to the bed and watched his father's face reflect pain from his leg when he tried to sit up straight.

Jake jumped up. "Dad, let me help you do that." He came closer and moved the lever on the bed.

Chet frowned at him. "You're worse than your mother, fussing over me."

Jake smiled. *He'll be all right. He seems to be back to himself.*

"That's why I sent her home," Chet told him. "That, and I think she needs a night of sleeping in our own bed. Poor thing looked pretty worn out."

Jake nodded.

Chet paused. "It's Wednesday, isn't it?"

"Yeah, Dad, it's Wednesday evening."

"I can't believe I've been in here since Sunday afternoon." Chet shook his head. "The mind sure can play tricks on you."

"Especially when you have a bump on your head the size of yours," Jake remarked.

Chet furrowed his brow. "I had the strangest dream that you

were asking me advice about women, and then you said something about an angel on a horse. Crazy, huh?"

Jake answered after a moment, "I really didn't want to say anything until you got home, but things have changed. And in some ways, not for the best."

"Get to the point, son. What's going on?" Chet frowned.

Jake told him everything except the intimate details of being with Cheryl.

Chet was quiet for a moment. "Your brother really tried to rape her?" His voice was deadly serious.

Jake slowly nodded.

His father quickly turned to the edge of the bed, but his leg reminded him to stay put. He turned to Jake with a pained expression, "When I get out of here I'm going to shove my good foot up his ass."

"Dad, you're not going to be able to do it for a while."

"What are you going to do about the beehive you've stirred up?"

"I don't know, Dad. I'm so mixed up right now. I don't know what to do. Either way, someone is going to get hurt, and what's it going to do to our family? I should've thought it out beforehand. I know it's a poor excuse, but it was like I couldn't help myself."

"The only thing I can tell you is that whatever you do, you'll have to live with it for the rest of your life."

CHERYL HAD BEEN UP MOST of the night crying on the telephone with Dori. At the end of their long conversation, they reached a conclusion: Now that Chet had awakened, there could only be one explanation why Jake hadn't tried to get in touch: He was going to be with Susan.

Neither woman wanted to believe Michael's story, but the evidence was clear. *Jake must have told Michael about them. How*

else would Michael have known so quickly that they'd been together?
Was it possible Jake used women like his brother but managed to keep it
a secret? Or was she the only fool?

She pulled into the church parking lot and scanned it for
Lucille's car, but not seeing it meant nothing — the woman was
always late. Dori had convinced Cheryl to attend the quilting
session and act like nothing had happened. If Lucille knew about
them, she likely wouldn't acknowledge it to the women and
tarnish her son's reputation. No matter what the outcome, life
would go on. *I need to lose myself in something … I need to quilt.*

Cheryl could smell the fresh coffee and the aroma from some
sort of hot dish as she walked down the church basement steps.
Alma, always the delightful hostess, greeted her with a nice hug.
The women were seated around a table waiting for everyone to
join them.

"I'm afraid our group is going to be small today," Joan said.
"Of course, Lucille won't be here and Patsy is out of town for a
meeting. Gert is home sick with a cold and Sophie's son is here
from Mankato."

"I guess we can serve lunch now, since the remaining six of
us are here." Nell got up to help Alma get the food on the table.
Once lunch was served, the group talked while they ate.

"The way it's sounds, Chet is going to be okay," Nell said.
"Thank God."

Everyone at the table agreed with a nod or a "Yes."

"If he wouldn't have been okay, Lucille would've had her
hands full with them boys," Mary stated.

"What do you mean by that, Mary?" Nell took the bait.

Mary sighed. "You know I don't like to gossip, but …"

Yes, you do, Cheryl thought.

"Mom, I told you not to bring that up," Joan snapped.

"What's that?" Nell's curiosity started to boil.

"I may as well tell you all, but please don't say I said it." All
eyes were on Mary as she continued, "You all know Erma
Bensfield?"

Everyone nodded except for Cheryl.

"Well, her daughter-in-law, Sharon, is a nurse at the hospital in the intensive care unit. She said while Chet was in the hospital, things got heated up between the older two boys, Michael and Jake."

"During a crisis, that can happen." Nell shrugged her shoulders.

"Yes, it can, but it wasn't about their father," Joan joined in. "Those two were in an argument about a woman. It's seems Jake, the older one, who is engaged, must have been with the woman the younger one, Michael, is interested in."

Cheryl felt her heartbeat quicken and she told herself, *Relax. Don't freak out. Take a breath.*

Nell's eyes got big. "I wonder if Lucille knows about this?"

"She does. Sharon said when the fists were flying, Lucille went in and broke it up," Joan answered. "After she calmed them both down, she convinced the older one to stay with his fiancée and forget about this gal."

Feeling the need to get away from the circle, Cheryl stood and started to clean up. In the kitchen, she could still hear the conversation through the open partition that was now completed. She stuck her hands into the hot, steamy dishwater and felt a tear run down her cheek then wiped it away with her wrist. With her back to the women, Cheryl held her breath but continued to listen.

"Who do you think the woman was those boys were fighting over?" Nell mused.

"Sharon didn't hear her name clearly but she thought they said Carol. Apparently, she must not be from the area," Joan answered.

Cheryl released a breath of relief learning the nurse didn't hear her name correctly. The rest of the afternoon she worked on the quilt but didn't say much.

On the way home, Cheryl told herself for the hundredth time to forget about Jake. When her eyes filled with tears, she was forced to pull her truck over to the side of the road. She rested her forehead on the steering wheel and wept. Now it was confirmed. What Michael had said about Jake was true. He was going to marry Susan.

AT THREE-THIRTY, Cheryl heard the bus pull away while she sat at the kitchen table peeling carrots for supper.

Taylor let the screen door slam as he came in.

She looked up and smiled. "How was your day, sweetie?"

"Good. We got to go outside and look for caterpillars and other bugs. We used stick pins and stabbed them on a board." Cheryl grimaced, but Taylor elaborated, "Some of the girls didn't like it and I let my caterpillar go before the teacher could poke him."

"It sounds like you had an interesting day. Why don't you change your clothes, then you and I can finish cleaning out the garden this afternoon."

Taylor went into his room to change. Cheryl went back to the carrots when she heard a vehicle in the driveway. Her heart did a complete flip when she pulled back the kitchen curtain and saw Jake's truck parked in front of the house. She quickly untied her apron and threw it over a chair. Glancing at her reflection in the side of the toaster, she smoothed her hair back on the sides of her head and down the length of her long braid. He knocked on the frame of the screen door, but before turning to answer the door, she unbuttoned the top button on her blouse.

"Hi." She felt shy with his eyes on her.

"Hi, how are you?" But before she could answer, he asked, "Is your boy home?"

She stared at him. "Yeah, why?"

"I need to talk to him."

"About what?"

"I need to talk to him about something I have to know. It's important to me. Can you trust me and let me talk to him?"

"Just like I trusted you, and then you told Michael and Brett all about us?" she fired back.

His eyes narrowed and he tilted his head. "What are you talking about?"

"Michael was here. He said you told him what a good piece of ass I was, and how you hoped I wouldn't think it was anything serious." She tried to keep her injured emotions out of her words.

"That guy is unbelievable," Jake said and shook his head. "I never told him anything. That asshole figured it out when he overheard Pastor Timms talk to me at the hospital. Oh, yeah, just so you know, the good pastor saw us that night at the fellowship hall."

Cheryl gasped with her hand to her mouth, horrified.

"Michael just put two and two together and confronted me. Then he comes over here with a pack of lies to tell you. Now that you know the truth, are you going to let me talk to your boy?"

Cheryl nodded slowly. She wanted desperately to ask him what his feelings were toward her but didn't want to face what he might say. "Taylor, could you come here?" she called.

Taylor came to the door and stood next to her.

"Would you come out here on the porch so we can talk, buddy?" Jake asked.

Taylor looked up at his mother.

"It's okay, honey," Cheryl assured him. "He just wants to talk to you about something. I'll be right in here if you need me."

The boy slowly opened the screen door and stepped out onto the porch. Cheryl moved back from the door but stayed close enough to see and hear them.

"Come over here, Taylor, and let's sit down," Jake told him.

Taylor gingerly sat down on one of the porch chairs and Jake sat down on the chair next to him.

"So, have you caught any more toads lately?"

Taylor shook his head no.

"If I asked you something, could you be completely honest and tell me the truth?"

"Yeah, I guess."

"Do you remember the bazaar a while ago when you said a lady had taken your ball and threw it in the direction of the Jenson twins and the dog?"

Taylor looked down and answered slowly, "Yes sir. But no one believes me about the lady."

"I believe you."

Taylor's head shot back up and his blue eyes got wide. "You do?"

"Yes, I certainly do. But what I want to know is what the lady looked like? What color hair did she have? What was she wearing?" Jake asked.

Why would he care? Cheryl thought.

"She had brown hair. I don't remember what she was wearing."

Jake hesitated for a second. "Did she have on a necklace?"

Taylor's face lit up. "Yes, she did," he exclaimed. "It was a butterfly that sparkled real pretty!"

Jake stood up and took out his wallet. He removed a picture and showed it to Taylor. "Is this her?"

Cheryl couldn't make out the image from inside the house. *Where would he get a picture of the woman? Unless he knows her somehow.* It took a moment for the notion to sink in. It was *her!* Susan was the dark-haired woman who threw Taylor's ball!

Taylor looked at the picture. "That's her. That's the lady who took my ball. She pointed to my mom and asked if she was my mother, then she took my ball."

Jake studied Taylor's blue eyes. "You're absolutely positive that's her?"

"Yes, sir," Taylor answered, and nodded with a big smile.

"That's all I need to know. Thank you, Taylor. Say goodbye to your mother for me."

Why can't he say goodbye himself? I can tell by the way he's acting, he's going back to that evil woman. I hope you get everything you deserve, Jake Cameron.

He glanced a couple of times in the direction of the screen door but he walked over to his truck. He opened the door and paused for a moment, then got in his truck and drove away.

MICHAEL CAME DOWNSTAIRS HEARING his mother's joyous voice from the kitchen in a conversation with Brett and Irene. She stopped in the middle of her sentence when Michael entered the room.

"Good morning," she told him with a wide smile. Lucille looked nothing short of radiant, dressed in a red pantsuit with a red and white print silk blouse.

He nodded and walked over to the cupboard and took out a cup. He filled the cup with coffee and sat down next to Brett at the table.

"As I was telling your brother, you and he are going to have to do chores this morning yourselves. Irene said Jake left early this morning for Minneapolis."

She took a deep breath that ended with a pleased smile. "It's such a relief to see things are back to normal for him and Susan. Well, I better get going to the hospital. Have a nice day, you two. I'll call you later, Irene." Lucille grabbed her purse and left with a bounce in her step. Irene took Lucille's coffee cup stamped with red lipstick to the other side of the kitchen and put it in the sink.

"I suppose that news makes you happy, doesn't it?" Brett asked Michael.

Michael blinked his eyes innocently at him and then towards Irene. "Whatever do you mean?"

Brett stared at him. "Don't act stupid. You know what I'm talking about. Jake and Susan together. Now you think there's nothing standing in your way. The thing I can't understand is, why you can't leave Cheryl alone?"

Michael took another swallow of his coffee and asked in a low voice, "Why? So, you can have her and that farm? I'm not going to let that happen. And as for her, she's going to get what she's got coming."

Brett closed his eyes briefly and shook his head. "Okay. You win. I'll give you the money for the bet and declare you the winner if that's what it takes for you to stop harassing her."

"You think it's just about the hundred dollars?" He chuckled. "This winner's going to be your next-door neighbor."

Michael whistled all the way to the barn when they went outside to do chores. Driving out to the pasture with a load of feed for the cattle, he smiled at himself in the side mirror of the old truck. The second the chores were done, Michael didn't waste any time. He put the keys to the farm truck back on the hook in the shed and started for the house.

"Where are you going?" Brett called after him.

"To take a shower. It's Friday, and I feel like doing a little celebrating."

Brett looked at his wristwatch. "It's nine-thirty in the morning."

"I'm taking the rest of the day off," Michael replied. He stopped and turned toward Brett then looked around. "I don't see anyone around here who's going to stop me."

17

J ake knocked on Susan's apartment door and heard her call from inside, "Who is it?"

"It's Jake."

She flung the door open. "Jake, what are you doing here?" Her hair was wrapped in a towel and she wore a white robe. "It's not even seven-thirty. Oh, my God, you must have left your house before five a.m. to be here now. Don't just stand there, come on in."

She reached for his hand and pulled him into her apartment. He came in quietly and she shut the door behind him. Then standing on her tiptoes, she pressed her lips to his to give him a quick kiss. She looked down at her robe. "I must look a fright. Let me get presentable."

She went into the bathroom and talked to him from in there. "Wow, this is a surprise. I wish you would've called because I have a meeting at nine. But maybe I could squeeze you in at one." He didn't say anything. "By the way, how's your Dad? I would have called, but I've been busy."

"He woke up Tuesday night," Jake told her and sat down on the couch. "I called but I couldn't get you."

"I'm so happy he woke up, and I'm sorry I wasn't here to

take your call. I've been *so* busy at work, and planning a wedding does take a little time, too, you know."

"Did you ever talk to Melody about standing up with Brett?"

"I'm afraid she just can't," she said flatly. "The Tribune is sending her out on location the whole week of the wedding. She just can't be everywhere, I guess. She told me she's hoping to get off a few hours to attend the reception."

"Do you really expect me to believe that?"

Susan came out of the bathroom with her makeup on and her hair in rollers. She looked at him with a blank expression and asked, "What? Why would you doubt it?"

"Sit down and talk for a minute."

She glanced up at the clock on the wall but sat down on the couch next to him.

"Remember that day at my church bazaar?"

"Yeah, what about it?"

"Did you see my brothers fighting?"

She let out a breath. "I told you, I didn't see a thing. I left the fellowship hall then immediately went to the parking lot and sat in your truck. What difference does it make if I did?"

He watched her eyes and continued, "I looked out the window when I was working on the stove and saw you bending over for something. What was that?"

Susan tapped her lips with her finger and paused like she was trying to recall. "Oh, I remember now. I took a small rock out of my sandal. I told you they really need to tar that parking lot. Why the inquisition about the bazaar?"

"You don't remember overhearing those two little monsters plotting anything, or throwing a boy's ball?"

She shook her head, then asked, "What are you talking about? I never overheard anything, and as far as throwing a ball, you know I don't play baseball."

"How did you know it was a baseball I was talking about?" He stared at her.

She gave me a dirty look. "I just assumed it was a baseball.

I'm done talking about this subject. It has nothing to do with me." She started to get up, but he grabbed her elbow.

"I'm not done with this subject. Sit down."

Her eyes got big but she sat down on the couch.

"My mother said she saw you going to my truck *after* the fight had broken out. And about that little boy, he identified you as the person who threw his ball toward the twins and the dog."

"So maybe I could have been wrong about my timing with the fight. But who are you going to believe about the ball? Me, or that little brat?" Her chest heaved with each breath.

"I believe Taylor," Jake said in an unrelenting voice.

"You know his name?" She stared.

"Yes, he's Cheryl's kid. But you knew that, didn't you? You asked him." She pressed her lips together and looked away.

"My question for you is: Why did you do it? Why didn't you stop those kids and why did you feel you needed to get Cheryl's boy involved?"

Her face flushed red when she looked at him. "Because I saw the way you couldn't keep your eyes off her. And I was right to think the way I did. I didn't answer the phone the other night because I knew it was you, and I was way too angry to talk to you. Michael called and told me all about you and the little country whore!"

"She's not a whore!"

Susan leaned her face closer to his. "Then what do you call a woman who chases after a man when he's promised to another?"

"She didn't chase me. It just happened between us."

"It just *happened*?" Her eyes flashed. "It just happened, Jake. I thought we meant more to each other than 'it just happened.' I forbid you to ever have anything to do with her again. And if Michael marries her, we are not going to have anything to do with those two!"

"I'm sorry ...." Jake took a deep breath as he stared into her eyes. His words came easier than he ever imagined. "Susan, I can't marry you."

Her eyes popped and her mouth fell open in disbelief. "What are you saying?" she slowly asked. "You want to be with *her*?" Her voice was loud as she shouted, "A couple nights in the sack with her and you're willing to forget about four years with *me*?"

"You know it's about more than sex. I can't handle how you mess with peoples' lives and you think nothing of it. I know it was you who got Milt fired from the restaurant."

Susan flinched but continued to glare at him.

"And let's not forget about your lies and deception," he continued. "But most of all, it hurts me that you don't take any interest in anything I do. And you sure as hell don't care what I want." Tears blurred his vision.

"Oh, yeah, and you believe she does? Other than you both being farmers and not being able to control your sexual desires, I can't think of a thing you two have in common." Susan was nearly spitting in her rage. "And let's talk about *her* integrity. Pretending to be interested in Michael, and the whole time trying to get you away from me. How can an uneducated, unsophisticated, lying little farm girl be better than *me*?"

He was quiet, then softly answered. "I guess I didn't realize it until now, but it's ..." He let it sink in for a second. "Because I love her."

She bent her head and started to cry. Her hands came together as she struggled to get the ring off her finger. Looking up, she threw it at him. "Your mother will never be happy about this, and your brother is going to hate you. And I ... will *never* forgive you. Get out of here, you country bumpkin," she sobbed. "You're making me late for work."

Reaching down, he picked up the ring and put it in his pocket. He set his key to her apartment on the end table and left.

THE SUN REFLECTED off the pool into Jim's apartment and made it feel like July instead of September. Michael sat on the patio and watched two girls who looked to be about college age sun bathe by the pool. Jim brought out an ice bucket and set it next to the empty quart of vodka on the floor.

"Man, I can't believe we've polished that off already," he said, and smiled at Michael. "But have no fear." He held up another quart of vodka in his hand. "I'll be right back with some more orange juice." Jim went back into the apartment and returned with a pitcher. He tossed a few ice cubes into both of their tall glasses and twisted the cap off the vodka bottle. He filled the glasses over half full with the clear liquid then topped them off with a splash of juice. He set the drinks on a small table between him and Michael then sat down on a lawn chair.

"So, your old man is going to be all right, huh?" Jim asked.

Michael was lying in a reclining lawn chair with his hands folded behind his head.

"Yeah, but he'll be out of commission for a while. He seems to be himself, but you know how he puts on a brave face."

"And your brother's back with Liz Taylor?"

"Yep, he went to Minneapolis early this morning," Michael said and reached for his glass. "I'm sure she's going to rip him a new asshole. I'd love to be a mouse in the corner to see that." Jim raised his glass to Michael's in a toast, which ended with them both taking a big swallow from their drinks.

"So, you got the green light then, on the Ice Queen?" Jim asked.

"I don't even want to talk about her. I'm really looking forward to paying her back soon, but not today. I just want to sit back, relax with a few drinks, and enjoy this beautiful day. Be happy my brother has come to his senses, and my father is going to be okay."

"Well, I do say, I'm impressed with this new attitude. I would have thought knowing your brother went back to his fiancée, you would want to rub Queenie's face in it."

"I haven't figured out the perfect way to tell her yet, but I'm sure something is bound to *come up*," Michael said, then laughed. Jim playfully punched Michael's shoulder then joined him in laughter.

THE VET STOOD up on his feet and gazed down at the cow lying on its side on the ground. He turned to Cheryl and David. "If I were you, I'd ship her while she's still alive. If I treat her, you can't sell or eat an animal with antibiotics in their system. But I really don't think she'll make it either way."

Cheryl rose from the ground and brushed the grass off her jeans then sadly looked to David.

"As soon as we're done with chores, I'll haul her in," he told her.

"No, I'll finish chores," she answered. "I don't want to take the chance of her dying before we can ship her." Both men nodded in agreement and the vet left shortly after he got paid.

With some prodding, they got the cow on her feet and loaded her into the cattle trailer. David waved to Cheryl as he drove out of the yard bound for the sales barn in Montevideo. She smiled and waved back feeling grateful for her hired hand, then continued to do chores.

In the chicken coop, she fed and watered the chickens, then began to pick the eggs. She made her way down each side of the small building and checked for eggs in the laying boxes then carefully placed them in a wire basket. She backed her way out of the coop and faced the door when she hooked it shut. Turning around to go to the house, Cheryl froze in her tracks. Michael's truck was parked in the middle of her driveway. He was leaning against the fender with his arms crossed while he watched her. When he stepped forward and staggered slightly, her heart hammered harder in her chest.

"What are you doing here?" she managed to ask when he was a few feet away.

"Just wondering if you have time to do a little visiting with a neighbor?" he answered with a provocative smile.

"Well, actually, David is waiting for me in the barn. He wants me to help him. If I don't get down there soon, he'll be up here looking for me."

He looked over to David's old red truck parked in the yard and stated, "Wow, that guy is really something."

"What do you mean?" She faked a smile.

"He must be some kind of magician or something, because I just saw him pull out of here a few minutes ago with a cattle trailer."

She took a deep breath then let it out. "I take it you were watching us from up on the hill?"

He nodded.

Letting her anger fuel her courage, she asked, "Look, I'm kinda busy. What do you want?"

He stepped closer and rubbed his fingers under her chin. "You know what I want, and this time I'm going to get it."

Cheryl could see his eyes had that cruel, dangerous look she'd seen the previous Sunday. She stared into those eyes without blinking her own, then in one quick move she threw the egg basket at him. The eggs scattered, hitting him and the ground as she ran for the house. She only got a few feet when he got a hold of her thick braid. Instantly, she went down in the dirt on her knees.

He twisted her arm behind her back and she screamed out in pain, "Michael, you're hurting me. Let me go!"

He pulled her to her feet and pushed her the rest of the way to the house. Going up the two steps to the porch, her feet touched only one of them. When he reached to open the screen door she saw an opportunity to spin around and break free. She turned but he promptly pushed her against the doorframe. She could smell liquor on his breath when he put his face close to hers.

"Do us both a favor and stop fighting," he said.

She brought her knee up, but he turned his body just in time. His eyes got big.

"You little bitch. You wanna play rough, huh?" He turned her around and tightened his grip on her arm.

"You're going to break my arm!" she cried out, "Please, Michael. Stop!"

She started to cry, but he didn't let up on his firm hold and shoved her across the threshold. Once inside, he pushed her through the kitchen, knocking over a chair then continued to move her through the house. When they bumped into a small table in the hallway, the lamp on it wobbled then tipped over and crashed to the floor. The door to her bedroom was halfway open when he kicked it the rest of the way. His body was close as they fell together on the bed face down. She heard him undo his belt buckle and pull it through the loops of his jeans. He pushed himself up, but kept her arm pressed to her back with his knee while he looped the belt through the buckle and around her neck. Cheryl moaned when he released her arm and a burning sensation went through her shoulder. Her other hand went to her neck where she gripped the belt and tried to pull it away, but he held it tightly. He pulled on the belt and forced her to sit up close to him.

"This is an insurance policy to make sure you're not going to scratch me again. If I were you I wouldn't try anything stupid. All you're going to do is hurt yourself."

"I don't understand. Why are you doing this?" she shouted. "You can get anybody you want to have sex with you!"

She could feel his hot breath close to her ear as he said, "Listen to you. I think you answered your own question, but you're only partly right. Don't you know you're the only woman I ever wanted that I couldn't get into bed? I did everything but beg you, and then behind my back, you screwed my brother. Did you do him in here?" He looked around. "Or on the porch?"

She didn't answer, so he pulled the belt tighter, causing her to clench her teeth together.

He brought his warm mouth closer, touching her ear. "Do you know where he is right now, Cheryl?" She remained silent, staring straight ahead. "He's in Minneapolis, most likely making love to Susan right about now. You remember Susan, don't you? The love of his life? The woman he plans on making his wife? You ...." He chuckled. "You were just the easy piece of ass he knew he could get. You should have heard him talk about how he loved screwing the shit out of you."

"That's a lie, and you know it," she responded through gritted teeth. "He told me you figured it out and that's how you knew."

Michael's eyes went darker. "You were with him again?" She didn't answer so he slapped her face.

She gasped and cupped her cheek with her hand.

"Answer me. Were you with him again?" he shouted.

"No, he stopped here to talk to Taylor."

"He stopped here to talk to your boy? And you expect me to believe that?"

"It's true, I swear."

His eyes bored into hers. "I don't like getting lied to. What did he talk to Taylor about?"

"Something that happened at the bazaar."

He was quiet for a second before saying, "I don't believe you. I'm going to punish you even more for lying to me." He got up and pulled the belt down, which made her go to her knees. "Beg me to forgive you and then beg me to make love to you." Michael reached into his jeans and took out a large pocketknife and opened the blade.

Seeing the knife, Cheryl felt light headed. She swallowed and closed her eyes, *Oh God. He's going to kill me. Who's going to raise Taylor? I'm never going to see his blue eyes again. Taylor will be the one to find my body.* She started to pray in her mind. *Oh, God, please no!*

He shook his hand that held the belt. "Come on, say it." She tried to speak but choked and he lessened his grip on the belt. "Make it easier on yourself. Say it."

"Michael, please forgive me. Please m-make love to me." Tears began to pour down her cheeks. He smiled, then ripped her shirt open and put the knife up close to her heaving chest. She let out a scream when he cut her bra in the middle and it sprung to the sides of her breasts.

"Take your hair out of that braid," he ordered.

While she undid her braid, he set the knife down and ran his fingers through her hair. He pulled it apart making it fluffy on both sides of her head.

"I forbid you to ever cut it short."

He must have seen her frightened eyes dart toward the knife because he picked it up and slowly turned the sharp edge in her direction. "Now, take your boots and jeans off. While you're doing that, I want you to promise you'll never be with anyone else again, but me."

She took off her boots and jeans but didn't say anything.

He screamed, "Say it!" He poked her chest with the tip of the knife and she gasped.

"I promise I'll never be with anyone else but you." Her voice trembled and broke into a cry while her shoulders shook. He had a pleased look on his face. He enjoyed breaking her down.

"The sooner you realize you and this farm are going to belong to me, the better off we'll both be. But I'll be fair, and let you make the decision about what we're going to do about it after we make love."

She held back a sob long enough to ask, "What do you mean?"

"Here's the deal. You have two options. You can decide what you want, it's up to you." "If I'm forced to take you down, you will lose this farm. Or ..." He smiled. "We could get married. Either way, honey, I'll end up owning it."

"I'll never marry you!" she hissed.

"I know you love this farm. You'll change your mind." He adjusted his grip on the belt then used his body to push her down on the bed. Now on top of her, he covered her lips with his.

From out of nowhere, a hand grabbed Michael by his collar and pulled him back.

"What the hell are you doing?" Jake shouted.

Michael's mouth fell open and his eyes turned cold. "This doesn't concern you. This is between me and her. Get out of here."

Jake's eyes flashed. "You're raping her, and it doesn't concern me? You sick son-of-a-bitch. Are you drunk?"

Jake grabbed the wrist of Michael's hand that held the knife. Michael released the belt from around Cheryl's neck but managed to hang on to the knife. He didn't quite have his balance when he swung at his brother and missed. Jake punched him in the face and he fell sideways back on the bed, just missing Cheryl as she rolled out of the way.

Michael managed to spring up and snarled at Jake, lunging at him with the knife. "Why do you care what happens to her?"

Jake grabbed Michael's arm again and pushed him back against the dresser.

"Because what you're doing is wrong," Jake grunted back. "And ... I love her."

Hearing Jake say those words seemed to enrage Michael further, and gave him an apparent burst of strength to pull his arm free.

"I knew it all along," Michael screeched with a detectable cry in his voice. He pointed the knife at Jake who stepped back. "I should kill you. Better yet," he reached out and grabbed Cheryl by the hair and pulled her to him. She screamed when he put the knife to her throat.

"If I can't have her, neither will you."

Jake's eyes got huge and he quickly blurted, "Michael, don't do this. This isn't what you want to do. Let her go," he pleaded. "Tomorrow, things will look different. Go home and sleep this off."

Eyeing Jake closely, he asked, "Why did you have to step into her world? You knew I loved her and yet you had to have her anyway. You already have the woman most guys would kill for. Can't you let me have this one?"

"Susan and I are no longer together," Jake said. "And what happened with her," he nodded at Cheryl, "I didn't plan it. I swear. I didn't mean to hurt you and I don't believe she did either. Let her go. She has a little boy to raise," he pleaded. Cheryl stood completely still, barely breathing, eyes wide with terror. "The kid will be an orphan and you'll be sitting in jail with that on your conscience for the rest of your life. You don't want that, and I don't want that for you. Let her go and none of us will ever mention this ugly mess."

Still holding the knife to Cheryl's throat, Michael stared at his brother for what seemed to be eternity. "If I let her go, do you promise me you won't tell Mom and Dad or anyone else?"

"Yes, Michael. I give you my word."

Michael shook his hand that gripped Cheryl's hair and she winced in pain. He turned her head to face him and clenched his teeth. "If you tell *anyone*, I will come back and finish this. I promise you." He took the knife away from her throat and pushed her towards Jake. "Here. Take your little whore. And just you wait. She'll break your heart, too." Michael closed his knife and shoved it into his jean pocket. He started to walk out of the room when Jake jumped in front of him.

Grabbing Michael's collar, Jake pulled him close to his face. "Just so you understand, Michael. If you ever touch her again, I will kill you." His voice was deadly serious.

Both brothers glared at each other for a moment before

Michael pulled away. He took a few steps toward the door then punched a hole in the wall next to the doorframe on his way out.

Cheryl gasped and Jake pulled her shaking body into his arms. The screen door slammed and soon after they heard Michael's truck pull out of the driveway, spraying gravel in its wake.

Jake gently pulled Cheryl to him and sat on the bed where he continued to hold her. She clung to him and sobbed while his hands lovingly rubbed her back to soothe her.

"He's gone. He won't hurt you anymore. I promise."

She stopped crying and lifted her head. "And how do you know that?"

"I know my brother. He won't be back."

Pushing away, she stood. "Jake, we need to stop him from doing this to anyone else," she said frantically. "We have to call the sheriff."

"Cheryl, sit. Let's talk about it first. We have to consider everyone involved."

"He viciously attacked me, and you don't think he should be arrested?" Her heart raced.

"He should pay for what he did and I would like to see it, but it's not just about him."

"What do you mean?"

"If you press charges, he will deny them and my mother will stand by him. Dad knows what happened between you and Michael on the day of his accident. And knowing my father, he'll want to do the right thing and prosecute Michael. Don't you see? If we act on this, it will likely destroy my whole family."

"So, you want me to pretend nothing happened?" she snapped.

"No." He stood up and held her shoulders. "I just want to have a life with you. I want to start it out new and not have to relive over and over all the terrible things that happened."

"Are you saying that because you gave Michael your word?"

"I would have told him anything to convince him to let you go."

"Jake, I need to know." She sniffled. "Do you love me enough to testify against Michael?"

"When I saw his truck and the broken eggs, I made the decision right then and there to kill him." His voice quivered. "But seeing the knife, I couldn't think of anything else but you. I thank God you're okay and that I didn't kill him. What he did to you was so wrong, I don't know why I didn't."

She stared at him.

"Maybe it's like you said; love can bring out the best in you. Cheryl, all I know is I love you and I want a future with you." He blinked back his tears. "But if testifying against him is the only way to put all this behind us ... I will."

Cheryl stared into his eyes for a long moment, considering. "I love you too," she said. "But you have to understand that if he even looks at me wrong, I will contact the sheriff." She wrapped her arms around him. "As much as I'd like to see Michael pay, I can't do it. I couldn't bear to see you in any pain. The only thing I want is a chance at a new beginning. With you."

18

The late morning sun shined brightly on the freshly washed windows of the fellowship hall. Cheryl sat on the bench outside and watched Sophie unlock the door for the quilting group.

When the older woman noticed Cheryl walking toward her, she waited on the step before going inside. "My dear, you sure must be excited to have our first quilting circle here. You're a half hour early. I hope you didn't wait too long for me," Sophie told her.

Cheryl smiled. "My friend dropped me off a little early, but it's a gorgeous day." She looked around at the maple trees mixed in with the pines around the churchyard. Some of their green leaves had transformed into deep shades of red and made a vivid contrast against the brilliant, sapphire sky. "I didn't mind waiting. *Some things are just worth waiting for.*"

"My, you're sure dressed up today. I love the scarf you're wearing."

"Thank you," Cheryl answered and managed a small smile. She adjusted the scarf that hid the bruises around her neck. Those purple marks were a reminder that the love she'd waited for hadn't come without a price.

The ladies sat at the table and talked while they waited for everyone to arrive. Most of the conversation was about how blessed they were to have the new facility.

It was time to serve lunch when Joan asked, "Does anyone know if Lucille is coming?"

"Pastor and I were out to their farm yesterday and Lucille told us she doesn't want to leave Chet alone just yet," Patsy Timms told her. Soon everyone else was there and Patsy cleared her throat. "Let's give thanks for the building and the people who helped build it." They kept their heads bowed and she continued, "May all who enter this building be blessed by God, and time spent here be dedicated to his will."

The prayer ended with an enthusiastic, "Amen." They finished their lunch and not long after they began to stitch.

"Most of you all know my girlfriend, Helen, who works down at Ekberg's." Mary had the floor. "Well anyway, she said that Lucille called and said she wanted to cancel the alterations on her gown for her son's wedding. Well, Helen told her, they'd started to work on the gown and she would have to pay for the work so far. She advised Lucille if it were her, she would just go through with the alterations and finish the dress. What would a person do with a half-altered dress? You certainly can't take it back to the store like that. I wonder if she found a different dress elsewhere or if her son is still getting married?"

"Lucille told me if anyone asks about her son's wedding here today, I could announce for her that there isn't going to be one," Patsy said with a sigh.

Everyone looked at each other with astonished reactions except for Cheryl.

"She didn't mention any details, so please don't ask me," Patsy continued. "All she said was, Jake called the wedding off."

A few minutes later, Patsy left the room and Joan's head immediately swung to the women seated around her. "I bet Jake Cameron's wedding was called off because of Carol, the woman him and his brother Michael were fighting over at the hospital."

"Wasn't Michael sweet on our girl Cheryl for a while?" Alma asked. All eyes went to Cheryl.

"Is he still trying to get you to go out with him, Cheryl?" Nell asked.

Cheryl shook her head no, but said nothing.

"I wonder who this woman is?" Joan remarked. "She really must be something to have two fine-looking men like them fighting over her."

"How well do you think Lucille is handling her son not marrying into that Petrich family?" Nell piped up. "She sure was on cloud nine when she told us about her son's upcoming marriage to the lieutenant governor's niece. I'm sure she isn't happy he broke off the engagement. But it goes to show you that you can't pick the ones you want your children to marry. That's the funny thing about love, it doesn't always grow where it's planted, but sometimes it grows wild where you least expect." She tilted her head at Cheryl with a sad expression. "Don't you worry girl, you'll find love growing somewhere again, someday."

Cheryl shrugged and continued to stitch the quilt. Patsy returned and the conversation quickly turned to new recipes.

Around three o'clock they started to wrap up when someone said, "Look, there's Lucille's son, Jake."

Everyone turned to see Jake through the large windows, about to come in the door.

"Speak of the good-looking devil, here he is now," Joan said to Mary.

Patsy frowned at her. Jake stepped in the door and smiled as he walked toward the group of women.

"Hello, ladies. How are you all doing this beautiful afternoon?"

"Fine," they answered almost simultaneously.

He looked at Cheryl. "Are you ready to go?"

The room went silent when Cheryl grabbed her purse and walked over to him. Mouths fell open when he extended his arm and she took it. Before Jake opened the door for Cheryl he proudly smiled at her then back at the group of women.

"I'll be damned, if that don't beat all, Carol is *Cheryl!*" Joan said out loud to the group.

Most of the women giggled, but Patsy pursed her lips and shook her head at Joan.

THE SETTING SUN CAST A SOFT, orange glow around the porch at Cheryl's house. Taylor was nuzzled between Jake and his mother on the wicker love seat. A warm breeze floated through the room while they sipped iced tea. He proudly showed Jake the baseball from his dad.

"That's a special ball. I can see why you're so careful with it," Jake said.

"Will you come over earlier tomorrow and play catch with me for a while? Then you can stay and have cheese noodles and hot dogs for supper."

"Okay, buddy, I'll be here early." Jake quickly glanced over at Cheryl. "Is that okay with you, Mom?"

"If you're okay with having that for dinner," Cheryl smiled.

"It sounds wonderful," Jake answered.

"It's time for you to get ready for bed, young man. You have school tomorrow."

"Can't I stay up a little later?" Taylor moaned.

"No. You were pretty tired this morning. So, go brush your teeth and I'll be in there in a minute to tuck you in."

Taylor turned to leave the room but stopped and ran back to Jake. He threw his arms around his neck. "Good night, Jake."

"Good night, buddy." Jake wrapped his arms around the boy's small frame.

Taylor skipped out of the room with a big smile.

Cheryl checked on him then returned to the porch and slid in close to Jake on the love seat. She laid her head on his shoulder.

"Who would've believed in the beginning of the summer we'd be sitting here right now in each other's arms?" he asked. "It's weird, but the beginning of the summer seems like it was a year ago." He suddenly sat up and inquired, "When did you first know you loved me?"

"You really want to know?"

"Yes, of course."

"I believe it was that night at the fellowship hall."

"When you were drunk?" He looked amused.

She shook her head. "No, when you asked me if I was going to stay and I couldn't come up with one reason to leave. I really wanted to stay and talk to you. It just felt right. I guess the longer we talked, the more I wanted you. When did you know that you loved me?"

He smiled. "Do you want to know when I first felt it, or when I admitted it to myself?"

"Both times," she urged.

"The first time I admitted it to myself was when I was breaking up with Susan."

She blinked her eyes. "So, when did you feel it?"

A big grin appeared on his face and he blurted out, "When I saw you swimming nude in the river."

Cheryl put her hand up in front of her eyes. "It was *you*?" she squeaked.

"Yep," he answered with a gleam in his eye. "Tell me, Mrs. Langtree, is that something you do often?"

"No," Cheryl snapped back. She suddenly gasped and searched his eyes. "Please tell me you were alone."

"I was with my dad and both of my brothers." His voice was serious.

Her face got hot and she dropped her chin to her chest.

He snickered and hugged her tight. "No. I was alone. I thought I saw a coyote or something go in the woods up farther by the river and went in to check it out, and found a goddess instead. I was so shocked when I saw you, I couldn't take my eyes off you. I thought, I am the luckiest man on earth. When you dove under the water, I moved closer not wanting to lose sight of you. I could have kicked myself when I stepped on that branch and alerted you that someone was there. That's when I first felt I loved you, but I didn't want to admit it. That vision of you is still in my mind ... and will be forever." His lips claimed hers in a kiss filled with a deep fervent longing for her.

They stayed out on the porch and talked about the future long after the sun disappeared behind the trees. Cheryl thought about how life had taken her on a full circle journey back to the very place where she began. It was where she belonged — on her wicker love seat in the arms of the man she loved.

THE END

I hope you enjoyed reading this book as much as I did writing Cheryl and Jake's story. If so, please help me on my writing journey and post a review. If you want more exciting modern history romance read Revenge in a Heartbeat — the next book in the Heartbeat Series.

ABOUT THE AUTHOR

Donna Lovitz grew up near Clear Lake, Minnesota, but considers tiny nearby Palmer her real home town. Her parents owned and operated the only bar and restaurant there, so she spent her early years meeting and observing a variety of interesting people. She married the love of her life, Rick Lovitz, and lived in Sauk Rapids, Minnesota, for 33 years before moving to Lake George, Minnesota, where they currently reside.

Along with writing, Donna enjoys snowshoeing, ice fishing and gardening, and has also added wine making to her lists of interests. Though winters in the Northland can be long, Donna doesn't mind. The calm beauty and serenity in the forest where she lives often kindle her creative spirit, and the nature around her home inspires her writing adventures.

Donna is a member of Romance Writers of America and has had articles published in the St. Cloud Times and poetry published in the literary journal "St. Cloud Unabridged." She is also a prolific creator of slogans and has won several contests for her creations.

Heartbeat of Desire is the first book in the Heartbeat Series. Donna plans to release the second and third book in the series — Revenge in a Heartbeat and Only a Heartbeat Away in the first half of 2021. The books in the Heartbeat Series center around a wealthy family of sugar beet farmers in Central Minnesota.

It has always been a dream of Donna's to write romance novels, and now she is making that dream a reality.

If you would like to know more about Donna, visit her website at: http://www.donnalovitz.com or visit her on Facebook at: http://www.facebook.com/donnalovitz

Other books by Donna Lovitz

Ryley — A Christmas Romance

ACKNOWLEDGMENTS

I am grateful to everyone who has helped and encouraged me on my writing journey. I am especially thankful to all my readers. Their support motivates me to do the thing I love to do — write! I would also like to thank Katie Schlomann, Wendy Gilbert and Florence Kahlstorf for their help in getting this book ready for publication. I am forever thankful to Patricia Jackson for inspiring me to design my own book covers. Finally, I would like to thank all of the members of the Northern Lights Writers, a Minnesota chapter of Romance Writers of America.